TALKING BUSINESS

I finally said, "Well, aren't you going to tell me about the robbery?"

Sundance grinned, for he'd known all along what I wanted to hear. "We rode in about one o'clock in the afternoon, and Butch took the lead in the bank. It didn't take any time to line up the customers and cashiers and go down the line, transferring money into the sack. Then it was the vault. The whole thing took ten minutes at the most."

"Too long," I muttered.

Sundance was quiet for a minute. Then, "You think you could have done it faster?"

"Let me try next time," I said, trying to put a joking tone into my words.

He ignored me. "What happened that was bad," he said, "was that the sheriff's office was directly across from the bank—who would have thought it?—and the sheriff, he looked out and saw all those people in the bank, waving their arms in the air. Didn't take him any time at all to mount a posse. We left with only three minutes to spare."

"You should have gone into town and checked the location of the bank," I said.

"And advertise ourselves as coming to rob?"

"Next time," I said slowly, "I'll be a widow woman looking to buy property, and I'll visit the bank."

He looked appraisingly at me. "Just might work," he said. "It just might work. . . ."

SUNDANCE, BUTCH AND ME

JUDY ALTER

LEISURE BOOKS NEW YORK CITY

A LEISURE BOOK®

July 2002

Published by

Dorchester Publishing Co., Inc.
276 Fifth Avenue
New York, NY   10001

ISBN: 0-8439-5042-0

The name "Leisure Books" and the stylized "L" with design are
trademarks of Dorchester Publishing Co., Inc.

Printed in the United States of America.

Visit us on the web at www.dorchesterpub.com.

*For my brother John,
who, like me, left behind a Chicago childhood
to live in the American West and fall in love with its spirit,
its life, and its history.*

SUNDANCE, BUTCH AND ME

Chapter One

No one knows where I came from—some say Wyoming, but most think it's Texas. I used to hear rumors that I was a teacher, even a Sunday school teacher, or that I was the runaway daughter of a rich cattle baron. Some say I died last year, struck by an automobile in El Paso. Others still believe I died in that hail of gunfire in Bolivia, when Butch and Sundance were supposed to have been killed. I once heard that I died of appendicitis in a Denver hospital. But none of it is true. I am here in Fort Worth, Texas, living as Eunice Gray and running the Waco Hotel. Still, everyone remembers Etta Place . . . and whispers follow me to this day.

Just yesterday I met that talkative cattle buyer, Luke Moriarity, on the street. He had with him his son, a child of five or six perhaps—who am I to judge the age of children?—and he poked and prodded the child to speak politely to me. Finally the little one said, "Good morning, Mrs. Gray," and I smiled and said, "Good morning."

But Moriarity must believe deafness comes with age, for as I turned away I clearly heard him tell the child, "Always remember, son, that you've said good morning to Etta Place."

"Who's that?" the boy asked.

1

"Never mind," replied his father. "Someday I'll tell you the story."

Well, I don't want to wait for someday. I want to tell the story now, tell that I didn't die in El Paso or Bolivia or Denver, tell that I was believed to be Mrs. Harry Longabaugh and still have the wedding photograph to prove it. And perhaps most of all I want to tell where I came from and what happened that could make me live outside the law. To my mind, loving a man isn't enough reason for some of the things that I did when I was young and wild.

I wasn't always called Etta Place. Fact is, I was born Martha Baird in a dogtrot cabin near Ben Wheeler in East Texas. How I came to be called Etta Place comes later, but my story really begins in that cabin in 1891.

Ben Wheeler wasn't in the Piney Woods where those tall trees give a sort of grace to the land and deep lakes make you know Texas has some pretty parts. No, our trees were a tangle of cedar and oak and hackberry, so thick that clearing the land to plow was a chore for any man and more than my father wanted to take on. It was a land of certain weather—certain to be unbearably hot and muggy in the summer, certain to be bitter and cold in the winter, and you could count on torrential rains in the spring and fall.

Ben Wheeler was a strange name for a town, but Mama told me the town changed its name—who knows what it was before?—after the Civil War, in honor of a postman who refused to carry the mail for the Confederacy.

Ephraim Baird, my father, had come to Texas from Kentucky long after what he called the War of Northern Aggression. He wasn't any happier with the Confederacy than Ben Wheeler had been. Though he was a man more given to laziness than anger, he was bitter about being driven from his home by the war. Of course, Pa was just a boy when the war was over, so it wasn't as though he was directly driven from his home, like so many who boarded up their houses and wrote "GTT" for "gone to Texas." It was just, he said, that a man couldn't make a living back there in Kentucky. I never understood why he complained so about East Texas, since life back home in Kentucky was no more than a shack in the mountains from all I heard, a shack not much better than what we had in Texas.

Of course, he didn't make a good living in Texas, either. Pa grew corn and sorghum on our little patch of East Texas, but he was as likely to spend the day fishing or hunting as he was working his crops. Then he'd send me out to pull the weeds, muttering about a girl having to earn her keep.

When he wasn't fishing or hunting, Pa was often in the saloon at Ben Wheeler. It wasn't much of a town—a general store, a livery stable, a Methodist church, a saloon, and perhaps ten houses, all looking as hastily built as ours. Mama had heard that the town was about to build a schoolhouse and hire a teacher, but Pa said it would only cost money and she could go on schooling us. "Don't take much schooling nohow," he scoffed. Since we didn't go to church or school, I knew no one in town except the Newsomes, who ran the store. To most of the town, I was simply "that Baird girl."

In the saloon a man could sit and talk about the indignities of life, about how by God no one was going to push him around. And others who had come to Texas from Kentucky and Tennessee would pound their fists on the table and agree with him. Pa would come home in what Ma called "a mood."

"A man oughta be able to grow a crop," he'd growl, sitting at our rickety, homemade table and drinking from the bottle of whiskey on which he'd spent what little cash he had. "It ain't right, I tell you!" His fist would rise in the air, then fall hard on the table, and we children—my little brother Ab and I— would scamper to the far corner of the room in fright. Mama just went about her cooking, trying to ignore him, but I could always see a trace of fear in her eyes.

The next mutter was liable to be "If I didn't have you'uns to take care of . . ." The threat would drift off, and I would wonder secretly what life would be like without Pa. By the time I was ten I was firmly convinced we would be better off, and I prayed for something to happen to him. The Lord, I reasoned, would forgive me. He knew what Pa was like.

The dogtrot we lived in stood a bit askew. Like everything else he did, Pa built it with little effort and less care. On either side of that central breezeway or dogtrot was a room of medium size, with space for one window cut out in each wall. There was no glass in the windows, and the only way to see out or let fresh air in was to go outside and lift up the heavy wooden shutter. Winter winds whistled through the cracks in the walls, and spring rains leaked through the roof so that Mama forever had to put buckets all around, even on the open dogtrot itself. And Pa had built in a low place, so that when it came a heavy rain the ground around became a lake. Once I remember the water edged up onto the floor of the dogtrot, and Mama stuffed sheets in the doorways to keep it from seeping inside.

Pa provided us with the essentials—a tin plate and cup for each of us, an iron pot for Mama to cook in, and a big pot for washing, which was done out of doors. Mama had a spider, that funny skillet that sat on three legs, that she used to make hot-water corn bread, and a gridiron, and once, as a great treat, Pa had brought her a coffeepot. Beyond that our provisions consisted of sugar, dried beans, rice, salt, and, when it wasn't too dear, coffee. Sometimes we had cornbread, sorghum, and milk for breakfast, dinner, and supper, and Mama counted us lucky that Pa hadn't sold the milk cow. We ate wild greens and, when Pa's aim was true and steady, fried rabbit or squirrel stew. But Pa would only hunt rabbit in months that had the letter R in them, a bit of Kentucky superstition to which he clung.

Mama was a puzzle to me . . . or maybe it was Pa—certainly, it was how the two went together. Where Pa was loud, sometimes profane, and not given to thinking much, Mama was quiet, soft-spoken, and always a little afraid of Pa. Not that she hadn't good reason. When he'd been too long in town and come home to find his supper cold, Pa had been known to take his anger out on her. More than once she kept her head turned from me, trying to hide the red print of a hand across her cheek.

One particular time stands out yet in my mind, maybe because it eventually had something to do with the direction of my life. A traveler had come to the cabin, late on a stormy night, lost and hungry. Pa was in town, but Mama had done what hospitality dictates—she welcomed him, fed him, and offered him the dogtrot as a place to sleep, whispering to me that Ab and I would sleep in the kitchen *with the door closed*. While the visitor ate corn bread and fried rabbit—Pa had some luck the day before—he told us he was headed for San Antonio, what he called the Queen City of Texas. As he raved on about

4

the city, streets of brick turned to gold in my mind, and I saw San Antonio as the most wonderful place ever. It was instantly the center of my dreams.

When Pa came home from town, unsteady on his feet, he tripped, literally tripped, over this stranger on his floor. At first, frightened, he let out a yowl. Then his fear turned to anger, which vented itself in profane hollering. I lay silently on my pallet and held out a hand to reassure Ab. The next morning, both Pa and the stranger were gone, and Mama wore a scarf pinned awkwardly around her neck. Her voice was hoarse, and she spoke little to us, but when the scarf momentarily slipped, I saw angry red fingerprints around her throat. San Antonio, like all dreams, was maybe not worth the price paid.

Where Pa had no schooling, Mama had an education. She spoke perfect English and insisted that Ab and I also did, and she taught us our lessons. By the time I was ten, I had a good understanding of mathematics and could write handsomely. Of literature, I knew only what she told us, for the Bible was the only book we had. Pa used it to frighten us, citing a vengeful God. Mama, though, told us about a loving and forgiving Lord, and I chose to believe her.

Mama was pale and fair and had probably once been pretty, though now she was just tired, with dark circles under her eyes and that haunted, scared look in them that I recognized even as a child. I marveled at the rosy color of her cheeks, but that was a childish misunderstanding—I didn't know Mama had consumption. Her name was Elizabeth, but Pa always called her "Lizzie," and I fancied she shied just a little every time he said it.

"Lizzie, you'll have to milk the cow. I done hurt my back," and he'd plop himself down on the cornshuck bed, moaning in misery, though to my mind he didn't look one bit miserable.

Or maybe he'd say, "Lizzie, this ain't fit to eat. Why can't you put a decent meal on the table?"

And she, pale and obedient, would apologize, when I wanted to shout, "If you'd provide better staples, Mama could put a better meal on the table!"

I asked Mama boldly one time why she had married Pa. She raised her chin in the air and stared out the doorway of the room that served as kitchen and living quarters. "The war . . ."

she said vaguely. "I had no one to take care of me. It was time to get married." I wanted to suggest she might have done better taking care of herself than she had counting on Pa to do the job, but I kept my tongue.

This unlikely couple had produced the two of us. Even as a youngster, I knew just exactly how they had produced us, too. Summer nights Ab and I slept outside on the dogtrot to catch whatever breeze might stir through the mugginess, but in winter we slept on pallets before the cast-iron Franklin stove. If there was any warmth left in the day's fire, we'd get it. No matter the season, Mama and Pa slept in the room across the dogtrot, but on all but the coldest nights, the doors to the rooms stood open. Thus they had a certain visual privacy ... but I could hear clearly. What I heard was Pa grunting like a wild hog does when it's rooting, small sounds that build to one long, louder one, and then within minutes the sound of his snoring. Mama never made a sound.

While I, with what I considered misfortune, favored Pa with his dark hair, Ab took after Mama, right down to the paleness and the rosy cheeks. Pa was hard on Ab, even when he was five or six years old. "Boy's got to learn to take it," he'd thunder. "Nothing in his life is easy." He'd send poor Ab out in a thunderstorm to check the milk cow, with Mama warning, "He'll catch his death of cold," and he'd send him out at midday in the midst of summer to gather kindling for fuel for the outdoor fire over which Mama cooked in the hottest months, even though she would protest, "I have plenty, Ephraim. It can wait till the evening cools some."

"It'll toughen him," Pa said, and brooked no argument.

Ab never seemed to get any tougher. If anything, he grew weaker, more afraid of Pa, more anxious to please. By the time he was eight, it was obvious, even to me, that everything was hard for him. I'd do his chores when Pa wasn't watching, and I'd look out for him as best I could, but I couldn't protect him every minute. When Pa took the belt to Ab's legs, I could only watch, shaking with fury. "Where are you, O Just Lord?" I wanted to cry out.

When I was fifteen and Ab nine, he didn't get up one winter morning.

"Get him outta bed," Pa said. "Gets movin' around, he'll be all right. You're babyin' that boy, not doin' him any favors."

"He's burning with fever and barely conscious," Mama answered, her eyes filled with tears. "I doubt he'll last the day."

Pa just scoffed and stomped off into the woods, calling to me to check the cow, gather twigs, tend the stove, and clean the cabin—my chores and Ab's, which I did willingly all the time anyway.

Mama sat by Ab's bed all day, some of the time with her head bent over to rest on his small chest, as though she could not get close enough to him.

"Can I go for the doctor?" I asked, desperate to be of help and to stave off what seemed an inevitable tragedy marching toward us.

"There's no doctor can do him any good now," she said softly, and I detected resignation in her tone.

"I don't care. I'll go for Doc Mason in Ben Wheeler," I protested. "He's a doctor. He can do something!" My tone rose in desperation.

She reached a hand for mine. "No, Martha, the doctor would not do anything I'm not doing. You stay with me. I need you."

And that filled me with pride . . . and a certain measure of acceptance. "Can I bring you something, Mama?" I must have asked that question twenty times that day.

Once she said, "Some fresh water, as cool as you can get it, for his head."

Pa, with the help of some of his friends from the saloon, had dug a well not far from the house. The water was a little brackish but the best we could do. One of my earliest lessons was that it was easier to carry two buckets of water—one in each hand—than to try to balance one. This day I ran to the well and hauled furiously on the buckets until I had two half full of water. Then I walked carefully without spilling a precious drop.

"Thank you, Martha," Mama said, rising to put her arm around me briefly. "This will ease him some."

Ab didn't seem to be in any pain. Indeed, he was asleep most of the time. Sometimes Mama could spoon a little broth into his mouth. She'd killed a chicken and stewed it, once Pa was safely out of sight, and I was hoping he'd be too drunk to count the chickens when he came home.

"Mama, drink some of the broth yourself," I said, handing her a cup.

She nodded absently and took a few sips, but soon the cup was put aside, her hands busy stroking Ab's head.

Toward evening he opened his eyes and said softly, "Mama?"

"Yes, Ab, I'm right here."

"Good," he murmured. Then a deep sigh, and he closed his eyes again.

Mama began to sob ever so quietly, still clutching his hand in both of her own.

"Mama?"

"He's gone," she whispered, "gone to the angels."

Mama sat there a while longer, and then, businesslike, she rose. "We must dress him," she said, and we put on one of his better white cotton shirts, a pair of coveralls, and the scuffed boots that were almost too small for him. "Can't have him going to heaven barefoot," she told me, with a slight smile.

"Pa did this," I said angrily.

"No, Martha, Ab had the consumption. I knew all along we could not keep him forever. Your father had nothing to do with it."

But in my heart I knew better. If Pa hadn't been so hard on Ab, if he hadn't tried to "toughen" him, I'd still have had a brother.

Pa came home late, noisily, but I pretended to be asleep on my pallet. I heard Mama talking to him in low tones and heard him say with the most grace he could muster, "Sorry about the boy, Lizzie."

Within minutes, the grunting started. Nothing, apparently, not even death, deterred Pa. I hoped the Lord was listening.

Next day Pa took some used boards, with which he always intended to build a barn—or so he said—and fashioned a coffin. It was rudely put together, but I think he tried. He grunted and sweated but managed to dig a small grave at the edge of the clearing that held our cabin, and then he went to Ben Wheeler to bring back the Methodist preacher. Mama and I sat silently by that small coffin. There was nothing more for either of us to say.

Pa was gone a long time and returned smelling strongly of whiskey. Behind him rode Brother Davis, who was good enough to come bury Ab even though he never saw the Baird family in his small congregation. Pa didn't believe in making the effort to go to church on Sunday morning. "You can thank the Lord for all his blessings right here," he said, but I knew Mama longed to go to church and visit with the other ladies. And she wanted us to have a Christian upbringing.

"Mrs. Baird, I'm sorry about your loss," Brother Davis began, "but we know that Abernathy is with the Lord."

"Right, Brother Davis, right. Now let's just get on with the burying," Pa said impatiently.

We three stood together in that clearing while Brother Davis asked the Lord to welcome Abernathy Baird, a child to be loved. Pa looked appropriately grief-stricken. Ab was, after all, his son, and I told myself to remember that. If it had been me in that box, Pa would have grieved. I needed to believe that. Pa put the coffin in the ground, Brother Davis said the Lord's Prayer, and Mama threw a handful of earth on the coffin. Then, grasping my hand firmly, she turned back to the cabin. She couldn't, I suppose, bear to watch Pa fill in the grave.

"Brother Davis, may I offer you some coffee?" she asked, and I marveled at her manners. I knew she wanted to bury herself in the bed and cry until she could cry no more. I also vaguely knew how much she needed the company of other women at that moment. I did the best I could, but I was too young to have a woman's understanding of grief and its inevitability. I still railed against the injustice of my brother's death.

"Why didn't Mrs. Newsome come with the minister?" I asked. Mrs. Newsome was the one woman both Mama and I knew in town.

"I don't suppose your father told her about Ab," Mama said wearily.

Chapter Two

Mama didn't last out the next summer after Ab died. Like my brother, she died of consumption, but there was more to it than that. She died of a broken heart, grieving for Ab, and she died of being just plain worn out. In my heart, I blamed Pa again, but I said nothing.

This time I was the one who dressed the deceased, carefully shaking out a dark wool traveling suit I'd found in her trunk. It was faded and streaked by folding and dust, but it was far better than the calico she wore daily. I had looked at her wedding dress—it was of ivory silk, made to wear over the crinoline she no longer had—and deliberately put it to the bottom of the trunk. Somehow it didn't seem fitting to me that she go to her grave in the dress that had united her with my father. The traveling suit was probably her honeymoon outfit, but I put that out of my mind. There were no other choices.

Pa went to town for a coffin this time. The stack of barn wood did not offer enough for an adult. I have no idea how he paid for it or what kind of credit he had to beg for, but I knew that Mrs. Newsome was generous to a fault. She had given Mama credit from time to time, and I used to fancy that she worried about Mama because she was married to such a lout.

10

Pa came home with a fine, sturdy pine coffin . . . and two men to help him dig. They dug the grave close to Ab's. This time when Brother Davis came out from town, the Newsomes and his own wife accompanied him. It made more of a farewell for Mama, and I was grateful to them for coming.

Before the ceremony, Mrs. Newsome pulled me aside. "Martha," she asked, "can I do anything for you?" I swear she looked over her shoulder at Pa as she said it.

"No, ma'am," I said, "but thank you."

"If there is ever *anything* I can do, I want you to come to me," she whispered, adding, "no one else."

"Yes, ma'am," I said, wondering what she meant and yet recognizing that she knew something, understood something that I didn't. Little did I know how soon I would turn to her.

Pa, looking hard at me, cleared his throat and said, "Well, let's get on with it."

Mrs. Newsome turned and went to stand at her husband's side by the newly dug grave.

Once again Brother Davis asked the Lord to welcome a worthy Baird to heaven and to bless the grieving father and daughter left behind. I stole a glance at Pa to see if he was grieving, but he simply stood, wearing his one boiled shirt and black coat, with his eyes downcast. I suppose in his own way he was grieving, but when the minister afterward grasped his hands and kept trying to offer comfort, Pa thanked him gruffly and pulled away as soon as he could.

"Don't know why that man came out here," Pa grumbled as I put johnnycake and syrup before him that evening. "Only asked him to speak over Ab because it would comfort your ma some. I don't need him tellin me the Lord loves me. Hah!" He almost spat in his anger.

"I didn't bring him," I reminded him, "you did."

He just gave me a dark look and turned back to his whiskey.

Pa and I passed by each other without speaking for days, and I was just as happy. I fed him and saw to the house, just as Mama had done, and he spent his days outdoors. But we had nothing to say to each other. I guess, though, that Pa began to think of me as Mama's replacement.

One night, some six or seven days after she died, I was awakened from a deep sleep by a rough hand over my mouth. Without Ab, I'd taken to sleeping indoors, where the air was close and stale. Even though I was grown—well, almost so—and pretty much fearless, I didn't take to sleeping outside alone. Now, before I could struggle to rise, the arm attached to the hand over my mouth held down my shoulders so firmly that I could not move.

I squirmed and tried to shout through the hand, but Pa simply held me down and said nothing, while he fiddled with my gown, pulling it up to bunch around my waist. Then his other hand roughly pushed my legs apart, and suddenly I was rent apart with a searing pain. My scream, kept silent by that huge hand over my mouth, echoed in my head but did nothing to blot out the familiar grunting sounds. With each thrust, his rigidness pushed into me, sending rivers of pain throughout my body, while I squirmed and wriggled and did everything I could to get away from him. The unmovable arm held me firm, and the pain, I found, grew worse when I tried to get away.

Then, with one loud groan, he was through. He rolled off me and stood up, turning his back to me while he buttoned his long johns. All he ever said, and that over his shoulder, was "A man has his needs."

I was left soiled and sticky on my pallet, shaking from sobs that I did not want him to hear. Within minutes, he was back in the bed across the dogtrot, snoring away. Ever so quietly—who would dare disturb him?—I crept to the washbasin outside and cleaned myself. Dressed in a clean gown—one of Mama's that still smelled of her perfume, though by now I fancied it smelled of him—I lay shaking on my pallet until dawn.

When I arose to fix his breakfast, I had made one firm decision: He would never again lay a hand on me.

That morning, he never said a word or indicated that anything between us had changed. "How," I wanted to demand, "can a man do that to his own daughter?"

But he sat there and held his cup out for more coffee, said he guessed he'd go hunting and might be late getting home that night, and walked out without giving me a second glance. He went not to the woods with his rifle but to the wagon. He hitched the horse and headed for town.

"To drink away his guilt," I scoffed.

* * *

I went back to sleeping outside and vowed I would even when winter came. I sharpened the butcher knife and took it to bed with me every night, hiding it alongside my pallet where I could reach it easily with my right hand, even if my shoulders were held down. And I learned to lie awake until I heard Pa snoring. Only then did I feel safe enough to sleep . . . and at that, I never slept soundly. I was always alert for another attack.

I took one other precautionary measure: I kept most of my clean clothes in a pillow sack along with a miniature of Mama and a handwritten note she had once left for me, telling me how much she loved me. It was all ready to snatch up in a moment if I had to flee. And I took Mama's hidden egg money from deep in the trunk where she had buried it and put it in the bottom of the pillow sack.

I was like a squirrel putting up nuts for the winter, but I knew that my winter would come soon. I wasn't sad about it. No, I was ready to leave that dogtrot, but I somehow needed Pa to do that outrageous thing to justify my leaving. Maybe it was because I was leaving Mama and Ab when I went. Whatever, I knew that I would not live on that poor piece of dirt much longer, and I made my preparations.

Meantime, life went on with a terrible dreariness. If I had missed Ab sorely, there was no way to put into words the emptiness that I felt without Mama. I had soon almost blotted Pa's attack out of my mind—not that it didn't happen or wouldn't happen again, but that I wouldn't think about it. But even were he innocent of that, Pa was poor company for a girl alone. He was sometimes drunk, often angry, never encouraging. I longed for Mama, the loving arm around my shoulders, the words of encouragement.

When Mama was alive, I used to dream of taking her and Ab with me to San Antonio and starting a new life there. Maybe it was because of tales she told me of the Alamo and the Kentuckians who had behaved there with more courage than Pa would ever have; more probably it was that dimly recalled memory of the traveler who said it was the finest city he'd ever visited. But I had no way to get to San Antonio, no way to support myself when I got there. Right then, it seemed to me that I could flee only if Pa provoked it, if he attacked

13

me again and gave me reason. Later I knew that I should have left before he had another chance. But, for then, I made the same choice Mama had.

Pa's next attack came a full two weeks after the first one. He had fallen to snoring, and I'd let myself drift off. Like a reenactment of a horrible nightmare, I felt his weight across me, his arm holding both my shoulders down. This time he didn't bother with the hand across my mouth. Who would have heard me scream besides him? And maybe he didn't care.

"Pa," I said levelly as he hitched up my gown, "don't do this again. I'm warning you. . . ."

He grunted, and his free hand reached between my thighs.

My hand reached for and found the knife hidden on the right side of my pallet. I brought it up, plunging it into his side, blindly, without aim. Only later would I suspect that I had hit directly into his heart. At the moment, I was acting out of desperation, unsure that I would even dare to break the skin.

Instead of those small, satisfied grunts, he let out a howl. The arm on my shoulders relaxed, and he slid sideways enough that I was out from under him. In a flash I was on my feet.

"You . . . you've killed me," he gasped, clutching at the wound that was gushing forth an amazing amount of blood.

I turned my eyes away. "I warned you," I said.

"A man . . . has his needs." He struggled to say it and then lost consciousness.

I didn't wait, never tried to see if I could help him, and later that would haunt me. I simply went into the house to grab my sack of clothes and leftover corn dodgers from supper. Then, still in my nightgown, I fled into the darkness, stepping over Pa's unconscious body as I left.

In the barn I changed into my best cotton muslin dress, a blue gingham that Mama had trimmed with scraps of white pique that she got I never knew where. Then my nervous fingers struggled to get the harness off its hook and put it on Dan'l, the workhorse that Pa kept but rarely put to work. Dan'l was gentle but old and tired, lazier than Pa, and I wasn't sure he'd take me as far as even Ben Wheeler.

I stood on a crate and hoisted myself onto the horse's back, just as I'd done the few times Pa made me ride the horse while he guided the plow and the even fewer times I'd ridden Dan'l just to be riding—and away from the farm.

Now I hitched the dress up to my knees and began to drum my heels on the horse's sides. "Come on, Dan'l, get going," I said in a voice so harsh I didn't recognize it myself.

It took me several strong words and a lot of drumming of my heels to get that old horse moving, and all the while he stood still my fear rose until it sat like bile in my throat. I fully expected Pa to rise up—from the dead?—and come after me. Was Pa dead? I neither knew nor cared. I simply wanted to be far away from there.

Finally Dan'l inched down the road with a slow and rough gait. Then, as though he got into the spirit of the thing, he began to pick up speed until he was moving at an awkward trot. I was bounced unmercifully on his back, every bone in my body wanting to call out to him to stop and only my fear silencing my voice. As I rode, I looked over my shoulder from time to time, expecting Pa.

I have no idea what time we reached Ben Wheeler, except that it was the dark of night. The town was pitch black. Not a light shone, and nobody appeared on the streets, which suited me just fine. I tied Dan'l behind the Newsomes' store and began to wonder how I'd get Mrs. Newsome's attention. She and Mr. Newsome lived in three rooms tacked onto the back of the store.

"Call me," she had said, adding, "no one else."

Ever so softly I tapped on a windowpane, whispering so low that even I could barely hear myself saying, "Mrs. Newsome? Mrs. Newsome?" There was no response. Desperation made me bolder, and I knocked more loudly, though I still hesitated to raise my voice for fear of rousing half the town. Still no answer.

I went around to a window on another side and knocked again, loudly this time. A murmur and a distant noise of stirring told me I had roused someone. I prayed it would be Mrs. Newsome and not her husband, but of course he was the one who came to a nearby door.

"Who's out there?" he demanded loudly. "What d'ya want, waking a man in the middle of the night?"

"Please, sir," I said, "could I see Mrs. Newsome?"

15

"Who is it?" he demanded, his voice still angry and a little fearful. "Who wants my wife in the middle of the night?"

"I'm Martha Baird," I said as strongly as I could.

"The Baird girl?" he asked, his voice rising in surprise but no longer angry.

"Yessir," I answered, hating every syllable of it, "the Baird girl."

"Mrs. Newsome," he called, "come here. There's somebody that needs you."

The Good Lord was awake and concerned, I decided. Otherwise Mr. Newsome would simply have turned me away in the middle of the night. But if He was watching, what did He think about Pa . . . and what I'd done?

At Mr. Newsome's bidding, I stepped closer to the door. He disappeared into the house and returned with a lantern. By the time his wife appeared, I was framed in the circle of light made ghostly by his unsteady hand.

"Lord in Heaven," she cried, "it's Martha Baird."

"Yes, ma'am," I said. "I . . . I have to leave . . . I . . .." And then the truth of it hit me, and I could not say another word.

Mrs. Newsome was more than equal to the task. "Come in, child, and tell me what's happened."

Once inside, seated at a scarred but comfortable kitchen table, I could do no more than shake. Mrs. Newsome stood before me, while her husband leaned against a door frame and yawned openly. I wished he'd go back to bed so that I could talk to her privately. What I had to say, I thought, should be between women.

She gave me a shrewd look. "He's bothered you, hasn't he?"

I nodded, realizing she knew before I did what would happen and what kind of a man Pa was. It would take me years and a lot of bitter experience to learn that what gave her that insight was generally called women's intuition.

"Some men have no good in them. . . ." Her voice trailed off, as though her anger was too much for words. After a minute she asked, "And you've run away?"

I nodded again.

"I won't let him come after you," she said in a reassuring tone.

Only then did I raise my head and take a long look at her. She wore a flannel nightgown with a matching bed cap, both faded from many washings, and her face was lined with fine wrinkles, the sort that come from kindness rather than meanness. Now her eyes were soft and caring, but her mouth was drawn into a hard, determined line.

In response to her promise of safety, I could only sob loudly.

Mrs. Newsome may have been nobody's fool. "There's more you need to tell me, isn't there?"

I took a deep breath. "I think I killed him."

"Lord God-a-mighty!" Mr. Newsome exploded. "How could a child kill her own father?"

I turned now to look at him. Unlike Pa, he did not sleep in his long johns but wore a nightshirt, a big long affair that hung awkwardly just below his knees. His feet and skinny ankles were covered by black socks, which looked ridiculous against the light pattern of his flour-sack nightshirt.

"Hush, James," Mrs. Newsome said. "We've got to hear what this child has to say." Then she turned to me and in a carefully controlled voice asked, "Why do you think you killed him?"

A giggle rose unbidden in my throat, and I wanted to say, "Because he told me I had." Instead I said as calmly as I could, "I stabbed him when he laid on top of me. I . . . I didn't mean to kill him, but I . . . I swore he'd never hurt me again."

She didn't flinch. "He'd done it before?"

"Yes, ma'am, once, just after Mama died."

Mrs. Newsome put her arms about me, murmuring, "Poor child, poor child. It'll all be all right." She made me think of Mama, and I bit my lip to keep from dissolving into sobs.

"How's it gonna be all right?" Mr. Newsome demanded. "She's a murderer. We're harboring a criminal."

"Hush, James. We've got to think this through. I have no idea if Sheriff Wilks would believe her story or not. . . ."

"Do you believe it?" he demanded.

She fixed him with a straight gaze, while I sat holding my breath. "I do. I've known about Ephraim Baird from the first day I set eyes on him . . . and the bruises his wife used to try to hide only confirmed what I knew."

"He said," I ventured timidly, "that a man has his needs." I truly thought for a moment that she would pick up the lantern and throw it, so great was her anger.

17

Finally she demanded, "James, what more do you need to know?"

He shook his head as though to say "nothing."

They talked between themselves for a bit, while I sat at that table, dazed now by what I'd done and the predicament I was in. At long last, I found my voice. "San Antonio," I said. "I want to go to San Antonio."

Mr. Newsome whirled on me. "Why ever do you want to go there?"

I couldn't explain about the traveler who stopped at our house or the tales I'd heard. I just shook my head and repeated, "San Antonio."

Mrs. Newsome was silent for a bit, and then she said, "James, there's a train from Palestine to San Antonio. You hitch up the buggy and take this child to Palestine."

"That's near fifty miles," he yowled. "Be noon tomorrow 'fore we get there, even if we start now." He yawned again.

"Well," she said practically, "I can go if you want, and you stay here to open the store in the morning. Wouldn't do for both of us to be gone and have the store closed. Everybody, including the sheriff, would smell a rat then."

"You can't go off to Palestine alone," he thundered. Then he had another thought. "How's she gonna pay for the train fare? And what's she gonna do when she gets there?"

She shook her head. "I don't know the answers to those questions, but I know what we have to do. We can't let her stay here and be branded a murderer, just for defending herself."

"You don't know he's dead!" Mr. Newsome countered.

"I think he probably is," I said miserably. "He was bleeding pretty bad."

Mr. Newsome gave me a long look, and I knew once again that I should have stopped to help Pa. There was no way to explain to another man what had happened or how I felt. "I have some money," I said. "Probably enough for the train."

"And when you get to San Antonio?" Mrs. Newsome asked, and there was a softness in her tone. She was protecting me, but she wasn't going to let me turn helpless.

"I'll take care of myself," I said with more confidence than I felt.

18

And that's what happened. Mr. Newsome had to get dressed in the middle of the night and hitch up his buggy to drive me to Palestine. It would be the afternoon of the next day when we got there.

As we left Ben Wheeler, I wanted badly to throw my arms around Mrs. Newsome and thank her, but I was shy, held back maybe because I'd never known many people outside my own family.

"Will you . . . will you see that Pa gets a decent burial, next to Mama and Ab?" I asked.

She reached a hand to smooth my hair. "Yes, I will."

"And . . . ?"

"And we won't either one say anything about having seen you tonight. James simply had to go to Palestine for supplies for the store."

"Why?" I asked.

"Because there are some things no one should be allowed to do and get away with. You aren't a bad person, Martha Baird. You were just put in a bad place." She turned to her husband. "In the morning, I'll mention to the sheriff that Ephraim Baird's horse wandered into town without a rider. I expect he'll go out there and find the man fell on his own knife and killed himself . . . by accident, of course."

For years afterward I remembered her words: *You aren't a bad person, Martha Baird.*

I never ever went back to Ben Wheeler, never went to see those three graves out there on that poor patch of land. I wrote Mrs. Newsome, once I was settled in San Antonio, and told her that I was all right. But how I got settled is another story.

Chapter Three

Mr. Newsome was plainly nervous about me. When it was dark, we rode in silence, casting sideways glances at each other from time to time. Sometimes I dozed off, sitting upright on the bouncing seat of the buckboard, but then Pa's face would swim before me, and I'd jerk myself back to the present.

Mama had died in the middle of July. It was now early August, the hottest time of the year in East Texas. The air was heavy, muggy, seeming to sit like a bale of cotton on my chest as we rattled over the rutted roads. Daybreak was always the coolest moment, and yet even it was hot and discouraging that morning. When it began to turn light, I could see that sweat ran out from under Mr. Newsome's hat—he wore a derby, like a city man—and I could feel beads of wetness on my upper lip and forehead. But his team forged ahead, slowly but steadily taking me toward a future that loomed blank and empty.

"Sure is hot, isn't it?" he finally said with forced good nature.

"Yes it is," I answered. I'd never been around enough people to be good at making conversation, though I could talk to Mama for hours.

He looked ahead at the road for a long spell. Then, finally, he turned to me. "Why'd you do it? Couldn't you . . . couldn't you have done somethin' else, anything?"

"No," I said. I wanted to cry out, tell him how awful it was and how wrong of Pa. But I didn't. He wouldn't have believed anyway, and I suspected he took Pa's part.

But then he surprised me.

"What your pa did is . . . well, it's the worst thing I can think of a man doin', and I'm holdin' no brief for him. But to kill a man . . ."

"I didn't want to kill him," I said fiercely. "I didn't mean to. . . . I just wanted to be sure he'd leave me alone." I bit my lip to keep from crying, lest he think I was using tears to get sympathy.

"There, girl, you don't have to get mad at me. I think I understand. Just don't know how a girl like you is gonna live with this on her conscience. How're you gonna make a living? 'Course, there's some things a woman can do . . ."

I had no idea what he was talking about, fortunate thing that was! "Pardon me?"

"Well, you know, in San Antonio. What you plan to do?"

"I'm a fair hand at keeping house," I said. "Mama taught me to cook and clean . . . and I can read and cipher. I reckon somebody'll want help."

"You may find in San Antonio . . ." He left the sentence unfinished, though after a minute he took a different tack: "Dressed like you are, you look like a schoolgirl."

"Mama taught me at home," I told him, "but I'm of an age to be in school." Naively I took it as a compliment that I looked like a schoolgirl.

"Well," he drawled, "you might just do better in San Antonio if you looked a little older. You know, different kind of dress." I looked at the new muslin dress I was wearing, a ready-made that Mrs. Newsome had insisted I have before we left.

"Well," he said, "you know . . . silk might be better." Then he added hastily, "But don't you ever tell Mrs. Newsome I said that."

I thought it was a strange conversation, and we didn't talk much for a long while. In midmorning we stopped under some trees and ate the biscuits and cheese Mrs. Newsome had sent, and by early afternoon we were in Palestine. Mr. Newsome found a saloon that served food, and after being sure I had money to pay for my own meal, ordered us greasy steak and potatoes. I picked at it but didn't eat much.

"Might be you don't know where your next meal's coming from," he said. "Ought to eat while you can."

But I continued to pick.

The train ticket took all but two dollars of the money I had and brought the discouraging news that the train wouldn't leave until midnight.

"You her pa?" the station agent asked Mr. Newsome.

"No . . . no, I'm not," that man answered nervously. "Uh . . . family friend. Just brought her to the train. Now, Martha, you curl up on that bench yonder and have a nap. I got to head on back."

I nodded, glad to be rid of him, and watched as he walked away, throwing me a nervous look over his shoulder. Then he hesitated, stopped a moment, and turned toward the ticket window. As I watched curiously, I heard him ask, "Got a pen and a piece of paper?"

The clerk nodded and supplied the items. Mr. Newsome wrote hastily, handed the pen back, and then came toward me.

"Here, girl, you take this. You go see this woman . . . tell her I asked her to look out for you." He handed me the scrap of paper; on it was written "Mrs. Fannie Porter, 505 San Saba, with regards from James Newsome."

I took it and stared at him, wondering what it meant.

"But don't you ever tell Mrs. Newsome I gave you that name," he said, his voice so stern that I thought a threat crept into it.

"No, sir, I won't," I said. And then he was really gone, while I sat and held the paper. The station agent came to check on me once I settled down on a bench. It was hard and uncomfortable, and my small bag of clothes made a lumpy pillow. But I was exhausted and almost asleep when I heard a deep voice ask,

"Where you from, miss?"

Sitting bolt upright, I found myself face-to-face with the agent, who had hunkered down so that he was at my level. "Uh, what?"

"Where you from?" he repeated, somewhat insistently.

My mind raced, and I knew that Ben Wheeler was the wrong answer. "Marshall," I said. "I'm from Marshall."

"That's good," he said, rising again to his full height. "Word came in over the wire 'bout some man from Ben Wheeler being found dead and his daughter missing. Didn't think that would be you, what with that family friend that brought you here and all."

"No, sir," I said with a forced laugh, "that wouldn't be me." I held my breath from then until the train finally arrived.

"All 'board" were the sweetest words I'd ever heard, though I was such a newcomer to trains—and to the world outside Ben Wheeler—that I barely knew what to do, how to behave. Timidly I chose a seat by a window and then waited breathlessly to see if I would be asked to move—maybe someone had a reserved seat?—or if some terribly unpleasant or nosy person would sit next to me. Tired as I was, sleep wouldn't come. The seats were prickly and uncomfortable, and the train was noisy, its great engine belching out a loud mournful sound at each road it crossed. Sometimes I would just begin to doze when the train lurched mightily and I was thrown awake again.

But it was mostly Pa that kept me awake. Now that I knew for sure he was dead—the stationmaster had confirmed it for me—I felt a terrible guilt. His face swam before me, and I heard him say over and over, "You've killed me." I was convinced that Pa—and that awful expression on his face, a mixture of surprise and horror—would haunt me the rest of my life.

I tried to call Mama's face up, but she never seemed as real to me as Pa, and I couldn't fathom Mama's reaction. She would have been horrified at what Pa had done, angry beyond belief and beyond her usual manner, but she would never have killed anyone. If that had been in her, I believed Pa would have been dead a long time ago. That conclusion made me think that probably I was more my father's daughter, prone to violence and wild behavior, than my mother's. And that was a sad thought, but I think it was one that right then began to shape my life. I was not as Mrs. Newsome hinted, fit to be with ordinary house folk.

Finally I slept fitfully, waking off and on, once when I thought I heard Ab calling me as though he were in pain. Then I stared out the window the rest of the trip and practiced mak-

23

ing my mind blank of any thought except the resolve that I would not cry and I would not spend my life seeing Pa's face before my eyes.

San Antonio was a puzzle to me, so different from East Texas that I could hardly believe I hadn't traveled days to get there. The size was one thing—in Ben Wheeler, I could stand at one edge of town and see the other end, but here the city stretched beyond me in every direction I looked, some of its streets paved, many still dirt. The paved streets usually had electric street-lights, the first I'd ever seen, and when the first electric trolley clanged by me on Commerce Street, ringing its bell, I must have jumped a foot. The thing ran on little metal tracks that were sunk into the brick of the street, but I couldn't see how it would stay on those tracks. At least it didn't go as fast as the railroad train.

Clutching Mr. Newsome's slip of paper in one hand and my bundle of clothes in the other, I began to walk aimlessly, partly searching for San Saba Street but mostly wondering at the city and its people, feeling suddenly as though I'd left Ben Wheeler far behind me. Reluctant to ask directions for fear someone would jump out and say, "You're the girl from Ben Wheeler, aren't you?" I naively believed that I'd come upon San Saba Street if I just kept walking. How big, I thought, can this place be?

Wandering first in one direction and then another, I passed fine large homes, so big that I thought surely several families must live in them, and then I passed small brown homes—I didn't recognize adobe—that looked substantial but poor. People had built strange fences around them, with small branches or limbs running straight up from the ground close together instead of rails lying across posts like a fence ought to be. These fences were all skinny tall posts.

The people were different, too. More of them, of course, than in Ben Wheeler. But there I'd known what the people looked like—everyone sort of looked like everyone else, though some had dark hair like me and others were fair like Mama and Ab. In San Antonio I saw Mexicans with flashing black hair and eyes and dark, rich-looking skin, and I saw a good number of fairly fat, light-haired men, with intense blue eyes, and many with blond beards on their faces.

There were policemen everywhere I turned, it seemed, and soldiers, men walking singly or in groups, or men and women together. But no women alone, none that I could approach safely and ask the way to San Saba Street.

Once I looked at the street numbers—I don't even remember what street I was on—but there were 2709 and 2711, and I thought I must have come a long way past my destination.

Another time, in what was obviously the Mexican part of town with those small brown houses, strange fences and bare dirt in the yards, I saw a woman sitting outside as though she were sunning herself. She was wearing a faded dress but was wrapped, even in the August heat, in a colorful shawl.

"I—Can you tell me where San Saba Street is?" I asked.

She smiled happily at me and murmured something in Spanish, but of course I had no idea what she was saying.

People in this part of town stared at me, for I was obviously an outsider, but their looks were neither angry nor distrustful. A group of children playing mumblety-peg in the dirt stopped to look up at me, and one shyly said something, though the only word I caught was "señorita."

No sense asking them about San Saba Street, I thought as I waved a hand at them. A part of me wanted to kneel down in the dirt and ask for a turn. But I had never played mumblety-peg with other children—only Ab.

Finally I came to a market square, with men and women behind stalls of fruits and vegetables, each one calling out loudly how fresh their goods were. Some called in English and some in Spanish, and the resulting chorus echoed in my ears like nonsense. I picked one stall where a Mexican woman was selling some sort of food I didn't recognize and loudly proclaiming, in English, that hers were the best in town.

"Excuse me, can you tell me where San Saba Street is?"

"San Saba Street?" She nearly shrieked. "No, you not go to San Saba Street." She shook her head back and forth firmly. The man in the booth—her husband, of course—spoke firmly to her in Spanish, and she answered him in a staccato that suggested she was giving him a tongue-lashing.

25

The man prevailed. "You wish to go to San Saba Street?" he asked politely in heavily accented English.

I nodded.

"It's west of the creek, San Pedro Creek," he said. "Here, I draw you picture in the dirt." He took a stick and began to draw, explaining carefully. But he never explained the woman's reaction, and I understood only later that San Saba was the street of whores.

It turned out I was only five or six blocks from San Saba, and I found it with ease, carrying the man's stick picture in my mind. Once on San Saba I had only to go another two blocks until I stood before number 505.

It was a large two-story house, not as grand as those I'd seen when I'd wandered south of the business district, but still a substantial house. Square in shape, it was covered with stucco—to me, of course, it looked like the adobe houses I'd seen earlier, though lighter in color and different in shape. There was a freshly painted picket fence around it and some grass in the front yard, even a shrub or two. While it wasn't exactly inviting, it did look as though a solid family lived there.

Then I remembered Mr. Newsome's nervousness and the fact that he hadn't referred me to Mr. and Mrs. Porter, but to Mrs. Fannie Porter, obviously an unmarried lady. And then there was the screeching Mexican lady in the market. Something was obviously different about this house and this street. I looked around, but the neighboring houses looked about the same—solid, substantial, not fancy.

I must have stood a long time, looking, gathering my courage, because when I finally approached the front door, with its impressive oval inset of cut glass, the door swung open before I could knock.

"Yes, miss?" A black man in a dark suit, high starched white collar, and white gloves made a semibow in front of me. Now, we had blacks in East Texas, and I was even on a "Howdy" basis with one or two families who lived around Ben Wheeler, but they never dressed like that!

"I'd like to see Mrs. Fannie Porter," I said as firmly as I could.

The corners of his mouth twitched just slightly. "Yes, ma'am," he said. "Please come in."

I entered a narrow hall with dark wood paneling—wainscoting—halfway up the walls and paper patterned with red velvet above that. Above me was a chandelier, with hundreds of pieces of glass that gave off a sort of sparkling light.

The man said, "This way, miss," and showed me through a curtained door—more red velvet—into a parlor. There was still more red velvet and two more chandeliers, but what puzzled me was the number of small sofas all around the room, each looking like they held two people. At one end was a small bar, bigger and much fancier than the one in the saloon Pa had frequented in Ben Wheeler, and a white piano with gold flowers and curlicues painted on it.

I perched on the edge of a straight chair near the door and studied the room. It was not a room where a family lived, that was for sure! It seemed forever that I waited, but it probably wasn't more than five minutes. Once I got up and peeked through the door. With no one in sight, I was so bold as to look into the room across the hall. It was almost identical to the one where I waited. I went back and sat on my chair.

Then a woman came through the swagged curtains that only partially covered the doorway. She was no taller than I but a big woman, not fat or badly proportioned, but generous. Her hair was light, like Mama's, but instead of pulled severely back from her face like Mama's, hers was fashioned in a great roll around the upper part of her face. It gave her height and a certain dignity, which was emphasized by her dress of voile, with silver and pink stripes going up and down—rather than around, where they would have called attention to a certain roundness about Mrs. Fannie Porter. My eyes were drawn again and again to the gold watch she wore on a slim gold chain around her neck. It was the first piece of real jewelry I'd ever seen, and I wanted one just like it so badly that the want was almost an ache.

Briskly she asked, "You wanted to see me?" Only after she'd said that did she look at me, and then her expression changed to one of surprise.

"Yes, ma'am," I said, rising and holding out my slip of paper. "Mr. James Newsome of Ben Wheeler gave me this and told me to come to you when I got to San Antonio."

Judy Alter

She held the slip of paper at a distance, and I thought I saw the same twitch at the corners of her mouth that the man had shown when I first got there. "And what did Mr. Newsome think I would do for you? Why are you in San Antonio? Alone, I presume. And what should I call you?"

Her questions were fired too rapidly for my tired brain, and I sorted them out. "My name is Martha—Martha Baird. And, yes, I'm in San Antonio alone. I'm . . . an orphan, and Mr. Newsome thought you would find work for me."

"Oh he did, did he?" Now she looked angry and muttered almost under her breath, "The low-down scum. . . ."

Fleetingly I thought that I'd never heard a woman use such language—certainly Mama would never have thought of it. I didn't know whether to be shocked or impressed. But weariness was overcoming me so strongly that my knees nearly buckled, and I longed to sit again on that uncomfortable straight chair. I forced myself to stand straight before her.

Mrs. Porter looked long and hard at me, saying nothing, until I wondered what she could possibly be thinking. But still I stood straight before her, my mind forcing my weary body to obey. Finally, she said, "I think you better sit down and tell me the whole story. You look exhausted, and I imagine you haven't eaten in a good while."

I nodded. It had been a long time since Mr. Newsome had advised me to eat heartily, but until that moment I hadn't thought about food.

She clapped her hands, and the black man appeared. "Hodge, what's for supper?"

"Fresh vegetables, sliced roast chicken, bread, and custard pudding," he told her.

"Bring this child a plate right away," she said, her voice pleasant but commanding.

He gave his little half-bow and was gone again, only to return in minutes with a tantalizing plate of the promised chicken, accompanied by potatoes, green beans, squash, and fresh light bread. My mouth watered.

"Eat first," Mrs. Porter said, "and then tell me your story. Here, let's take it to a table so you can eat more conveniently."

She picked up the plate and carried it back through the curtained doors, motioning with her head for me to follow. We

28

went down the entry hall into another hall that ran perpendicular to the first. Along the back wall of the passageway, a narrow staircase rose to the second floor. At the foot of the stairs, a doorway opened into the dining room. It was a good-sized room, but I was puzzled that it held not one long dining table, as I'd expected, but several small ones. I wondered who would eat at all those tables in this house, which now seemed quiet and empty.

When we were seated, she again commanded me to eat, and though I was suddenly ravenous and wanted to tear at the food, I ate daintily, aware that she was watching me intently, and blessing Mama for the manners she taught me. It wasn't just that I was hungry—the food was delicious. Pa's vegetable garden had never produced green beans or squashes that large or flavorful. When I had licked the last of the custard off my spoon, she said, "You have good manners. Someone's taught you well."

"My mother," I said, wiping my mouth carefully and folding the napkin. It was heavy fabric and crisply white.

"What happened to her?"

"She died. My . . . my little brother died of consumption, and I think Mama died of a broken heart. But she had it too . . . consumption, that is." In spite of myself, I could feel a tear or two in my eyes. *It's just because I am so tired*, I thought, and willed the tears away.

"And your father?"

I opened my mouth, but no words came. She waited patiently, her expression neither compassionate nor unkind. I tried again to bring up the lie I'd made up: Pa had abandoned me, just up and left one day, and after a week I went to the Newsomes for help.

But the words wouldn't come.

"I killed him," I said evenly, though I felt the words come against my will. Maybe I badly needed to confess.

"He must have needed killing" was her only response. "Tell me about it."

The story came out slowly. As deliberately as I could I told about Pa and a man's needs, and about my warning, and then back to the way Pa had treated Mama and bullied Ab and how what he did to me was the final insult on a long string of bad

29

deeds. I managed to get through it without once ever seeing Pa in front of me. "I know it was wrong, and I guess I'll have to go to jail . . . maybe even hang . . . ," I concluded.

This last only then occurred to me, with a terror I can't describe.

"They don't much hang young girls, especially not those raped by their fathers," she said dryly, "and I see no reason anyone else ever has to hear this tale . . . that is, if you can keep from telling it anymore. You say James Newsome knows? Will he tell anyone?"

"Mrs. Newsome won't let him," I answered before I thought how that sounded.

She laughed aloud for a minute. "I thought he was that kind. Now, you've eaten, and you're obviously beyond tired. I . . . have a spare room. You sleep, and tomorrow we'll talk about work for you."

Hodge showed me to a room on the second floor, furnished with only a bed, a small chest of drawers, and a chair. "Chamber pot's under the bed," he said. "And lock's on the inside. You lock the door, and don't let any noise you hear bother you."

I thought it was the strangest piece of advice I'd ever been given, but I did as he said and locked the door before changing into the one clean gown I'd brought. I crawled into the bed, between clean white sheets that smelled from having been hung on the line in the sunshine. Within seconds I was fast asleep, and through the night I was dimly aware of sounds—music from far away, laughter and voices coming and going closer to me— but I slept on. When I woke, the sun was high in the sky.

Chapter Four

"What kind of work can you do?"

It was early afternoon, and I'd had a good dinner of chicken salad: yesterday's chicken, probably, with tomato aspic—a new taste for me—and more fresh bread and custard pudding. Julie, who was apparently Mrs. Hodge and who cooked for Mrs. Porter and lived with Hodge in a small building behind the house, had served all this in the kitchen. Once again the house seemed eerily quiet, and I remembered the vague sounds I'd heard during the night.

Now I had been summoned to Mrs. Porter's bedroom—boudoir, Hodge called it—and I silently practiced saying the word to myself until I could make it sound as he did—"boodwahr." The boudoir was not upstairs where I'd slept but a large room off the rear of the parlor. It was in fact almost a separate apartment, with two other smaller rooms across a short hall.

She was propped up by dozens of pillows, or so it seemed, in a great, canopied bed, with sheets that looked shiny pulled up over her and her lunch tray abandoned on the bed beside her. She wore a wrapper of the same material as the sheets—shiny and rich-looking, not feed-sack cotton like the wrappers I was used to. But even as she sat in bed, ·her hair was perfectly combed and it seemed to me there was just a hint more than natural color on her cheeks.

I stood before her, dressed in one of the two cotton everyday dresses I'd brought, this at least made of store-bought calico that Mama had traded for with her eggs and butter.

"What kind of work can you do?" she repeated without inviting me to take a seat.

"I can cook, sew, and clean house. If necessary, I can weed, plant, hoe a garden, but I'd rather not."

That loud laugh again. "I'm sure. I'd rather not too."

Before she could say more, I told her, "I know that you have Julie and Hodge to do those things for you, but I thought perhaps you could refer me to some friends who need help."

"Honey," she said, throwing the covers back and swinging her feet off the bed and into some sort of shoe with fur around the top of her foot, "I wouldn't trust my friends with you. What kind of a place do you think this is?"

"I don't know," I admitted. "I'm puzzled. It's a big house, but it seems empty . . . and it's fancier than anything I ever imagined I'd see."

"Yeah, it's fancy," she said, rising to pace around the room. "But it's not empty. There are five other women living here, up on the second floor where you slept last night. They stay up late at night, and they sleep away the day." She paused a moment, bent to stare in the mirror at her dressing table and carefully smooth her hair.

"This is a female boardinghouse. We entertain gentlemen here in private—for money. Do you know what I mean?"

I nodded. Somewhere I'd heard about prostitutes. Surely not from Mama—maybe Papa threatening to visit one. I wasn't sure, but in the back of my mind I knew that some women let men do what Papa had done to me, only they charged money for it. I never thought, though, that they lived like Mrs. Porter. "It's a whorehouse," I said boldly, and then, even more boldly, asked, "You?"

She eyed me. "Sometimes. Not often. I own this house, and I run it. The girls work for me."

It all made sense to me now, and, uninvited, I sank down onto the fainting couch next to the dressing table. She seated herself before the array of bottles and brushes and waited for me to speak.

"Mr. Newsome thought you would hire me to do that," I said. There was no question in my voice.

"Yes, he did. It was a damn fool thing to think of, but that's how men's minds sometimes work. Long as your father had done what he did, you'd been 'initiated,' you might say, and you might as well make a living at it. Is that what you want to do?"

I stood up. "No, ma'am, I don't. I'll just be leaving now. And thank you for the meals."

"Sit down," she said in a voice that was almost a roar. "I wouldn't hire you even if you wanted me to. You're too young, and no one's ever going to say that Fannie Porter lured a young girl into the life. But we've got to figure out something for you."

"I can cook and clean," I repeated, feeling a surge of despair.

"Do you want to spend your life cooking and cleaning?"

Not Pa, but Mama, floated into my vision—Mama scrubbing old board floors on her hands and knees, poking at dirty clothes in a washpot over a fire, baking bread when she was too exhausted to knead. "No, I don't."

"How much schooling have you had?"

I shrugged. "Mama taught me at home. I can write a good hand, and I know mathematics. I have read some of the Bible, but we didn't have any other books. Mama used to talk to us about Shakespeare and things, but I've not read much."

"Your mother was a remarkable woman," Mrs. Porter said, "and I think I want to make one of her dreams come true."

Puzzled, I waited.

"I'm going to send you to school, make a lady of you."

I opened my mouth to protest, but she waved a hand for silence. "No, I'm not going to take you on as a daughter or try to mother you. You're near grown, and you'll have to do the rest of it on your own. But I'm taking you on as a project . . . I want to show the world that Fannie Porter recognizes class."

Too stunned to speak, I watched her pace the room, her head bent as though she were deep in thought. "The Ursuline Academy," she muttered, "but first clothes . . . and a place to stay. . . . She's got to meet the girls, and I've got to lay down the law." Then, looking at me, she announced, "We have a lot to do to get you ready for school in the fall."

She clapped her hands, and Hodge appeared. "Hodge, I want my second sitting room fitted into a bedroom for..." She turned to look at me. "We can't call you Martha Baird. What shall we call you?"

"Martha Baird's my name," I said in protest. I wanted a new life—but the thought of a new name was unsettling.

"Well, that won't do for reasons you and I both understand. We'll call you ... how about Etta? ... I've always been partial to the name Etta. Nicest girl ever worked for me was named Etta—not that that's an omen or anything, mind you. And a last name? Porter? No, sounds like my daughter, and that would give you a burden to bear. Newsome? We could make it a wry joke on that slimy ... How about Place? Because you've found yourself a place. Etta Place."

She looked at me for agreement, and I nodded, silently repeating to myself, "Etta Place, Etta Place." It sounded all right on my tongue, and I knew I couldn't go around admitting to being Martha Baird, the girl who stabbed her father to death.

"It has a fine ring to it," Fannie concluded. Then she was back to business. "And, Hodge ... bring me the morning newspaper and send for Mrs. Carrerra, the dressmaker. Right away. And tell the girls we'll meet at four this afternoon in the parlor. Oh—and I'll need the carriage in thirty minutes. I'll drive myself."

Hodge, apparently having no trouble sorting out all those orders, bowed and disappeared.

"Now, we have to have a background for you. Logically, you'll be my niece ... let's see, the daughter of my recently deceased brother. Oh, don't look so startled—I don't really have a brother. It's not as though I were wishing bad luck on a real living person. Where would you like to come from? Someplace far away."

"Up north," I said promptly.

She shook her head. "We're going to erase East Texas from your speech, but right now there's just enough of it to convince anybody you're from somewhere in the South. How about Atlanta?"

"Georgia?"

"Right. Atlanta, Georgia, but in the country nearby, not in the city. That'll give you leeway to be a little bewildered about

34

city ways." She went to a chifforobe and began looking through the dresses hanging there, holding out one and then rejecting it, taking another out for inspection. At last she threw a gray crepe dress on the bed. "My respectable clothes," she said, and laughed.

Then she was serious again. "You'll have to amuse yourself for a few hours," she told me by way of dismissal. "I have to dress and go out. You best wait in the kitchen with Julie . . . you can use those cooking skills to help her. I don't want you meeting the other girls, though, until four o'clock. I'll do the introductions."

"Yes, ma'am," I said.

"None of that 'ma'am' business. You call me Fannie."

I nodded.

Three hours in the kitchen was not nearly as endless as I'd expected, with Julie filling me in on the various residents of the house. Someone called Juniper had been there the longest, she said, "near on to ten years, and that's a long time for a girl to be on the line. She must be near thirty year old, time to be gettin' herself a different line of work. 'Course," and she shook her head, snapping a green bean extra hard, "ain't much else she can do." She rinsed the beans with a dipper of water, put them aside, and picked up several ears of corn.

"Here," I said, "I can do that."

"All right, honey, then I be starting some biscuits. Now, that Lillie Davis, she's new and right smart, knows she doesn't want to stay here forever. She's from somewhere in East Texas . . . ah, Jerusalem—no, Palestine, that's it."

"Palestine!" My voice rose in spite of myself. It was too close to home. "How long has she been here?" I cursed myself for a fool. Did I think she'd just arrived yesterday?

"Been about a year now. Miss Lillie must be . . . oh, twenty-one. How old you be?"

"I'm sixteen," I said.

She rolled her eyes heavenward. "And you're gonna work here? That don't sound like Miss Fannie."

Hodge came into the kitchen then. "Don't be talkin' so much, woman, when you don't know nothin'. Miss Etta, she's going to school. The Ursuline Academy, Miss Fannie tells me."

"Well, I'll be . . . I don't know what's goin' on in this world."

"Miss Etta," Hodge said, "your room is ready for you. I got that no-good Juan to help me move a bed in—we've always got extra beds—and I put in a nightstand, a chest of drawers, a dressing table, and an upholstered chair. Miss Fannie says you'll be needing a desk, but I'll have to do some bargaining to get that."

A bedroom of my own, with a desk in it, was a dream beyond belief. I had to bite my tongue to keep from crying or gushing or doing something silly, but it worked. I was amazed at the self-control I'd learned in the last two days. "Thank you, Hodge. May I go look at it?"

"Yes, ma'am. I put your things in there, but I 'spect you'll be havin' new things before long."

The room was not large, but to me it was as big as a ballroom, the bed the softest I'd ever felt. I put my few belongings in the drawers, lay down to test the bed, and was instantly asleep, exhausted by the rapid turn of events in my life. I wondered, as I drifted off, what Mr. Newsome would say next time he came to visit Fannie. A horrible thought struck me: Maybe he'd been planning to ask for me to "entertain him." The idea of his disappointment made me giggle.

I must have slept only minutes when Fannie shook me awake. "Sorry, Etta, but Mrs. Carrerra is here to measure you. I told you we had a lot to do."

As I slowly sat up and rubbed sleep from my eyes, she waved a hand at the room. "We'll get a throw to match the curtains— Mrs. Carrerra can see to it—and a rug of some sort. And I told Hodge to get a desk. . . ." Just the littlest bit of impatience crept into her voice.

"He said he'd have to bargain for it," I told her, feeling myself rush to Hodge's defense.

She nodded, apparently already dismissing the desk as a problem, and led me into the third small room in this wing of the house. It proved to be her sitting room, and a short, smiling Mexican woman waited there, tape measure in hand. She said something in Spanish to me, and Fannie immediately translated, "*Buenas días*. It means good day. It's the way you greet people. We'll have to get you some everyday Spanish right away."

As I stood still in the middle of the room, Mrs. Carrerra measured and Fannie ordered. Told to strip to my camisole, I'd been forced to admit that I owned none and had nothing on beneath the cotton dress I wore. Camisoles—seven of them, trimmed with eyelet lace—were first on Fannie's list, followed by wrappers in a variety of fabrics and prints—flannel for winter, cotton and muslin for summer, one good wool. Then came a bewildering variety of dresses with only one thing in common—they were to be either black or dark gray.

"My niece," Fannie said carefully, "is in mourning for her late father, my brother. Young as she is, it's only appropriate that she wear clothing befitting her grief."

I'd never had anything black in my life, but until that moment I had never thought about the way I looked. Suddenly I worried that black might be unbecoming to me, but I said nothing.

The measuring was soon over, and Mrs. Carrerra left with a promise—in Spanish, of course—to deliver one or two dresses within days.

"Meantime," Fannie said, "you'll stay in the house and wear wrappers of mine or the girls."

She left the room and returned in minutes with a wrapper of sheer gauze over a deep rose pique. "Here, put this on. Here's a ribbon for your hair that will match . . . sort of."

"I can't. It's too fine." I was absolutely thunderstruck by this magical and airy creation that she handed me.

She stared me down. "Put it on, and then come let me fix your hair. Can't have you meeting the girls looking like that."

I wanted to bristle—Mama had always told me I was pretty—but I knew that Fannie was right, and I submitted to her ministrations. She fixed my hair in a softened version of her own—more suitable, she said, for a young girl. While she worked on my hair, she told me she'd read the newspaper thoroughly and there was indeed a small article mentioning that a man near Ben Wheeler had been found stabbed to death, his daughter missing. The knife with which he appeared to have been stabbed was left at the scene, and the local sheriff suspected the daughter. "Newspaper says," she said ironically, "that Martha

Baird was considered a fine young woman and no one can fathom—that's the reporter's word—why she did this terrible deed." She raised her hands in exasperation. "Damn fools should be able to figure it out. Only one thing could make a girl that desperate."

"Thank you," I said. There didn't seem to be much else to say, but if Fannie understood, maybe Mama would have too.

By then it was four o'clock, and we could hear the chattering of female voices in the main parlor. The girls had assembled to meet me. With my nervousness hidden but nonetheless present and accentuated by the unaccustomed outfit I wore, I followed Fannie through the curtains.

"Evening, ladies," she said brusquely, and I watched with admiration as the businesslike, no-nonsense woman, the woman who had first talked with me, replaced the chatty, talkative woman who had revealed herself in the last hours. Such was to be the pattern of our relationship—I knew a different Fannie from the madam who had, I would later learn, a reputation for being hard and shrewd and who ran her business with a firm hand.

"This is my niece, Etta Place," she said, without a hint of doubt in her voice. "My dear brother—Herman Place—died recently in Atlanta, and Etta has made her way to my doorstep. Of course, I had no idea she was coming, or I'd have told you before this. Etta will have a room next to mine and will attend school in San Antonio this fall. She will *not* entertain customers, and until I decide otherwise, she will not be present in the public parts of the house during working hours."

So I was not to get to watch for James Newsome or stare at the men who frequented the house—or watch the girls in operation. I very much wanted to do the latter—I wanted to see how women behaved with men, because I felt my knowledge about that was limited by Pa's awful nature. It didn't dawn on me that watching whores at work would be just as limiting.

"How come her name's Place, not Porter?" one asked.

Oops, I thought. She should have stayed with Porter, as was her first inclination.

But Fannie warmed to her story. "I'm a widow, Lillie. You know that. The late Mr. Porter died suddenly . . . of a gunshot. But I was named Place when I was a child."

"Etta," said another girl. "We used to have an Etta who worked here." She looked a little puzzled. "It isn't a common name."

Again Fannie invented as she went along. "That's true. It is a coincidence, isn't it. Now each of you introduce yourselves, please."

The first was Lillie Davis, the girl from Palestine, as young as Julie had said and very pretty. "I'm just here temporarily," she said with a winning smile, and I thought she could have been a classmate of mine at the school I was about to attend. Wearing a flowered cotton wrapper, she sat on one of the parlor sofas, her legs demurely crossed at the ankle, feet on the floor, as though my mama had told her how to sit.

"Maud Walker," said the girl next to her, obviously older than Lillie by at least five years and as dark as Lillie was fair. An angry resentment burned in Maud's eyes as she looked at me, and I made a mental note to avoid her. She sat and stared a minute, then added in a low tone of voice, "From St. Louis."

Juniper was next, the one Julie said had been with Fannie the longest. Her eyes were tired, and there was a sad look about her. She was clearly older than the others, and I'd watched her earlier shepherd the others into the room. "I'm Juniper," she said. "Been here so long I don't know where else I'm from."

The others laughed, but Lillie said, "You won't be here forever, Juniper. You wait and see." She nodded at the next girl.

"I'm Wallie," said an overweight girl with rouge high on her cheeks—Mama would have been horrified! But when I thought that I almost laughed, because Mama would have been horrified at where I was anyway. Her hair was a strange shade of red too—I didn't know about henna, of course, but it was an unnatural red with a lot of orange to it. She looked exactly like what I had thought all the girls here would.

"Wallie?" I asked incredulously, my tongue working before my brain.

Just a hint of humor flashed through her eyes. "My pa ran out of girls' names by the time I came along. I was number ten. I'm from Oklahoma." A tinkling little laugh followed, as though she had said something funny. To me, the laugh sounded forced and funny.

39

Last was Cassie, who looked to be not more than my age, though, remembering what Fannie had said, I assumed she must be older. I hadn't really noticed her before, but when I looked closely I thought there was some Indian in her. She had coal-black hair and eyes as dark, with dramatic dark eyebrows, high cheekbones, and pecan-colored skin. It was her manner that I most noticed, though—she held herself straight and kept back from the others a little. "I'm from San Angelo," she said, and then, unexpectedly, added, "My brothers are all outlaws. They brought me here."

Was she waiting for my reaction? I swallowed hard and managed to say, "Pleased to meet all of you," as distinctly as I could. It wasn't enough, but I was at a loss for manners at the moment, especially after Cassie's disclosure of her family background. I don't suppose I'd even seen an outlaw—or even thought about seeing one.

"Some business," Fannie said briskly. "Wallie, that Ben Coleman came in here drunk as a hoot owl again the other night. You are not to entertain *anyone* who is rowdy drunk, not even your favorite regular."

Wallie sniffed and raised her chin a little, but she said, "All right. I'll warn him." And then she giggled again.

"Lillie, you missed your doctor's appointment last week. See that you keep it this week."

"I don't need—" Lillie began.

"Do as I say." Fannie had almost a motherly tone in her voice.

"Juniper, I want to see you in my sitting room right after this. I . . . I may have found something for you."

Juniper's sad eyes lit up for a moment. "Thanks, Fannie."

"That's all," Fannie said. "Supper is on, and we open in two hours."

Such was my introduction to life in a whorehouse. That night as I lay in bed and listened to the distant sounds of a party, I puzzled over the turn my life had taken—and how I felt about it. In a way, I'd been rewarded because Ma died and I killed Pa—didn't I have my own fancy bedroom, a new wardrobe, and the longed-for chance to go to school? But on the other hand, I was in a whorehouse—clearly, to be a whore was not as bad as to murder, but both were beyond the path of respectability.

And by going—even happily—from one to the other, I'd sealed my fate. I would never, I then knew, live the everyday life of a schoolteacher or the wife of a doctor or merchant. I was outside the law, if not exactly an outlaw.

Chapter Five

"What do you know about nuns?" Fannie asked. She wore another of her "respectable" outfits—a gray suit of China silk piped in black braiding, with white gloves and a small white hat with an enormous feather that swooped down over one side of her face and destroyed all the respectability gained by the rest of her clothing. We were in the carriage—she had again told Hodge she would drive, and she did it with such command that I was impressed.

"They're Catholics," I answered.

Mrs. Carrerra had brought me three tailored skirts—one each in black, navy blue, and gray—and three crisp white shirts with tucked fronts. Today I wore the navy skirt—the one color Fannie hadn't specified.

Fannie's mouth twitched just a little, a sign I was beginning to learn to look for. "Yes," she said, "they're Catholics. So what?"

"They're popish. That's what Pa always said. They'll take over the country and give it to the Pope if we give them leave. Then the Pope will tell us all what to do." It was a litany I'd often heard repeated late at night in our cabin.

"I really am sorry I never had the chance to know your pa," Fannie said, clucking to the horses as they crossed Delarosa Street. Three young Mexican children ran in front of the carriage, spooking the horses with their screams, but Fannie's hands on the reins were firm.

"I don't think you'd have liked him," I said primly, and then instantly knew that I'd been gullible again.

Fannie's laughter roared to the surface. "Liked him?" she exclaimed. "I'd have cut him to size in nothing flat. Can't stand men like that—stupid but opinionated."

"He didn't like women like you either," I said. "I mean . . . I don't think he liked women that didn't do what men told them to."

She laughed again. "I'm sure he didn't. But look at the daughter he raised." She took her eyes off the horses and the street to look at me.

"My mama raised me," I said fiercely.

"All right. Let's go back to the nuns. Do you know how they dress? That's my real point. They wear long black gowns—lots of layers of heavy black cloth, even in this god-awful hot weather. And they've got these things on their heads—wimples, they're called—that barely leave their faces poking out. I always wonder what's happened to their hair, shut under those things day in and day out."

I simply stared at her, unable to imagine the outfits that she was describing. "Why?"

"Why? I don't know. Guess they think that's what the Lord . . . or maybe the Pope . . . wants. But I wanted you to know, so you wouldn't gape at them."

"Yes, ma'am," I said. "I won't gape."

But I almost did. When Mother Superior Theresa Alberta at the Ursuline Academy ushered us into her private office, it was all I could do to keep from asking her what color her hair was. I had to admit, silently to myself, that she had a sweet face. The kindness that shone from it was missing from Fannie's or Lillie's or Wallie's or even from my face. Mother Theresa had not known life in a whorehouse or with an abusive father, that was for sure.

"Etta?" she said. "A lovely name. Unfortunately, not related to any saint that I know of, but . . . Tell me of your schooling, child."

Judy Alter

While Fannie told her our story, now firmly imprinted on both our minds, about how I was her niece, the daughter of her recently deceased brother, I took secret looks around the Mother Superior's office. The walls were bare except for a cross with Jesus hanging from it—crucifix, Fannie told me later—and the curtainless windows were high so that they let in light but you couldn't look out. We sat in straight wooden chairs, and Mother Theresa sat behind a plain wooden desk, her own chair as uncomfortable as ours.

When she asked about my schooling, I explained that until her death my mother had taught me at home. "My father . . . ah . . . he wasn't happy with the school in Atlanta," I said, with some confidence, "and Mama preferred to keep me at home with her, sick as she was."

Mother Theresa clicked her tongue sympathetically. "We'll start you in the fourth form in the fall"—she laughed a little, as though to reassure me—"though I'm sure you'll advance rapidly. But I feel that's what we must do."

"The fourth form?" I asked.

"Girls about nine or ten," Fannie said dryly. "You'll advance, Etta, don't worry about it."

And so I began to spend my days with girls six and seven years younger than I, while I spent my evenings in the company—sort of—of girls much more worldly.

Actually I didn't see Fannie's girls from day to day. The house was deadly quiet when I arose to go to school—Julie woke me and fed me, and Hodge drove me in the carriage, but Fannie didn't even stir. And when I came home from school, there was just the faint murmuring of a household coming alive for the day, this at four o'clock in the afternoon! Sometimes I had supper with the girls, but they generally clustered together at two or three of the tables while I sat alone at another. Only Lillie ever really tried to talk to me.

"Why're you going to school?" she asked casually one night. "I quit as soon as I could."

"Fannie is good enough to send me," I said, "and I want to be a schoolteacher someday." It was the future that Fannie had laid out for me and that we both talked about, in spite of my certain knowledge that I could not live enough within the law to be a schoolteacher.

44

"A teacher! Land, can you imagine going back into the schoolroom when you didn't have to!" She laughed a little and then said seriously, "I'm waitin' for some tall, dark, and handsome man to take me away from all this"—she waved a hand expansively—"and I'm gonna be a housewife. Just like my mama." She laughed nervously. " 'Course, Mama didn't start in a place like this." And then, for just a minute, I thought I saw a tear in Lillie's eyes.

"Some outlaw's gonna take me away," Cassie said. "I'm gonna ride with him and his gang, find me some adventure."

Juniper, who usually stayed aloof from the other girls and ate alone in silence, muttered softly, "Probably no one is gonna take either of you anywhere 'less you take yourselves."

Maud Walker just stared at me, her expression unfriendly.

"Well," Lillie said happily, "I didn't say he had to be honest. Just rich. That's all I ask."

They seemed to believe that life was just beginning for them and that adventure and excitement lay straight ahead. Increasingly since I'd come to Fannie's, I shared that feeling—deep inside I knew I wasn't going to the Ursuline Academy forever, and I wasn't going to live in a whorehouse. What puzzled me was what form my future would take, where the excitement would come from. Mostly I tried to tell myself that the future would sort itself out in time, and I had only to be patient . . . and watchful. Meanwhile, life in Ben Wheeler, even Mama and Ab, seemed increasingly remote, almost as though that had been another person in another lifetime. Only Pa continued to haunt me.

Fannie often took her supper alone in her rooms, but sometimes she joined the rest of us, and then she ate with me, which was fine except that she had a tendency to quiz me unmercifully about what I'd learned in school that day.

"Sometimes," I said one evening, "it's not easy to say exactly what you've learned. I think it all goes together somewhere in my mind, but I can't tell you specifically. Oh, maybe I learned that King Richard III called out 'A horse! My kingdom for a horse!' when he was defeated in battle, but that probably won't do me much good. Today I practiced pouring tea and serving little tiny sandwiches to the other girls. I could demonstrate. . . ."

Behind me I heard a giggle—Lillie, no doubt. Fannie, mollified, finished her supper in silence. It was the first time I'd ever bested her, and I relished it.

But when the customers—guests, clients, whatever they were called—began to arrive, I was banished from the public parts of the house. Once in a while, when I was supposed to be studying, I crept to the door to the parlor and peeked around the curtains. What I saw excited me in a strange way. Oh, not sexually. It was the freedom and the happiness—at least, that's how it looked to me, after all those years shut up in a cabin in East Texas with a grim father and a cowed mother.

Most evenings a man played the piano that sat at the end of the parlor, plunking out lively tunes while the girls and their "guests" gathered around, drinks in hand. Frequently a girl would take her guest to one of the sofas, where they would sit in earnest conversation . . . or once in a while I saw a couple kissing. As I'd watch, one couple and then another would detach themselves from the group and head to the doorway. I knew they were going up those stairs, but I always had to bolt back to my room first so as not to be caught peeking.

The men fascinated me. Though none looked like Pa, they were a wild variety. There were men in business suits who looked to be bankers and lawyers; others looked like Mr. Newsome—men who owned small businesses and came to the city to escape their lives and maybe their wives. And then there were men whose dress and manner clearly indicated that they were cowboys—denim work pants, denim shirts, boots. I'd heard Fannie say that all guns had to be checked with Hodge at the door, but some of them surely looked like they normally wore six-shooters. But there were no farmers among them—Pa would not have known how to survive, let alone behave in a place like this. When I thought that, I asked myself why Pa was still the measure by which I interpreted things. Could I never put him behind me?

The girls seemed evenhanded in the distribution of their favors, making as big a fuss over the cowboys as the bankers and lawyers. And make a fuss they did—patting the men's cheeks, fingering the lapels of their coats or the collars of their shirts, laughing into their eyes and whispering in their ears, generally behaving in ways that would have scandalized Mama . . . and

46

which now intrigued me. Without knowing it, I learned a lot about flirting from my secret hiding place.

"And just what do you think you're doing?" Fannie's voice, stern now, jolted me out of that speculation. While I thought she was in the dining room, she had come from behind me.

"I . . . I was just . . ."

"You were just peeking," she said without the slightest bit of amusement in her voice. "Do you want to go out there and join them?"

"No," I said quickly, "no, I really don't."

"Then I'd suggest you get back to your books. And don't let me ever find you 'peeking' again."

"Yes, ma'am." I barely had time to notice that Juniper stood behind Fannie, her eyes red as though she'd been crying. As I turned into my room, I heard Fannie say,

"Juniper, you go on upstairs and take the night off. We'll work on this."

Work on what? I wondered.

Twice the first year I lived there Fannie closed the house because a special group of men arrived. The first time I was ordered not to leave my room, the order so sternly delivered that I was cowed and did not disobey. But to me the usual noises of the night were exaggerated—the men's voices, the women's laughter were all louder. And late at night, as I lay in my bed, I heard a man come back to Fannie's room with her. The door shut tightly, and I heard no more, but I was left with more questions than usual. The second time it happened, I was determined to find out who these men were. Though I dared not creep all the way to the parlor, I did go as far as the stairway hall where I could hide in the shadows under the stairs. I had to wait longer than usual for any couples to go upstairs—apparently, from the sounds of it, they were all having a riotous time in the parlors. Finally, though, they began to drift upstairs in pairs—these men were cowboys. At least they wore denim pants and shirts, leather vests, kerchiefs about their necks, and carried Stetsons. They looked, somehow, rougher than Fannie's usual clientele did—I didn't know what made me think that, maybe beards and mustaches, maybe their swagger as they walked. Whatever, there was something different about them.

And also something remarkable—most wore gun belts, and Fannie apparently overlooked her rule about checking guns at the door. These men, whoever they were, were a group apart for Fannie and the girls.

The second time they came, the men stayed four days and Fannie closed the house to all others the entire time. I found it tiresome, because I was confined to my room, unless I could sneak into the kitchen to visit with Julie and Hodge. But even they were less talkative and more on edge than usual, and they absolutely refused to tell me anything about our "guests."

Finally, the men left. That night, Fannie came into my room to, as she put it, check on my studies.

"How's school?" she asked brightly. "Haven't had much of a chance to check on you the last few days."

"You've been busy," I muttered. Then, boldly, "Who were those men?"

"Men?" she asked vaguely, which made me explode at her.

How dumb did she think I was? "The men," I said patiently, "for whom you closed the house, the men who stayed four days instead of one night, the men who apparently wore their guns to bed."

"How do you know that?" she snapped. "You've been peeking again."

"Just from behind the stairwell," I said. "If you'd told me who they were, maybe I wouldn't have peeked."

She looked at me for a long time without speaking. "You're right," she finally said. "I should have told you. They're outlaws." She waited to see if I would be shocked.

"I'm an outlaw," I said. "At least, I'm on the outside of the law. Why are they outlaws?"

"They rob banks and trains, and they come here to celebrate—sometimes to hide—after a job. They're . . . they're good customers."

"I can imagine," I said dryly.

It was a long time before the subject of outlaws came up again.

"Etta, can you read the next passage from the reader?" Sister Magdalena looked at me with her bright smile of anticipation.

I rattled off the passage, missing not a word. Behind me I heard a whisper and a giggle.

"Children, children, we will have order when one of our number reads aloud." Sister was indignant, as though misbehavior was beyond her comprehension.

I knew what the whisper was and why they giggled. Word had spread throughout the school that I was the girl who lived in a whorehouse—oh, they called it a female boardinghouse, the euphemism of the day, and most of them probably didn't even know what it meant, but they knew it was dirty. *Tarnished* was the word that came to mind. And I was the object of jokes because of it. I was getting very tired of the fourth form.

Within a month, I was promoted to the fifth, then the sixth form, and finally I was with the small group of girls my own age that still remained in school. Sister Theresa assured Fannie that I was making remarkable progress, but still two years yawned before me like an endless time. I wanted the schooling desperately, but I found I hated school—rather like writer Mark Twain when he said he hated writing but liked having written. I would have liked having been schooled—in the past. The lessons were easy for me, the sisters treated me as though I was breakable, and the other girls acted like I was a freak. I cared nothing for any of them.

"I'm Elizabeth, and I know where you live," said a girl in the upper level. She was pretty, probably too pretty for her own good, with curly dark blond hair piled around her face and caught with a fashionable ribbon at the back of her neck.

I nodded. What, after all, could I say?

"You must hate it," she said, drawing on what she must have thought was a deep well of sympathy.

"No, it's really quite exciting."

"All those men . . ."

"Some of them are quite handsome." I was deliberately making fun of her, though she had no way of knowing it.

"Do you . . . will you . . ."

I knew what she wanted to ask and thought it rude. "No," I said, though more and more I wondered what I would do when I finished school. My choices seemed limited, but it was not a problem I could discuss with Fannie. And I sure wasn't going to talk to this Elizabeth about it.

There was one good thing about the school that I much appreciated and that made me think of Mama: They taught manners. We had high tea, just like the English, every afternoon, and each of us in the upper forms had to take turns being hostess. That meant not only pouring the tea and serving the crumpets but also graciously leading the conversation.

Sister Theresa would give us the topic of the day. It might be the government's treatment of the Indians or whether or not women should have the vote or what was the United States's proper response to the growing unrest in Cuba. We were expected to be able to converse intelligently on these matters.

There was only one girl who truly became my friend at that school. Her name was Jolié, and her French parents had recently settled in Castroville, south and west of San Antonio. Jolié attended the Ursuline Academy as a boarding student. She was my age or, most likely, even a year or two older, and there was a certain worldliness about her. Like me, she would never have the innocent shine of Sister Theresa's face. "I hate it," she said vehemently, pushing a loose strand of black hair out of her eyes. "The girls, they are all so childish! And there are no men. And no one who speaks French."

I laughed. "I can't speak French to you, but I can sympathize about the girls. They're dumb and boring. But I don't miss the men."

"You don't?" She looked at me in disbelief.

I shrugged and bit my tongue to keep from telling her I knew where the men were if she was interested.

"I want to bring a friend home from school," I said boldly that evening. "She's a boarding student, and she hates it."

"I am truly sorry about that," Fannie said, sarcasm creeping into her voice, "but I imagine her family would hate it a lot worse if you brought the girl here."

"I don't want to be ashamed of where I live," I countered. "I did that all those years with Pa. . . ."

Fannie never minced her words. "Don't try the pitiful act on me, miss. I know you never had any friends, and I'm sure it's hard for you to make friends at the school. But I won't pity you because of what happened to you before . . . and I won't let you bring another young lady home here.

"And there's one more thing: I've watched you with Lillie. She's young and friendly and, in her own way, very naive. I don't want you to make friends—close friends, the confiding kind—with any of the girls. You may think some night late that you're sharing confidence and that you can unburden yourself of the story of your father, but you can't. Whores are not to be trusted—never met a one I would really trust—and your story would be all over the house by the next morning and the city by that night. You understand?"

I nodded. Fannie had read my mind, for I still longed to tell the story again to someone, if only to banish the ghost of Pa that I kept seeing.

"You keep your confidences for me," she said, but she had on her businesslike tone and not her laughing, happy personality. It didn't inspire confidences.

I never did bring Jolié home, though Fannie bought tickets so that Jolié and I could attend the opera when it came to San Antonio. Jolié thought that was every bit as wonderful as visiting me, and she remained the only friend I had in school.

What the Ursuline Academy taught me, besides education, was to be complete unto myself. I never got over wanting friends, but I learned first in Ben Wheeler and then at Fannie's that they were a luxury I could do without if I had to.

Isolation was nothing new to me, nor was loneliness. Though I missed Mama desperately, I refused to think about her, to think what she would say if she knew where I was living. Maybe, just maybe, she'd say, "But, Martha, you're getting an education, and maybe it's the Lord's way." But I couldn't be sure of that. I couldn't think about Mama and whores at the same time, and she would have hated that my name had changed.

If thoughts of Mama troubled me, Pa haunted me, late at night, when I was alone in my bed. I'd sometimes wake in terror, reliving that last night, thinking that he was crawling into my bed again. And then I'd see his face and hear him say, "You've killed me." My heart would pound, and I wanted badly to cry out for Mama to come put her arms around me. But Fannie was not the sort I could call to, and I forced myself to lie quietly in my bed. Sometimes sleep never came until almost morning.

Chapter Six

One incident remains forever clear in my mind from the years I lived with Fannie and attended the Ursuline Academy. A strange covered ambulance stood outside the house when I arrived from school one afternoon. Inside, everything was commotion—a police officer stood at the foot of the stairs in the front hall, Julie hovered toward the back of the hall wringing her hands, Lillie and Cassie were collapsed on sofas in the parlor, clinging to one another and sobbing, and Fannie was nowhere to be seen.

"What . . . ?"

"Miss Etta, you best go direct to your room," Hodge said in a tone with much more authority than he usually mustered. Even though he had just come in the door with me, he was apparently wise enough in the ways of the world—and of whorehouses—to understand the situation immediately. His warning was, of course, enough to make me go directly to Fannie's room instead of to my own.

The room was darkened, curtains pulled, and Fannie lay like a mound in the middle of the bed.

"Fannie!" Creeping closer, I could see that she had a cloth laid across her forehead—I guessed that it was a cold cloth against a headache, like those Mama had occasionally used.

"Go away, Etta."

Even in a short time, Fannie had taught me well. "I will when you tell me what's going on."

That made her angry enough to sit up in bed, flinging the cloth to the floor. "Why, you ungrateful little . . ."

"I'm not ungrateful," I said, almost repentant but not frightened by her. "I know something bad has happened, and I want to know what it is. Then maybe I can be of some help." I paused a minute. "I was raised to be helpful, you know."

She buried her head in her hands, and I could barely hear what she said. It began with "Juniper . . ." and trailed off into muttering I couldn't understand.

Something struck clear to the bone in me, and I remembered Juniper's red eyes the night Fannie caught me peeking. Sitting on the bed to put an arm around Fannie's shoulders, I asked gently, "What about Juniper?"

"Laudanum. She took laudanum. I . . . I never had a girl even try that before."

I had no idea what laudanum was, of course, but it didn't take much to guess. "Is she . . . is she . . . ?"

"She's dead," Fannie said bluntly. "Lillie found her 'bout an hour ago. I called the police. I . . . I guess they'll take her away."

Juniper, who had always been sad, was sad no more, I thought. "Why did she do that?"

Fannie sighed, pushed the pillows behind her to prop herself up, and looked at me. "She was caught in the life," she said, "couldn't see any way to get out of it. And she was getting too old."

"Too old?"

"A whore's not a lot of use after she's thirty and something," she said bitterly. "Remember that if you're ever tempted to take up the life."

I wanted to tell her that I knew that the life wasn't what was waiting for me any more than teaching was, but I didn't think this was the time to say it. "I thought you were going to find some place for her to go."

Fannie shook her head miserably. "I tried. Thought I found a family that had kids and wanted a nursemaid. Juniper, she was raised in a big family, and then once she had two children of her own . . . She'd have known how to raise those babies."

"Two children of her own?" I echoed in disbelief.

"That was why she was so sad, mostly. They drowned, fell into a stock tank when her husband was supposed to be watching them. You can imagine one falling in, but both of them? It . . . it just broke her apart. She left home and never went back."

I felt I was drowning in misery myself, as though Fannie were piling detail on detail deliberately to make me sad. Maybe, I thought, there's some kind of moral lesson here I'm supposed to understand. "Juniper didn't get the position as a nursemaid, did she?"

"No. They decided they couldn't have a fallen woman as a nursemaid. That man—I ought to tell you his name—he's spent more time and money in this house than almost anyone in San Antonio. And then he turns righteous!" Anger was replacing her despair.

I could see lots of complications she apparently overlooked— mostly the man's wife and her apparently justifiable opinion of Fannie and a woman who had worked for Fannie—but I didn't say that.

"We've got to arrange the funeral," Fannie said, suddenly her old decisive self again.

"Does she have family?" I thought about Mama's pitiful funeral and hoped that Juniper had people who would grieve over her.

"Just that no-account husband, and she sure wouldn't want him around. No, we'll be her family." Within seconds, she was in her wrapper, her hair fixed, her nose powdered, ready to do whatever she had to.

"Fannie," I said softly as she headed out the door, "how old are you?"

She turned a wise eye on me. "Twenty-seven. I've got three more years." And then she was gone.

I didn't believe her for a minute.

Fannie had an awful time trying to find someone to talk over Juniper at the city cemetery. She tried the Catholic priest, who was horrified, and the Methodist and Episcopalian ministers, who declined as politely as they could. The problem, of course, was twofold: Juniper's "profession" and the way she had died.

Finally, though, Fannie found a relatively young and new Disciples of Christ minister who agreed to say the words.

For that one day I was allowed to act like the rest of the girls—or at least to join them. It was a dreary February day, and we gathered in the public cemetery, a depressing place where the grave markers were either plain or nonexistent. Fannie had once driven me through a private cemetery on one of our Sunday drives, and I'd seen the elaborate markers rich people put up for their loved ones. In the city cemetery, the graves I'd fixed for Mama and Ab and Pa would have fit right in. There were no trumpeting angels, no smiling cherubs, no tall pointed spires that led the soul right up to God.

"God," the minister intoned, "we ask you to bless this woman whose life was marked by trouble so that she became an outcast of society. . . ."

The words came to me with a ferociousness that I felt in the pit of my stomach. My life had been marked by trouble, no doubt about that, and I was an outcast from society. If my true identity ever got out, I would be forever shunned—and for something a lot worse than living in a whorehouse. In the midst of the minister's prayer, I gave my own silent prayer to Fannie for having saved me from that fate.

"She was a victim, Lord, of your terrible vengeance, but also a victim of the world in which she lived. We leave final judgment up to you, O Great Lord, but ask you to look with pity and tenderness upon this thy servant, Juniper."

There was a loud honking noise, and, startled, I looked up to see Hodge blowing his nose vigorously, while Julie wept openly into a handkerchief. Lillie looked terrified, as though she'd never believed death could come that close to her. Even the flamboyant Wallie was subdued, and Cassie looked upset though she had no tears in her eyes. Only Maud remained unmoved, staring stonily at the casket poised above the unmarked grave.

Fannie closed the house that night, out of respect, she said, but the next night it was business as usual. And I went back to school feeling more removed than ever from my classmates, who had not an inkling of whores and laudanum and abusive fathers. Even Jolié, I decided, wouldn't understand, and I was relieved that Fannie had not allowed me to bring her home. I had been in San Antonio six months and it seemed in some ways like forever.

Fannie was in no hurry to find a girl to replace Juniper. For months—almost a year—there were only four girls in Fannie Porter's house. It didn't seem to slow business down much, and it didn't seem to worry Fannie. How one went about recruiting for such a position, I didn't know and I didn't ask.

Finally, in December of 1893, Annie Rogers appeared in the parlor one evening and was properly introduced, just the way I had been a year earlier. For once, I was allowed—even invited—to the meeting. She was unusually tall but thin, not a big woman like Fannie, and she had fiery red hair—not Wallie's funny henna color—and green eyes that looked as though they were sizing you up. When she appeared at that meeting, Annie wore a conservative white shirtwaist and brown skirt—the sort of thing I would have worn to school—but she didn't look like a schoolgirl. There was something about her that made me think she knew where she was going, what she was after.

When she introduced herself, she just said. "I'm Annie Rogers" and never told us where she was from, where she'd recently been, not a thing. She was friendly in turn to each of the girls, but when I was introduced—with Fannie's cautionary "She's not one of the girls"—Annie gave me an appraising look that cut to the bone.

By now I was seventeen, nearly as old as Cassie had been when she came to Fannie's, I was sure, and I was beginning to feel self-conscious about my protected status. I was literally a schoolgirl among whores, and I thought that perhaps it was a weakness in me, a lack of daring, that I was not in the parlor at night with the other girls. Yet I knew that surely was not the direction of my future. And I also knew by now that Fannie would have never let me make that my direction.

"Pleased to meet you," Annie said, looking directly at me. "I used to be a teacher. Maybe we've got something in common."

Maud Walker gave a sort of half-laugh, half-snort, but Lillie said, "What a nice idea. I think Etta's lonely a lot."

I knew right away that I was going to disobey Fannie: Annie Rogers was going to be my friend.

For a month or so, Annie and I simply nodded and smiled in the dining room, much as I did with the other girls. But when we'd all eat, I'd see her watching me, her eyes speculative. The girls all liked her, and she talked animatedly with each of them, but it was sort of like she wasn't paying full attention to them. Annie Rogers was a puzzle.

In spite of Fannie's warnings, I continued to peek at the curtain some nights. I noticed that Annie was as popular with the men as she was with the girls. She soon had several "regulars" who came to visit her, and I'd watch her make each man feel that he was the only man in her life—her eyes laughing at him, her attention focused on him, her posture inviting and yet ladylike. I began to model myself after Annie. Late at night, when everyone's attention was anywhere but on me, I would practice in front of the big mirror that stood in a walnut frame in my room. Annie had, I decided, the air of being a lady, and that was important to me—a kind of self-assured sophistication that dictated slow, controlled movements, an ability never to look flustered, trip over the carpet, or bump into the furniture. And she was just mysterious enough to hint to the men that if they got her alone . . .

Annie had been at the house about three months when one night at supper she picked up her plate and glass and brought them over to the table where I sat alone. A silence you could almost feel came over the room as the other girls stared at her, knives and forks and glasses suspended in midmotion.

"Mind if I join you?"

"Of course not," I said smiling, glad that at last we were going to be friends.

Her movements were deliberate as she set her dinner down, arranging the plate and glass to suit her, then seating herself and ever so carefully spreading her napkin on her lap. Fannie always insisted on linen napkins, and each of us had a special napkin ring so that we could save our napkins and use them more than once. A touch of elegance I'd never dreamed of in Ben Wheeler.

She took two or three bites before she spoke to me, and by then the other girls had gone back to talking among themselves. "Why're you here?"

"I'm Fannie's niece," I said, repeating the story that was now so familiar that I almost believed it. "She took me in to educate when my father died. . . . I'm from Georgia. Atlanta."

Her eyes twinkled. "What if I told you I don't believe a word of that?"

I thought for a minute, and then I said softly, "I think you best not say that to Fannie."

Her laughter was much softer than Fannie's roar, but it was just as genuine. "I don't intend to," she said. "But you aren't a niece . . . and you're hiding something, though I'll be dadblamed if I can figure out what." Fannie's warning echoed in my ears— tell a whore, and it'll be all over the house by morning, the town by the next night.

"I don't know what you mean," I said distantly.

She sighed. "I didn't think you would. But can we be friends anyway, without solving my suspicions and your distrust?"

"Of course," I said, putting aside Fannie's other warning: Make no friends among whores.

She took another tack. "Do you like school?"

I looked at her for a long minute before I spoke. "No, not at all. I'm glad to learn, but I'm bored with it. I . . . well, I feel there's adventure ahead of me, and I'm just putting in time at school waiting for it to happen."

She laughed again. "Lots of girls would think living in a whorehouse was adventure enough. But I guess we all feel that way, as though something great was just around the corner."

I was a little deflated to think that my sense of impending adventure was not mine alone but shared by all the others. Oh, I knew Lillie expected to be swept away by a dashing stranger and Cassie expected to ride away with an outlaw, but I dismissed those fantasies as childish. My own undefined dream was more true.

After that Annie ate with me frequently, and we traded guarded confidences. I never told her about Ben Wheeler and Pa, though I talked often of my mother and my brother, and she never told me where she was from, but she talked of a lost love who had been life itself to her and had died tragically. We didn't trade details, but we shared feelings.

Fannie came to my room late one night. "You're taking a real shine to that Annie, aren't you?"

"She talks to me," I said, "like I was a real person. The others . . . they resent me, because of the way you treat me."

Fannie was in one of her kind and generous moods, rather than her businesslike-madam stance. "I know that," she said, "and I'm glad you have someone to talk to. Just remember what I said: Don't talk too much."

"I know," I said, with just a trace of annoyance creeping into my voice. How, I wondered, could I resent someone who had done for me all the things Fannie had done. And yet, childlike, I resented her authority over me.

Maud Walker was so full of her big news at dinner one night that she forgot she usually didn't talk to me and included the whole room in her conversation. Excitement was rare for the usually silent Maud, and I listened with interest. Thank heaven Fannie was eating alone in her room.

"Got a telegram," Maud said. "Kid Curry's comin'. Says he pulled a big job."

Lillie was on her in a minute. "Shhh. You know you're not supposed to say that."

Maud shrugged. "Everybody here knows." Lillie cast a significant glance in my direction. "All right, except her. But you know Fannie's told her. Anyway, he's comin' and he's bringin' Will Carver with him. How about that, Lillie?"

Lillie blushed, of all things. "I guess I'd like that," she said.

"Who are these people?" Annie Rogers asked unbelievingly. "You'd think the Crown Prince of England was coming here."

Lillie giggled. "I guess he probably wouldn't stop on San Saba Street if he ever did come to San Antonio. They're outlaws from Wyoming, Utah . . . up that way somewhere."

"Now who's talking too much?" Maud asked sharply. "I bet you best shut your mouth before Fannie hears what you've been saying."

It was Lillie's turn to shrug.

Annie lingered in the dining room after the others left. "You know these men?" she asked.

I shook my head. "Fannie makes me stay in my room when they're here. That is, if they're the ones I think they are."

Annie wrinkled her nose in distaste. "Doesn't sound like fun to me."

Without meaning to, I stared at her. Whoever these men were, no matter if she found them disgusting, she would have to sleep with one, two, or three of them—more than once. I wanted badly to ask why she did it, how she could make herself do it. Memories of Pa floated before me, and I remembered my sick disgust. Inanely, I said, "Well, back to the books."

Instead of leaving, Annie sat down in the chair next to me, just as I started to rise. I sat back down. "You're amazing," she said. "You live in a whorehouse, and yet you manage to remain somehow free from it. What are you hiding . . . or hiding from? I don't understand it." She shook her head in puzzlement.

I studied her face for a minute and found nothing there but honesty. So I said what had been on my mind for a long time. "I think there's a story behind you that I don't understand. I've thought so ever since we first talked."

She raised her shoulders just a bit and turned to stare out the window. "I don't mind talking about it now, not like I used to. My father raped me almost every day for several years. Started when I was ten. My mother . . . she knew, but she didn't do anything."

"You didn't kill him?" I asked. Having tried so hard to think I was justified in killing Pa, I came to believe it was the way everyone acted.

She looked astounded. "Kill him? Of course I didn't. I just ran away from home."

"I killed my father," I said, shutting my ears to the tiny voice inside me that chanted Fannie's warning about telling secrets to a whore. In Annie I saw the one person who understood, because the same thing had happened to her. I guess I thought if she was that honest with me, I owed her equal measure. I still believed that if I talked about it, the memory would stop haunting me. And Fannie had long ago stopped letting me talk about it.

"You what?"

"I killed him. The second time he came to my bed. I . . . I warned him that he would never do that again. I was sixteen." It sounded more awful in the telling than I had expected.

She looked at me with a certain wonder. "You were stronger than I was . . . and older. I . . . I didn't know I could do anything but run away."

Surely she didn't admire me for having taken a life. I had to change the subject quickly. "You said you were a teacher?"

"I was. In Kennedale, Texas. Sort of helped the real teacher in a one-room school, because I'd had lots of schooling. What your father does to you at night isn't supposed to keep you from going to class the next day." Her laugh was bitter. "But I . . . I couldn't keep on teaching. I felt tainted, dirty . . . so I do what gives me a reason for feeling that way." Her eyes were out the window again. "But I'm not going to do it forever!"

"No," I said, "I know you're not. And I'm not ever going to do it."

"Good for you," she said. "Well, I got to get ready for the night. See ya, Etta."

"See ya," I echoed. Relieved to have shared my burden, I refused to believe that Fannie was right that I was foolish to confide in Annie. She was my friend, bound to me by a tie stronger even than that by which Fannie claimed my loyalty.

As I wandered back to my room, I wondered when the outlaws would arrive.

They came four days later, making a lot of noise late in the night. I wasn't sure, but I thought there were other customers there when they arrived—and that the other customers left fairly quickly. There was a lot of shouting and two gunshots. The next day I saw that one of Fannie's crystal chandeliers—the one in the front parlor—was shattered. Two days later, without any comment by anyone, it was replaced.

I peeked that night for sure, but I didn't have to go far to do it. I was actually asleep when they arrived, wakened by their shouts. But what brought me out of bed, some two or three hours after they arrived, were voices in Fannie's room—loud voices.

"Curry, you get out of that bed!" It was Fannie's voice at its most strident, raised in a tone that even I had never heard.

A masculine voice answered, and though the speech was slurred, I could understand the words. "I'm gonna sleep here, Fannie. You wanna sleep here too?"

"Curry, you go upstairs with Maud where you belong. . . ." Fannie's voice had begun to take on a pleading tone.

Then Maud's voice joined in. "Come on, Curry, let's go upstairs."

Judy Alter

The masculine voice grew stiff. "You go on upstairs, Maud, and you take whoever you want. I'm staying here."

There was a kind of muffled talking, a door slamming, footsteps walking away—the disappointed Maud, I supposed—and then silence. Finally I went to sleep.

Next morning I heard from an excited Julie that Kid Curry had slept in Fannie's satin sheets with his boots, pistols, and hat still in place. All I could surmise was that he had lain very still all night long. I never did speculate on where Fannie slept.

"They were a mess." Annie had caught me in front of the house, before I got in from school the day after the outlaws left.

"They were noisy," I conceded.

She looked sideways at me. "That's not all they were. Too damn big for their britches, that's what! Lord deliver me from any more outlaws."

"You didn't like them?" It sounded naive even as I said it.

"No," she said emphatically, "I didn't like them. And that Kid Curry was the worst of them all—mean-spirited, selfish, son of . . . I can't imagine why Maud hangs on his every movement." Her voice trailed off, and something made me wonder if maybe she despised Kid Curry so because he had paid all his attention to Maud, except the night he slept in Fannie's bed—and ignored Annie. I guessed I would never understand whores.

"I hope they never come back," she said vehemently.

"Me too," I said, though I realized that our reasons were a little different. But we both agreed that we wanted nothing more to do with the outlaws—and that seemed another bond between us.

Chapter Seven

Sundance. Butch always called him "the Kid," as though every third outlaw throughout the West were not Kid something or other. For Butch, there was no other Kid. For me, there was no one but Sundance, and I always called him that, even after I found out that the name came not from his magic charm but from the much less romantic fact that he had spent time in the jail at Sundance, Wyoming, when he was younger.

He appeared at Fannie's one day in the spring of 1894. When I came in from school in the afternoon—I was in my last year at the academy, and Fannie was beginning to talk about teaching positions—he was sitting at one of the small tables in the dining room, talking with Fannie.

I stood in the doorway a moment and watched them. Fannie was listening intently, leaning toward him, paying him much more attention than she did most men who came to the house. In fact, I'd never seen her look at a man like this, and maybe that's what first caught my attention.

Slouched back in his chair, casual and comfortable, he looked to be between Fannie and me in age, probably at least ten years older than I was. But the years had not been hard on him, and he looked sort of boyish. He wasn't tall, just medium height, and slightly built, but he had an easy grace about him. His hair was dark reddish-blond and thick, matched by a neatly trimmed mustache. And he was carefully dressed, his suit of dark gray broadcloth—no outdated nankeen for him—and he wore a linen shirt, with a black silk cravat, tied bow-fashion under the collar. Before I heard him talk, I would have told you he was from the East and a city man.

"Hello!" He dragged the word out into several syllables and added the sound of surprise to it. Then I knew he was a westerner, and suddenly I knew that he was an outlaw, though I don't know how that knowledge came to me. He was certainly better looking and better behaved than Kid Curry, at least according to what Annie had told me. "She's my niece," Fannie said sharply, turning to look at me in displeasure.

"Of course she is," he answered smoothly as he got up and came toward me, his hand extended. "Harry Longabaugh. They call me Sundance."

I was almost rooted to the spot, mesmerized by those blue, blue eyes. But I did manage to extend my hand. He bent to brush his lips across it, a kiss that I felt up my arm, clear to the top of my head.

"I'm Etta."

He just smiled and held a chair for me to seat myself between him and Fannie.

She was looking her most severe. "Etta is in school at the Ursuline Academy," she said.

"Of course she is," he repeated, but he never took his eyes off me, and I, in confusion, looked down at the books I carried.

"Sundance will be here for a while," Fannie said, and her tone carried a clear warning that she did not expect time to breed familiarity between the two of us. "He'll sleep in that extra bedroom upstairs."

"Alone," he added with a mischievous grin, staring at me until I blushed. "Where are you from?" he asked, leaning forward and stretching his hand out as though he would grasp my hand in his. He stopped just short of that, under Fannie's watchful eye.

"She's my niece, I told you," Fannie said. "Raised outside Atlanta."

"Georgia?" he asked, incredulous, just the edge of laughter sneaking into his disbelief.

"Yes, Georgia." Fannie held her ground.

"Why, Fannie, I never knew you had relatives back there." He said it in mock seriousness, playing with her to my discomfort.

I realized I had said only two words in that whole long exchange, and now I gathered myself together to ask, "Have you known Fannie long?"

"You mean," he asked, whirling from Fannie to me, "that you don't call her 'Aunt Fannie'?" His grin was infectious.

I grasped for words, but Fannie interrupted me in a dry, nononsense tone of voice. "All right, Sundance. She's my niece. You don't need to know her life story, because you aren't gonna see any more of her."

"Why, Fannie . . . you purely amaze me." Then he turned toward me, almost as if she hadn't spoken. "I've known your . . . ah . . . aunt for several years, been a visitor in her house from time to time. Enjoyed the hospitality, I must say." He favored Fannie with a huge grin.

"Etta," she said sternly, "I think you best go tell Julie you're home and then get to your books."

"Yes, ma'am." But I rose reluctantly, and as I left the room I turned to look again at him. He was staring at me.

Outside the dining room, I almost bumped into Annie, who had apparently been peeking around the corner of the door—I wasn't the only one in this house given to peeking.

"Who *is* he?" she asked.

"An outlaw," I said serenely, sailing past her with my books in my hand.

Annie was right behind me. "How do you know?"

"I can tell."

He didn't appear at supper that night, and I admit to some disappointment. Annie was relentless.

"Where's your outlaw?"

"I don't know," I replied, feigning disinterest.

"I saw how he looked at you this afternoon. You better watch out. You know what Fannie thinks about your—what's her word?—fraternizing with the customers."

65

I wanted to reply hotly that he wasn't a customer and I wasn't fraternizing with him. But I knew another blush would give me away. I managed to say, "He's . . . he's staying a long time. He's not just a one-night visitor."

Annie smiled, her look full of anticipation, and I knew full well what she intended. I felt like reminding her that she was the one who hated outlaws, not me.

That night I was the one who peeked. The formal parlor was full of loud noise, voices overcoming the piano. Several men stood around the piano singing, their voices straining to match the "Sweet Adeline" that was being banged out by the piano player. The girls hovered around them, and I saw instantly that Annie stood with her arm casually around Sundance's shoulders. He sang heartily, at least pretending that he was unaware of her presence. And never once, while I watched, did he turn his head to smile at her, the way I'd seen men do too many times in my peeking.

Later that night, after I had really and truly been studying for a while, I crept back to the first hall just in time to see Annie go up the stairs with a man I didn't recognize. Though he was smiling and joking with her, she almost stomped her way up the stairs. A few minutes later Sundance went up those stairs, and as he had forecast he was alone.

I went to bed, a certain gladness filling my soul. I was too naive to fantasize about Sundance and me, to build a dream life—or even a dream encounter—for the two of us. But I was certainly glad he hadn't gone up those stairs with Annie or one of the other girls. I never did figure out where he got his supper.

In the next two days I saw him occasionally, usually from a distance. He would appear at odd hours and be missing at times I expected to see him, like supper. When we met in a hallway, he flustered my soul by looking hard at me, but always with a smile.

Three days after his arrival, he appeared at Fannie's front door riding a fine Thoroughbred and leading another. I had just gotten home from school and put my books on my study table when I heard Hodge calling ever so softly, "Miss Etta. You best come out in front. Mr. Sundance, he done brought two horses. He says for you to come out there."

Two horses? Whatever for? But quick as a flash I was out the front door.

There he was, wearing another fine suit, sitting astride a beautiful chestnut. One hand held the horse's reins while the other led a second, equally fine horse.

Grinning, he asked, "You ride?"

"I—I've ridden a workhorse," I said. And then I felt compelled to add, "Never with a saddle."

His laughter echoed across the street. "I thought so. Atlanta, my foot! You're from the country, girl!"

"Fannie told you 'outside Atlanta,'" I reminded him.

"More likely, outside San Antonio," he hooted. "You ever ride sidesaddle?" Before I could answer, he went on, "No, of course you haven't. All right, I'll give you a lesson."

With that he dismounted, hitched his own horse to one of Fannie's fancy hitching posts—they were cast metal, shaped like little black boys holding their hands out for the reins—and handed me the reins to the led horse. "Here, hold this while I demonstrate."

Now, a sidesaddle is at best an awkward affair. There's a curving horn on the left side around which you're supposed to hook your left knee, and then you ride with both legs on the same side of the saddle. It's made more graceful when your legs are covered by countless yards of riding skirt, but when a man in trousers tries to demonstrate, it's purely ridiculous. Of course, until Sundance showed me, I didn't know a thing about sidesaddles, but I knew enough to laugh at his posture as he tried to show me how to mount. In fact, I laughed aloud.

"How did you ride that damn workhorse?" he demanded.

"Astride," I answered. "I pulled my skirts up to where they didn't get in the way."

Now it was his turn to laugh. "Well, I don't hardly think I can take you riding in San Antonio that way. You'll have to master this blasted saddle."

He helped me up, his hands moving my legs into position and sending that same electric thrill through me that I'd felt when he kissed my hand two days earlier. I managed, however, to keep my composure and end up seated on the horse, though it was an uncertain seat at best. Fortunately, the horse was calm and stayed fairly still through this whole procedure. My skirt was a plain broadcloth cut for school—not the yards of cloth meant to cover a sidesaddle—and I was sure I looked ridiculous. But I didn't care.

Without my noticing her, Fannie had appeared on the porch. I wondered later if Hodge had summoned her.

"I'm just taking your niece for a ride," Sundance called happily. "She needs the fresh air."

I guess Fannie knew that she couldn't make a fuss in public. She shrugged and went inside, but I could tell from the set of her shoulders that she was angry. Hodge followed nervously behind her. And I thought I saw Annie peeking out of one of the upstairs windows.

Riding sidesaddle was not easy. I felt as though I would slide off the horse at any minute—on the left side, of course. Sundance was good about keeping the pace slow.

"Want me to keep the reins?" he asked. The idea that any man had to hold the reins to my horse galled me, and I said no, I could manage by myself. But between keeping my seat and guiding the horse, I was hard put.

We rode through the city streets. "You mean you've never seen the Alamo?" He was incredulous. "You've been here how long, and you've never seen it?"

"Nobody ever offered to show it to me," I said, feeling as though my education and background were lacking just because I'd never seen one famous ruined fort.

"You know what happened there?" he demanded.

"The Mexicans killed some Texans."

His laughter rolled over me. "I'm not a Texan, but I can even do better than that at telling the story." And then he launched into a tale about Davy Crockett and Jim Bowie and Colonel Travis, who drew a line in the sand and dared men not to be cowards. "I . . . if I'd been there, I'd have been with Travis," he concluded. "I'd never have run."

"You'd have died," I said. It seemed a simple choice to me: run or be killed.

"I'd have died knowing I was doing the right thing."

I didn't tell him I thought that was a strange sensibility for an outlaw.

The Alamo really was just a hollow shell of a building, with a couple other falling-down buildings and a wall that had great, gaping holes in it. The roof was mostly gone over the main building, there was brush and cactus everywhere, and in one corner a pile of dirty blankets seemed to indicate that someone was living there.

"Don't you just feel the spirit of those men?" he asked.

I shook my head. "It's dirty and falling down. Why don't they just tear it down?"

"Because," he said sarcastically, "it's a shrine. Some Texan you are."

Outside he bought chili from an old woman with a pushcart. It was spicy and hot and burned my tongue, but he ate it without blinking and went back for seconds. The old woman smiled at him and said, "*Muy bueno.*"

"You, too," he said, and then, with an apologetic smile to me, "I don't speak Spanish."

"Tell her *gracias*," I said.

It came out like "grassy-ass," and I giggled at him.

We were mounted again—me still sliding off that sidesaddle—and we rode through the market area, passing stands where they sold fresh vegetables and poultry, wagons full of hay or wool or hides.

"This is such a wonderful city," he said enthusiastically. "I love all the different people and things. You can get Mexican food, German food, look at the river, sit in the park. . . . I envy you living here."

"I've never seen it like this," I said. "I just go to Fannie's and school. No one has shown me the city . . . and Fannie sure wouldn't let me wander around alone."

He was amazed again. "You live in San Antonio and you haven't seen it? It's not just the Alamo you missed—it's the whole city."

We had come to a park, a green openness with lush palm trees and beds of roses. Sundance dismounted and helped me down. After he ground-tied both horses, he surprised me by producing a blanket on which we could sit. We sat in silence for several minutes, he comfortable and me anxious.

"You aren't from Atlanta . . . or Georgia," he said. "Want to tell me about it?"

I considered for a long moment and then said, "No."

Sundance laughed—I soon learned that his laughter always bubbled to the surface, and it was one of the things that made me love him. "All right, I'll tell you about me."

"Please," I said.

He looked startled, as though no one had ever wanted to hear about him. "My family," he said, "generally doesn't want to hear my stories. They'd some of them like to forget I was ever born a Longabaugh."

I could have told him I was sorry, but I didn't think he wanted sympathy. Besides, of all people, I knew that sometimes family were wonderful, like Mama and Ab, and sometimes, like Pa, they were a burden. "Are you going to begin with 'I was born . . .'?" I asked.

Grinning, he said, "All right, I was born in Pennsylvania, the last of five children. My pa, he farmed some but his heart wasn't in it, and there . . . well, we were pretty poor. I read a lot as a kid—read about people who lived different from me, and I swore I'd live better than my folks."

"Do you rob people to do that?"

His eyes flew wide open, and he almost jumped up from his seat on the blanket. "What do you mean, rob people?"

"You're one of Fannie's outlaws, aren't you? From—what do they call it—the Hole-in-the-Rock?"

He threw back his head in laughter. "Hole-in-the-Wall! Wait till I tell Cassidy that one!" Then he really was on his feet, asking anxiously, "How did you know about that? Did Fannie tell you I was one of them?"

I shook my head, looking up at him. "I guessed . . . somehow I knew when I first met you. And I knew about the whole bunch ever since Harry Logan was here—Kid Curry, I think they call him."

"Mean son of a bitch," he muttered, and then quickly said, "Pardon me. . . . You didn't . . . you didn't have anything to do with Curry?"

I wasn't sure how he defined "to do with," but I quickly reassured him. "Fannie doesn't allow me to fraternize—it's her word—with any customers, and when outlaws are in the house she practically locks me in my room." His opinion of Kid Curry wasn't any better than Annie's, and yet they both associated with him—well, in one way or another.

Relieved, he sat back down. "Good for her. I don't trust a one of them—except Cassidy—and I wouldn't trust them around a schoolgirl, specially if there's liquor to be had."

"What is Hole-in-the-Wall?" I asked.

"A place," he said, "in Wyoming. Along what they call the Outlaw Trail. It's a canyon with rock walls, sort of part of the Big Horn Mountains. It's a place where outlaws hide and can't be found easily. Butch says a dozen men could hold off a hundred, because you can see for miles in any direction from the top of the wall."

"Is there a hole in it?" Somehow I envisioned a great round hole in a rock wall.

"Naw. There's a notch where you can run cattle through—and we've done that—but there's no hole."

I wanted to go there, to see it. "Finish your story. How did you get from Pennsylvania to the Hole-in-the-Wall?"

"I followed an older brother to Colorado, place they call Cortez in the western part of the state. My brother—George—he raised horses, and I wrangled for him. I know a lot about horses." He didn't sound boastful, just as though he wanted me to know the truth.

"I could tell," I said, but the corners of my mouth twitched.

"Aw, not the sidesaddle. That's not fair!"

Then I laughed aloud, and in an instant he joined me. When he could stop laughing, he said, "I know a lot about choosing good horses, horses that will last."

"Do you steal horses?" I was absolutely intrigued by the adventure, or what I thought of as the adventure, of his life.

"Horses? No, I don't steal horses—at least not too much anymore. Used to, though. That's how I got started."

"What'd you do, just say to yourself, 'I'm going to steal a horse today'?"

His hand reached out ever so casually and covered mine where it lay on the blanket. "Not quite. I . . . well, there were some other fellows living around there—Matt Warner, and Bill Madden, and a couple of others—and they'd been doin' it—rustling is what it's called when you steal horses and change the brand—and they kind of took me along. Not Cassidy—he was there, but he wasn't stealing horses."

"Who's Cassidy?" My hand turned and nestled into his, and he moved a bit closer on the blanket so that we were very close to each other but not quite touching.

"Butch. His real name's Robert LeRoy Parker, but he calls himself Butch Cassidy. He's . . . well, he's the best friend I got in the world, and I'd go to the end of the earth for him. He would for me, too."

I wouldn't have gone to the other side of San Antonio for Annie, and she was probably the best friend I had. The whole idea of friendship that strong fascinated me. But I already knew, too, that I would have gone, willingly, to the end of the earth for Sundance.

"Cassidy's in jail now in Wyoming," he went on. "Got framed. Bought some horses from an old guy without knowing they were stolen. Fellow he thought was his friend testified against him, and the court decided Butch stole the horses, sentenced him to the state penitentiary. Probably the dumbest thing they ever did—he'll come out an outlaw for sure."

"Why would anybody lie about his stealing horses?"

Sundance looked away, squinting his eyes a little as though seeing a land not anywhere near where we were. "Big ranchers up there in Johnson County and around, they're fighting against the small ranchers. Butch just got caught in the middle."

"Will you get caught too?" I asked. My hand was still inside his.

"Not . . . least I hope not. Don't intend to. . . . Hey! Look at that sun goin' down. We best get back. Fannie'll skin me alive."

"She's more likely to skin me," I said. "Are you afraid of Fannie?"

His grin was pure mischief. "Nope. I know how to sweeten her."

Naive, I didn't even think to speculate on what he meant. I was reluctant to leave, and he had to pull me to my feet. When he did I found myself face-to-face with him, our faces only inches apart. We stared at each other, eyes locked.

He reached for me, then seemed to hesitate, and with a shrug said, "No, not now." Then, almost briskly, "Come on, let's get you back on that saddle."

This time as he helped me mount, his hands seemed impersonal, and I felt no surge of thrill. Something had changed the mood of the afternoon, and I wished I knew what it was.

Fannie was waiting when we got back to the house. "Sundance . . . ," she thundered as we walked into the front hall.

"Fannie," he said patiently, a bit of exasperation creeping into his voice, "we went for a ride, and I told your niece the sordid story of my background. That's all." He thought a minute. "No, that's not all. She's a charming young lady, and I enjoy her company. I . . . I also respect her."

Fannie looked somewhat mollified, but she didn't want to give up her anger totally, so she turned it on me. "You go to your room. I'll be there directly."

Smarting, I did as she said. Good as she'd been to me, Fannie didn't, I told myself, have control over my life. That was my belligerent mood when she knocked on my door.

"Everything I've tried to tell you about whores goes double for outlaws," she said, standing before the desk where I sat.

I didn't answer. There seemed to be nothing to say. "You get involved with that man, you'll spend your life wondering where he is, when he's coming back, whether or not he's in jail . . . or hung from a cottonwood someplace. It's no life for a lady."

Suddenly I started to giggle, and the more I giggled, the angrier Fannie got at me. Her hands were akimbo on her hips, and her eyes blazed. Finally I managed to say, "I'm not spending my life with him, Fannie. I just went for a ride. He . . . well, I really like him."

"That's what I mean," she said triumphantly. "I can see it in the two of you—and I'm no dummy about these things—you really like each other. You're both headed towards trouble you don't know."

There was more to the story than what Fannie was telling me, but I couldn't make it out. She was angry beyond measure, if her only thought was to protect me.

I stood up to face her. "Fannie, I've had trouble, and you've rescued me, for which I'm more grateful than I can tell. But I'll have to find out some things for myself. And do what I think is right. Just now, that doesn't amount to much more than finishing school and maybe going for another ride or two with Sundance before he leaves." I was surprised at my own strength, but I stood my ground and looked directly at her.

"I oughta tell him he's not welcome," she mumbled, "tell him to move on."

"But you won't," I told her, "because then I'd have to leave with him." I didn't know that wasn't the only reason she wouldn't tell him to move on.

"It's that serious?" Her anger was replaced by surprise.

"It's that serious, at least for me. I can't speak for him." I hadn't, of course, thought of it as serious at all until that moment. The words surprised me as they came out my mouth, but they were true.

"I wouldn't count on him taking anything serious. You'll be buying yourself a whole peck of trouble. Believe me, I know." And then Fannie Porter did the most extraordinary thing. That hard-hearted madam, who seemed to tolerate me only because my presence built a new image of her, reached out and hugged me.

I hugged her back fiercely. We might never understand each other, but a strong bond would always hold us together.

I didn't see Sundance for three days, at least not to talk to. Oh, yes, I wondered—and at night, I'd peek through the curtains and see him laughing with Maud and Annie and the others. But he didn't come to supper, and he didn't bring a horse for me to ride, and he didn't tell me any more of his life story. I hadn't the nerve to watch each night and see if he went upstairs alone—I would have been too crushed if I'd seen him go up those stairs arm in arm with Annie.

It didn't occur to me that I didn't see much of Fannie during those days either. I did see Annie—oh, did I see Annie! She was a grab box of questions. "Where did you go? I watched you out the window." . . . "Did Fannie just kill you when you got back?" . . . "Did you tell him . . . you know, about your father?" "Where is he now?" Every time I turned around, it seemed Annie was behind me, asking another question.

"We went for a ride."

"No, Fannie didn't kill me. We talked."

"No, I didn't tell him about my father. Why should I?"

She shrugged. "I don't know. If someone cared a lot about me, I'd feel obliged to tell them."

"I've only known him six days . . . and only seen him twice. Why should I feel obliged?" I didn't tell her that my heart felt obliged.

She shrugged again.

Chapter Eight

Hodge brought me a note that Friday evening when I was studying at my desk. He knocked softly and seemed in a hurry to be out of the room. "Mister Sundance, he sent this. . . . I sure hope Miss Fannie don't find me delivering this to you."

"I'll be sure she never knows," I told Hodge as I reached too eagerly for the note.

It read: "Meet me on the front porch at 6:00 A.M. Sundance." He had, apparently, carefully planned this for a Saturday, when I had no school.

I was there, of course, dressed in my school clothes—a white shirtwaist and a tan broadcloth skirt. The morning air was cool, and I'd thrown a paisley shawl over my shoulders, but it couldn't stop my trembling, which came, I decided, from anticipation more than from cold. I waited almost five minutes alone on that porch, wondering if I'd been a fool to believe a note that I didn't even know came from him.

He appeared this time driving a small carriage, with another perfect Thoroughbred hitched to it. "Come on," he said in a sort of shouted whisper—plain enough so that I could hear, but also low so as not to wake the neighborhood—or Fannie.

"Where are we going?" I asked as I came down the walk.

He was out of the carriage and ready to help me in. "For a picnic. I'm leaving tomorrow, and I decided we should spend the day together."

"I haven't seen you in three days." It was less a complaint than a statement of fact that perhaps held a question behind it.

"Fannie," he said tersely. "She read me the riot act after we went riding. She really cares about what happens to you, and she's afraid I'll hurt you."

"Will you?" I was seated in the carriage now, next to him, and I turned to look directly at him.

"Probably," he said. "But we could have some wonderful times first."

I turned away, and I would have gotten out of the carriage if he hadn't put out an arm to stop me. "Wait. I won't ever deliberately hurt you, but I can't always guarantee what will happen to me . . . or what I'll do. I'd always try to keep you safe, but I can't always promise to keep me safe or by your side. Do you understand?"

I didn't. How could I, at seventeen, understand the life of an outlaw? In that idyllic moment, how could I have foreseen the future? Fannie tried to tell me, and Sundance in his own way tried to tell me, but I was blinded. In some senses I was as blinded as Mama had been when she married Pa, but I didn't want to make that comparison.

"Are we going away together?" I asked. "I . . . I haven't finished the semester."

By now we were far enough down the street that his loud laughter wouldn't wake Fannie. "Lord help me," he called. "I'm talking to a schoolgirl, talking about ruining her life by running away with an outlaw, and all she can say is that school isn't out yet!" He reached an expansive arm around my shoulders and pulled me toward him for a quick kiss, planted on my nose.

Then he was solemn. "No, we're not going away together. Not now. I've some business to attend to, but I'll be back for you. Sometime. Someday. It may be a while. But I'll come back someday."

I was absolutely uncertain how I felt about that promise, but I said nothing.

Judy Alter

We rode through the silent streets of the city, just beginning to come alive for the day. "Where are we going?"

"West," he said. "Just west. See what's out there."

"Hills, I think," I told him.

There were indeed hills—enough that the horse tired from pulling us up and down. But the scenery was remarkable, and for long periods we rode without speaking, looking at those gray-green hills, the streams that cut through them, the long vistas from hilltop to hilltop.

He had, as he'd said, brought a picnic lunch. "Julie packed it," he said. "She and Hodge are more on my side than they'll let on to Fannie. Julie said you particularly like chicken. So there's roast chicken, carrots and celery, light bread, and . . ." He dug into the basket he had pulled from the floor of the carriage. "Chocolate cake! Why that devil! Julie must have baked it special." Then, with a funny look, he admitted, "I asked her two days ago to put together this lunch. I bet she did bake it special for us."

It was delicious—moist and rich with dark chocolate, the icing even better than the cake.

We picnicked by a river in a town called Boerne. Sundance had brought a blanket again, and we spread it on the ground and laid out our sumptuous feast. After we ate, he leaned back on the blanket, closed his eyes, and appeared to go to sleep. I sat watching the river and some water birds that landed on it and then quickly took off again. He must have slept fifteen minutes.

When he awoke, he said, out of the clear blue, "I'm down here because I'm afraid I killed a man."

There wasn't much I could say except "Oh?"

"I said," he repeated impatiently, "that I think I may have killed a man. I've never done that before."

"It's hard, isn't it." I wanted to reach out and take his hand, reassure him somehow, but I was still shy.

"How would you know?" he muttered angrily. "I . . . I didn't mean to. He wanted to arrest me, and I shot—it was self-defense."

"I understand about self-defense," I told him, though to myself I admitted that was a questionable application of the word.

78

"Well," he answered, still almost angry, "you don't understand about self-defense to save your own life. You couldn't."

It was, I decided, time to tell him. "You're wrong. That's exactly what I do understand."

"How could you?"

"I killed my father to save myself," I said, thinking I could not have put it more straightforward.

"You what?" His voice almost screeched on the last word.

"You heard me." I wasn't about to repeat it.

He sat up abruptly, staring at me as though he'd never truly looked at me before. It was enough to almost cause me to forget the confession I was about to make.

"I killed my father because he tried to rape me. A second time. After the first time, I swore he'd never do it again—and he didn't." In spite of myself, I began to shake with hidden sobs. I hadn't cried when I'd told Fannie, nor when Annie and I talked, so why was I so weak now? I forced myself to a stiff silence.

Still he stared at me, but one hand reached to smooth my hair away from my face. "I can't imagine . . . I mean, it's one thing to shoot a sheriff—he was a sheriff, blast the luck—in a robbery, but to kill your own father. How do you live with that?"

"I see his face every night," I told him, "and I wake thinking he's creeping back into my bed. But that—my secret—is why I feel so tied to Fannie. She made it all right—at least as much as she could—and gave me a chance at a life."

He was thoughtful for a long time. "She knows," he said. "I . . . I guess I'm not surprised. But she didn't tell me."

I wondered why he thought she would.

We sat in silence for a long time, though every once in a while he would raise his head and look at me. Finally, he asked, "You use a gun?"

"No. A butcher knife." Why, I thought frantically, would he want the details?

He let out a long whistle. "Guns are neater. Ever shoot one?"

I shook my head. "Pa had a shotgun, and I used to unload it of a secret at night when he'd had too much whiskey, but I never shot it."

He scoffed. "You don't need a shotgun, but someday I'll teach you to shoot a rifle. Meantime, try this." He pulled his coat aside to reveal the pearl handle of a small pistol protruding from a pocket near the waist of his pants. He pulled it out, cracked it open to check the bullets, and took off the safety. "Here, hold it straight out in your right hand—you are right-handed, aren't you?" He took my hand and fitted it to the gun, index finger over the trigger.

With his hand over mine, I felt that same tingle again. Afraid I was blushing, I stared intently at the pistol.

"Now point at that tree. No, wait. Put the gun down by your side for a minute."

Puzzled, I did as he said. He took the handkerchief from his breast pocket and stuffed one end into a crack in the tree, so that the piece of silk hung there like a flag. Instantly he was back at my side. "Now raise your arm, hold it straight out, and shoot at it."

"I'll ruin your good handkerchief," I protested.

Dryly he said, "Doubtful. You probably won't even hit the tree."

Determined to show him, I aimed the pistol carefully and so slowly that he said, "Speed is usually important. Whoever you're shooting at won't give you time to aim. Hold your arm steady, now."

I pulled the trigger, surprised at the way the little gun jumped in my hand. But there was a black hole in one corner of Sundance's handkerchief, and he was saying, "I don't believe it. Beginner's luck. You couldn't do it again."

I raised the gun again, felt it jump, and saw a tear at the edge of the handkerchief. It was a five-shot pistol, and when I had fired all five shots his handkerchief had three holes. When I pulled it loose from the tree, I saw the monogram *HL* in one corner.

"Three out of five," he whistled. "I'm impressed. I may take you with me to rob a bank sometime."

"I'd go, you know," I told him. Even then I knew that our words would become self-fulfilling prophecies, and one day I would ride with Sundance. And I also knew that he didn't hate me for having killed my father. When we returned to San Saba Street, Fannie was less angry than I expected.

"You've made your choice, girl," she said, "and you're the one who's going to have to live with it." There was real sadness in her tone.

"I haven't made any choice," I told her. "He's leaving tomorrow, and I don't know when I'll see him again. I'm going to finish school, get a job teaching, and do the things you wanted me to."

She eyed me shrewdly. "I know you mean that, but I think he'll be back here for you, and then you'll go with him, no matter where he leads."

I couldn't argue with that.

Sundance didn't leave the next day. In fact, he stayed four more days, and we had one more long afternoon together. This time we sat in the formal parlor—the girls were all still asleep or busy upstairs, and the house was quiet. Fannie, knowing full well that we were there, left us alone. There was no sentimental parting speech from him. Instead, he regaled me with the story of his outlaw life.

"Tell me how you got the name Sundance," I said.

His eyes sparkled with laughter. "I stole a horse, a saddle, and a gun from a man named Craven, up in Montana. Sheriff caught me some four months later and kept me in the jail at Sundance for a couple of months. Then he decided to transfer me to . . . I honestly don't know where I was going, but we went to St. Paul and then got on another train, maybe to Rapid City in the Dakotas. Anyway, the sheriff—guy named Ryan—went to the bathroom, and while he was gone I picked the locks on my cuffs and then I jumped off the train." He paused a minute, then added, "Of course, I had help. Cassidy was on the train. I expect it was running a hundred miles an hour when we jumped. That was some jump!"

A hundred miles an hour! "Were you hurt?"

"Bruises and bangs," he said, shrugging. "Nothing important. Guess rather than being hurt, my ego was inflated 'cause I had escaped from a sheriff. 'Course, they caught me again. I was convicted and sentenced to eighteen months, but they kept me at the Sundance jail because I was under twenty-one. I kept trying to escape, but it never did happen, and I was finally released. I swear, I'm never going to jail again!"

"If that's true," I told him, "you better change your way of life."

"Can't do that. Once you've done the things I've done, the world won't let you go straight. They always want you for the last thing you've done."

"Killing the sheriff?" I asked.

"And the Malta train robbery. It was three years ago, but those railroad folks are slow to forget."

"Tell me about it."

"It was a blundered job, for sure. The work of amateurs. But Madden and Bass and me, we were looking for a little excitement. Weather was so cold everyone was out of work, and we . . . well, we just thought it was the thing to do. Train stopped at Malta—that's in Montana—early in the morning, about three o'clock. After it pulled out of the station, Madden and I jumped on the baggage car, made our way to the engine, and told the engineer to stop at a fire about a mile out of town—'course, it was Bass who built the fire. When it stopped, we told him to make the mail clerk open the mail car."

He laughed. "Trouble was, there wasn't anything there. So we went to the express car and told the messenger to open the safe. We got about twenty dollars in cash, two small checks, and a whole lot of nothing. The messenger swore he didn't have the combination of the bigger safe, and we believed him—usually only station agents have it. Newspapers later claimed we missed $25,000 that was in that big safe—damn the luck! We were cold and mad—but then, so were the trainmen. So we all had a drink and then we sent the train on its way.

" 'Course, pretty soon there was a big reward out for us—big deal, we didn't get a hundred dollars and they've got a five-hundred-dollar reward offered. The Great Northern hired some detectives, and they found Bass and Madden at a saloon. Then—damn the luck!—they got me as I was getting on a train going east, figuring to get away for a while. I got away finally, but when Bass and Madden came to trial, they apparently said I was with them. Fine friends those—Cassidy would never have done that to me. That's when I went to Hole-in-the-Wall."

"And the ones who were tried?" It seemed to me that he was particularly unsympathetic toward them. They may have identified him, but, after all, they were caught and he escaped.

He shrugged. "They served time—still are. That's the chance you take."

"Was that your first big . . . uh, robbery?"

He stared at me and reached a hand across the back of the sofa to rest it ever so casually on my shoulder. "Why are you so interested in this?"

I never flinched as I looked at him and said, "I figure it's going to be important for me to know."

He grinned. "It probably is. You're right." And then he leaned toward me and kissed me, ever so gently. Other than the hand that still rested on my shoulder, he didn't touch me.

"All right. There's the bank robbery at Telluride, four or five years ago. No one knows for sure that I was there. We knew the town marshal, Jim Clark, would be out of town, so we rode in a couple of days before the robbery. Just kind of hung about town, drinking in the saloon, getting to know what was goin' on. Decided to try it about noon one day when there wasn't much going on. Matter of fact, it turned out there was only one teller in the bank—it was the San Miguel Valley Bank—and he had a pile of money in front of him. I held the horses out back—that's how come nobody knows I was there—and Matt Warner went inside with Tom McCarty. Matt held a gun on the teller, Tom watched out the door, and Matt scooped up the money—twenty thousand dollars of it."

"Twenty thousand!" I'd never imagined so much money in my life. "You're rich," I said.

"Will you marry me for my money?" he asked jokingly, then turned serious. "We split it three ways remember, so it's not all that much. And being an outlaw is like a lot of other things—a lot of your work comes up empty-handed."

"What do you mean, empty-handed?"

"Well, look at the Malta train robbery. We didn't get enough to make it worth all the trouble, not to mention the risk of getting caught."

"Probably you need to plan better," I told him, my mind racing ahead, thinking how I could help him plan his robberies. *Mama*, I thought, *if you're in Heaven and you're listening to this, I'm sorry*. But I knew nothing, not even Mama's memory, would stop me from being with Sundance.

Judy Alter

"Let me finish about Telluride," he said with a grin. "I told you I never killed a man 'cept that sheriff by accident. But that bank teller—he was such a coward, shaking and trembling and begging them to remember he was the sole support of his mother. Matt said he was tempted to shoot him or at least beat the tar out of him, just for being so scared."

I pondered a minute. "So it's bravado that does it?"

He looked at me long and hard, and then he said, "Yeah. But you already know that. Figured it out all by yourself. That's why you scare me, Etta Place."

Next morning, as he prepared to leave, I handed him a folded silk handkerchief, with the monogram HL in one corner. "To replace the one I ruined," I said.

"Did you embroider it?" He fingered it carefully, shook it out, and fanned it into his breast pocket.

"No. I can't embroider. Julie did it."

"Then my thanks to both of you." He smiled at me, those blue eyes looking right through my facade of composure.

"Oh," he said, as though it were of no consequence, "one thing I forgot to tell you. I have a wife. Anna Maria Thayne. She's in Castle Gate, Wyoming." He put one hand on the back of my head and turned my face toward his for a bittersweet kiss that held the promise of much more to come.

Chapter Nine

I didn't hear from Sundance for nearly two years. He had left in late summer, and too soon the next spring dragged into summer. Wildflowers bloomed around the city—bluebonnets with their purple color and bright orange paintbrush and yellow squaw blossom—and then died in the South Texas heat, which was hotter than anything I'd ever known in Ben Wheeler. Maybe not as humid, but hotter.

I was through with the Ursuline Academy, almost as glad to be shed of it as I had been to leave Ben Wheeler. I would miss Mother Theresa, whose kindness to me had been gentle and reassuring, and I would miss Jolié. Beyond that, I was glad to leave behind empty-headed girls and a stern way of life.

Jolié had bid me farewell by saying wistfully, "I wish we had been better friends, Etta." She pronounced it funny—"Et-*ta*"—and her accent made me smile.

"I wish we had too," I said truthfully, but I could say no more. She would go back to her family home in Castroville, but she had hinted that there was a young man from France who would come to claim her one day soon.

"I will be the bride," she said, "and he will make me happy."

I envied her the settled future, the sureness that someone would take care of her. It was all too plain to me that I would have to take care of myself, even if Sundance did come back for me. The one thing that Fannie told me and I really believed was that I couldn't count on him forever. Nor would Fannie shoulder the burden of my protection forever—she had done me a tremendous kindness by educating me, but I was going to have to find my own life. *Sundance*, I cried aloud at night, *when are you coming back?*

"We'll have to find a teaching position for you," Fannie said briskly one day. "May not be in San Antonio. I think some of the smaller towns around here need teachers pretty badly. Do you good to get away from this house." She had on her no-nonsense voice.

"I would hate to leave," I told her truthfully. "You and Julie and Hodge have been family to me."

The no-nonsense hat dropped away. "Lord, child, I know that, and I will miss you. Makes me feel good to have you around, but we've got to think of your future. No decent man is going to marry you if you live in a whorehouse."

"No decent man," I retorted, "will marry me if he knows I killed my father."

In one of her rare gestures of affection, she put an arm around me. "No matter who he is, he's never going to know that. Honey, you just have to erase that from your mind."

Easier said than done, I thought. In truth, though, Pa had stopped visiting me so much at night, just because I had other things on my mind: Sundance's sweet parting kiss, the puzzlement of a wife he'd mentioned so casually, and, of course, the long silence. I would never ask Fannie about any of it, particularly the wife, and I couldn't talk to Annie either. Oh, Annie talked to me. A lot.

"He's an outlaw," she ranted, more than once. "You're moping around here, looking like you're going to the gallows tomorrow, all because of an outlaw. You haven't heard from him"—she knew that much—"and you won't. Ask Fannie, she'll tell you they think they're a law unto themselves. Nobody else matters to them. You think Maud has heard from that Kid Curry?"

She hadn't. I knew from listening to her talk at the dinner table.

Another time: "You know what's the matter with you? You haven't known any men. Don't know how they treat women. I mean, there was your father, and maybe one or two neighbors back wherever it is you really came from."

I could have told her about Mr. Newsome and his plans for my future, but I kept silent.

"Fannie ought to at least let you out in the parlor, so you'd not be so sheltered."

"And what if some man wanted to take me upstairs?" I asked as coolly as I could.

She shrugged. "Might not be the worst thing that ever happened to you."

Pa's face loomed before me, and I shuddered visibly. Instantly, Annie was at my side with an arm around me.

"Honey, you can't tell me a beautiful girl like you is going to go through life having nothing to do with men just because of what your pa did to you . . . ah, twice."

Or, I wanted to argue, because of what I did to my pa.

"What," she asked, "if Sundance wanted to take you upstairs?"

"He wouldn't," I said.

And then she dropped her bombshell: "Don't fool yourself. Sundance is no gentleman. Where do you think he spent the nights when he was here?"

I wanted to shout, *Upstairs alone! He told me that.* Instead, I just looked at her.

"He slept with Fannie most of the time," she said, her voice even and without emotion.

It was a joke, of course. What else could it be? Fannie wouldn't do that. She never slept with customers—and Sundance, he was special . . . to me. Slowly it dawned on me that Annie wasn't joking. It was true: Fannie had invited Sundance to her bed, and he had accepted—or maybe Sundance had invited himself, and Fannie had accepted. Either way, they slept together. And neither one of them would see in any way that their behavior compromised their separate and very different relationships with me.

87

A kind of white rage went through me. For just a flash, I was almost out of control, speechless, shaking, filled with an anger that was beyond anything I thought was inside me. It wasn't the cold, determined anger that I'd felt toward Pa—this was instant and absolutely without reason.

It subsided as quickly as it had come.

"Are you all right, Etta? I . . . gosh, I'm sorry I said anything."

"No," I said, striving for control, "you're not. It's a secret that's been burning a hole in your tongue. And it's better out. I'm all right."

I left the room with all the dignity I could muster, moving slowly rather than rushing in anger. But behind me, I could still feel Annie's eyes boring holes in my back. And I could sense her wishing she knew what was going on inside my head. I never gave her that satisfaction.

Later, lying in my bed, I reviewed it all in my mind, trying to be as clearheaded as I could. Fannie granted her favors to a very few men—I knew that, though I never figured how she chose them. Still, how could anyone resist Sundance? She would not see that as a betrayal of me—indeed, she might think she was helping me by keeping Sundance busy elsewhere. But I didn't fool myself that altruism had any big part in Fannie's motivation.

And Sundance? In long sleepless nights after Annie's revelation, I told myself that he kept apart from me because what was between us was special. What he did with Fannie was casual and physical. What he and I had was spiritual—well, maybe that was too much, maybe emotional was a better word. In my mind I rehearsed long and earnest conversations with him, and he always explained things just the way I thought.

For days I was distant to Fannie. I longed to shout and scream and accuse, but for a lot of reasons that was useless—and self-defeating. I had no claim on Sundance that would have kept her away from him. She knew I was interested in him, but she disapproved of that interest—and maybe she had shown her disapproval in the ultimate way.

Fannie knew that I was keeping myself distant, and I'm sure she knew why, but she never said a word. Fannie Porter didn't have to explain herself to Etta Place . . . and never would.

In the end, we never again talked specifically about Sundance's visit. But I did notice that she grew rather harsh with Annie, as though she was angry with her, and Annie, in turn, grew churlish with me. She avoided me at supper, and often, from another table, sat staring at me in an angry way.

Sundance had set in motion a chain of dominoes that hadn't fallen until he was safely away.

"Being as it's summer, there won't be any teaching positions available immediately," Fannie said one day. She sat in her bed, surrounded by her breakfast tray and the morning newspaper. I had been summoned to her presence. "I'll ask Mother Theresa if she knows of a position taking care of children in the home."

This time it was not Pa's face but that of Juniper that swam before me. "You think she can find a family who wants a girl from a whorehouse?"

Fannie looked wounded. "You aren't a whore," she said. "And Mother Theresa doesn't tell everything she knows."

Mother Theresa knew a woman in the parish who needed help daily, four hours in the middle of the day. She had five young children, and they were too much for her to manage alone.

I would be less a teacher than a nursemaid, and I would be paid a pittance.

"I will turn my salary over to you," I told Fannie.

"Honey, I make enough money. Balancing the books has nothing to do with what's between us. You keep that money. Buy yourself a pretty gown, put it away for a rainy day, do whatever you want with it."

And what's between us? I wanted to ask. *Sundance?* But there was nothing for me to say to Fannie, and I still debated what I would say to Sundance when, if ever, he reappeared.

Annie had set me to thinking about more than Fannie and Sundance. If he was that kind of man—that kind being the men who frequented Fannie's house—then maybe his promise to come back for me was spun of air and smoke. That doubt flitted through my mind, but I refused to believe it. I held on to my faith that he would be back for me. But sometimes, in the dark of the night, doubts crept in, and then I would hear

89

Judy Alter

Annie's voice saying, "He's no gentleman. . . . He slept with Fannie."

What I learned that long summer was to put my feelings into compartments: My affection and loyalty to Fannie went in one pigeonhole in my mind, my feelings for Sundance in another, and my jealousy for whatever went on between the two of them in a smaller, darker compartment in the very back of my mind.

I went every morning to the Brewster household. Mr. Brewster was a banker who left home promptly at eight every morning, his wife having fed him a substantial breakfast. He returned home at noon every day for an equally substantial dinner. It was at noon that I saw him, and, the very first day, I took an instant dislike to him.

"Nelda, my coffee is cold!"

"I'll just get some fresh, Jonathan. You sit right there. No, Charlie, don't bother Mother right now." She brushed a child away as she went for the coffee, and Mr. Brewster totally ignored that child—and the other four.

The children were Susanna, age seven; Jonathan, Jr., age six; Annabelle, age four; Charlie, age three; and the year-old baby, Samuel, whom Mrs. Brewster affectionately called "Sammie." Mrs. Brewster reminded me of Mama so sharply that some days I could hardly bear to be around her. It wasn't a good reminder. She brought back all the bad about Mama's life—she was tired, pale, and determinedly cheerful even when I knew she didn't feel it in her soul. I could imagine where all those babies came from: Mr. Brewster was probably as relentlessly demanding in the night as Pa had been.

He only tolerated my presence. Once I heard him say to her, "I don't know why you have to have that girl around here. We don't know a thing about her." Mrs. Brewster answered serenely, "Mother Theresa at the academy recommended her. She's here because I need help, Jonathan. She keeps the babies while I prepare your supper."

Thoughts of his own satisfaction must have quieted him, for he said no more. But I saw him watching me over his dinner plate while I fed little Sammie or mopped up after Charlie, who was wildly destructive. Mr. Brewster's eyes were dark and . . . well, sinister. I wondered if he was a patron of Fannie's house.

Finally one night I asked, "Do you know the Brewsters? Mr. Brewster, he . . . ah . . ."

"He's a wretched man," Fannie said so vehemently that I was taken aback. "Pious. The kind who denounces the sins of the flesh in church but comes to the whorehouse on Monday night."

"Does he come here?" I asked cautiously.

"Not anymore. I made it plain he wasn't welcome a year or so ago . . . He slapped one of the girls, hard, for no reason."

I was incredulous. "Why did you send me to work in his house, then?"

She sighed. "Because I felt almost as sorry for his wife as I have in the past for you. And because I knew he wouldn't do anything in his own house. You're safe. . . . And finally I guess there's the thought that I want you to see that the so-called proper side of life—those upstanding citizens—often aren't any better than those of us who admit to our sins openly."

If I hadn't been so busy puzzling over what she'd said, I'd have laughed at the idea of Fannie confessing to sins. But she was right in her logic, though it didn't work to any goal she had in mind: Mr. Brewster probably did as much as anyone to convince me that running away with Sundance was the right thing for me. Certainly, he showed me that marriage, like his or like Mama and Pa, was not for me. I wasn't going to live that way!

Once during that long summer, Fannie absently talked to me about her background. I have no idea what prompted her confession, or what she thought I'd learn from her story. But she looked at me one evening as I sat in her sitting room—a thing I did more since I'd been out of school and had no studies for her to shoo me back to my desk—and she said, "I was married, you know, respectable-like, the whole business. It was seven . . . no, eight years ago, in Stephenville, His name was J. T. Evans—I called him Jimmy, and I thought I'd found my life's love."

Amazed, I put down the book I was reading. "What happened to him?"

"Killed in a fight in a bar," she said matter-of-factly. "Jimmy was ever one to seek out trouble, if it didn't find him first."

Outlaws being much on my mind, I asked, "Was he an outlaw?"

Fannie's familiar deep laughter roared through the room. "Lord, no. Jimmy wasn't smart enough to be an outlaw. He was just a troublemaker." And suddenly she was sober. "But I loved him. . . . I really did, and after that . . . well. . . ."

She shrugged, and I imagined that I was supposed to understand that the loss of Jimmy had sent her into the life. I didn't think much about that, because I was puzzling over the fact that Jimmy wasn't smart enough to be an outlaw—did that mean she admired Sundance for his brains? Was she, who always warned me against the outlaw's life, making a comparison I didn't understand? Was she going to be my rival for Sundance?

She read my mind. "I don't know why I'm telling you this, except to tell you that you can't rely on any man to take care of you—I don't care if it's Jimmy, or Sundance, or Mr. Brewster, or that . . . what's-his-name from your hometown that told you to look for me. One way or another, they'll end up letting you hang for yourself."

"Not Sundance," I whispered to myself. But even as I smiled at Fannie, I knew deep down that Sundance, too, would let me "hang for myself." Still, when your heart is determined, no amount of logic will change your course. Fannie knew that, and so did I. But we didn't talk about it.

One day toward the end of the summer, Mr. Brewster was in a particularly foul mood. There was, as far as I knew, no explanation for it, beyond the heat that depressed all of us. But he claimed his ham steak tasted "off" and the green beans were cold.

"The steak is fresh cut from the butcher's this morning," Mrs. Brewster said in a soothing tone, "and I'll put the beans back on the stove. They sat too long while you attended to your toilet."

He rose angrily from his chair, a hand raised in the air. "I won't have you saying it's my fault my dinner is cold." The raised hand came crashing down on Mrs. Brewster's face.

Almost simultaneously, Susanna and Annabelle began to scream, although Mrs. Brewster uttered not a sound. She put a hand to her face, almost tentatively, then turned back to the stove. Mr. Brewster sat down in his chair at the table as though nothing had happened. But after a minute he looked at me and said, in an ugly tone of voice, "Can't you make them be quiet?"

Inside I was quivering. Once again, Pa's face, leering over me, flashed through my vision, and I felt that cold, detached anger. The girls were looking to me, not to their mama, for reassurance, and I pushed the anger away. Boldly, I said, "Not as long as you hit their mother."

Mrs. Brewster gasped, a sound of fear. Mr. Brewster's eyes flew open, and he started to say something. But I turned my back on him and shepherded the children, including the two still-screaming girls, up the stairs to the bedroom. I never knew whether or not I would have stabbed him if I'd had a knife.

I didn't go back to the Brewsters after that day.

"How can you abandon that woman?" Fannie asked indignantly. "She needs help."

"She'll have to help herself first," I said, and my thoughts tilted sadly toward Mama and all that she and Mrs. Brewster had in common. I was beginning to see that dying had been Mama's way of helping herself, and I hoped it wouldn't be Mrs. Brewster's. Even more than I had needed Mama, those little children needed her.

"If you've been helped yourself . . . ," Fannie began, her tone preachy.

I drew myself up. "I have been helped, and I'm grateful beyond measuring, but I helped myself first—if you want to put it that way."

I'd expected indignation or anger, but once again Fannie's laughter filled the silence. "I guess you did," she said, "and you probably aren't the first one to justify murder as 'helping yourself.'"

I thought of Sundance and the sheriff he shot in self-defense. Was it, I wondered, the same thing? Where and when did self-protection become lawlessness?

No job teaching in a small town materialized, and I did not have to leave Fannie's. In September I began to teach the younger children at the Ursuline Academy. Fannie made the arrangements without consulting me and then told me that Sister Theresa had hired me. Angrily, I told her that she was treating me like a schoolgirl, making my decisions, and that she had to let me grow up and take care of myself.

"You will," she said with a shrug. "You start Monday at eight." And that was the end of the discussion.

At first I dreaded going back to the academy, which, with a few exceptions, had always been to me a cold and uncaring atmosphere.

Susanna Brewster would be in the class where I was helping, and I was truly glad to see her again. She came toward me diffidently the first day.

"Miss Place? I'm glad to see you again."

"Thank you, Susanna," I said, putting an arm about her shoulders. She was far more subdued than an eight-year-old should be, and her round eyes were wide with a kind of perpetual fear. "How are things at your house?"

Even as she said, "Fine, thank you," she shook her head, her gesture contradicting her words.

I knelt in front of her and looked her straight in the eyes. "I will do anything I can to help you, Susanna, you and your brothers and sisters. You know that, don't you?"

She nodded solemnly, her gaze avoiding mine.

"You'll have to tell me what I can do."

She nodded again and turned away with a shy. "Bye."

Susanna, I decided, was just like her mother. She didn't have the spunk to help herself. But then I thought that a harsh judgment—she was, after all, only seven or eight. Would she endure this life until she was eighteen or twenty and then marry someone just like her father? Moral interpretation did not come easily to me, but I wondered if I was beginning, in my own mind, to justify my crime by looking at the misery of others, to approve my own action by the inaction of others.

To my surprise, I enjoyed teaching third grade. The academy had enough teachers—principally the sisters, but with laypersons like me to take on the extra burden—that we were able to study reading and arithmetic with small groups of children, listening to them recite individually. I spent hours helping Susanna and her classmates trace the figures of the Spencerian system of penmanship, encouraging their neat, round penmanship.

"You look happy," Fannie announced one afternoon as I came home from school, a stack of childishly written papers in my hand for my evening's reading.

"I am," I told her. "I enjoy the children more than I expected . . . and I like the academy better than when I was a student there." I didn't add, though, the thought that was always on my mind: *Besides. I won't be doing this forever. Sundance is going to come—soon—to take me away.*

It was approaching two years since Sundance visited San Antonio, and I'd had no word from him. Many a day I told myself I was foolish to believe he'd still come back for me. He was, as Annie and Fannie each told me in their own ways, an outlaw without a sense of honor . . . or commitment. A man unable to love. I had been swept away by a naive infatuation, and to continue to believe in it for two years was childish beyond belief.

But then I'd remember the way he'd talked about taking me to a bank or the funny way he'd mentioned that wife—was that it? had he reconciled with his wife?—as though I should know about her, and I'd know that Sundance would come back for me sometime.

Fannie never mentioned him anymore, and even Annie stopped talking about my outlaw. As far as they were concerned, I guess, it was a flash in the pan, something over and done with, about which, if asked, they could say "I told you so." Except that I remembered that Fannie had long thought he would come back for me. Some days I longed to ask her if she still believed that, but I kept my own confidences. In late March of 1896 I received a letter—not from Sundance, but from that Butch Cassidy he had talked about so much.

"Dear Miss Place," he wrote,

My good friend Sundance has told me about you, and I must say I am looking forward to meeting you. Up until recently, my time has not been my own—I remembered that he was in jail for stealing horses—

But now I have joined up with Sundance again, and he has, as I say, told me about you. He is not much of a hand to write letters, but I enjoy it, so I told him I would write you in his place. I hope that by fall you will be with us in Hole-in-the-Wall. I think Sundance hopes that too.

The letter went on to describe what they were doing, though there was no mention of bank robberies or train holdups. To read Butch's letter, you'd have thought they were a pair of ranchers, trying hard to remain peaceable in a kingdom that was torn apart by the battle between small ranchers and big cattle barons. They, Butch assured me, stayed out of trouble by remaining beyond the reach of the big ranchers, safely in Hole-in-the-Wall. But Butch's letter, in plain and unemotional language, told of the hanging of one of their friends by vigilantes. "He had too many cattle to suit them," he wrote. And then, describing Hole-in-the-Wall, he concluded,

It really is a wonderful place, and I know you will like it.

Yours truly, Butch Cassidy

P.S. Sundance sends his best regards.

I read that letter five times without stopping, locked in my room where no one would disturb me. Sundance was coming for me! I hadn't been childish and naive—I had known true love when it walked right up and hit me in the face. But what did "best regards" mean? And if Sundance and Butch were living together in Hole-in-the-Wall, where was that blasted wife? The letter, which answered so many questions, raised an equal number of new ones. Still, it left me walking on air.

"Understand you got some mail," Fannie said that evening as the two of us sat at a table apart from the others to eat our supper.

Hodge, I thought, *do you have to tell everything you know?* "Yes, ma'am, I did."

"Sundance?"

I shook my head to say "no."

"All right, missy, tell me who the letter was from?"

She knew that no one had ever written to me in all the years I'd been with her, and there was no one to write but Sundance. Her puzzlement was obvious on her face.

"Butch Cassidy," I said, and offered no further comment.

"Butch! He's out of jail! Well, good for him." Then, almost in a rush, "What'd he say?"

"Would you like to read the letter?" I thought this bold offer would call her hand, but once again I underestimated Fannie.

"Yes," she said decisively, "I would."

Without a word, I left my supper cooling and went to my

room to retrieve the letter from under my pillow, where I'd hidden it. When I returned, still silent, I handed it to her.

She read slowly and carefully, sometimes mouthing the words silently as she read. When she finished, she put the letter carefully between the two of us and looked at me. "Well?"

"Well what?" I asked. "There's nothing to say. The letter is . . . well, it's not from Sundance." I had started that sentence out boldly but finished it rather lamely.

Fannie laughed. "You surely didn't ever expect Sundance to write to you, did you?"

I shook my head. I would never have admitted to her that yes, I had thought at first that he might. Now, after Butch's letter, I simply expected him to ride up to her house one day.

As though she read my mind, she said, "Sundance will just ride up here one day, and you'll be gone." Then, with a catch in her voice, her hand reaching to cover mine, she said, "And I'll be lonely without you." She raised her head and stared as though looking a far distance away. "Girls come and go here, and I don't mourn over a one of them—save maybe Juniper— but you're different. And Lord knows, I'll miss you, Etta Place."

"I won't ever go forever," I told her. "And I'm not like Sundance. I'll write letters."

"Lord love you," she said, "I know you will."

It was a good thing that school was out in May, for from that time on I had a hard time concentrating on my duties.

"Miss Place," Susanna asked on the last day of classes, "will you be here when we come back to school?"

"Of course, Susanna," I said instinctively, and then thought that the child deserved more honesty. "Well, maybe. I'm not sure."

"Would you . . . could you come help Mama again this summer? She really needs you." The blue eyes were solemn, and I thought I saw tears welling up in them. Carefully, Susanna ran a hand across the lower lids of her eyes, "Mama says we're going to have another brother or sister sometime this summer."

I bit my tongue to quiet the protest that rose in my throat. "What good news!" I said with deliberate cheer. "I'm sure you're excited."

Susanna shook her head. "Mama says I'll have to take care of the others and learn to help her cook for Papa."

I could see the weight of the world settling on this child. "I know you'll be a big help to your mama," I said. *Fannie*, I wondered, *can't you take this child in when I'm gone?* But Fannie was not in the business of raising abused children. I was a one-time experiment, and I knew that. I worried about Susanna—and the other small Brewster children—but I knew that once Sundance came for me, I would turn my back on San Antonio . . . and Fannie, and Susanna, and Hodge and Julie, without a backward glance.

I lived in anticipation.

Chapter Ten

He came for me one day in June—really one morning. I had taken the habit of sleeping late—not as late as the girls—now that school was out and I had no daily schedule. So it was close to nine o'clock when I wandered into the kitchen, wearing a light lawn wrapper, my hair still in tangles about my face.

He was sitting on a stool in the kitchen, watching Julie knead bread. It was her startled look that made him turn toward me, and then his face broke into a grin. "Good morning. You're looking particularly lovely this morning."

Embarrassed, I turned to leave, but his hand reached out and grabbed my arm gently. "No, don't go, I meant it. You look wonderful."

"I haven't made my toilette," I stuttered.

"I know. I like you this way." And then Harry Longabaugh kissed me—not the gentle kiss he'd given me when he left, but a strong kiss from a man to a woman he loves. My mouth tingled, and I felt a strange pull in the pit of my stomach. Instead of backing away, I moved instinctively toward him, my mouth working to meet his.

Hodge coughed discreetly. "Miss Fannie . . . she be coming into the kitchen any minute."

Sundance drew away but held firm to my hand. "She wouldn't be surprised, Hodge. She knows why I'm here." His smile wrapped around me, and I wanted to plant my mouth on his, to continue where we'd left off. He must have known, for he whispered to me, "We've plenty of time." Then, more loudly, "Come and have some breakfast before you do that 'toilette' or whatever you call it."

I ate biscuits and good homemade peach preserves, but they tasted like cardboard, and my coffee might as well have been water. My eyes never left Sundance, though I wondered inanely if I was going to be such a dolt all my days with him.

"So you're back!" Fannie strode into the kitchen. She too was barely out of bed, but she had combed her hair and patted a little color into her cheeks. And her wrapper was flowing and satin.

"Fannie, how lovely you look!"

I couldn't tell if he meant it or if there was a touch of sarcasm in his voice. Fannie couldn't tell either.

"Don't try to flatter me, Sundance. I know why you're here."

He shrugged. "I guess we all know. I told Etta I'd be back for her."

Fannie whirled toward me. "And there's no sense asking if you'll go with him, is there? Even though it's been two years since you've heard from him?"

Sundance made no effort to defend himself or explain the two years, and I simply shook my head.

"Sundance," she said, "I expect people to make their own way in this world, and most times I think they get what they deserve. But this child—she was only a child when she came to me—got off to a particularly bad start." She stood before him now, her eyes boring into his. "I don't expect you to do anything to hurt her."

He shifted uncomfortably. "I surely wouldn't do anything deliberately, Fannie. I think you know that."

"It's the things you do un-deliberately that worry me," she said with acid in her voice. Then, turning to me, "Etta, my recommendation is that you don't go. But you know that, and I know that you won't listen. But you also know that I'm here if you ever need anything. You just send me a telegraph."

A softhearted Fannie made me squirm in discomfort. "Yes, ma'am, I do know that, and I appreciate it . . . and, Fannie, there's no way . . ."

She brushed me away. "Now, don't go getting mushy on me. What I did for you, I did because I wanted to. And you've made me proud. I suspect in some way you're still going to make me proud. I . . . I just worry. . . ." And with that she turned and fled to her bedroom, calling over her shoulder, "Hodge, bring me a tray!"

Sundance and I stood looking at each other, and I remembered one of Pa's old sayings that I always hated: "The fat is in the fire."

Sundance did not want to linger. I had one day to pack my clothes and books, tuck away my treasured pictures of Mama and Ab, and box up my school papers to be stored in Fannie's attic.

"You need new clothes," he said.

"I have plenty of clothes," I protested. "Fannie always bought me new clothes for school in the fall."

Laughing, he said, "It's bad enough that I'm stealing away a schoolgirl. I won't have you looking like one."

And so he took me shopping. His wallet apparently had no bottom, for he bought me a silver gray suit of china silk, with pink piping on the jacket and a hat with pink feathers to match. While I whirled before the mirror and a nervous saleslady hovered over me, Sundance lounged back on a chair, his eyes smiling with delight.

"My," he said, "won't you be the hit in Fort Worth!"

"Fort Worth? I thought we were going to Wyoming."

"We are. But the train goes through Fort Worth, and I can't pass Cowtown without stopping."

Then there were dark skirts and brightly colored shirts for everyday wear—none of the white batiste I'd been wearing!—and practical wrappers of cotton and flannel. "It gets cold in Wyoming," he warned.

But the most outrageous and the outfit that delighted my heart was a silk serge suit of dark brown, almost a mahogany, piped with black cable cord. It fit tightly at the waist and flared into a gored skirt, the kind newly fashionable. It made me feel sophisticated.

"Where will I wear it?" I asked.

"We'll find a place," he assured me. "You'll wear it for me."

My heart did one of those little jumps, and I had to look away from him.

Then there was the matter of nightclothes. I blushed furiously when Sundance said to the salesgirl, "Bring us a selection of nightgowns."

That poor woman, probably thinking there was a honeymoon in the future—well, in a way there was, wasn't there?—brought filmy creations of satin and silk, things that Fannie would have worn.

"No." Sundance waved his hand to brush her away. "We're going to Wyoming. It's cold. Do you have anything warm?"

In San Antonio? I wanted to ask, but I kept quiet, while the saleslady trotted out one or two flannel wrappers.

"Sundance," I whispered, "I have warm wrappers aplenty."

He shrugged. Then a smile lit his face, and he said, "Let me see that pink satin one again. Here, hold it up to her."

The puzzled saleswoman obliged, and it seemed that the wrapper would fit me. "We'll take that, too," he said.

"What about the cold weather?" I asked.

"It's for Fort Worth," he said.

"You need a valise," he said. "What were you planning to do? Put your clothes in a pillowcase to carry them on the train?"

"I never had a valise," I told him. "I never had enough clothes to worry about before Fannie started to dress me."

He looked askance at me. "And she'd have you looking like a schoolgirl forever. Come on, girl."

We bought a small, calfskin-covered trunk, and then more clothes than I could fit into it.

Sundance stayed at Fannie's two nights before we left, and he slept upstairs—alone. As I lay in my bed, I wondered why he was not next to me, why he showed no interest in sleeping with me. Was it Fannie? I'd think yes, that was it, and then I'd know that Sundance was not a man to be intimidated by Fannie. It was a puzzle—daytimes he was affectionate, even nuzzling my neck in front of Fannie or Julie or Hodge—but at night, he gave me a swift peck on the cheek and went upstairs. I knew that he went alone and stayed alone, because Annie reported to me.

"He isn't staying with Fannie this time," she said in a conspirator's tone. "He really did go upstairs alone at night . . . and I saw him leave that room in the morning."

"And what," I asked archly, "were you doing awake so early in the morning?"

When she answered, "Watching out for you," I felt guilty and gave her a hug.

"Oh, Etta," she said, "I . . . I worry about you, but I'm also as jealous as I can be. I want to be out of here . . . to do something exciting. Do you suppose I'm going to stay here forever, until I'm too old . . . ?"

"No," I assured her, "you're not." But I had no idea then what Annie would do to escape her life at Fannie's.

Fannie turned uncharacteristically sentimental when the carriage pulled up to take us to the train station. She started out full of bravado.

"Sundance, you take good care of this girl, or I'll . . ."

"You'll what, Fannie?" he asked, his eyes dancing with laughter.

"I'll sic every lawman in the West on you, that's what I'll do."

He threw up his hands in mock surrender. "I believe you, Fannie, I do. And I'll take as good care of her as I can." He turned to look at me. "But she'll have to learn to take care of herself, too."

"I believe she's already proven she can do that," Fannie said dryly. "Perhaps you best watch how you behave, Sundance."

I didn't share in their laughter.

But when I'd said my goodbyes to Julie and Hodge and Annie—the other girls simply peered out of an upstairs window with a kind of bored curiosity—Fannie came forward, and though she was dry-eyed, I saw real sadness on her face.

"I'll . . . well, hell, kid, I'll miss you."

It was one of those rare times when Fannie and I hugged, and this time I made the first gesture. "I'll miss you, Fannie . . . but you must know that I will always be grateful to you. I owe you my life—and more."

"Hogwash," she said impatiently, trying to brush away a tear so that we wouldn't see it. "If it weren't for me, you wouldn't have hooked up with this lowlife." She jerked her head in Sundance's direction, and he replied,

"Always a pleasure, Fannie. Thanks so much."

"Go on with you," she said, raising a hand as though she'd swat him.

As we drove away, she walked to the porch of the house and then turned to raise a hand. It made me cry, but Sundance only said, "Don't worry about her, Etta. She's not that sad. That's one tough woman."

I raised my head almost angrily. "So am I. And she is that sad . . . because I am too." I would not have let him see a tear for the life of me.

It made him laugh again. "All right," he said between chortles, "all right. I know you're strong, and I'm forewarned."

Vaguely, I noticed that he had substituted "strong" for "tough." There was a difference, but I wasn't sure yet what it was.

Once I boarded the train, I felt like a new person. In part, it had nothing to do with Sundance. I realized, almost instantaneously, that I was a different person from the girl who had ridden the train from Palestine to San Antonio some five years earlier. Age was part of the difference, of course, but I had gone from a sheltered country girl, usually barefoot and in a cotton dress made from a flour sack, to a young woman, well educated, the product of a whorehouse. Oh, I guess Sundance was part of it—he had, after all, dressed me in the most sophisticated clothes I'd ever had, and he was treating me as though I were a woman of the world. Only he and I knew that I was still a schoolgirl.

But the thing that most made me a new person was that I had left yet another life behind me. Five years ago, I'd fled from Pa, his hardscrabble farm and barbaric ways, and I'd even taken a new name to completely change my identity. This time I'd take that name—Etta Place—with me, but I'd left the whorehouse behind for good. But my change of identity—and of life—would be as great. Did I feel a certain sadness, a tie to San Antonio? Not at all. I was ready for whatever came next.

But I was a bit puzzled. If I expected Sundance to whisper sweet nothings in my ear now that we were away from Fannie and off, as it were, on our life together, I was disappointed. He treated me cavalierly, holding my arm as we boarded the train, bowing me into the seat, leaning almost across me to point to something out the window, and, always, smiling at me as though he'd just invented me. But beyond casual touches of the hand, there was no passion—nor any hint of passion to come.

I was, of course, nervous about the passion part of our relationship. He was a man used to physical pleasures, and I was a girl raped by her father, albeit one who had lived in a whorehouse and seen the casual acceptance of coupling by others. But never by myself. A part of me was frightened—would it be as painful and unpleasant as it had been with Pa? But another part of me was impatient—there were those feelings deep in the pit of my stomach that welled up when Sundance even looked into my eyes, and that electric tingle when he touched my hand.

He seemed oblivious to all that and more concerned about what we would get to eat when the train stopped in Austin. We got off and went into the station, where food was available. We studied the menu crudely printed on a blackboard, and I announced I'd have the chicken salad.

"Uh, I wouldn't do that," he muttered in my ear.

"Why not?" If I wanted chicken salad, then I wanted it.

"Well . . . no telling when it was made, or how clean it's been kept. Stick with something that doesn't spoil."

"Such as?"

He shrugged. "A sausage sandwich is pretty safe."

"I don't want sausage," I said, "I want chicken." If he thought he was going to start this relationship off by telling me what to eat, I'd show him. I hadn't been around Fannie all those years for nothing. I would not be Mama or Mrs. Brewster!

"Suit yourself." He shrugged and ordered himself sausage in a roll. "The lady'll have chicken salad," he said.

"The lady" was faintly sick by the time we reached Fort Worth, and desperately so when we got to something called the Maddox Flats. It wasn't a hotel—in fact, dimly, I thought it might be a whorehouse—but a woman came out of the back to greet Sundance joyously. He, however, rushed through the formalities in order to get me upstairs, where I promptly hung my head over the chamber pot and disposed of the chicken salad.

He was amused, but he was sympathetic. "Can I get you anything?"

I shook my head, miserable because I felt so bad and because I was embarrassed. But a part of me was also mad. I'd given him a chance to say, "I told you so." Fortunately, he didn't say it. He simply sent for hot tea, and when I collapsed on the bed, still wearing my traveling suit, he put cold cloths on my head.

"I'll just step outside," he said, "and you get into one of those warm wrappers. Ah . . . ah, forget that satin thing for now."

Dimly I realized that the "satin thing" was meant for this, our first night together, and my dinner of chicken salad had spoiled all our plans. But I was too sick to care. With Sundance pacing outside the door—I wouldn't have cared if he'd stayed inside the room—I pulled off the suit, left it in a heap on the floor, pulled on a wrapper, and crawled into bed.

"My, my, aren't we neat," he said when he came back into the room, eyeing the crumpled clothes on the floor. With careful precision, he hung them in the wardrobe and then deliberately and slowly undressed down to his underwear. Carefully, he climbed into the other side of the bed.

I lay curled into a ball of misery on my side, my back to him.

He leaned over, kissed me on the forehead, and said, "Good night, Etta." Then, as he pulled away, he said, "There will be better nights, I promise you."

Thinking I heard just the faint touch of laughter in his voice, I turned toward him. "Are you mad at me?" It was an instinctive reaction, probably born of too many years with Pa.

He laughed softly. "Of course not. But I did tell you not to eat that damn chicken salad. Maybe next time you'll believe me."

I reached for his hand. "I might," I said.

And that's how Sundance and I spent our first night together, lying stiffly next to each other in a double bed, me racked with misery and he—well, I don't know exactly what he felt, but I'm sure things hadn't gone as he'd planned.

It would not be, I decided firmly, an omen of things to come between us.

Chapter Eleven

During the night, I really began to believe that Maddox Flats was a whorehouse. It was a big house like Fannie's, and in my misery that night I heard the familiar sounds of men's voices—loud voices—and the occasional softer laugh of a woman. Beside me, Sundance slept soundly, snoring softly.

"Are we staying in a whorehouse?" I asked in the morning.

"Shame on you!" he replied indignantly. "Mrs. Maddox would never want to hear you say that. She runs a respectable boardinghouse."

"Does she serve breakfast?" I asked, my stomach now recovered enough to feel empty.

"No. I went out while you were still sleeping and bought some penny rolls from a cart in the street." He reached into a sack and held out a fat roll, glazed with syrup.

The fact that she didn't serve breakfast confirmed my suspicion. No one in a whorehouse got up early enough to eat breakfast, but everyone in a "respectable" boardinghouse expected eggs and hotcakes.

The roll was delicious, but so sweet and sticky that I could hardly open my mouth to ask, "Is there any coffee?"

He shook his head. "The pitcher's still full." He nodded toward a pitcher and basin set on the bedside table. Two glasses sat by the pitcher, but when I poured the water it was lukewarm and not very good-tasting. I made a face.

"Etta," he said with real impatience, "one thing you've got to learn about this life . . ."

"What life?" Every reference to "the life" I'd ever heard had meant being a whore.

"The outlaw life!" he exploded. "You just can't always have the comforts you got used to at Fannie's."

"But we're not outlaws right now," I pointed out. "We're paying customers—we are, aren't we?—in a boardinghouse that ought to provide better for its guests."

"I'm going downstairs," he said, turning his back on me. "Get dressed, and I'll show you Fort Worth."

"I don't want to see Fort Worth. I want to go to Denver and on to Wyoming."

"There's no train until tomorrow," he said. "You can either see Fort Worth with me or you can sit in this room and remember how you felt last night."

Sundance, I was discovering, could give as good as he got. "I'll be downstairs shortly," I said, and then dressed so leisurely that he was nearly out of patience when I appeared.

We rented a carriage at a livery, and he headed the horse west along the bluff behind the pink granite courthouse. To one side of us was the city, with its mix of rough frontier days and up-and-coming business. On the other side, below the bluff, the prairie stretched endlessly before us.

Next thing I knew we were in a residential section far different from that which housed Maddox Flats, much finer. The houses were grand—some of wood, some of brick, one of granite like the courthouse. All were large and square, with even rows of windows marching across them, chimneys emerging sedately from the roofs. Imposing front lawns and walkways directed the eye to front doors of leaded glass.

"Bankers must live in these houses," I said. "Are there very many rich people in Fort Worth?"

"You've got an obsession with bankers," he said, "and blinders on about what they're like. Someday you and I are going to live in a house just like these. Bankers are going to help us get there." Then he laughed. "I'm a banker, of sorts, after all."

I considered for a minute. "Will we live in Fort Worth?"

"Maybe, maybe not. How about South America? Butch is always wanting to go there."

"I don't think they have houses like this in South America," I said. "I think there they would be more . . . well, like San Antonio."

"And what would you like?" he asked, amused at me.

I looked straight ahead at a three-story redbrick home, with a green glazed tile roof, tall columns on the front, and wraparound porches at the second story. "I want that house," I said. "And I want it in Fort Worth."

I had no idea why the city fascinated me. I had been there less than twenty-four hours and had spent much of that time sicker than I wanted to recall. "I want to live in Fort Worth," I said with determination. I meant, of course, after we'd saved up a fortune by robbing trains and banks and gotten all that adventure out of our systems.

Sundance reined the horses to a stop and sat staring at me. "You really mean that?"

"Yes," I said firmly, "I do."

Laughter again. "All right, my lady, you shall have your wish. . . . I just can't tell you when."

Neither of us knew how prophetic those words were, nor the twists and turns our lives would take before I returned to the Queen City of the Prairies. But I knew even then that I would be back.

That night we dined on quail and roast beef at a place called Peers House. "Better than Julie's cooking," I said, eating the last bite of a fruit trifle laced with bourbon, even though I had already eaten twice as much as usual.

"Julie's not cooking for bankers in Fort Worth," he said, and then laughed at me.

A short but dapper-looking man in a vest and top hat came by, barely glanced at me, and then bent to whisper in Sundance's ear.

"No. Thanks, but not tonight," Sundance replied.

"We'll miss you."

Judy Alter

Sundance tipped an imaginary hat in his direction and said, "There'll be other times."

"A poker game," I said.

"You're clairvoyant, too! Of course it was a poker game. I told him I'd prefer your company."

My heart sank just a little, for I knew what he meant. "I believe I'd like some more claret," I told him.

"I believe you wouldn't," he said. "Remember the chicken salad."

When we got back to our room at Mrs. Maddox's, I retired behind the folding screen and emerged wearing a long-sleeved, high-collared wrapper.

Sundance stood looking out the window, though he stood to the side of the window and reached one hand to part the curtains ever so slightly. Through this slit, he looked down at the street. I would learn that this was the way he always looked out of windows, a habit of caution that had become part of him. He still wore his pants, but he had discarded his shirt and was down to an undershirt.

"Come look," he said. "You won't see this much activity again for a long time." He hadn't even turned to look at me, but when I walked to his side his free arm went quietly around my waist. If the wrapper bothered him, he said nothing.

"See that lady of the night down there? She's old . . . and kind of pitiful. I've a mind to go give her a dollar."

"For what?" I asked.

He turned toward me. "Not for what you think," he said. His face was now very near mine, and he stared intently at me. Then his hands reached up to hold my face, and he kissed me long and gently. "Get in bed."

I did as I was told, still wearing the wrapper, shaking in anticipation as I waited for him to come to bed. I didn't know which I hated more—my own nervousness or the fact that the nervousness made me lose control of the situation.

Sundance, however, was in perfect control. He kissed me gently on the forehead, took extra blankets from the wardrobe, and made himself a pallet on the floor. "Sleep well, Etta."

I sat up in astonishment. And then disappointment washed over me like a flood. "You're not sleeping in the bed?" I asked stupidly.

"You're not ready for me to," he said.

I lay back down, arms behind my head, thoughts racing. I wanted him—I wanted him to show me how it could be so different from Pa. But every time I thought about that, Pa's face swam before me. I remembered the pain, and I heard him say, "A man has his needs." And I remembered my vow never again to be that helpless.

Sundance was snoring softly. And I knew that sleeping on the floor on a pallet gave him more power than if he had forced himself on me.

I jumped out of the bed and stood over him. "Sundance," I said, "I . . . I want to sleep with you." It took every ounce of courage I had to say that, and as I said it I felt that lurching in my stomach.

"You sure?"

I nodded, and crawled into bed.

"I'm used to women taking off their clothes before they get into bed with me," he said softly.

I was flustered. "I . . . I didn't know. . . ."

"My pleasure, ma'am," he said as he unhitched his suspenders and let his pants fall, revealing the long cotton underwear that he apparently wore summer or winter. Then he was in the bed, lying next to me, his head propped on one elbow. "You all right?"

From what I knew of Pa and what I heard of men at Fannie's, most of them didn't care how you were. Sundance, I told myself, was different.

"Uh-huh," I murmured. Suddenly, though it was hot as could be in that room, I was chilled through and through—the shaking kind of a chill.

He knew, of course, but he said nothing. His hand began to stroke my forehead, brushing my hair away from my face. For several minutes, he said nothing but only stared intently at me, his hand always moving. And then the hand traveled, first down to my neck and shoulders, and then, ever so tentatively, he unbuttoned the wrapper and reached inside to touch one of my breasts. I was still shaking.

"Etta," he whispered, "don't think about your father. Don't think about anything." His mouth came down on mine, gently at first and then demanding, working, insisting on a response.

111

Thinking I didn't know how to respond, I found my kisses meeting his, my mouth working on his.

Now he lay beside me, his length pressed against my body, and one hand reached up under the bottom of the wrapper. He stroked my belly, sending sudden sensations through my stomach that startled me. And then he was stroking my thighs, all the time talking to me in a low voice. I stopped shaking as a kind of electricity seemed to flow through me.

"Trust me, Etta. Let me show you what it can be like. Don't think about your father. Think about me. Think about us."

By the time Sundance had wriggled out of his underwear—when did he do that?—and pulled the wrapper over my head, I was in a trance, soothed by his voice and transported by his touch. When he entered me, I felt nothing but pleasure, a rising pleasure that met his every movement until both of us lay panting.

"You want to go back to Fannie's?" he asked at last.

"Well," I said, "now I know that maybe I could make a living there."

He jumped from the bed and, standing stark naked before me, shouted, "That's what's wrong with females. You're an ungrateful lot." Then he was back in the bed, kissing me and holding me tight. "It wouldn't," he whispered, "be the same with anyone else."

"I know that," I told him. "Let's go to Wyoming tomorrow."

This time I was the one who began the stroking. When again we lay panting, he said, "I do believe you're a quick learner, Etta Place. Will you learn to be an outlaw as quickly?"

At that I laughed aloud.

"I knew I could make you laugh again," he said slowly, "but I'll be damned if I know what was funny about what I just said." He shuddered just a bit as he said that, and I didn't know if it was from passion or from brief sight into the future.

I didn't tell him that I'd laughed just because I felt like laughing. It was a new feeling to me.

We went by train to Denver, and I watched the landscape in fascination. The prairie around Fort Worth turned progressively flatter as we moved north, the land rolling occasionally into deep cuts. There were wildflowers because it was June—carpets of gold flowers that disguised what would in a month be bare and brown—and there were plum thickets, their bloom already gone for the season. But there were no trees.

Sundance pointed out various places for me, telling me, for instance, when we were in the Panhandle. "The Staked Plains," he said, "Llano Estacado. Story is the early Spanish explorers put stakes down so they wouldn't lose their way back."

I could see why. In some places the land was perfectly flat and unmarked by trees, giving you the impression you could see forever. But at other places, it rolled into deep cuts and gorges, revealing rocky red soil.

We went north to Colorado, then straight west across empty plains where there was little vegetation. Even now, in spring, there was only a cracked and brown soil, as though it had been dry for centuries. Occasional fences rose from the ground, where some poor soul was trying to raise corn or melons or whatever he could—dryland farmers, Sundance told me, as he pointed out the scattered dugouts to me.

"Look," he said, and my eye followed his finger to a rise in the ground. "Someone lives there."

"Underground?"

Patiently he explained about dugouts, those half-in-the-earth dwellings that offered better insulation against heat, cold, and storms but no creature comforts. "Dirt falls into your soup," he said. "But you'll find that out in the Hole."

"You live in a dugout?" I asked.

He shook his head. "No, but there are some there. If it's a bad winter, we'd be glad of one."

I shook my head. I never wanted to live half in the ground. That wasn't part of the dream I carried in my head.

My first glimpse of the mountains fascinated me. They rose in the distance, faint and purple, like small hills on the horizon. I thought we would reach them quickly, but in two hours they were no closer, no larger.

"By sundown," he said, "we'll be there."

It was barely noon, and I could not believe it would take all day to reach those tiny hills. Of course, at last, as we grew nearer, they grew larger, until they loomed like giants. No longer faintly blue, they were dark gray and black and forbidding, with no green softening their rugged edges.

113

"Do people live in the mountains?" I asked.

He smiled. "Of course. In the foothills leading up to them, in the valleys between. They're not solid walls of rock—they just look that way. There are thousands of trails and entries into them, if you know where you're going."

"Can we go there?"

He shook his head. "No, we're going to Wyoming. You'll see mountains there—probably more than you ever wanted."

"Come on," he said impatiently. "We're getting off here."

"Here? In Denver? Even I know it's not near Wyoming, and you're in a hurry to get to Wyoming."

"It's closer than Fort Worth," he said with a grin, "and I'm not in that much of a hurry. We have some shopping to do."

I followed him down the aisle of the train car. At the end, he stood aside with gentlemanly propriety so that I could go first. The conductor assisted me down the steps, and then I turned to Sundance: "My trunk!" I hadn't seen the new calfskin trunk he'd bought me since we boarded in Fort Worth.

"It'll be held for you at the station until we go north tomorrow," he assured me.

"We need to make sure it's taken off this train." I wasn't about to trust anyone with my trunk and fully intended to stand there and watch while it was unloaded.

He chuckled. "No, Etta. It will be fine."

Once again we stayed in a boardinghouse that he knew and where he was greeted like a king. I had half hoped for an elegant hotel, and when I finally mentioned it, he said, "Hotels are too public. No telling who's watching in the lobby."

Once we deposited our hand-carried bags in the room, he was impatient to be gone. "We've got to shop," he said. "Get you some winter clothes. Fort Worth was no good for that. Never gets cold enough down there."

We spent the afternoon in mercantile stores. Sundance held flannel shirts and huge sweaters up against my shoulders, and if they were anywhere close to the same size, announced, "That's fine. We'll take that . . . and this . . . and that." Apparently the fit, beyond a rough approximation, wasn't important.

I went away with two warm jackets, several sweaters and heavy shirts, white shirtwaists, two pairs of heavy boots, and—most amazing of all—three split skirts.

"People will think I'm improper," I complained. Fannie, I knew, would have been scandalized if I'd worn a split skirt.

"People you're going to see won't think anything except that you're smart," he said. "You don't want to be riding sidesaddle all over Wyoming, do you?"

Remembering the discomfort of our first horseback ride together, I laughed aloud. "No, I don't."

"Then you'll wear split skirts," he said, swooping the packages up off the merchant's counter and holding his other arm out for me. "And you're laughing again."

I still felt like laughing all the time.

I made no modest toilette that night. And we had no supper. As we deposited our new purchases—he had also bought himself a new heavy jacket, three pairs of pants, and some shirts—he said, "Try on the split skirt."

Surprised but not unwilling, I picked it up and headed for the screen that served to hide a dressing area.

"No," he said huskily. "Here. In front of me."

I stared at him for a long time. Then, slowly, I backed up to him so that he could undo the tiny buttons that coursed down the back of my blue faille dress. Each time he loosened a button, he brushed his lips gently—tantalizingly—across my back. By the time he reached the buttons below my waist, I was quivering.

"The split skirt," he said calmly, pulling the string that loosened my petticoat.

Wearing only a camisole, I stepped into the skirt and then walked boldly across the room. It swirled about my legs in a way that skirts never did and, at first, threatened to bunch between my legs and trip me.

Sundance laughed aloud. "It'll probably be better ahorseback than on foot," he said. "Kind of like boots." And with that he reached down, deliberately, to pull off the black leather boots he wore.

In a flash I was beside him, dropping the split skirt onto the floor. Then, as deliberate as he had been, I peeled off his jacket and began to unbutton his shirt, using my mouth to tease with each button released.

115

Sundance moaned and reached for me, and we became a whirlwind of activity, each peeling off the other's clothes until we ended in a frantic, passionate coupling in the bed.

"You're wanton," he said, "absolutely wanton."

"Only with you," I told him, "only with you."

Chapter Twelve

We took the train to Cheyenne and changed there to the Chicago & Northwestern for Casper. Outside Denver, the landscape changed dramatically, almost with every mile. Closer to the mountains, the Colorado plain had turned to green. It was, Sundance told me, the foothills, with forests of pine and meadows ripe for grazing livestock. Now, though, the green gave way to a dry brownness, and the land flattened. There were always mountains in the distance—but they were less spectacular, the brown, bare mountains of southern Wyoming. The land close to the train was dismal and barren.

"Is this what Hole-in-the-Wall looks like?"

"Naw," he said, "it looks worse." Then he grabbed my hand and laughed. "No, there's grass, and a stream—Buffalo Creek—and a few trees. And the walls are sandstone—bright red. It's got a lot more color than this place."

"It better," I muttered. I couldn't imagine living in a place this much worse than East Texas.

"I can get you a train ticket back to San Antonio," he said softly. " 'Course, I won't go with you, but . . . ."

I shook my head. "No." To turn around for San Antonio—sometimes a tempting thought—would have been cowardly. No, I didn't want to be apart from Sundance.

Casper wasn't much—mostly a collection of wooden buildings that looked to be no more than a few years old and were already falling down. The main street wasn't even one block long, and I counted eight saloons in that small place. There were few women on the streets—almost none, in fact. All I saw were Indians and cowboys.

Casper had, he told me, been the site of a gold strike, but by now everyone figured out that the "rich vein" was only asbestos. These days the excitement was oil—the first refinery had been built last year—and oil had brought lots of roughnecks to town.

I watched carefully as my calfskin trunk was unloaded from the train and carted into a mercantile store. Then I followed Sundance.

"Howdy, Mrs. Johnson," he said cheerfully to a rather sour-looking woman behind the counter. "Want you to meet Etta Place. Etta," turning to me, "this is Mrs. Johnson. She and her husband run this store. They're good folks."

Did he wink at me as he said that?

"I'm glad to know you," I said, extending a tentative hand.

She ignored the hand, nodded at me with obvious disapproval, and said, "You can change in there." She jerked her head in the direction of the back of the store, as though having Sundance bring a woman in were a common occurrence.

Head high, I went to the back of the store and soon emerged in a split skirt and a white shirt.

"I need to get into my trunk," I said.

"Etta . . ." His voice was a cross of question and pleading, as though he was saying "Please don't make me go to all that trouble."

"I need to get into my trunk," I repeated.

He threw his hands up. "All right. What's so dadblamed important in that trunk? You can't wear silk where we're going!"

"Just get it for me," I said.

My back to him, I unlocked the trunk and dug down carefully until I found my miniature of Mama. Then I locked the trunk and carefully tucked the picture into the bedroll he had prepared for me.

Sundance, seeing what I had gotten, never said another word. He simply hoisted the trunk and took it back to the storeroom.

That settled, I took my first good look at him. He had somehow, somewhere changed out of his suit and into denim pants, now tucked into high boots, a crisp chambray shirt, a kerchief around his neck, and a Stetson on his head.

"Now you look like an outlaw!" I spoke before I thought.

He was definitely not amused, nor was Mrs. Johnson, and I slunk out of the store without thanking her for her hospitality.

Two fine horses were saddled and hitched to the bar outside the store. One was a bay with a dark mane and tail; the other, bigger one was a chestnut so dark it almost looked black. Both were powerful, muscled horses meant for the distance. Behind them was a mule.

"Whose horses are these?" I asked.

"Ours. Boys brought 'em in for us. I wired ahead."

"How did you know exactly when we'd arrive?"

"Didn't. Horses have been down to the livery stable for a week or more now. It's all right, Etta. Don't worry about it. Just try not to talk about outlaws anymore."

I blushed furiously and was not at all reassured to see that he was laughing at me.

It was midday when we rode north out of Casper onto broad, sweeping plains, green with grass but with absolutely no trees. The land seemed to roll around us in bluffs and small hills, so that sometimes we could see for a distance and other times I could not tell where we were going. Overhead the sky was a bright blue, and the temperature was cool enough that the sun felt good on our shoulders as we rode. It was the wind I noticed. It blew my hair into my face, ruffled the wide legs of my split skirt, whipped at Sundance's hat—and it never stopped.

"Does it always blow like this?"

"Most of the time," he said. "Better than the heavy wet air that settles on you in San Antonio this time of the year."

We rode through deep grass, sometimes startling up prairie hens or an occasional cottontail, even a jackrabbit or two. Once I pointed at a bird circling overhead, and Sundance said tersely, "Hawk. He probably wants that cottontail that just skittered in front of us."

I watched in fascination, hoping to see the hawk swoop down. But it never did, and eventually it gave up and flew away.

119

There were deer—mule deer, he told me—and lovely packs of antelope that ran like lightning when they saw us.

But I saw no mountains.

"I thought you said Hole-in-the-Wall was next to the mountains. Where are they?"

"Wait."

"Wait? What time will we get there?" I fully expected that mountains would materialize out of the horizon any minute.

"Day after tomorrow," he said.

"What?" I screeched, for I had fully believed that I would sleep happily at Hole-in-the-Wall that night. "Two days?"

He nodded. "Tomorrow night if we ride hard, but I don't 'spect you want to do that."

My legs were already a little sore, and my bottom was tired of the bounce of the saddle. No, all I wanted was to be down from that horse. I'd not foreseen hard riding as part of my adventure.

Sometimes we rode for long periods without speaking. I'd look at him and find him contentedly staring ahead, a slight smile on his face. I decided he was glad to be back in this part of the country, and I said nothing.

We rode in silence, but I was thinking about bank robberies, how they were planned, how a woman, dressed in the fine dresses in my calfskin trunk, could make inquiries in banks that Sundance never could. In my mind's eye, I could see myself walking into a bank, asking the banker's help with my widowed status, gradually gleaning information from him. My years with Fannie had taught me, among other things, how to use flattery with men.

Out of the blue, late in the afternoon of our first day of riding, he said, "I have a wife you know."

I turned to look at him. "You told me that in San Antonio. Her name's Anna Maria, and she lives . . . I forget where.

"Castle Gate."

I laughed, but this time it wasn't that happy laughter that had bubbled up in me over the last few days. "Good thing I wasn't expecting you to marry me," I said.

"She says she's gettin' a divorce," he answered somewhat angrily. "Thought she was marrying a substantial fellow, someone who would go to work in the bank in the morning and come home at night. She can't handle the outlaw life." He looked sideways at me, as though waiting for a reaction.

What Anna Maria Thayne wanted was just what I wanted to avoid—boredom!

"You don't seem heartbroken," I said.

"I loved her," he said. "Why else would I have married her? She's beautiful and she made me feel wonderful—all the things you are, Etta." He reached for my hand, but I withdrew it. He shrugged and went on. "But she wanted me to be something I wasn't . . . and then the love wasn't there anymore. Do I love her? Not anymore."

I asked the question most on my mind. "Was she smart?"

He looked startled. "Smart? She'd been to school . . . but, no, she didn't read much, and she didn't want to have to think. She wanted me to do that for her."

I dug my heels into the horse's sides and galloped away, leaving him well behind so he wouldn't see the smile on my face. When he caught up with me, he grabbed the reins of my horse and brought us both to a halt. Then, leaning from his saddle, he kissed me soundly.

That afternoon, as the sun began to move toward the west, big black clouds boiled up in that direction. Storms in Texas are sometimes fierce, but they never seemed to come from the distance that this one did as it rolled toward us.

"Sundance? It's going to storm."

He had already noticed, of course, but he seemed particularly unperturbed. "Looks that way." He shrugged.

"There's no place to get out of it," I said. "No trees, no houses." It was a statement of the obvious, and I bit my tongue the minute I said it. I didn't want Sundance to think I was afraid, and I really wasn't scared. I just didn't particularly want to get wet.

"We'll sit it out," he said. "I've got slickers for us and tarps to put over our bedrolls. We'll be fine."

With that he dismounted, unrolled his pack, and took out the slickers. I put on the one he handed me—a rubbery affair with a hood to cover my head—and watched while he donned the other one and then wrapped both our bedrolls in another long piece of rubberized something.

By now the sky to our left was flashing with lightning, and the horses were beginning to act skittish. Sundance looked at me, as though appraising, and said, "I think we best stop. Don't want the horses running away in a storm."

In that wilderness where there were no trees—I swear I had not seen a one the whole afternoon—he found not only trees but a fallen log, which he dragged away from its small stand of scrub pine to use as a hitching post for the horses.

"No sense in hitching them to a patch of trees lightning might strike," he said as he tied the reins around the log. "I'll probably just hold the reins in case it gets bad enough to really spook them."

And so that was how we sat and waited for the storm—me burrowed down in my slicker as close to Sundance as I could get, him holding the reins of both horses and staring nonchalantly at the sky.

It was a thunderstorm unparalleled. The sky burst with great sheets of lightning, thunder rolled around us as though the god's bowling game was really grand, and large drops of rain pelted us. In the end, the rain was really less than the thunder, lightning, and wind.

"I really like a good storm on the plains," he said.

I thought about hitting him. Rain was blowing in my face, and slicker or no slicker, my hair was getting wet and I could feel water trickling down the back of my neck.

"How long will it last?" I asked, thinking of the storms in Texas that sometimes blew up in seconds and were gone as quickly. This one seemed to me to have settled in for a longer stay.

"I don't know," he said slowly. "God hasn't confided in me." Then he laughed. "It's just a late-afternoon thunderstorm, Etta. Happens all the time in summer."

We had hunkered on the ground less than an hour when it was all over, and blue sky—now dimmed by twilight—began to appear to the west.

We rode for another two hours before Sundance deemed it time to camp. Then he opened the packs on the mule and drew forth a small tent, plus cooking utensils and preparations for supper.

Oh, it wasn't an elegant supper. We ate cold biscuits and jerky and beans—courtesy of Mrs. Johnson, he told me, though I couldn't imagine any courtesy from that grim woman. It was not the finest meal I'd ever had.

"I hope we get there tomorrow," I said.

"If you want to ride that hard," he replied.

"I'm game," I told him, deliberately using a phrase I'd heard from him.

We slept apart that night, each rolled in our separate blankets, and I appreciated what he had said about nights being cold even in summer. I was grateful for the blankets and would have been even more grateful for his warmth. In the morning he made coffee, tried to fry the leftover biscuits—a greasy disaster—and we rode on.

"I'll ride hard," I said. "I want to be someplace, not just out on the plains."

"All right. You may get hungry."

"I may get sleepy, too, but I don't want to eat your campfire cooking again."

He laughed aloud.

It was a day like the previous one, except that the storm clouds didn't boil up in the late afternoon. Instead, miraculously, I saw mountains ahead—hazy at first, as though I was imagining them, and then more solid. Real mountains rising to the very clouds, but they were far, far away. On our side of the mountains was a ridge, so red it took my breath away.

"They call it the Red Wall," he said. "It's one of several hogback ridges leading up to the Big Horn Range. If we were coming in from the east, you'd really see it. But we'll come in from the south end of the wall. Between it and the mountains is the valley—it's . . . it's a special place, wide and hidden and . . . well, you'll see."

Emotion colored his voice when he spoke of this place. I'd thought of it as a hideaway, but now, from his tone, I saw that it was in some strong sense a home to him, a place where his heart lived.

"Will we ride through the hole?" I asked. Somehow riding through that much-talked-of Hole-in-the-Wall seemed a fitting entrance into outlaw life.

"No. It's north. We'll just slide in between the beginning of the wall and the mountains. They'll know we're coming."

"Who?" I asked.

"Butch and the others."

"Everyone there is an outlaw, then," I said, imagining an army of men.

He laughed aloud. "Lord, no, we've got honest neighbors who run a few head of cattle and raise hay. But they protect us."

"Who's 'us'?" I asked.

He shook his head. "Never can tell at any one given time. Population changes. But Butch is always there . . . and mostly, so am I." He grinned at me. "When I'm not in San Antonio." A pause, and then he said, "You'll probably see Kid Curry."

"I saw him in San Antonio," I said, "and I didn't like him."

"You probably won't like him any better here," he told me, "but try to get along. He's dangerous. One thing I don't like about him."

After a long silence he said, "They'll want you to cook for them, you know."

"Who will?" I asked. Cooking was definitely not what I had come to Wyoming to do.

"Butch and them," he said. "They do their own cooking, but it isn't very good. And they'll figure, you being a woman and all . . ."

"They can figure again," I said. "I haven't cooked in years."

"You do know how, don't you?" He was laughing.

"I can cook," I told him.

He smiled. "And will you?"

I thought about it. I didn't want to cook, never had liked it, never thought I was any good at it. But cooking for them might be a way to get Butch and the others to accept me. Little did I know that I would come to enjoy it and take pride in the meals I put before Butch and Sundance. I never cared what Kid Curry ate.

We rode past the point where the red wall began to rise out of the plains and into a valley. The walls were indeed red, steep, and absolutely bare and stark, rising sharply in layers from the valley floor. Before us was what I could only call scrub ground—brown and dry, the summer heat apparently having burned it even this far north.

Late in the afternoon we came to a smallish river. "Middle fork of the Powder," he said. "Buffalo Creek heads up this way." He jerked his head toward the northwest.

We followed Buffalo Creek until we came to a point where the wall turned east, away from us.

"There," he said, "that's the hole."

I couldn't see much. Maybe a slight shift in the direction of the sandstone and maybe a bit of a dent in the top of the ridge, but nothing that I could pinpoint and call the "hole."

"That's it?" I asked, disappointed.

"That's it," he said. "Did you want a road sign there pointing it out?"

"No, but I wanted something that I could identify."

He laughed and shrugged. "Come on, we're not far from camp. Blue Creek takes off in another mile or two."

Blue Creek, I learned, was where Butch Cassidy had taken up a squatter's claim—and where I would live for the winter.

We came rather shortly to a small, almost square cabin—not a dugout but a building that sat on the ground, if not exactly firmly or squarely. Somehow it had a slightly askew look, as though it might shift an inch or two at any moment or perhaps settle a little nearer to the ground. Already, it looked as though a tall man would have difficulty standing straight in it, and I wondered if Butch was any taller than Sundance.

Around the cabin were several brush corrals, with only three horses now in them. Some scrub trees grew haphazardly around, but the ground was mostly bare, and there was no creek in immediate sight. They probably, I thought, had to draw their water from some distance away. I vowed I wouldn't be the one to draw and carry water. Cooking was enough of a compromise.

The cabin nestled against the low wall of the rising mountains, affording a clear view down the trail toward the notch in the wall. It was well suited for watching who was coming your way, and I saw why this Cassidy person boasted you could hold off a hundred people from here.

"Hallo the house!" Sundance called loudly.

"They know we're coming already," I said.

"Sure. Someone's had us in their sights since we passed the notch."

125

Two men came banging out the door of the cabin, letting it slam wildly on its hinges behind them. One raised a hand to shade his eyes and look in our direction, but the other looked away, and even from that distance I could see that his expression was sour. His whole posture spoke of anger.

The angry one was, of course, Kid Curry. I recognized him and instantly liked him no better than I had at Fannie's.

The other man walked quickly toward us. When he stood within a few feet of our stopped horses, he said, "Sundance," and Sundance replied, "Butch."

I looked at Butch Cassidy, about whom Sundance talked so much, the man for whom he'd go to the ends of the earth. Cassidy had a round face, which had broken into an easy grin when he greeted Sundance. But his jaw was square, and his face one of strength, yet friendly enough that he reminded one of a happy child. Much stockier in build than Sundance, he was a slower man. He reminded me of a teddy bear.

He caught me looking at him. "You're Etta," he said, his voice almost shy.

I nodded and smiled.

"Well, it's a real pleasure to have you here, ma'am."

Kid Curry had joined us by then, but he looked sour and said nothing. He was dark-complected and unshaven and generally unappealing. But it was his eyes that drew my attention and that I remembered from Fannie's. They were dark and small and smoldered with perpetual anger.

"Sundance," Butch demanded, "you gonna help that lady off that horse?"

Sundance sat unmoving, but his face was creased with laughter. "You're so anxious to get her down off it, why don't you help her?"

"Well, I guess I just will." And with that Butch came to offer a handheld step for me and help me down.

Just as I turned to thank him, Kid Curry said, "You shouldn't have brought a whore here, Sundance. They ain't none of them nothin' but trouble."

I froze and then turned slowly to look at him. He was staring at me, his look challenging and angry. Sundance, for once stunned, still sat on his horse.

126

I knew I had to deal with Kid Curry right then or I'd deal with him forever. Maybe I just acted on instinct, or maybe I knew from life with Pa what happens when a woman lets a man bully her. Probably I knew Curry and I couldn't live together all winter without clearing the air.

I moved without hesitation—or so it seemed to Sundance and Butch, though to me it was an eternity while I walked the few steps it took to put me squarely in front of him, my face inches from his.

He stared at me with an arrogance that made me sure he expected me to explain, conciliate, even beg.

Instead, I reached up and slapped his face as hard as I could. "Don't you ever again call me a whore," I said.

Instinctively he covered his red cheek with one hand. But I saw the other hand go to his gun.

Sundance was now off his horse, faster than I'd ever seen him move. "Curry," he said, his tone soft and slow, "don't do it. Don't make me fight you."

"She slapped me," Kid Curry said in disbelief.

Butch shrugged almost philosophically. "You called her a whore. Sounds like a fair trade to me."

At that, Sundance burst into laughter. I knew later that it was deliberate rather than spontaneous, his way of defusing the situation. And it wasn't until much later that I saw the humor in Butch's statement. But what Butch said and the way Sundance laughed worked—Kid Curry turned away.

"Keep her outta my way," he muttered.

Sundance, now bold, replied, "Sure, Curry. You don't have to eat what she cooks."

Later Sundance came as close to anger at me as he ever had. "He could've shot you right there," he ranted. "I wouldn't put it past him. I . . . I've seen him shoot a man for no good reason. You took a foolish chance."

"I'd have taken a worse chance," I said, "if I let him go on thinking of me as a whore."

Sundance finally grinned. "Etta Place," he said, "you are something different. I don't know how long we'll last, but it's a pure pleasure, ma'am, it surely is."

Chapter Thirteen

Sundance and I were outside, wandering around the bare ground, but he had gotten over his anger—or scare—at my encounter with Kid Curry. I had not gotten over my anger.

"I won't sleep under the same roof with Curry," I said.

"There's a curtained-off sleeping area." His voice was soothing, and I knew he was trying to lull me into acceptance. "That'll be for us. Butch and Logan will sleep in bedrolls, outside as long as it's not too cold."

"I mean it," I repeated. "I won't ever sleep under the same roof with him. If I do, I'll take to putting a butcher knife by my side again."

Sundance whirled to look at me, his eyes wide with surprise. Even between us the subject of my father and my use of a butcher knife was forbidden. That I had brought it up myself testified to how strongly I felt.

"We can sleep in a tent," he said.

"And freeze?" I asked.

"Not us," he said, leering at me, "not us."

Sundance pitched a tent for us some hundred yards from the cabin. The canvas floor was made soft by featherbeds, and there were more comforters to cover us when the nights turned chilly.

For now, it was warm enough for light blankets.

It was a commodious tent—not a Sibley, he informed me, like the ones the army said held seventeen mounted soldiers, as though anyone would be mounted in a tent! This was like the tents the army issued, with a stove—Libbie Custer had slept in one with the general before he got slaughtered. Sundance said we'd never use the stove even on cold nights, lest we burn up or suffocate ourselves. Besides the stove, there was room for a chair or two and poles on which I could hang most of my clothes.

I liked it a lot better than the cabin.

"I can fix you sort of a table, if you've a piece of mirror," he said. "And we've enough lanterns." He was trying hard to please me, and I loved him for it. But I wasn't going to give an inch on my hatred of Kid Curry.

"Do I have to cook supper tonight?"

"Up to you," he said. "Butch'll probably do it, but it'd be better if you did."

"I'll start tomorrow," I said, but Butch's rendition of stew made me regret that I hadn't started right away.

Denver seemed a long time ago, and Sundance and I had had no comfortable privacy since, being either on trains or sleeping by campfires. Sometimes that long first day at the cabin, when he looked at me a certain way I ached with wanting him.

Etta Place, I'd say to myself, *you vowed no man would ever do that to you again, and now, in less than seven days, you've gone weak-kneed over him. You can't be an outlaw if all you want to do is run off into the woods with Sundance!*

But my lectures did little good. When Sundance and I were alone at last, I turned to him almost frantically. He was deliberately slow, teasing with his hands, his mouth, his tongue until I moaned and almost begged, and when at last we came together I cried out in pleasure.

"You're right, Etta," he said, and I could hear the laughter and happiness in his voice, "a curtained-off area would never have done."

Still panting, I managed a little laugh. "I . . . I won't do that again," I said.

"Yes, you will," he said. "At least, I hope you will."

I couldn't get Curry out of my mind, even with Sundance's loving. "He's . . . he's not the same kind of outlaw as you and Butch," I said. "He's mean, evil . . . I wouldn't cry if he went to prison."

"And if he was hanged?" he asked.

Startled, I sat up. "Hanged? None of you will be hanged."

He shrugged. "It could happen. Of course, I prefer to think not, but . . . Besides, Etta Place, think about you. You're not the kind of woman that people think of as a murderer. But here we both are."

Yes, I thought, here we both are. And I couldn't be more pleased. But there was still Curry. Somehow I had to get him out of the way. "I don't like the way Curry looks at me."

"He'll never lay a hand on you, Etta, I promise you that. Even Curry wouldn't dare do that." His voice was solemn and hard now. "Can we please stop talking about him now?"

Funny how little we understand about the future, and how things can go just the way we were sure they wouldn't. But we didn't know that then, as Sundance took me in his arms again. This time his urgency was greater than mine, but I never could make him cry out. At least he never grunted like Pa.

I began to cook for them, though the kitchen was pitifully supplied with utensils—there was a cast-iron spider in which I could fry and make gravy, and a handled griddle for pancakes, and a shallow granite oven that someone had let get rusty. Only three of us could eat at any one time, there not being any more of the chipped enamel plates. But wonder of wonders, there was a corn bread pan like the one Mama had, where the corn bread comes out shaped like little ears of corn. I made corn bread until they were tired of it. Of course, before I could use any of it I had to give all the utensils and the whole cabin a thorough scrubbing.

"I keep it clean," Butch protested, sitting with his feet up on the table and watching me while he sipped coffee.

"Do you know how much grease was on this spider?"

Coming through the door, Curry said, "Don't go washing the coffeepot. It'll taint the coffee."

I ignored him and deliberately plunged the coffeepot into hot, sudsy water. I never had believed that old cowboy tale about coffeepots "seasoning" with use and ruining with soap.

"Bitch!" Curry turned on his heel and left.

"Why do you deliberately make him mad?" Butch asked.

I shrugged. "I don't like him."

He smiled a little. "He doesn't much like you either."

Almost always, Butch and Sundance and I ate together, but sometimes Kid Curry was there. Then I made him wait until one of us was through and I could wash the plate and give it to him. It struck me it was like feeding a dog after the family had eaten. If he resented it, he never showed it. Curry ate as heartily as any, and I had fleeting thoughts of Lucreztia Borgia and her poison ring that scattered lethal droplets into the food of her victims. Other times there were other men at the cabin. My favorite was Elzy Lay, who apparently left behind his bride, Maude, and their new baby, born too soon to be healthy. And there were one or two others who were never even introduced.

I cooked mostly what they brought me—some days a fat sage chicken or a plump young rabbit that I larded with bacon and let roast most of the day. Sundance was a great hand to shoot squirrels and clean them—I never would clean the game they brought—but I didn't even like to cook the tiny varmints and made a face every time he brought the things. Still, they made a good stew, with fresh new potatoes and turnips, bought from a farmer down the valley.

Some days Sundance packed me off to the mountains early in the morning. We had two or three favorite streams we went to, where we'd catch grasshoppers and make birch fishing poles. The trout ran freely, all silvery gray with dark speckles and shades of rose and orange dotting their flesh. Sundance and I would pack potatoes and buttered bread and lard to cook the fish and have a feast, way up there in the mountains by ourselves, and then the others would be angry when we came back and they had no supper. I told them there was jerky in the shed, and when Curry flared in anger, as he usually did, I saw a slow smile creep across Butch's face.

Sundance and I would ride high enough that the pines whispered as we passed under them, following the creek until the air was clear and keen, almost biting with its smell of sage and pine, and alive with the song of the meadowlarks. There were green, grassy meadows, surrounded by quaking aspen, whose

131

leaves had not yet turned gold in anticipation of the first frost, and cottonwoods and rabbit brush that grew shrub high with bright yellow flowers.

Sundance used to watch me as I rode through this land. He knew that it was unlike anything I'd ever seen, and he knew, without my telling him, that I felt truly free here. I wasn't Etta Place, the farmer's daughter, nor the madam's protégé. I was just me. Sundance might have reminded me that I was now an outlaw's woman, but I didn't look at it that way.

But days wore into weeks, and no one talked about robbing a bank, stopping a train. They talked about hunting and fishing and maybe going to Denver for a change of scenery. They didn't seem to need much money, and when supplies were needed and Butch went to town, there was always enough cash. His first trip to Kaycee, the nearest town, he brought back my trunk that had apparently been shipped from Casper. I never did figure out how the Wild Bunch arranged some of these mysterious things, like the horses that were always waiting for us at the right spot.

But I was overjoyed to have my trunk back. I searched its contents carefully.

"You think Mrs. Johnson stole something?" Sundance asked as I shook out fine dresses of crape, voile, silk, and challis.

"Never can tell," I replied crisply. "She didn't like me. Thought I was a whore."

He laughed. "That wouldn't make her steal your clothes. In fact, it'd probably have just the opposite effect."

"Sundance, I'm . . . well, I'm bored."

"Shame on you. And I work so hard at night. I'd, ah, never have guessed you were bored."

I threw a shoe at him. "I'm not bored at night, but I thought I was coming to live with outlaws. All I see is a lazy bunch of men, sitting around fishing and talking and not doing anything."

He turned serious. "You can't rob trains every day. It's not like going to the office every morning. When we run out of money, we'll start to plan again."

"When's that?"

He shrugged. "I warn you, Etta, nobody but me's gonna take kindly to your butting in. I know you're smart, and I bet you have some good ideas. But you tell Curry that . . ." His voice trailed off, the grim prediction left hanging. Then he changed the subject.

"You know how to shoot a rifle?"

"I know how to shoot a pistol," I said smugly.

"I know," he said grinning. "I remember. But what about a rifle?"

When we practiced with a rifle, I was not nearly the success that I had been in San Antonio with a pistol. I shied from the kick of it, and my shots went wild. He made me try again . . . and again, and he gloated with satisfaction when I hit one of the tin cans he had finally found somewhere. If I missed, he'd simply say, "Try again." I thought I was using untold quantities of ammunition, but he always said, "Bullets are cheap. Your life isn't. You may *need* to be able to do this one day."

The day I shot a rabbit was triumphant for Sundance and bittersweet for me. The small, gray critter was still warm and soft when I picked it up—gingerly—by the hind feet.

"Good shot," Sundance exulted. "Rabbits are hard, 'cause they're so fast. They kind of dart out of your sights. You're learning, Etta. You're going to be a real shootist."

That night Sundance skinned my trophy, but I refused to cook it.

Evenings, when we were headed back to Hole-in-the-Wall from a day in the mountains, the sky would be the most astounding shade of violet and then, before our very eyes, it would turn to amber and rose. We'd ride into a canyon and the world would become dark, as though night had fallen suddenly, but then, up on the next ridge, we'd be treated to those violent colors again. Finally, the whole world would turn a dull gray, and I'd be left longing for the brightness of sunset. Sundance always knew how to time it so that by the time the world turned gray we were almost back at camp. We never rode long in the darkness, and I was grateful. Once in one of those canyons I saw a wolf sitting on the rim, watching us curiously, as though trying to appraise these intruders into his land. When Sundance reached for his rifle, I held out a hand and said, "No." The wolf watched another minute, then was gone. In later nights, when I heard howling, I wondered if it was that wolf . . . or the coyotes that tried so hard to get the few good banty hens that

Butch insisted on keeping in a small fenced area.

"Winter be here in another month," Sundance told me one day as we sunned in a meadow, having just filled ourselves with gooseberries I'd picked.

"Another month! It's only August." Here I sat, perspiring—forgive the word—in a cotton shirtwaist, and he was talking of winter!

"In Wyoming there are three seasons: winter, July, and August. You've had July and now we're on August. Then it's winter."

"Winter doesn't come until November," I protested. "Maybe sometimes a cold snap in October, but . . ."

"That's Texas," he said, and laughed. "This is Wyoming. We best get those sheepskins aired out from the shed and put them in our tent."

Butch Cassidy was a real puzzle to me. The others deferred to him, even Sundance, and he was clearly the leader. But I thought him too soft, too gentle to be an outlaw. Curry was too hotheaded to be in charge, but Sundance . . . No, Butch had some kind of power over the others.

Whenever the talk turned ugly—especially when Kid Curry was around—Butch would rise up and say, "You won't be swearing in front of a lady." Curry would hush, but his look was resentful.

Sundance sometimes fell into a fit of bad language as well, but he always looked sheepish when Butch reminded him there was a lady present. And once, when he and I had quarreled—the matter so minor that I don't now remember it—Butch all but ordered him to apologize. Sundance bristled, as though he'd fight, and then all the starch in him collapsed, and he looked at me and said, "I'm sorry." But even then there was laughter in his eyes. Behind him I heard Curry mutter, "By God, I'd never apologize to a whore." This time, I chose to ignore him.

In those long August evenings as we sat around a late-night fire outdoors, Butch would sometimes talk to me, as though he longed for a woman to talk to.

Butch had been born Robert LeRoy Parker in Utah and was thirty years old that year at the Hole. His family was strict Mormon, and Butch had known hard work all his life.

"First time I ever got in trouble," he said, staring off into the firelight, "I rode into town to get some overalls. Store was closed, but I didn't want to have to come back—it was a long ride, maybe seven, eight miles. So I let myself into the store— didn't bust anything—took the jeans, and left a note saying I'd be back to pay. Had the money in my pocket and everything. But the storekeeper, he didn't see it that way."

"What'd he do?"

"Swore out a complaint. Embarrassed me. I was raised to believe a man's word is good, and you take him for it. Made me doubt the law."

I almost hooted at the difference. I had ended up outside the law because I'd killed my father; Butch, because he'd "borrowed" a pair of overalls. It was like Sundance told me, justice really was blind.

"Seemed to me," Butch went on, "that neither the law nor the Mormon Church were doin' me much good, just hemming me in with don'ts and punishing me for things I didn't do. My pa, he lost his land when the church ruled against him. I pretty much saw that being a saint wasn't an easy road. Guess I was ripe when Mike Cassidy drifted by Marshalls' ranch one summer while I was working there."

"Cassidy? Is that how you got your name?"

He grinned, like a child caught in an embarrassing moment. "Yeah. I guess I sort of had a case of hero worship. Mike Cassidy was lots of things, but the one I saw most was he was a rustler. To me, coming from where I did, it wasn't only exciting—it was a way out, an escape. And I took it, took his name." He turned thoughtful. "But it was only part hero worship. I have enough love and respect for my family that if I'm gonna break the law, I don't want to carry the Parker name into it." This time his embarrassment seemed to come from revealing a soft spot. He looked deliberately away for a long time before he took up his story again.

In Telluride, Colorado, he was jailed for stealing a colt, but it was, he told me, a misunderstanding just like the overalls. "Made me mad all over again at those who have control . . . and I swore I'd get even, give some power to the little farmer like my pa."

Another night, almost out of the blue, he said, "Al Hainer and I raised horses outside Lander," continuing the story of his outlaw career as though he'd only left off five minutes before.

" 'Course, in winter, our herd didn't multiply much. Too cold for us to go out and gather in strays." He had an amused look on his face as he said it.

"You were rustling," I said.

"Lord, yes, but we only took from big ranches. Anyway, that's where we got caught for horse stealing. Don't know why it took so long, but they took two years trying us. Then, for some dad-blamed notion I still don't understand, they let Hainer go and sent me to the state penitentiary. They was all full of wanting me to stop stealing horses. Told 'em I would if they'd pay me to quit." He laughed loudly at his own joke. Then he turned solemn. "Governor finally pardoned me after I done about seven months. When that sheriff wanted to shake my hand, I refused. I figured if they were going to think of me as an outlaw, I was going to be the best outlaw in the whole northern plains states."

I began to see why Butch was the leader, and I could surely identify with his determination to be the best outlaw in the region.

"While you were languishing in that jail," Sundance broke in, "Madden and Bass and me robbed the Great Northern at Malta."

"You told me about that," I said.

"Yeah." Butch laughed. "I heard later you only got about twenty dollars and missed twenty-five thousand."

"Not true, Cassidy, and not funny either." Sundance's temper flared, and we all sat in silence for a while.

"Etta?" Sundance's voice was impatient when he spoke again. "I'm turning in. You coming?"

"Sure, Sundance," I said, reaching out for a hand to help me off the log where I'd sat too long and grown stiff. " 'Night, Butch. I want to hear more later."

Butch just grunted.

"I want to hear more later," Sundance mimicked, sitting on the stool in our tent. "You and him sure are getting thick as thieves."

"I think," I said, "that you've chosen an unfortunate figure of speech." I lay naked under the light blanket of summer covers, having expected him to join me in our bed. Instead I was treated to this pouting complaint.

"Well," Sundance said haughtily, "you aren't with him. You're with me. And I don't think either one of you should forget it."

He blew out the lamp, kept his back to me as he undressed, and then crawled into the covers, staying as far as possible from me.

I laughed aloud at him. "Sundance? Do you think I'd cheat on you with Butch?"

"Quit laughing," he said, but his tone was not quite so complaining.

He was being so childish that I considered turning my back to him. But I didn't. I began to rub his back. "He's a wonderful man, Sundance. I like him as much as you told me I would. But he's not you." I inched closer and closer, until my body pressed against his back. Then my hands explored his shoulders, his back, on down to his thighs.

He moved and twisted a little, and then he was turned toward me, his mouth coming down hard on mine. After a minute he rose up to say, "I . . . I don't want you to ever be with any other man," he said, his strength and assertiveness now returned.

I pulled his head down to my breast, and words were lost to us.

Afterward, as we lay close together, I poked him in the ribs. "You didn't really think Butch and I . . . I mean, really you didn't." I laughed again.

He raised on an elbow to stare deep into my face. "Don't you ever tell anyone about that," he said, and I read a threat in his voice, though I didn't know what the penalty would be for transgression. Then he lay down on his back, hands locked behind his head.

"Besides, Butch has a woman."

I was startled, a little at the news and more at the quick fire of jealousy that ran through me. I didn't want Butch Cassidy for a lover, but I didn't want to share our closeness with another woman. "Why isn't she here?"

"She married someone else while he was in jail. But he goes to see her occasionally. She wasn't tough enough."

I pondered that for a minute. Tough enough? Or maybe she was like Anna Maria Thayne—too tough, too smart to ruin her life waiting for an outlaw. Or maybe she just didn't want excitement.

"Would you wait for me?" Sundance asked.

"Depends on how long the sentence was," I said. My thoughts went back to Butch. "Those nights he just disappears—that's where he goes?"

"Doesn't take a damn detective to figure that out," he muttered, moving toward me and pushing the blanket even farther away. "I don't want to talk about it anymore."

And talk was silenced again.

Later, Sundance told me that Butch had been released after more than two years in prison for stealing that colt. What Butch hadn't told me was that he'd been released on a promise never to come to Wyoming again.

"We're in Wyoming!" I said.

Sundance smiled. "So's Butch. What they don't know won't hurt them." And then he was thoughtful. "Or maybe it will. Butch carries a grudge."

Elzy Lay was more like Butch than Sundance, a tall, gentle man, soft-spoken. But like Sundance he was apparently well-educated. He always tipped his hat to me and said, " 'Morning, Etta," or, as he left, "Thanks for the meal, Etta. I'll be seein' you."

Once I asked if the baby was better, and he grinned and said, "Thriving. She's just beautiful. Doesn't cry nearly as much anymore, either. Maude's feeling a lot better too, now that she can get some sleep."

"Why don't you bring Maude and the baby with you? I'd enjoy the company of another woman around here, and I'd like to see that baby."

He lowered his eyes and watched his toe draw a circle in the dirt. "She doesn't know . . . where I go when I come here. She . . . she wouldn't understand." Then, in a rush, as though it explained all, he added, "She was raised a strict Mormon."

"Why do you do it, then?"

Elzy sighed. "You always keep thinking that the next big strike is going to get you out of it. After that bank . . . or that

138

train . . . or that herd of horses . . . you're going to have enough to go somewhere new, start over again, and live like an honest man."

"And are you?" I asked.

He shook his head. "Probably not. Probably most of us will be killed doing this . . . and I'll leave Maude behind, for her family to say, 'I told you so,' and I'll leave that baby. . . ." His voice broke, and he turned away from me.

Later, when I asked him to play on his guitar, he chose "The Girl I Left Behind Me."

They were planning something. Elzy Lay came by more frequently, and he, Butch, Sundance, and Kid Curry would sit around the scarred board table in the cabin. Sometimes when I was outside I could hear their voices raised, often with a touch of anger, but whenever I went into the cabin, they stopped talking. I would see maps spread out on the table before them, with penciled lines showing the way they planned to get from here to there, but I never got a close look at the maps. Elzy always took them with him when he left.

One night as they sat around the kitchen table, I deliberately busied myself at the rough shelf where I cooked, dried dishes, and did all those other domestic things.

"Get her outta here," Curry muttered to Sundance.

I looked long at Sundance, and he simply ducked his head.

"Etta can stay," Butch said.

Curry stood up so fast his stool went over backward. "Then I ain't," he said, and stormed out the door.

Just as Sundance murmured "Good riddance," Butch said, "He'll be back."

I hoped Sundance was right.

"If we hide horses off the trail here, about ten miles from Montpelier . . . ," Butch said, and they were poring over their map again. This time I stood and listened and studied the maps.

Chapter Fourteen

I went to Butch, not to Sundance, and later that made Sundance angry again. But I knew that Sundance would agree with me when he was in front of me and then hang his head and look at the floor in front of Butch and the others.

"Butch, I want to go with you to Montpelier."

He didn't laugh like that was the funniest joke he'd ever heard, and he wasn't patronizing. "I know you do, Etta," he said soberly. "I been thinking about it."

"And?"

"I don't know. More than the thing about you bein' a woman, it's kind of like havin' a new man along. Boys don't know you that well. But we can't leave you here . . .'less one of us stays. And I know you want to go."

"Sounds like it would be easiest to take me with you," I said practically.

This time a grin covered that wide face. "One thing about you, Etta, you got it all figured out way ahead of the rest of us. Let me think on it a day."

Sundance had been out in the brush corral, feeding the horses, while Butch and I stood outside the cabin and talked.

When he headed our way, Butch turned and went into the house.

"What you and Butch talking about so seriously?" he asked, laughing as though it were a joke.

"Montpelier," I said.

It was no longer a joke to him. "What about it?"

"I want to go."

One of Sundance's rare bursts of anger flew over him. "I thought you and I would talk about that first." His voice was low and even, a bad sign in him.

I shrugged. "I knew what you'd say. 'It's all right with me, Etta, but the others . . .'"

"What did Butch say?"

"That it's a lot more complicated than that." I turned and went into the cabin to start supper, and for the remainder of the day Sundance and I avoided each other.

That night, Curry returned, sullen, silent, and angry. But he was back. When they gathered at the table, he said nothing until Butch announced, "Etta's goin' with us. She'll hold the horses at the first change."

Curry exploded in a rage. "You can't take a whore with us! I ain't goin'!"

"That's right," Butch said calmly. "You're not going, Curry. You're goin' to stay here and watch the place."

I had to turn my face to hide both my pleasure and my amusement that someone would be appointed to "watch the place." What was to watch? I didn't know, of course, that Curry's assignment would be to watch for law officers.

"You see anything out of line, you'll know where to find us." His finger traced a route on a map.

"I—" Curry began to protest.

"Shut up, Curry," Sundance said. "You heard Butch."

"And you," Curry said, a tone of threat in every word, "brought that whore here."

It was another of those quick, instinctive moves on my part. I had been disjointing a prairie hen for stew. Coming from behind Curry, I took the knife, still dripping chicken blood and entrails, and pressed it to his throat. "Don't call me a whore ever again," I said, letting him just barely feel the pressure of the knife.

Elzy and Butch were openmouthed, but Sundance, in his calmest voice, said, "She knows how to use it, Curry. Believe me, she does."

As quickly as I had threatened him, I moved away and washed the knife so that I could continue cleaning the hen. Behind me was a great silence.

That night, when we were alone in the tent, I moved toward Sundance, expecting passion. But he backed away.

"Etta, someday you're going to push one of them too far. You'll get in trouble you don't expect. I just hope you don't take me with you."

In that instant I had a very clear picture of Sundance's loyalty: It was to himself. Whatever existed between us was not the kind of love that drew Butch to Lander yet kept him, from respect and concern, always at a distance from the woman he loved. Standing there, staring at Sundance, who was watching me warily, I thought about leaving, going back to San Antonio.

But I hadn't been to Montpelier yet, I hadn't ridden with them and known the excitement of the chase. And truth to tell, I didn't want to leave Sundance.

He was by now sitting on the edge of the bedroll, taking off his shoes. I sat next to him and wordlessly slipped my hand into his shirt, loosened his belt, and moved my hand downward. We began the deliberately slow ritual of undressing each other, a ritual that always ended in frantic haste.

That was why I stayed with Harry Longabaugh.

We left the next morning. All Butch said to me was, "It'll be a hard ride, Etta."

I nodded, and we rode off. Curry was still asleep.

Sundance and I rode together, companionable as though we were riding off for a day of target practice in the mountains. "Butch has been there," he said. "To Montpelier. Says there's plenty of money in the bank. It's a prosperous town."

I wondered if he really knew that, or if this would turn out like the baggage car at Malta.

"We got the getaway all figured—where the creeks are for water, holes we can hide in. You'll hold the horses at the first relay, about fifteen miles out of Montpelier."

Fifteen miles! I wanted to be part of the robbery, not miles away. I bit my tongue, though, because at least I was allowed to go along. Next time I wouldn't hold the horses.

"That's the most important stop," Sundance said, seeing the look on my face and reading it easily. "That first change of horses can make the difference in whether we get away or not."

We rode north and west, across the Green River Valley, then the Wind River range of mountains and down into the Sweetwater country. Always we were leisurely, and often we rode far apart from each other—Butch and Elzy some miles ahead.

"Four of us might be suspicious," Sundance told me. "Folks might remember seeing four men riding together."

"But not a man and a woman?" I asked.

He laughed aloud. "You don't look like a woman right now, Etta. You look maybe like a fifteen-year-old boy."

I looked down at myself and joined him in laughter. I wore a pair of his pants—tight-fitting on him, they were baggy on me—and a denim shirt. My hair was tucked up under my hat. But my face was smooth and had, I knew, the look of an unshaven youth—and my features were far too delicate to have fooled anyone except at a distance.

"That," Sundance pronounced, "is one reason you're not going in the bank with us."

I didn't explain that my mind had been working for weeks on ways I could take advantage of being a woman to help them.

We camped three nights, and the last night we made a cold camp. In the morning, I gave them each cold biscuits wrapped in paper and watched them ride off. I was left alone in a thicket about a quarter mile off the road.

"You be all right all day?" Sundance asked, giving me a quick peck.

"I brought a book," I said, retrieving a copy of a Charles Dickens novel from my bedroll.

"A novel! You go to rob a bank and you take a book? Etta Place, you are purely original." He kissed me again, this time more soundly.

"You want to ride with us, Sundance?" Butch asked, the patience in his voice clearly ironic. And then, to me, he said, "Remember to be ready when the sun is about a third of the way down. We won't have seconds to spare."

It was a long day. The sun took forever to climb to its height, and I thought it never would go down. I had no appetite for cold biscuits and no taste for reading. I paced, watered the horses in the nearby creek, paced some more, stared at that blasted sun until I saw spots. Gradually, though, it began its descent, and I unstaked the horses and held the reins, two in each hand.

I heard them long before I saw them, a noise in the distance that gradually grew into the roar of pounding hooves. Then suddenly they were before me.

"Everybody muffle two horses—no whinnying, no stamping . . . and no talking." Butch spoke low and fast, and we did as he said.

It seemed to me we stood that way forever in silence, but Sundance later told me the posse was only three minutes behind them. Then it came again, that distant noise growing into a roar. Only this time it went on past us and gradually grew faint, and then we could hear it no more.

"Mount up," Butch said. "Turn those other horses loose."

We left the tired horses behind for someone—who, I never knew—to pick up, and we rode silently off through the trees, away from the road.

After some miles, Butch said we'd split up, Elzy would go to his wife, and Sundance and I to the Hole. "We'll meet there in five days," he said. Before he left, he winked at me and said, "Let your hair down, Etta, and wear that split skirt. You're a lady again!"

Then he went one direction, Elzy another, and Sundance and I went home by way of Montpelier.

"We can't ride in there!" I said.

"Why not?" he asked lazily. "My wife and I, we've been over to Boise to see her family, and now we're heading back to Cheyenne. I had a bandanna over my face and my hat pulled down low. No one will ever recognize me. You just go on and change, like Butch said."

I did, and that was just the story Sundance told when we stopped at the saloon in Montpelier to order coffee for me and a beer for him.

"Where's everybody?" he asked innocently, looking around the empty saloon.

"You folks come at a bad time," the bartender said. "Every man in town 'cept me is gone off chasin' bank robbers. Just happened little over a couple hours ago."

"Bank robbers!" I pretended great alarm. "Harry, we . . . we mustn't stay here."

"Oh, it's all right now, ma'am," the bartender said soothingly. "They sure won't be coming back here. Only hope the posse catches them bas—'scuse me, them fellows, and hangs them from the nearest tree limb."

I hid the shiver that went through me, and what had threatened to well up as laughter was now stilled. Sundance, though, thought it funny and could hardly hold his laughter until we got well away from town.

"Did you hear him?" he crowed. " 'They won't dare come back to town!' If he'd known I was sittin' there with half his bank's money in my saddlebag . . ." And he was off into great roaring laughter again.

I looked at him and finally laughed too. It wasn't just the passion that kept me with Sundance: It was his sense of fun. And more than that, it was his sense of adventure, his daring. You couldn't help admire a man who would ride right back into a town where he'd just robbed the bank—and get away with it. At least, right then, I couldn't help but admire.

We rode lazily through the same country we'd crossed only days earlier. At night we made big showy campfires, cooked small game that Sundance shot, talked late into the night, and made love wrapped in blankets against the early-fall chill.

The first night as we sat with our hands wrapped around coffee cups, I finally said, "Well, aren't you going to tell me about the robbery?"

"What's to tell? I 'spect we made about seven thousand dollars. That what you want to know?"

"No," I said coldly, "that's not what I want to know. Tell me about it, everything that happened."

He grinned, for he'd known all along what I wanted to hear. "We rode in about one o'clock in the afternoon, and Butch took the lead in the bank. It didn't take any time to line up the customers and cashiers and go down the line, transferring money into the sack. Then it was the vault. The whole thing took ten minutes at the most."

"Too long," I muttered.

Sundance was quiet for a minute. Then, "You think you could have done it faster?"

"Let me try next time," I said, trying to put a joking tone into my words.

He ignored me. "What happened that was bad," he said, "was that the sheriff's office was directly across from the bank—who would have thought it?—and the sheriff, he looked out and saw all those people in the bank, waving their arms in the air. Didn't take him any time at all to mount a posse. We left with three minutes to spare."

Three minutes seemed like no time at all. I remembered how close behind the posse had been at the first change of horses.

"You should have gone into town and checked the location of the bank," I said.

"And advertise ourselves as coming to rob?"

"Next time," I said slowly, "I'll be a widow woman looking to buy property, and I'll visit the bank."

He look appraisingly at me. "Just might work," he said, "it just might work." And then, "I'm tired of talking."

We were at Hole-in-the-Wall three days before Butch arrived. Curry left for a while, and we had a wonderful time that first day, playing in bed until midmorning, eating when we wanted, joking about where Butch was and why he was so slow.

That night, when we went to feed, we played hide-and-seek in the moonlight that danced on the corrals. We snuck around posts and fences and behind bushes and pretended to call like owls—Sundance was better at that than I was. But then suddenly he was gone—there were no more owl hoots, and the silence grew until it frightened me.

"Sundance?" I called over and over, and each time my call was a little more frantic. Suddenly I was aware that I was alone, miles from anywhere or anybody, in the pitch dark. What if . . . *Stop*, I told myself. *Nothing can possibly have happened to him. He'll turn up in a minute.*

But he didn't. I waited maybe fifteen minutes, though it seemed like fifteen hours to me, and then I began to feel my way along the corral fence, to head for the cabin and the comfort of a lantern.

"Got ya!" He jumped from behind a post, scaring me so badly that I screamed aloud and then turned on him in anger.

"Harry Longabaugh, don't you ever do that to me again."

"It was a game," he said lamely. "I won."

"You lost," I said. "And if you ever do it again, I'll shoot you." My voice was cold with anger.

"I believe you would, Etta," he said.

Later what bothered me most about the whole thing was that fear had made me lose control. I vowed that would never happen again. But then, I'd made other vows. . . .

Next morning Sundance was gone when I woke up. I finally found him sitting at the notch. Hand shading his eyes, he was scanning the horizon, looking mostly to the north.

"You're watching for him," I said. Unspoken was the question of why. It could only be that Sundance was worried.

"I just want to know he's not rotting in some dumb Idaho jail," he said.

"How long will you watch?"

He shrugged.

"What if it's three weeks?"

He shrugged again, obviously made uncomfortable by my probing. "That'd be too long. I don't know. Guess I'd give up."

"You wouldn't go looking?" I thought surely he'd trail Butch, find out what happened.

"There's a whole world between here and Idaho," he said, "too much space to be lost in. Butch wouldn't expect me to do that."

There it was again: Sundance was loyal, but only up to a point. I remembered that he'd once told me he'd go to the ends of the earth for Butch. Maybe it depended on how far the ends were—or what the odds were.

He watched for two days. When dusk came and it was pointless to watch from the notch, Sundance would come down to the cabin. He'd eat a silent supper, picking at whatever I fixed for him, and when we went to bed, his lovemaking was fierce, almost desperate. I missed the laughing Sundance and marveled that one man could be so dependent on another, though Sundance would have denied that loud and long.

Butch was neither jailed nor hanged. Neither was he left for dead, a bullet in his heart, in some hidden draw between Montpelier and Kaycee. He came riding in on the eighth day, jogging across the plains as though he hadn't a worry in the world.

I saw him first, the tiniest of specks on the horizon. "Sundance?"

He stared for a long time. "That's him," he said, and his whole body relaxed. "Let's go back to the cabin."

"We aren't going to wait here and welcome him?"

Sundance looked astounded. "Welcome him? After I've spent two days of my life sitting on a damn rock waiting for him? I'm going to have a drink, that's what I'm going to do."

By the time Butch reached the cabin, Sundance was on his second whiskey, while I sipped at the first he'd poured for me.

"Hello" was all Butch said, slinging his saddlebag into a corner of the room.

Sundance had put his feet on the table and leaned so far back in his chair that he was almost horizontal to the floor. He tilted his hat back on his head, as though to clear his eyes and see this intruder into his world of peace and comfort.

"So where you been?" Sundance asked casually, though I knew the real question was. "Where you been while I've been sitting on a damn rock looking for you and worrying about what happened to you?"

"Well," Butch drew his answer out, "I kinda meandered around, wanting to be sure no one followed me here. And then . . . I stopped in Lander."

"That a new ring?" Sundance asked.

Butch wore an opal ring on the third finger of his left hand. "Yeah," he said, "it's new."

Sundance eyed him. "What's it say on the inside?"

"None of your business," Butch replied.

"Strange thing to inscribe on a ring," Sundance answered, laughing.

Butch had stopped to see Mary Boyd, and she had given him that ring. And maybe he and Sundance were close, but Butch didn't share anything about Mary Boyd, not even his feelings. I never did know what was inside that ring, though I had a pretty good idea.

"Want to take Etta to Denver?" Butch asked.

"Sounds like a good idea to me." Sundance never gave any sign he'd been worried.

"I've been to Denver," I said.

*   *   *

We went to Denver.

"You haven't really seen the city," Sundance told me on the train from Cheyenne to Denver. "Remember?" And he leered at me.

Butch looked away in embarrassment. He knew how we'd spent our time in Denver.

"This time," Sundance went on, unperturbed, "we'll stay in one of the grandest hotels in all the country. Brown's Palace Hotel."

"You said," I reminded him, "that hotels were too public for outlaws."

Butch sat up straight in his chair. "You told her that?"

Sundance shrugged. "I wanted privacy." He looked completely satisfied with himself.

"And now we'll be public?" I asked. "Even though there's just been a bank robbery?"

"Shhh," Sundance said, clapping a hand over my mouth and looking nervously around to see if anyone had heard. Now Butch was doubled over with laughter—anyone else would have been angry.

Sundance didn't know whether to be angry—and stern with me—or give in to his inclination to join Butch in laughter. He chose the latter, and they were like girls with the giggles: The more they tried to stop, the harder they laughed.

"You're making a scene," I whispered. "Now people really are looking at us."

That only set them off again, and it was several long minutes before, panting and exhausted, they sat quietly in their seats. But each avoided looking at the other, and I, angry by now, stared determinedly out the window.

Brown's Palace Hotel *was* the fanciest place I had ever seen—Sundance had been right about that. It was richer and finer than anything I had ever imagined, and I always thought my imagination was pretty good along those lines, being as reality for so long had been just the opposite.

The building was a triangle—it didn't even have four sides, like buildings are supposed to. And the corners didn't meet like corners should—they were round, so that the lines of the building seemed to swoop around.

Inside the lobby soared higher than any room I'd ever been in, and the furnishings were rich and lush—deep red velvet Oriental rugs on the floor, shiny brass spittoons, great tall plants.

Sundance sauntered through the lobby as though he lived this way every day instead of just having come from sleeping in a tent and eating in a ramshackle cabin. Butch, on the other hand, stood openly staring, taking in every detail.

"You haven't been here before?" I asked him.

He jumped, as though my voice had brought him back to reality. "Oh . . . yeah, Etta, I have—twice. But it's new and wonderful every time. I never thought, growing up poor as I did, that I'd ever see anything like this."

No, I thought, but I intend to live this way from now on. That I didn't was one of those tricks that fate plays on us.

We had adjoining rooms, almost identical, with dark wainscoting and, above it, floral wallpaper rich with mauve tones. The bed was mahogany, with a high headboard and a footboard almost four feet tall, and there was a matching marble-topped table, with pineapples carved into the wood beneath the marble. Sundance collapsed into a Morris chair with blue and purple cushions, while I hung out our clothes. For me, there was a ladies' rocker, with a tufted back in mauve that matched the wallpaper. Lace curtains hung at the windows. It was much grander than any bedroom at Fannie's.

We ate oysters and champagne.

"What is that?" I screeched as a platter of soft gray things, resting on shells, was set before me.

"Oysters, Etta. Lower your voice." Sundance spoke calmly.

"Oysters?" I echoed.

"Raw oysters," Butch explained helpfully.

My voice rose three octaves. "Raw oysters?"

"Put lemon and that sauce on them," Sundance said patiently.

We were in the hotel dining room, an elegant room with dark paneling, crisp white linen tablecloths, heavy silver flatware, fresh flowers on the tables, and soft music from a string quartet. When the waiter shook my napkin open and placed it on my lap, I almost thought he was being forward.

Sundance grinned at me. "I'll have to take you out in style more," he said.

Yes, I thought, he would. I wanted to learn the ways to behave in places like this. "I like the champagne," I said. "The bubbles . . ."

Sundance looked at me. "Don't drink too much of it. Remember the chicken salad."

I lifted my glass to him in a toast, while Butch, bewildered, asked, "What's chicken salad got to do with oysters and champagne?"

We finished the meal with ice cream molded into the shape of seashells. "Are you sure it's not oyster ice cream?" I asked, and the two of them howled as though I were the funniest person they'd ever met. We had all three had too much champagne.

"Etta?" Sundance said softly that night when we were in bed.

"Hmmm?"

His hands began to stroke, touching places that ordinarily turned me to fire. I kissed him soundly, thinking I was ready for a night of passion, but then, just as quickly, I fell asleep in spite of his whisperings and soft blowing in my ear. I remember waking once to realize that he was rubbing my back, and I tried to rouse myself, but it was no good. I sank back into sleep.

"I told you champagne was worse than chicken salad," he said, and there was a touch of anger in his voice.

"Sorry," I mumbled.

The next morning I awoke with a great thirst and drank heartily from the water pitcher. Immediately a great wave of nausea came over me.

Watching me from the bed, Sundance said dryly, "I forgot to warn you about that. You shouldn't drink water with a champagne hangover."

When I recovered, I said weakly, "I think it's worse than the chicken salad," and he laughed at me. Or with me.

One night Sundance joined a poker game in the hotel, though Butch twice warned him against it.

Judy Alter

"I'm going to increase our investment," he said, grinning and trying to be nonchalant as he walked away. But I saw him turn and take one more look at Butch, to see how serious he was.

Butch's big hand reached out and covered mine. "You go on, Sundance. I'll just take care of Etta here."

Sundance wavered, but only an instant, and then he was gone into the men's parlor.

"I envy you and Sundance," Butch said slowly, watching him walk away. "I'd like . . . well, I'd like to have a woman in my life all the time—not just these stolen visits."

It was the first time he'd ever talked to me about Mary Boyd's existence.

"Tell me about her," I said.

"She's about the prettiest woman I ever saw," he said, and then caught himself suddenly, " 'cept of course you, Etta. You and her, you're mighty close in looks."

"Do you mean we look alike?" I asked, laughing. "Or you can't decide which of us is better-looking?" I was joking, but there was a touch of vanity in my question.

He spoke low, quietly. "You're a mighty beautiful woman, Etta." Then he added, "So's Mary. But in lots of ways I know you better than I do her."

"Thank you, Butch," I said.

He never did tell me much more about Mary, beyond that she had married while he was in jail, and now he and she both regretted it but they were honorable people and would not tarnish her marriage vows.

"I would take my happiness where I found it," I said.

Butch looked sideways at me. "No, Etta, you wouldn't. You just think right now you would."

"Sundance would," I said.

"You're right. Sundance would."

We were both silent a minute, my thoughts on Anna Marie up in Castle Gate and Sundance's casual abandonment of her.

Then Butch spoke softly. "Etta, you know whatever Sundance does or doesn't do, I'll always look out for you. He's my best friend, and I'd do anything for him . . . except let you get hurt."

I reached out to take his hand. When I did, to my astonishment, I felt that same tug in my stomach that I felt when Sundance looked directly at me.

152

Butch and I stared long and hard at each other, and then Butch pulled his hand away, saying, "Guess we might as well turn in. Sundance'll be in there all night."

We had to leave Denver the next day. Sundance had lost everything except the money Butch had held back to pay for the hotel.

"You don't," Butch said righteously, "walk out of a hotel without paying your bill."

I had thought he'd be angry at Sundance, but when he heard of the loss Butch just shrugged and said, "Easy come, easy go."

Chapter Fifteen

It was a long winter.

"We don't work in the winter," Sundance told me. "Too cold." He was grinning. "But not too cold for other things." He drew me into his arms, but I surprised both of us when I resisted.

"What he means," Butch said, "is that you can't plan too good in winter, 'cause you could get caught in a blizzard or something. It just ain't a good time to be robbing banks."

"I think," I said slowly, "it'd be the perfect time, because no one would expect you."

"Etta," Sundance said with exasperation, "we been doing this awhile. Trust us."

And so we settled in for the winter at Hole-in-the-Wall. Butch had brought me reading material from his last trip to Lander—stacks of old *Harper's Weekly* and *Leslie's*, three dime novels about Buffalo Bill, and a copy of Cooper's *The Pioneers*—and they had a chessboard, over which they spent long hours. Butch was remarkably good at that, slow and patient and thoughtful. Sundance would play for a while, then do something foolish out of his impatience. More than once, he jumped up and overturned the board.

"That," Butch said, "is a breach of manners."

"Breach? Where'd you learn that word?"

"From you."

It snowed a lot that winter, and on sunny days we played in a white wonderland. Butch didn't much like snowball fights and stayed in the cabin, but Sundance and I were like little kids. One morning early I dragged him out of bed to make a snowman. It took a lot of groaning on his part, and a lot of coaxing on mine—with some promises about what we'd do after the snowman was built—but I finally got him up and dressed. Wearing two sweaters, a split skirt, heavy wool stockings, and a hat that came down over my ears, I was so bulky I could hardly move. When I tried to walk in the boots Sundance had gotten me by mail order, I floundered and once fell.

"See?" he demanded. "This is a bit of damn foolishness. Let's go back to bed."

I blew smoke rings with my breath. "Of course we're not going inside! If you help me build a snowman, I'll make you an extravagant breakfast."

Sundance was meticulous about the snowman once he got started. "No, you've got to roll that smoother."

I'd rolled and rolled the large ball for the main part of the body, but no matter what I did it was lumpy. He stood watching me—and not helping.

"Can't have all those bumps on it," he said with an air of authority. "Snowmen are round and smooth."

"You start on the second ball," I ordered him, and he seemed to obey. But when I turned my back, still smoothing the first large mound of snow, something wet suddenly hit my back. As I whirled, I saw Sundance reaching into the snow for another handful. He shaped it carefully into a small ball and took aim again.

"Sundance, don't you dare!"

He laughed and sent it speeding toward me. This time it hit me square in the chest and splattered snow into my face. He laughed aloud.

"All right," I said, grabbing a handful of snow. I rolled it in my hand a little, and threw it in his direction. It disintegrated before it was a foot from me.

"Texans!" he called in glee. "Don't even know how to pack a snowball. Want me to show you?"

Judy Alter

"No," I shouted, my dander up by now. "I don't want you to." I grabbed another handful of snow and began to shape it as I'd seen him do, but when I saw him standing there looking smug, as though he knew I wouldn't ever be able to hit him, petty anger overcame me.

"I . . . you show me how to pack it," I said, holding the snow in both hands and walking toward him.

He watched me, his face beaming with a know-it-all air of superiority.

When I was right in front of him, he reached for my snow and said, "You see, you got to pack it—"

Sundance never finished the sentence, because I ground the snow into his face with the palm of my hand. When I drew back, he looked like Old Man Frost.

Sputtering and yelping, he brushed at his face with a heavily gloved hand—too heavily gloved to do him much good. "That's war," he declared. "No quarter given." With that, he bent down for a handful of snow, but I, being forewarned, darted away from him and around a small bush.

He chased me as I floundered in the snow, screaming so loudly that Butch appeared at the doorway of the cabin just in time to see Sundance grab me, pull aside the scarf around my neck, and dump his handful of snow inside the back of my jacket. It was my turn to yowl in real pain.

We ended in a rolling, laughing mess on the ground, both of us covered from head to toe with snow.

"You children brush off all that snow before you come in the house," Butch said with a straight face. "And, Etta, I'm 'bout ready for breakfast."

I was tempted to tell him I was too and why didn't he cook it. But I knew that his pancakes had the texture of old rubber.

Sundance was now standing over me, where I still lay on the ground, panting half in exhaustion and half in laughter. He reached a hand to help me up.

"You need to dry out before you cook?"

I shook my head. "If I get out of this outside layer, I'll be fine."

So we trooped into the cabin and shed our clothes. I wasn't really fine, for the back of my sweater was wet and cold. I figured it would dry as I worked around the stove. I fixed flapjacks and

156

sent Butch out to the shed for the sausage that was curing there. We drank countless mugs of steaming coffee, and it was noon before we finished breakfast.

Christmas found us huddled in the cabin while a blizzard raged outside. We ate canned tomatoes, biscuits, and potatoes, because neither of them had been able to hunt, and we had no presents to exchange for we'd not been even to Kaycee in weeks, not that shopping there would have been any good.

"You were any kind of useful woman, you'd have knit me a scarf," Sundance said.

"You'd never have worn anything I knit," I retorted. "But you could have thought ahead and gotten me diamonds in Denver."

"Yeah," Butch said, "but he lost the money. Remember?" He stared at Sundance, who looked uncomfortable, and then Butch burst out laughing. "Wasn't the first time you did somethin' dumb, Kid. Probably won't be the last."

"Thanks," Sundance said dryly. "I got a lot of faith in you too. Taking eight days to get back from Idaho."

We had all been cooped up together too long, and it was only Christmas. An endless winter stretched before us.

The snow stopped by New Year's. None of us stayed up to watch in the year, but the next day we had a really good meal because Sundance brought me a fat grouse.

"To 1897," I said, lifting a shot glass of whiskey, which was all we had to toast with, "a year of success." I wouldn't have drunk champagne if it had been there. In fact, I never did drink it again in my life.

"That means," Sundance said, "that we don't get caught."

Sundance and I still left Butch the cabin and stole away to our tent, even on the coldest of nights. And Sundance could still set me on fire with his hands, his tongue, his whole body. Some days we spent as much time in bed as we did out of bed, and we rose exhausted. Butch never said a word, even in jest, but when we'd been a long time in the tent, I often avoided looking at him. He never did get to Lander that whole winter, because the weather was bad.

Butch and I had no more long talks, for Sundance was always with us, and he was petulantly jealous when Butch and I talked. But there was one night . . . Sundance had flat out had too

157

much to drink, and he was slurring his words, nodding in his chair.

"I'm goin' bed," he said. "You comin'?"

There would be no passion that night, I knew. "In a minute," I said. "I'll finish cleaning up."

Without another word, Sundance staggered out the door. Sober, he would have insisted I come with him—or planted himself obstinately at the table to wait. But now he went uncomplainingly.

Butch watched him with amusement. "Sundance is okay," he said. "He just hasn't figured himself out." Then, out of nowhere, he said, "You know, Etta, you ought to go back to San Antonio."

"San Antonio?" I echoed in surprise. "To Fannie's? To the life? I would never!"

He shrugged. "Hard for me to say, but it might be better—in the long run—than staying with us. No telling what's gonna happen someday."

"What do you mean?"

"Sundance and me . . . we could get caught again, we could get killed." He turned and stared at me. "You could end up in jail, Etta . . . or worse."

"Nothing will happen to any of us," I said with a confidence that covered the tiny nagging fear in the back of my mind.

He stared at some imaginary distance. "Sundance thinks he's always gonna be the one in charge of himself," he said slowly, "just 'cause so far we've been lucky, jumpin' off trains and the like."

"You've both been in jail," I reminded him.

"Yeah," he shook his head, "but not for too long, not in bad places. It can change . . . something in my bones tells me it will change."

I gave him a swift hug and left for the tent. As I closed the door, I saw Butch pour himself another shot of whiskey.

I lay awake a long while that night. Beside me, Sundance was snoring loudly, but I never touched him. I was busy with my thoughts, examining Butch's grim prediction from all sides. "No," I whispered fiercely, "I won't let it happen. We won't get caught." And then I reached for Sundance, as though the reality of his body would comfort me. But stroke and whisper as I might, he never said more than " 'Night, Etta."

Two things broke the monotony of that winter. The first involved the Donaldsons, who lived down the road. All I really knew about them was that Sundance assured me the man was not an outlaw, and once when we rode by their cabin I saw the woman hanging out laundry with four or five stair-step children tugging at her skirts. I remember saying to Sundance, "Better her than me," to which he replied, "No babies, Etta?" and I said firmly, "No babies."

One day in March, when the sun, brighter than usual, almost began to melt the snow, the Donaldsons drove up in their wagon. I was cooking supper and thought it strange, when I looked out the window, that Mrs. Donaldson was driving the horses. Mr. Donaldson was huddled on the seat beside her, holding his left hand, which was wrapped in a cloth. Behind them, the children sat silent and impassive, even though the snow blew in their faces and they must have been near freezing.

"What's wrong?" I was out the door and down the path, oblivious to the cold. Obviously Mr. Donaldson was hurt—in this country, no woman would be driving the horses unless something was wrong with her man.

"Sam's done hurt his hand," she said, jerking her head toward her husband, who sat with his head down, silently cradling his injured hand.

"Come inside," I commanded, turning to yell, "Butch! Sundance!" They were out in the corrals, caring for the horses.

The Donaldsons trooped into the house, and at a motion from their mother, the children silently lined themselves up against one wall. When she said, "Sit," they did.

"Let me see your hand," I said.

Mr. Donaldson peeled off the layers of dirty sheeting to reveal a forefinger swollen to twice its size and black on the tip. His hand was puffy, and red streaks led from the finger toward his wrist.

"What . . . what happened?" I fought for control, willing myself to quell the nausea that rose in my throat.

"Mashed it with the hammer," he said tersely. "Four days ago. It ain't gettin' any better."

And it's not going to, I thought, praying that Butch and Sundance would come through the door. "Have you put hot packs on it?" That was a suggestion born of desperation—I had no idea whether or not hot packs would help. It was simply a cure—for something—that I'd heard.

Mrs. Donaldson nodded. "Packed it in snow. Then put hot packs on it. Just keeps getting worse 'n' worse." Her look was grim.

"What's goin' on?" Butch burst through the door, then stopped suddenly when he saw Donaldson's outstretched hand. "What'd ya do?"

Donaldson, tight-lipped, repeated the story, and Butch bent closer to examine the finger. Behind him, Sundance peered over his shoulder.

"I can take care of that," Sundance said with a kind of cheerful confidence. "Just give me a minute." He rummaged in some cabinets, got out what appeared to be pieces of sheeting, cleaner than what Donaldson had been using. Then he turned back. "I've heard all my life that you got to tell if blood poisoning has set in."

Butch was watching Sundance warily, and I, somehow forewarned, backed away from the table where Donaldson sat.

"Thing to do," Sundance went on, "is have the patient put his hand out on wood—table here will do. Just kind of pull that finger apart from the others. Then the patient—that's you, Donaldson—has got to look at the sun. Somehow the rays of the sun go in your body, and if you don't look—but I do—I'll be able to tell if there's blood poisoning. Mrs. Donaldson, you best look at the sun too."

By now I knew that something awful was going to happen, and I couldn't believe that both of them obediently looked out the south window of the cabin, Donaldson even bending his head down a little to get a direct view of the sun.

When Sundance took the cleaver from the wall—the one I used to cut up small game—I clapped a hand over my mouth just in time to quiet a scream. Butch was silent, but his eyes were wide and unbelieving.

Within a second, it was done. Sundance lopped the finger off below the second joint. Donaldson yelped in pain, then demanded, "What the . . ." And the children began to wail in fright. Instead of comforting them, Mrs. Donaldson almost curtly ordered them to be quiet, and they, apparently used to such orders, silenced immediately.

"Gangrene," Sundance said calmly. "It was either that or you take about a week to die. You want to quarrel?" He was busy wrapping the sheeting around the stump of finger. "Etta, bring me a needle and thread."

But I had fled the cabin. For one awful moment, when that cleaver descended and the blood spurted, I saw Pa again, saw him lying on the floor bleeding, heard him say "A man has his needs."

The moment passed—Pa disappeared again into the recesses of my mind—and a few minutes in the cold revived me. When I went back inside, Sundance had pulled skin up over the stump of the finger and stitched it. He was pouring whiskey over it as I came in. Then he wrapped the finger again in a piece of clean sheeting.

"Here," Sundance said, holding forth the bottle of whiskey. "Take a good slug of this. Matter of fact, take the whole bottle with you."

We gave them coffee and some corn bread left from breakfast, and the children ate ravenously but silently. There was no talk in the cabin. Mr. Donaldson was pretty much stunned, though he managed to mutter, "Thanks to you. I'm obliged." And Mrs. Donaldson just nodded her thanks.

"Get him to Kaycee to the doctor," Sundance said to the woman. "That was just a stopgap. He needs real care. See those streaks running up his hand . . . ?"

Mrs. Donaldson nodded solemnly and motioned for the children to climb into the wagon. I shaded my eyes against the sun shining off the snow and watched them disappear down the road.

"Sundance, we have to go check on them in a day or two," I said as soon as they were gone. "Those children are hungry . . . and they're too quiet."

"Etta, Etta, you can't change their lives. But, yes, we'll go."

"Didn't have to give them the last of the whiskey," Butch protested. "I mean, that was an amazing thing you did, Kid, and I . . . well, I hope you're around if I ever get gangrene. . . . No,

161

maybe I don't. But anyway, did you have to give him the last bit we got?"

"It isn't the last," Sundance said patiently. "There's another bottle in the cupboard." He reached into a shelf over the cook-stove.

Butch lowered his eyes. "I drank that," he said slowly.

"You drank it?" Sundance was incredulous. "You didn't share? Do you know how far it is to Kaycee and another bottle?"

"It gets cold of a night," Butch said, with almost a whine in his voice, "and I ain't got no one to keep me warm." His look at Sundance was clear in its meaning.

Sundance began to laugh. "That," he said, "is your own fault. You're not getting any sympathy from me. And you best get to Kaycee in the next day or two and bring us some whiskey."

"You don't need it," Butch said, his meaning again clear.

Sundance smiled and put an arm around me. "You're prob-ably right," he said, pulling me out the door.

I felt bad for Butch—and worse for Mr. Donaldson.

"Why were you so darned cheerful?" I demanded when we were alone. "You could at least have been sorry about having to do that."

He looked genuinely hurt. "If I'd come in there talking soft and tellin' him I was sorry, he'd have never let me do what needed to be done. I had to make him believe I knew what I was doing."

"Did you?"

He shrugged. "I knew the gangrene part had to come off 'fore it spread all through his body."

"But," I protested, "that part about wood and the sun. . . ."

"I made it up. Pretty good for the spur of the moment, don't you think?"

He was obviously proud of himself, and I finally told him he had a right to feel that way.

The second thing that happened was really in late spring—what would have been summer in Texas but in Wyoming still felt like winter. It also involved neighbors, people I'd never heard of before, but that Butch and Sundance knew.

Sometime in late April, Butch disappeared for almost a week, only to return leading a string of fine, proud horses—deep chested, long-legged Thoroughbreds. Butch and Sundance, who were sometimes careless about feeding the stock because they knew I'd do it, now became religious about feeding these horses. They were fed grain, not hay, twice a day. And the two of them rode each horse every day—they'd disappear early in the morning, and reappear in time for the midday meal. Then they'd switch horses and be off again. This seemed to go on for weeks.

But they lost one of those horses in a way that made them angrier than I'd yet seen the two of them. One day when the sun had already sunk behind the mountains and the evening cold had set in, there was a great shouting outside. "Halloo the house!"

"It's Curry," Sundance said.

"Wonder what he wants?" Butch mused. "Sure makin' a lot of noise."

"He's not eating," I said, and Sundance laughed.

Both of them stayed seated. I'd have thought they'd be up and out the door to see what was the matter. Within seconds, though, Kid Curry burst into the cabin.

"Gonna take one of them good horses out back," he said.

Quick as a flash, Sundance pulled a pistol, leveled it at him, and said, "No. You're not." With his head, he motioned for me to move across the room.

Curry snarled. "Put the gun away, Sundance. I gotta have the horse."

"Oh, swell," Sundance said, still pointing the pistol. "I know. You've led the law right to us."

"Not if you give me the damn horse and let me get away." Desperation made his voice crack, and I was amused to see fear—or at least anxiety—in the tough Kid Curry.

"What happened?" Butch asked it as though he barely cared.

"That fellow Dean, the Texan that the Johnson County sheriff hired. Caught him at Griggs's and would've had him dead center, but Mrs. Griggs, she grabbed the end of my rifle and pointed it up so all that happened was they got a hole in the ceiling. Dean, he got away, and I know he's after me."

Sundance was on his feet, indignant. "You shot up the Griggs house? With their kids there?"

"Naw," Curry said, speaking quickly, as though if he could get this over with, they'd give him the horse and he'd leave.

"Mrs. Griggs, she sent the kids down into the cellar."

Butch spoke as slowly as Curry did rapidly. "Those are our friends, Curry. You don't go shootin' up your friends' houses."

"But there was a lawman in there—one that's liable to get you for rustling those horses outside. You give me one, I'll lead him the other way."

"What're you leavin' us?" Sundance asked. "Some old thing you've run to death?"

"It's a good horse," Curry protested. "Just winded. It'll be all right."

As he rode away on the finest horse in the corral, Curry called out, "See you in Belle Fourche."

The horse was a good one—not as fine as Butch's string, but strong and healthy.

"Tell you, Sundance, I don't trust him," Butch said as they watched Curry disappear. "Someday he'll bring us all trouble. He's mean."

Sundance laughed. "Outlaws are supposed to be mean, Butch. You're just the one who's not."

For two days, we took turns watching from the notch, making sure that Curry hadn't led the law to us. It was cold, so none of us could stay up there long at a time.

"You don't have to watch," Sundance said once when Butch was at the notch and he and I were sharing a breakfast of flapjacks. I longed for eggs and grits and the lavish breakfasts I'd had at Fannie's.

"I'll take my turn," I said sharply. If I hadn't, it would have been because I was a woman . . . and not equal among them. "What's in Belle Fourche?" I asked, remembering Curry's parting words.

"A bank," Sundance said.

"And when were you going to tell me about it?" I asked.

"Ah, Etta, we're just beginning to think about it."

The string of fine horses and the long hours spent toughening them made clear sense to me then. And so did the fact that I wasn't in on the planning, at least the beginning stages.

"Isn't it time to get out the map?" I asked. "Where is Belle Fourche?"

It turned out that Curry had been riding the country looking for a likely bank. Belle Fourche in South Dakota was the place he said looked the best, with an easy getaway. A man named O'Day was going with us.

Sitting at the table, we worked out the plan. Mostly Butch worked it out, but I got in a word or two, and Sundance mostly insisted it wouldn't work.

"I'll leave in a week," Butch said, "and you two will leave two days after that. There'll be a buckboard and two harness horses in Kaycee, so you ride the two horses we least need to get away—the sorrel and that one that threatens to lame up all the time—and board them in Kaycee."

Sundance suddenly seemed to realize what Butch was saying. "A buckboard? Oh, that's swell. We'll really outrun a posse in a buckboard." He poured himself another whiskey.

"You'll look more like a couple traveling 'cross country in a buckboard," he said.

"And why don't you ride in the damn buckboard?"

Butch grinned ever so slightly. "Because you're the one takin' Etta with you. Besides," and he lowered his head slightly, "I got to go someplace first."

"Lander," Sundance said in disgust. "We can't even rob a bank without you havin' to go to Lander and tell where we'll be. Hope the law never finds out about her."

"She has to know, in case . . ." Butch spoke with quiet determination, but then his voice trailed off. In a moment, he was back to business. "We'll all meet about here"—his finger stubbed a point on the map—"ten miles out of Belle Fourche. We'll camp, send O'Day in to serve as lookout."

"O'Day?" Sundance asked. "Only thing he ever looked out for was himself."

"Town should be quiet," Butch went on, as though Sundance hadn't spoken. "They have a big veterans' celebration the weekend of June 26 and 27. We'll hit on Monday. Bank should be full, people tired."

"Good timing," Sundance admitted.

Butch left one week later, and Sundance and I spent two days alone at Hole-in-the-Wall.

"You want to ride up in the mountains?" I asked one day when the weather was cool and clear. "We can catch some trout for dinner."

"I'd rather go to bed," he said.

165

"Not," I said primly, "in the middle of the day."

"But there's no one here to know, 'cept you and me." He pulled me toward him and kissed me so hard that I almost gave in. But we went fishing and had fine trout for dinner.

"We are coming back here, aren't we?" I asked as we lingered at the rough wooden table over cups of coffee, his strongly laced with whiskey.

"If everything goes like it should," Sundance said. "I guess we'll come back as long as we're alive and not in jail."

"That won't happen," I said, still positive that nothing could touch us on this grand adventure. "But Butch doesn't believe that, does he? That's why he goes to Lander before any robbery."

"Doesn't take a detective to figure that out," Sundance said.

"Would you come see me before a big robbery?" I asked, knowing he wouldn't.

"I'm doin' better," he said. "I'm taking you with me."

"Sundance," I asked, "am I the only lady outlaw in Wyoming?"

He shrugged. "I've heard rumors of one or two—cattle rustlers. Don't think I know of any that rob banks, but probably some guy takes his lady with him, just like I do. Does it matter? You want to be the only one?"

"Yes," I whispered, "I do. At least, I want to be the boldest."

"That's some goal to set yourself in life, Etta." Even Sundance was taken aback.

"You're the best outlaw bunch. . . ."

"Yeah," he said, "and we keep getting blamed for botched robberies that amateurs do. Law doesn't even know professionalism when it sees it."

I laughed aloud and flew into his arms. Sundance, more than anyone I had met, could twist facts and interpretations until he was always on the right side. For him, there was none of Butch's moral deliberation.

"Let's leave the dishes till tomorrow," he said huskily.

We followed Butch's plan. A buckboard was waiting in Kaycee, two mules hitched to it.

"Mules! Damn mules! He said harness horses!" Sundance was beside himself with disgust as we rode away. "Just wait till I get Cassidy for this one. He did it deliberately."

"To humble you?" I asked.

"To ridicule is more like it."

June is beautiful in Wyoming. In Texas, it would already be sweltering hot, but here it was the kind of day that made you want to stay outside forever. We rode northeasterly—Belle Fourche was barely over the state line into Dakota, but north almost to the Wyoming–Montana line. As we went farther north, the grasslands finally changed into hills—the Black Hills, Sundance told me—and it was there, at a prearranged spot, that we met up with Kid Curry, Butch, and George O'Day. It was late Saturday, June 26, when we arrived.

O'Day was younger than the others, and more happy-go-lucky-looking. Short and sort of pudgy, he had eyes that laughed—not with the magnetism of Sundance's, but they were happy eyes. Outlaws, I still thought, should have the staring angry eyes of Curry. O'Day bowed charmingly over my hand when we were introduced and seemed not at all disturbed to hear that I would ride with them on Monday.

"She gonna' cook?" Curry asked.

"We'll take turns like always," Butch said. "I'll cook tonight."

"Never mind, Butch," I told him. "I'll do it." And then everyone except Curry had a good laugh about Butch's cooking.

O'Day rode into town the next morning, while the rest of us lounged around. I had the latest *Harper's Weekly* to read, and there was a stream nearby where we tried to fish but were so unsuccessful we had to eat bacon and biscuits for dinner. When he came back that night, O'Day nearly fell off his horse but managed to catch himself.

"Gran' party," he said, and the smell of stale whiskey and tobacco nearly knocked me over.

"You're drunk," Sundance said. "And that's dumb. You know, we don't drink when we work."

"Had t'look like I was one o' the boys," O'Day mumbled. "Be all right. Now they know me, won't sus-sus-pect when I ride in again tomorrow."

"Go sleep it off," Butch told him angrily.

George O'Day got no supper that night. But next morning he was up early, chipper as could be. "See ya in town," he called.

"Do you trust him?" I asked Sundance.

"Much as I trust anyone, 'cept you and Butch," he said. "You're different."

We left the buckboard and mules behind. "Someone will get them," Butch assured me—there it was again, those mysterious people who supplied buckboards, appeared with horses when needed, picked up loose horses left behind. The Wild Bunch had a lot of faces that remained, to me, still unseen.

We rode into town about one-thirty in the afternoon, riding leisurely. But Butch was looking intently for O'Day. Finally, as we passed the saloon, O'Day staggered out into the street. There was no other word for it. The man was drunk again.

"Damn," Sundance muttered.

"Curry, get O'Day's horse and then hold all the horses in front of the bank," Butch ordered tersely. "Etta, you come inside with us. Keep your rifle trained on folks, but please, please, don't shoot."

O'Day shambled into the bank with us.

"This is a stickup," Butch said, and I almost laughed at how corny that sounded. The five or six customers in the bank didn't think it corny at all and quickly lined up against the wall, Butch waving them that way with his rifle. Sundance, meanwhile, was forcing the clerks and cashier from behind the teller's cage.

"You can't do this," one clerk protested. "We just had our big celebration . . . and . . ."

"And there's lots of money in the vault," Sundance finished for him. "You just stand real quiet there, and no one will get hurt."

Dressed in Sundance's clothes, my hair tucked under a hat, my face slightly blackened with dirt, I thought I looked a credible outlaw as I held my rifle fixed firmly on the whole line of people. Instead of nerves—about which I had wondered—I felt a sense of exhilaration. Oh, I never would have shot those people, and I was even a little sorry for them, scared as they were—I think to this day that one of the tellers wet himself. But I was holding a rifle on people, I was the one in charge. Any minute a sheriff could come running in the door, and that danger even sent a thrill through me. I almost laughed aloud, but I knew better. It would have distracted Butch and Sundance, who were filling saddlebags with money from the vault and the tellers' cage.

Join the Western Book Club and GET 4 FREE* BOOKS NOW!
A $19.96 VALUE!

Yes! I want to subscribe to the Western Book Club.

Please send me my **4 FREE* BOOKS**. I have enclosed $2.00 for shipping/handling. Each month I'll receive the four newest Leisure Western selections to preview for 10 days. If I decide to keep them, I will pay the Special Members Only discounted price of just $3.36 each, a total of $13.44, plus $2.00 shipping/handling ($22.30 US in Canada). This is a **SAVINGS OF AT LEAST $6.00** off the bookstore price. There is no minimum number of books I must buy, and I may cancel the program at any time. In any case, the **4 FREE* BOOKS** are mine to keep.

*In Canada, add $5.00 shipping/handling per order for the first shipment. For all future shipments to Canada, the cost of membership is $22.30 US, which includes shipping and handling. (All payments must be made in US dollars.)

NAME: _____

ADDRESS: _____

CITY: _____ STATE: _____

COUNTRY: _____ ZIP: _____

TELEPHONE: _____

E-MAIL: _____

SIGNATURE: _____

If under 18, Parent or Guardian must sign. Terms, prices, and conditions subject to change. Subscription subject to acceptance. Dorchester Publishing reserves the right to reject any order or cancel any subscription.

One woman snuffled quietly, and I waved my rifle at her slightly. It seemed foolish of her to cry, and I wanted her to know that.

Too soon for me, Butch said, "You all go into that back room there." He motioned with his guns, and when they were all crowded into the room, he locked the door behind them.

"That one lady," I said, as we dashed for the door, "she had a ring I really liked."

"No, Etta," Sundance said sternly.

We jumped on our horses, nearly knocking O'Day out of the way, and were thundering out of town when Sundance said, "O'Day's not on his horse. We got the horse, but he's back there in town."

"We ain't stoppin'," Butch said. "I told him no drinkin'."

I didn't feel one bit sorry for George O'Day. Later, I would laugh at what happened to him, and, finally, I would be angry when I learned that half of what we took that day went to pay for the fancy lawyer who eventually had him acquitted of all charges. But that gets me ahead of my story.

Chapter Sixteen

There were fresh horses eighteen miles away, and we rode at a breakneck speed for them. Butch figured it would be dark before the posse reached the same point, and we could ride more slowly. At a certain point, where the ground was bare of grass and less likely to leave a trail, we turned sharply south. By midnight, we were at Rye Grass Creek, many miles from Belle Fourche, and Butch said we could rest.

That morning, at first light, we split up. Sundance and I were again to be an ordinary married couple traveling across Wyoming. "We've been to family at New Castle," he said, "and now we're heading home to Kaycee, if anyone asks." I had transformed myself into a woman, changing Sundance's hand-me-downs for a split skirt and white shirt, crumpled though it was. My hair was loose under my hat, and Sundance assured me no one would take me for a man, let alone a bank robber.

We did meet someone—a sheriff from Spearfish, up close to Belle Fourche—and he told us what happened to O'Day.

"Damndest thing," he said, telling us what he'd learned over the wire service while he was in Casper on business. "They left one man behind, or else he left himself behind. Word is, he was drunk. Anyway, when his horse went with the others, he supposedly went up to someone in town and asked as nice as could be if he could borrow a horse, because his had left without him. Then he hid in an outhouse, but someone saw him go in and threw down on him. He came out with his hands up, and all they could find on him was a pint of whiskey and some cartridges. But they turned the outhouse over and found a gun. Got him in jail. You ever hear of a dumber robber?"

Sundance forced a laugh and said no, he never had.

"Did they catch the other men?" I asked with wide-eyed innocence.

"No, ma'am. Lost the trail in the dark, and come morning they never could find it again."

I shook my head and made a *tsk-tsk* noise to show my disapproval, and Sundance muttered, "Damn shame." I wasn't sure if he meant O'Day or what, but the sheriff took it that he meant it was a damn shame the robbers had gotten away.

"It was sure to God that Wild Bunch," the man went on. "We'll get 'em. Well, you folks have a good day and keep your eyes open in this country. Never know when you'll run into one of them desperadoes."

As he rode away, he was still chuckling and saying, "Hid in an outhouse!"

Sundance rode silently, his jaw set, never looking at me, never looking back. After about five miles, he turned in the saddle and scanned the land. The sheriff was out of sight.

"Ride like hell," he told me, spurring his horse. Without a question, I followed his lead, and we rode until the horses had to rest.

"Why are we suddenly in a hurry?"

"They know it's the Wild Bunch—or think they know—and they'll be at Hole-in-the-Wall before we are if we don't hurry."

Butch had the word before we did, and he was at Hole-in-the-Wall, with freshly saddled horses and our belongings rolled into packs on them.

"I packed your mother's picture, Etta," he said softly, and I thanked him.

And so the next morning we rode away from Hole-in-the-Wall, so early that light had not yet climbed over the red ridge and spread down into the valley. Even in August, the air was chilly, and I was glad for a sweater.

We rode in silence, once again going the length of the valley—headed south this time—rather than up and over the notch, which was, even I knew logically, where the law would come from.

"How much money did we make?" I asked, for Butch still had the loaded saddlebags.

"Listen to her, will you!" Sundance said. " 'We.' "

Butch grinned. "She took the risk, so it's part her money. It's about six thousand, Etta, but a lot of it will have to go for O'Day's defense."

"Defense! He got drunk, could have gotten you all caught, and you're going to defend him? I swear I will never understand you."

"We can't let him rot in some jail for thirty years, Etta. He's one of us."

"It's tempting, though," Sundance said through gritted teeth. "I ain't been so mad at anybody in a long time."

"You wouldn't want us to do that to you if you got caught," Butch said mildly, and Sundance had the grace to grin. But he said, "I wouldn't have been drunk."

We'd reached the south end of the wall, and Butch said, "I'll ride up and take me a look. Etta, can you fix us a cold breakfast?"

I could and did, but all we had was jerky that was too spicy and hard to chew.

We rode again after only a ten-minute rest. Butch had seen nothing from the wall, not even with the binoculars he produced, much to my surprise.

"Where are we going?" I asked.

"You're sure full of questions," Sundance said, but he reached from his horse to cover my hand with his and gentle the teasing.

"Brown's Park," Butch said, "next stop down the outlaw trail."

"The outlaw trail?" I echoed. "What's that?"

"An old cattle trail," Butch went on. "Now, it's known as the outlaw trail—amongst us, anyway—because it has three really good hideouts. Hole-in-the-Wall to the north, Brown's Park in the middle, and Robbers Roost to the south.

I laughed with disbelief. "A whole trail for outlaws! You amaze me. How far does it go?"

"From Montana down to New Mexico," Sundance said curtly, once again put out, I suspected, because Butch was explaining something to me when he thought it should have been his duty—or privilege, I didn't know which.

"And where is Brown's Park?"

Sundance jumped in before Butch could speak. "Straddles the Utah–Colorado line, maybe lops over a little bit into Wyoming."

"Where will we stay? Another tent?"

"Naw," Sundance said, "probably Jarvie's dugout." He looked quickly at me. "Sorry, Etta, I know you don't like the idea of a dugout . . . but it'll be all right, it really will."

"I'm sure," I told him.

"Kid," Butch said, shaking his head, "I don't know what you did to deserve this, but you better enjoy it while it lasts. Someday, Etta may wake up."

I looked quickly at Butch, a dark look that threatened him into silence, and then turned the moment light with laughter. "I'm awake," I told them, "I wouldn't sleep through any of this for anything."

Neither Butch nor Sundance felt they could go into Rock Spring, the last sizable town we'd see in Wyoming. But they wanted badly to know what had happened at Hole-in-the-Wall, if anything. I rode into town to see what I could discover.

"Kind of try to spruce up," Sundance said, taking the blanket roll off my horse. "You know . . . you look like you've been riding for days."

"I have," I said sharply. But I combed my hair carefully, ran a wet finger over my eyebrows, pinched some color into my cheeks, and put on a fresh cotton shirt, though it was badly wrinkled by Butch's packing. I smoothed it as best I could and tied a black ribbon around the collar, thinking to draw attention away from the wrinkles.

"I don't suppose you have an iron," I said caustically.

Sundance laughed. "No, ma'am, I surely don't. But you look terrific."

173

We had camped some five miles out of town, and I rode that distance slowly, so as to appear casual and unhurried when I reached town—rather than frantic and on a lathered horse. Rock Spring was not large, and I wondered if it was even big enough for news—if there was any—to have reached it. The land around was barren and brown, with craggy hills bare of trees. A sense of desolation sat over the whole town. I was heartfelt glad I was only passing through.

It was midday, but there were a few people on the boardwalks, none of them hurrying. The August sun must have warmed them as it had me. Ahead on my left was the bank, a brick structure with double doors—I tried to appraise it as Sundance would but could reach no conclusions. At least it wasn't across from the sheriff's office.

The mercantile store lay beyond and across the wide, dusty street. I pulled my horse to a stop in front of the hitching post and dismounted, trying to be oblivious of one or two hard stares. Surely it wasn't unusual to see a woman in a split skirt riding astride in this town—yet the one or two women I saw had full skirts and dainty hats, and carried parasols. I was definitely not from the town.

In the store, I browsed for a moment, trying to quiet my beating heart. The unbidden thought came to me that the storekeeper would alert the sheriff who would arrest me and throw me in jail forever—or until I told him where to find Butch and Sundance. *Get hold of yourself, Etta!* I lectured silently.

"Help you, ma'am?"

"Oh, yes sir, thank you." I turned my warmest smile on the man who approached me. He wore a dark canvas apron over denim pants and a chambray shirt, and little round glasses perched on his nose, about halfway to his eyes. His hair was thinning—he was almost bald—and his ears stood out almost at angles from his head. Clearly he was a storekeeper. But just as clearly he was friendly and not one bit suspicious.

"New in town?" he asked.

"Ah . . . just passing through," I said. "My husband, he had to stay to fix a wagon wheel—we're camped north of here, some ten miles." In truth, we were five miles south—I thought my deception clever. Later Sundance would deride my naïveté.

"We need some coffee . . . and, ah, canned tomatoes. And I," I blushed, "would like some Lydia Pinkham's pills, please."

He looked understanding and sympathetic, as though we shared a secret. "Yes, ma'am. Fix you right up."

I wondered how he meant that.

"We've been traveling so," I said conversationally—he was my friend now, wasn't he?—"that we hardly know what's goin' on in the world. Have we missed anything important?"

He shook his head with a smile. "No, ma'am. No major disasters I know of. Country hasn't gone to war, praise be to God, and the bank hasn't been held up in two years."

I tinkled a little laugh. "Goodness, and you think that's good fortune?"

"Sure is," he said, "what with that Wild Bunch on the loose. Never know where they'll strike. But I guess they got some of 'em the other day. Word is they shot and killed two men at Hole-in-the-Wall."

My heart lurched, and I could feel my face getting red. Feigning interest in a bolt of material, I turned to finger it, even as I said, "That so? Well, I suppose it was deserved. . . ." My voice trailed off, then came back stronger. "Is there a newspaper in town?"

"Yes, ma'am. We've got this week's paper right here. Just came out today. I can add it to your purchases."

"Thank you," I said.

I paid in cash—was it traceable to the Belle Fourche bank?— and then, as my new friend loaded my things, reminded him, "I'm ahorseback. The wagon . . . my husband's fixing it."

"Oh, of course," he said. "Here, I can fix these in a roll and tie it behind your saddle."

I rode away after profuse thanks and turned once to watch him standing in the street, hand shielding his eyes against the sun's glare, watching me. Was it friendly . . . or suspicious? I would never know.

But I did know I dared not ride fast—and I had trapped myself into having to ride north for a bit, before I could head south. My detour north and then back around the town added a good hour to my journey, and late-afternoon shadows were beginning to fall when I finally rode into our camp.

175

Sundance was pacing furiously, and the minute he saw me, his fear turned to anger. "Where've you been? You find some storekeeper down there you liked?"

I felt as though he'd slapped me, and I sat silently on my horse looking down at him. We were at an impasse. He stood, arms akimbo in anger, staring at me. It was, of course, Butch who defused the situation.

"Let me help you down, Etta. Kid, you get those things out of that pack."

His face still angry, Sundance did as he was told, and I found myself off the horse, standing next to Butch, his comforting arm around me.

"What buggered you?" he asked.

"The storekeeper . . . he talked about the Wild Bunch, says they shot and killed two of them at Hole-in-the-Wall."

Now they both stopped dead and stared at me. "You sure?" Sundance asked.

I nodded, angry that he would think I made it up—or misheard what the man said to me.

Butch let his breath out slowly. "There wasn't anybody there what was with the gang. They've killed two innocent men . . . I wonder to God who they were."

Suddenly I felt sick. "What if it was . . . you know, what's his name? The man whose thumb you cut off, Sundance?"

Sundance looked as stricken as I was. "No," he said, "it can't be. . . . I mean, why would they shoot a man with little kids?"

It was Butch, though, who put into words what we all thought. "Please, God, let them not have killed innocent people in our place."

I pulled the weekly paper out and we scanned it, but there was nothing about shooting outlaws at Hole-in-the-Wall. We never would know who they shot.

Butch turned away, leaving us together, and Sundance looked at me from under lowered eyes for a long time. I stood perfectly still as he came toward me, his voice soft, as though he were gentling a wild mare.

"Etta," he whispered, "I was so frightened when you were gone so long. I began to think I shouldn't have sent you into town. . . . I thought of all kinds of things that could have happened to you. I'm sorry. I guess I just don't have a handle on my temper."

It was a big apology from him, and I knew it. I also knew better than to dwell on it. "I was scared too," I told him, "scared somehow I had an invisible sign on me that said, 'I'm with the Wild Bunch.' I even thought maybe they'd throw me in jail until I told them where you were." I laughed a little now at the silliness of it in retrospect.

He smiled just a bit. "I'd have busted you out, you know."

And then we were in each other's arms, kissing with a passion we hadn't shared since before Belle Fourche.

There was a soft cough behind us. "Etta," Butch said plaintively, "I'm starving." But the look on his face made it clear that he was pleased with our reconciliation.

We lay in our separate bedrolls that night, nestled close together, with Butch discreetly on the other side of the small fire they'd dared to build. "Will that Jarvis's or whoever's cabin have two rooms?" I asked.

He grinned and reached his head toward mine, his arms buried in his bedroll. "Might," he said. "Why?"

"I'd like some privacy," I told him unblinkingly.

He chuckled. "I'll see that we get it."

Brown's Park wasn't a lot different from Hole-in-the-Wall. Oh, maybe it was more lush, set in a great forest. But the ground near the dugout was scrubby bare and uncared for, and the dugout itself was, if anything, less inviting than the cabin. The only thing really to be said for it was that the Green River ran nearby, strong and burbling—a real river, as opposed to Blue Creek.

John Jarvie's dugout was empty—and, as I said, most discouraging. Built into the side of a rise in the land, it had a flat graveled roof, flat board walls inside and out, and a dirt floor. The furniture was like that we'd left behind—a scarred table that was obviously homemade, some rickety chairs that would have sat uneven on the best of wood floors and were worse on the dirt, an open fireplace for cooking, with a cast-iron Dutch oven lying amid old coals and a pot on a hook hanging above it. I'd have to scrub them both thoroughly before I'd use them.

That night we'd cook over an outdoor fire, as though we were camping.

"Where's Jarvis?" I asked.

"Jarvie," Sundance said impatiently, "John Jarvie. He's almost never here. We're just welcome to stop. And we do."

It was a strange arrangement to me. I sent them off to catch a fish or shoot a rabbit or do something so we'd have more than johnnycake and hardtack for dinner.

Sundance came back triumphantly waving a string of trout, though Butch was right behind him, protesting, "I caught two of those, Etta. One for you and one for me!"

I kissed Butch first and then Sundance, and said, "I'll eat one from each of you."

It was a bad fall, beginning with the news—brought by Butch from a foray into the town of Maybell, Colorado, where there was, he said, no danger of his presence being reported—that someone named Bob Meeks had been caught for the Montpelier robbery and been sentenced to thirty-five years.

"Thirty-five years," I breathed, aghast. "He'll be an old man before he gets out!"

Butch and Sundance both tried to shrug it off, but I could see in their eyes that they were stunned.

"He didn't even do it," Butch protested. "He wasn't there."

"Can we bust him out?" Sundance asked, and I could tell he was serious.

"Of the state penitentiary in Idaho? You crazy?" Butch looked astounded.

"Well," Sundance conceded, "maybe that wasn't a good idea."

"Will he tell them it was you?" I asked.

Butch shook his head again. "Nope, he won't." He seemed very sure, but I wasn't. If I were in jail, I'd have done anything—honest, dishonest, loyal, disloyal—to get out, or at least I thought I would.

Sundance must have been having the same thoughts about being in jail. "I'd escape, or make them shoot me," Sundance said. "No way I'd spend thirty-five years sitting in a jail."

Butch looked long and hard at him, and at last Sundance returned his look. As I stood watching both of them, it occurred to me that more than surprised, more than angry, they were afraid. They would never have admitted it, and I would never have brought it up.

The news got worse in November when Kid Curry found us at Brown's Park. He was once again on the run.

"What happened to your arm?" Butch asked him bluntly.

Curry raised his right hand—his gun hand—to reveal a large scar, still new enough to be angry and red. "Shot," he said in disgust. "Shot went through my horse—killed 'im—and got me in the wrist."

"Can you shoot?" Sundance asked.

Curry shook his head. "Not now . . . but it'll come, I know it will. I keep practicing to keep it limber."

And probably, I thought, irritating it so the muscles wouldn't heal. But I wouldn't put myself in sympathy with Kid Curry.

When his story came out, none of us had sympathy for him. It seems he and Walt Puteney and another man whose name I don't remember decided to rob the bank at Red Lodge, Montana. Knowing the city marshal and considering him a friend, they invited him to leave town before the trouble started—a bit of stupid impudence that left me speechless and apparently did much the same for the marshal, for he alerted the sheriff and the three were ambushed before they ever had a chance to rob the bank. The other two were captured immediately: Curry, his horse and himself shot, rode about a mile before his horse dropped dead. Then he too was arrested, and all three were taken to the Deadwood jail, where O'Day was already awaiting trial, having been taken there from Belle Fourche.

"So why aren't you still in jail?" Sundance asked suspiciously.

Curry began to swagger a little in the telling. "Broke out," he said with pride.

Butch asked, "How?"

Curry told his tale with glowing pride. "Jailer and his wife, they came to feed us. We jumped 'em."

"You jumped a woman?" Sundance was incredulous.

Now defensive, Curry said, "Well, it was that or rot in that jail. We didn't hurt her bad."

Later we would learn that was an understatement, and that they had indeed beaten both the jailer and his wife severely. Beating a jailer, Butch and Sundance could understand—jailers, like outlaws, took the risks that went with their jobs. But a

179

woman? It didn't sit well with either of them. But at that moment, they were still curious.

"How'd you get away?"

"Horses waiting," Curry said. "Never mind who. But Puteney and O'Day, they got captured again. Imagine they'll be looking at a long stretch now."

"Yeah," Butch said bitterly, "because you beat a woman."

"I wasn't the only one hittin' on her!"

Curry's protests fell on deaf ears. All Butch could say was, "We got to get some way of defending them. We need to plan." And then he and Sundance pulled stools up to the table, maps spread in front of them, and began to plan.

Curry, pacing the floor between the table and the door, threw me a dirty look. "You still lettin' that whore know everything we do?" he asked.

Sundance's voice was steel. "Don't ever call her that again, Curry, or I swear, I'll kill you myself. Save the marshals the trouble."

Curry laughed too loudly, as though laughing the threat away.

I left them, muttering over their maps, and went to bed, though I didn't sleep. Distantly I heard their low talk and wondered if Sundance would leave. When he came to bed, I whispered, "Do you have to leave?"

"No, Butch will go." He kissed me lightly but made no further gesture in my direction.

Butch left the next morning, and when I asked, Sundance said tersely, "He'll find a friend . . . someone who can take the money into Thermopolis and hire a good lawyer for them. It's the least we can do . . . and all we can do."

"Your money from Belle Fourche?" I asked.

He just shrugged.

The only blessing that I could see was that Curry left with Butch—and I presumed he wouldn't return soon.

Butch was back five days before Thanksgiving, and they decided to have a celebration. There was in Brown's Park more of a community than in Hole-in-the-Wall—families who looked after one another, shared joys and sorrows . . . and holidays. Sundance explained carefully to me that these people didn't mind outlaws, if the outlaws behaved while they were there and didn't bring the law down on the park.

"And we never do that," he said solemnly.

"Just like you never do that at Hole-in-the-Wall?" I asked, thinking of the two men killed there.

Sundance hung his head. "That was a mistake." But then he quickly added, "On the part of the law, Etta, not us."

Two days before Thanksgiving, neighbors' wagons began to pull up before the dugout with linens, silver, and dishes. The Johnsons brought two fine trestle tables—dismantled but easily assembled—and linen cloths to cover them. Mrs. Johnson's mother, the elderly Maybelle Waller, gently handed Sundance a silver tray that was, she said, for the turkey—nothing else. Someone else brought five perfect plates of fine English china and a sixth that was badly chipped—"I'll eat off that," I said— and another family arrived with three carefully wrapped water goblets—"All that's left of Mother's set," the man said gruffly.

There were promises of food. One family had pumpkins to make pies and another promised potatoes. Still another had canned green beans during the growing season and promised to bring enough for all.

It would, I assured Sundance, take at least three wild turkeys to feed this congregation.

"Three? Lucky if I get one in a week's worth of hunting," he complained.

"If you get three," I asked, "how am I going to roast them?" I had but one small oven, heated by an uncertain wood fire.

"Who invited all these people, anyway?" he fumed.

"You did."

It turned out to be fine, more than fine, and in a sense it was my first ever big holiday party. Thanksgiving and Christmas weren't much at Fannie's. But here was a group of people making absolutely foolish merriment over a turkey and dressing and corn bread and canned pickles and relish, and pumpkin and vinegar pies.

They sang everything from "She'll Be Coming 'Round the Mountain" to "Rock of Gibraltar," they danced when someone brought out a fiddle, and they laughed hysterically over things that were barely funny. The walls of that tiny dugout shook, until I wondered if the sod ceiling would fall in upon us, and the party spilled over to the outside, although the November air was crisp, clear, and very cold.

It was midnight before they all left, and two o'clock in the morning before I crawled, exhausted, into my bed, where Sundance waited.

Next morning I faced a mammoth cleanup chore, and both Butch and Sundance left early. "Going hunting," they explained. I rolled up my sleeves and settled into it, but the memory of the night before cheered me all day long as I worked. By evening, when they returned, the dugout was back to normal and most of the neighbors had come to pick up their belongings. Thanksgiving was, sadly, a thing of the past.

Chapter Seventeen

We went to San Antonio for Christmas. Sundance and Butch decided it was time to get away from Wyoming and Utah. Rustling and bank robberies had pushed the big ranchers too far, and vigilantes covered the area. The cry was out that the Wild Bunch had to be captured, dead or alive. Never mind that half the robbers the vigilantes wanted had nothing to do with the Wild Bunch and wouldn't have known Butch Cassidy or Harry Longabaugh if they'd run face-to-face into them at a bank robbery. Every cattleman from Rock Spring to Salt Lake City thought all his problems—from lost cash to stolen cattle—could be solved with the capture of the Wild Bunch.

"Narrow-minded, they are!" Sundance exclaimed. "They can't think beyond us. We're getting the blame for things we'd never think of doing." He was genuinely angry at the unfairness of it—at least, that was how he saw it.

I would never have said it, but somewhere in the back of my mind I remembered an old saying, "Live by the gun, die by the gun."

"Yeah, things we'd never have done—like beating a jailer's wife within an inch of her life," Butch mused. "It's time to go for a while."

Judy Alter

"How long?" I asked. I didn't want to leave Brown's Park, and I was sure we could outsmart the law if only we put our minds to it. If I'd told Sundance that, though, he'd have reminded me that they were the outlaws, they were the ones that knew what they were doing.

"Depends on how long Fannie can stand us," Sundance said lightly, and then added, "and how long we can stand it there. Get out your finest wool dress," he commanded.

"I can't," I told him, almost angrily. "It's at Hole-in-the-Wall. Butch didn't pack all my fine dresses."

He looked startled for a moment and then began to laugh. "We don't any of us have good clothes," he said. "We left them behind. Denver it is."

"Salt Lake City is closer," Sundance pointed out, but Butch vetoed the idea as too dangerous.

The day before we left, Kid Curry arrived again. I left the room when he came banging in the door, but his voice filled the dugout and I clearly heard what he said.

"Gettin' too close out there," he said. "Ain't no place safe, it seems. Them vigilantes are everywhere."

"They're not close to here?" Sundance asked nervously.

Curry muttered something, and it struck me that it would be a great irony if the vigilantes found us just as we prepared to leave for Texas.

"Where you all goin'?" I heard Curry ask suspiciously, apparently seeing the preparations under way.

When Butch muttered "Texas," Curry announced he'd been thinking of going down there himself. "Haven't been to Fannie's in a spell—the girls there, they miss me, I know they do!" For the rest of the evening, he bounced around the dugout in high spirits, crowing about the good time he'd have in San Antonio.

I stayed in the curtained-off bedroom, coming out only to offer a supper of cold biscuits, canned tomatoes, and jerky. When Curry frowned at the sparseness of the provisions, Butch said tightly, "She ain't cookin'. We're leavin' tomorrow."

That night Sundance tried to kiss me into silence as we lay in our bed, but my whispered anger echoed through the dugout. "Why," I demanded, "didn't you simply tell him he couldn't come with us?"

184

"Can't do that," Sundance whispered back, making his whispered voice as soothing as possible. "He's one of us, no matter what he's done. And we . . . we swore to look out for each other."

Honor among thieves again! "Well, I didn't swear any such thing," I retorted, turning my back on him.

I tossed and turned and slept fitfully that night, dreading what had once seemed a bright Christmas and now seemed an impossibly long journey. Once during the night Sundance reminded me, "We can't stay here, Etta."

And so we rode horseback to Denver, a long and difficult ride, with cold camps at night that left us shivering in our bedrolls. It was, Butch said, not a good idea to light a fire. Fortunately, early December that year was milder than usual, but the three of them watched the sky each day with worried looks. "Bound to snow soon," Sundance muttered.

"Naw," Curry said, staring at the sky to the west, "color's wrong. It's just colder than blazes."

Days we rode slowly in single file. Butch led a packhorse, but the rest of us had only bedrolls and a few belongings. We generally rode without speaking, which gave me a lot of time for thoughts I'd just as soon put aside.

"Been shorter to cross the mountains," Curry complained one night, rubbing his hands together to warm them. We had gone the long way round, skirting to the north of Brown's Park so that we crossed east in Wyoming rather than going diagonally in a straight line across the Colorado Rockies to Denver.

"And easier to get snowed in," Sundance said.

Curry just scoffed, and I saw Butch watching both of them from beneath lowered lids, silently assessing the potential for trouble.

Even Sundance and I barely spoke during those days, though he would occasionally reach out to touch me, as in reassurance. I always smiled at him, and I never knew if he recognized that my smile was forced. The comfort of Fannie's seemed a long way away . . . and maybe not worth the trip.

But then I'd remember Sundance's words: *We can't stay here, Etta.*

At last we turned south, following the eastern slope of the mountains, and here Butch declared it would be safe to have a small fire at night. "Colorado," he said, "isn't as up in arms as Wyoming."

I never realized till then what a blessing a small fire was. One day with the sun warm on us, the men shot four squirrels, and I stewed them at night. With full bellies, we sat around that flickering fire, warming our hands on cups of coffee to which Sundance had added just a little whiskey. For the first time in days I felt warm—inside and out.

Sundance sat next to me, and we all stared at the fire without saying anything. Occasionally he would turn to look full in my face.

"Sorry you got into this?" he asked once.

"No," I said truthfully. "But I've been happier . . . and I will be again."

He kissed me soundly, paying no attention to Curry's snort of disgust.

After a few minutes, Butch stood up, yawning, and said, "Come on, Curry, we'll spread out blankets over yonder. Leave the fire to these two."

"The hell I will," Curry muttered. "I got a right to be warm as them. They don't need no privacy. Nothing but—"

"Don't, Curry." Sundance's voice, like steel, cut him off in midsentence, but it didn't take much imagination to finish what had been left unsaid.

All four of us slept around the fire that night, Sundance's head next to mine, our hands clasped just inside my blankets.

Denver was a flurry of shopping and fine food and comfortable beds—the hardship of the horseback trip was out of mind in an instant. We stayed at the same boardinghouse as before— no Brown's Palace this time—and all three men were greeted like long-lost brothers. The first morning, Butch and Curry disappeared with our horses.

"Where are they going?" I asked curiously, my head fuzzy from a night of loving with Sundance.

"Sell the horses," he said.

My head cleared instantly. "You're selling my horse? The one you gave me?"

"Etta," he said with a chuckle, "we don't want to board it all the time we're gone. Don't know how long that'll be. We'll buy you a new horse."

"I like that one," I said stubbornly, and he threw his hands up in the air.

"Come on, let's go shopping."

It seemed to me I had just bought clothes I barely wore, left them behind, and then here I was buying more, trying on tailored plaid skirts and dark-colored blouses, daytime dresses of muslin and linsey-woolsey and cambric, elegant evening dresses of satin and silk trimmed in ribbon and spangles with leg-o'-mutton sleeves, and frothy wrappers that made some of Fannie's pink concoctions look downright plain. I bought slippers with tiny French heels and long pointed toes and tiny, feather-trimmed hats with bags to match. And I tried to forget the fine clothes packed away—maybe forever—in trunks in Wyoming.

"It's too expensive," I murmured over one dress of China silk that I would never have an occasion to wear—I knew that with a certainty.

"Buy it," he growled.

When we had taken all my packages back to the boarding-house, it was time to outfit Sundance. "We can't have you looking like a lady and me like this," he said, gesturing at the rough trail clothes he still wore. "Got to be a gentleman."

Butch went with us—Curry, it appeared, had met himself a young girl who would take him shopping. We had a high time picking suits with vests, shirts with starched collars, a watch for each man to string across his middle from the vest watch pocket, derby hats, even spats and gloves.

"My, my," I said as they paraded before me that evening, "a pair of . . . let's see, riverboat gamblers."

"No, Etta, they wore string ties and funny flat hats," Sundance said in disgust. "We're Denver businessmen . . . in Texas to look at some investments."

"If you believe it," I assured him, laughing.

"You better believe it too," he retorted, but he was smiling.

We stayed in Denver only two days, and I never saw Curry after the first five minutes. If the same were true in San Antonio, it might be a merry Christmas after all.

On the train to Texas, Curry sat apart from us and slept, and I was happier with Sundance beside me and Butch, riding backward, in the seat across from us.

"You pleased to be going home to Texas?" Butch asked innocently.

The pause that thought gave me must have shown on my face.

"Did I say something wrong?" he asked, almost apologetic.

I recovered quickly, aware that Sundance was watching curiously to see how I'd handle it. "Yes and no," I said. "I'm pleased to be going to Fannie's, but there are parts of Texas I'd just as soon never see again."

"Fair enough," Butch said, and changed the subject.

But when I dozed off Pa's face swam in front of me. I hadn't seen him for a long time, and I brushed my hand, as though to brush him away. Sundance caught the hand and held it, waking me.

There were lighter moments, too. Once the two of them got to whispering about how easy it would be to hold up the train, and they looked around at the other passengers, calculating how much cash and jewelry was collected in that one car alone. They got so silly they pointed at this passenger and that, imagining a sack of gold or a diamond stickpin or who knows what.

"And you," I whispered with a laugh, "have accused me of being indiscreet. I think you both best hush." But the idea of robbing a train had been planted and would take hold sooner than I could ever have imagined.

Fannie, forewarned of our arrival, had closed the house, even though there was no financial justification for it—"my" outlaws wouldn't bring her any business. Only Curry would choose one of the girls; Butch would smile and charm them all and walk away, as he always did, though the next morning he might complain about being lonely and cold at night. I was certain his loyalty to Mary Boyd back in Lander was strong enough to turn temptation aside. And Sundance . . . well, of course he wouldn't!

The three men made such a commotion getting our luggage from the carriage to the front porch—by now, we had six pieces of luggage among us—that Hodge was at the door before we could knock.

"Miss Etta, it surely is good to see you. Come on in. Miss Fannie, she's waiting in her room for you." He gave the men a dark look that indicated they were not to follow me. "I'll show you gentlemen to your rooms," he said.

Fannie waited in a chaise lounge, her hair stunningly piled on her head, her body—which had not grown any smaller—swathed in a wrapper of fine merino wool, her face carefully made up. Her room, always pink and lavishly decorated, had been redone with rose-studded wallpaper, new lace curtains under deep pink valances, and new furniture—a dainty desk meant to resemble a French antique but looking too insubstantial for Fannie, the chaise lounge, and a wing chair with ottoman, both upholstered in deep pink and sort of gray stripes. The latter pieces seemed meant for a man to sit and smoke his pipe.

Waving a hand in my direction, she favored me with a genuine smile.

"Lord, child, I *am* glad to set eyes on you again after all this time and—what was it?—three letters?"

"I . . . there wasn't much to tell, Fannie." I stood in the doorway. What, I wondered, would I tell her? Of Belle Fourche?

She swung her feet to the floor and pushed them into fur-trimmed slippers, pink to match the gown. Then she pushed off from the chaise and came toward me, arms spread, to gather me in a hug that so surprised me I near lost my breath.

"I missed you," she said, and if I hadn't known better I'd have thought Fannie was fighting back tears.

"I missed you too," I said, wondering how much truth there was in my words. Surely I had thought about Fannie, but Sundance had made my life so complete I missed no one—except Butch when he wasn't around and Mama when she crossed my mind fleetingly.

She held me at arm's length and scrutinized my face, while I tried to smile reassuringly. At long last, she said, "He's good to you."

"Yes, he's good to me. He loves me." There were a lot of things about Sundance—and Butch—that I wasn't going to tell Fannie.

189

"You brought Butch!" Her eyes lit up. "Let me go see him," she said, as though I'd been holding her back.

"We, uh, we brought Curry too," I said, and then rushed on to add, "I didn't want to, but Sundance said we couldn't leave him behind."

She shrugged. "I can handle Curry."

She never, it turned out, had to handle Curry. By the time we got to the parlor—surely we'd only spent five minutes in her room—Curry and Annie Rogers had found each other. Annie, who had always hated outlaws, was hanging on Curry's every word—and on his arm. He was spinning long stories for her, though I stayed far enough away that I didn't have to hear them.

"Where's Maud?" I whispered to Fannie, expecting a war between whores.

Fannie shrugged. "She's moved on. Annie can handle him."

For the rest of our stay, Annie "took care" of Curry, and he, surprisingly, behaved almost as though he was civilized.

When I finally got her alone, I demanded, "What are you doing? You hate outlaws, and Kid Curry is the worst of all! Don't you remember the last time he was here?"

Her smile was almost condescending. "You don't understand, Etta. You're not stuck here, with no prospects. Curry wants to take me away with him—and he's behaving better than he did that other time. I . . . he's kinda cute."

I gave up, though I ranted and raved to Sundance that night until he put his fingers to my lips and said softly, "Stop thinking about Curry and start thinking about me."

The best part about our stay in San Antonio was that I pretty much had Sundance and Butch to myself. The three of us toured the city, sometimes bought our lunch from street vendors, shopped in the market, walked along the riverbank, and laughed at our own jokes. Julie packed us lunches on warm days, and we picnicked in the same spots that Sundance had taken me to earlier, watching the sun go down before hurrying home to Julie's best cooking—the things we never had in our camp-sites, like roast pork or Cornish hen or bread pudding.

"Chicken salad for lunch?" she asked one day and never did understand why Sundance and I collapsed in laughter. Another time she made flan for us; neither Sundance nor Butch had ever eaten it, and Sundance claimed to love it, though Butch said a mouthful was enough for him—too slimy. I laughed at him and without meaning to hurt his feelings.

"I guess I'm just not sophisticated," he said, pouting.

For Christmas, Fannie had Hodge put up a cedar tree in the main parlor, and one morning when the girls were still asleep, Sundance, Butch, and I trimmed it with glass ornaments that Fannie had bought special and popcorn strands—Julie popped the corn and made poor Hodge string it. Then we carefully fastened small candleholders onto the tips of the most substantial branches and fitted candles into them, though I warned the men that we could not light them until Christmas Eve—and then we'd have to keep a bucket handy.

"A bucket? I swear, Etta, you're getting motherly and full of precautions. That tree isn't going to catch fire! I don't want you getting to be an old lady on me." Sundance seemed only to be half joking.

"A bucket," I said firmly. "Trees catch fire easily."

The house had been open every night after the night of our arrival, but for Christmas Eve Fannie closed again, and we all gathered around the tree. Carefully, under my supervision, Sundance lit the candles, once asking loudly, "You got your bucket ready, Etta?"

The new piano player—his name was Joe or José or some such—played "Silent Night, Holy Night," and "O Little Town of Bethlehem" and "Hark the Herald Angels Sing." Sundance knew all the words to all the verses, and I had to try to follow along. I barely knew the first verses, and it made me angry. Knowing all the words seemed to represent a certain kind of polish that I still hadn't achieved.

Butch stood on the other side of me, singing in a loud and clear baritone, and every once in a while I'd catch him looking at me. Once, when his look seemed ever so tender, I wondered if I was the one woman who could turn him from—or save him from?—Mary Boyd and all the unhappiness she meant to him. The thought made me so uncomfortable that I threw my arm around Sundance's shoulders and sang louder than ever.

Fannie had presents for all the girls, and for Julie and Hodge. They, in turn, had gotten together to buy her a lovely ice wool shawl in her favorite shade of deep pink. She draped it lavishly around her shoulders and paraded about the parlor in an exaggerated, hip-swinging walk that made the men shout and clap, the girls giggle, and Hodge frown with disapproval.

Fannie and I exchanged presents privately in her room—at her request. I had little for her, not from a lack of money—Sundance would have been generous. But my imagination was blank—the harder I thought, the more desperate I had become, until at last Sundance had said, almost angrily, "For God's sake, Etta, get her a tin of sweets and forget about it." I found, at a jeweler's in San Antonio, a trinket tray for her dressing table. Of silver, it was oblong, the smooth center surrounded by ornately worked rose blossoms. I had that smooth center engraved simply, "For Fannie, from Etta."

Fannie's smile told me she was pleased. She looked at the tray, then at me, then back at the tray, holding it at arm's length as though to get a better view—and then she carefully cleared a spot for it on her dressing table. With a grand gesture, she removed the diamond watch-pin she always wore and plunked it down in the middle of the tray.

"Looks grand, doesn't it?" she asked with a broad smile.

I nodded. "It does, Fannie. May you have a thousand diamonds to fill it."

She laughed aloud again. "It's about time, child, you had some diamonds. Here . . ." Awkwardly she thrust a small box into my hands.

I fumbled with the ribbon, nervousness making me slow. "Now don't worry, Etta, I haven't mortgaged the place to buy this. It's just something I thought you should have."

"It" was a magnificent brooch, an intricate working of pearls and tiny diamonds into a pattern of flowers and leaves, with gold vines twining them together. I fingered it and could say nothing. What I at last managed was neither graceful nor appropriate. "How can I wear this in a cabin in Wyoming?" I wailed.

One of the blessings about Fannie was that she understood. A casual hand plopped itself on my shoulder, and she said slowly, "I guess I give it in the hope you won't always be in the wilds of Wyoming." Then she laughed aloud. "I expect Sundance to take you someplace wonderful someday. You can tell him I said so."

I did tell him that night, after I showed him the brooch. He admired it duly, but he was blatantly jealous. "I wanted to buy you diamonds," he said, like a little boy who wanted to bring his mother flowers.

But then, when I told him what Fannie said, he was indignant. "She said that, did she? Well, I'll show her. I'll take you to the grandest places you can imagine, places Fannie Porter has never seen—"

I put a finger to his lips. "Shh. This isn't a contest between the two of you," I reminded him.

I had gotten Sundance a gold stickpin—with his money, of course—and he chortled over it, declaring we would dine out the next day so he could sport it. For me, he had a strange gift: a leather-bound book of blank pages.

He was almost embarrassed. "I know it's not as good as Fannie's brooch," he said, "but . . . I thought you'd write whatever struck you about your life these days. I don't know . . . maybe it's a bad idea. . . ."

"It's a wonderful idea," I told him, and meant it. I wrote my first entry that night, while Sundance snored gently in the bed. Almost without my willing my hand what to write, I began the journal with the story of my father.

Next morning, Sundance warned severely, "But don't ever let that fall into the wrong hands. Some law officer gets hold of a record of the Wild Bunch . . ."

Butch and I also exchanged gifts—scarves! I had picked a plaid woolen scarf for him, and he had chosen a wonderful piece of smoky blue silk for me. Perfect gifts, I thought, to express our feeling of family yet love for each other—or perfect gifts to hide the feelings we each fought. I kissed his cheek soundly, and he blushed but managed to hug me. The hug we shared was just a tad longer than it should have been, but Sundance didn't see.

Fannie's house resumed business as usual the day after Christmas, and it was busier than I thought I'd ever seen it. But beneath the flurry of daily activity was the planning for New Year's Eve—the biggest night on Fannie's calendar. There would, she told me, be champagne, and oysters on the half shell and fresh shrimp, hurried up on ice from the Gulf Coast, and dainty cakes that Julie was even now baking.

"Can I help?"

"No, Etta, you'd just get in the way. Julie and I are used to this."

"Can I come to the party?"

She looked long at me. "I guess you're old enough now," she said, smiling, "if you promise to behave."

"It's Curry you best worry about," I said.

She laughed—that light, forced tinkle of a laugh. "He's under control . . . or haven't you noticed?"

The celebration was not nearly as much fun as I'd thought it would be when I was seventeen and peeking through curtains at the hilarity. Everyone seemed drunk and loud—including Sundance—and the champagne made me hot and sleepy. Sundance could barely drag his attention away from the girls, I thought bitterly. Looking at me rather quickly once, though, he suddenly grabbed my arm.

"You," he announced, "need fresh air."

Sleepy and sullen from the champagne, I resisted, pulling away from him. "Just leave me alone," I said haughtily.

Sundance's only reaction was to laugh. "Sorry, Etta, Sundance knows best." And with that he swooped to pick me up and carry me, kicking and protesting, out the front door.

"Shhh," he said. "Even on this street, you'll have the police on us if you don't stop yelling at me."

That quieted me, and the cool air sobered me. It was a cold night, cold for San Antonio, and the air *did* feel good to me. We stood on the porch, not saying much, watching the early fireworks that shot into the air from the Mexican part of town. After ten minutes, I was wide awake, shivering, and apologetic for my bad disposition.

Sundance tilted my face toward his and murmured, "You're just like most women—can't handle anything stronger than sarsaparilla."

It wasn't exactly the most romantic thing he'd ever said to me, but I put my arms around his neck and kissed him.

"All right," he said, "we can go in now."

We returned just in time to toast in the New Year—Sundance filled my glass with barely a sip—and to shout loud boasts about what a wonderful year 1898 would be. Little did we know that for us, it would be a year on the run.

Chapter Eighteen

Butch came in early one morning waving the San Antonio newspaper and shouting, "Sundance! Sundance, where the hell are you?"

Sundance was as a matter of fact still in bed, and so was I. We were in the room adjacent to Fannie's, the room that had been mine when I lived there and was now, for the time being, ours.

Butch pounded on the door. "This country's goin' to war," he shouted.

"Who they going to fight?" Sundance asked lazily, winking at me. "East against West this time? We'll win."

"Come on, Sundance, this is serious. Get out here."

Resignedly, Sundance pulled on his long johns and then a pair of pants. With a kiss for me and a suggestion I put on my wrapper and come see about the fuss, he left.

I found them in the dining room a few minutes later. Fannie had joined them, and she and Sundance were listening to a wound-up Butch.

"We can fight for our country," he said, "and that'll erase all the things they think we did. We'll be honorable citizens again."

Sundance looked at me. "The Spanish, it seems, have blown up one of our ships—the *Maine*—in Havana." He shook his head. "Just when I'd been thinking Havana might be a good place for us to go."

"It is a good place," Butch insisted, "to fight."

Butch kept talking about the sinking of the *Maine* for days and was only distracted when he received a copy of the Lander newspaper. "Outlaws Kill Rancher." The byline said it was from Vernal, Utah, and we knew immediately that it was Brown's Park, though the best geographical description given was "the base of the Douglas Mountains." Vaguely the article said that a posse had cornered three outlaws and in the gun battle a rancher named Valentine Hoy was killed.

"Did you know him?" I asked.

Both men nodded. "He was all right," Butch said. "We stayed clear of him, and he stayed clear of us, and we howdyed when we met in town. No reason to shoot him. It's gonna make things worse than ever up there."

Fannie rolled her eyes heavenward. "That mean you're staying here forever?"

I knew she was joking, but Sundance's nerves were too raw with the news from Brown's Park. "We're paying you well, aren't we?"

"Sundance," I said that night, "we got to go. We can't stay here at Fannie's any longer."

"You, too?" he asked, and for once there was bitterness, not laughter, in his tone. "We're payin' the old . . . we're payin' her, and we can stay. We got no place else to go except maybe Fort Worth. We can't go back north, Etta, whether you understand that or not."

"What I understand," I said, my tone matching his, "is that innocent men are being killed in your place, and you're too damn comfortable in San Antonio to do anything about it."

"You want me to go up there, wave a white hanky in the air, and say, 'Here I am, boys! Come get me!'?"

"I want you to act like a man and take some responsibility for a mess you've created," I said angrily. And then, almost spitefully, "Butch's idea about serving your country might not be so bad."

"They'd hang us before they'd enlist us," he said, his voice now weary instead of bitter.

"You haven't killed anyone, so they wouldn't hang you. And they might let you enlist instead of serving time."

"They try to put me in prison, I will have killed someone," he said ominously, "and then they'll hang me. I can see it all happening." He was looking far away, as though watching a scene in the future play itself out.

Curry was not as cautious as Sundance. He left San Antonio soon after the New Year, impatient, he said, with inactivity.

"I didn't think you were very inactive," Butch said with a look that was the closest he would ever come to a leer.

Curry ignored him. "You can stay here all winter, do nothing," he said scornfully. "Me, I got to see what's goin' on up north."

"You go on back," Butch said quietly, "and see how things are. Spread the word we'll meet in . . ." He paused to think for a moment. "Steamboat Springs, late March."

Curry nodded and picked up his blanket roll to head for the door. Sundance's voice stopped him.

"Curry, you do anything dumb, I swear we'll leave you to hang."

He was indignant. "I ain't gonna do anything dumb," he protested.

"Watch your temper, then," Butch said, his voice quieter than Sundance's but still commanding.

Curry shrugged and left the dining room, where we'd all just finished breakfast.

Annie had watched Curry with calculating eyes during his speech but said not a word. Later she admitted to anger at his leaving but said, "A whore can't be too demanding, I guess. Maybe he'll be back."

"And would you go with him, Annie? He's a killer." The words were out of my mouth before I realized that I sounded just like Fannie.

"You went with Sundance, didn't you? Of course, I'd go north with him if he asked me."

I wanted to shout, *There's a difference! Can't you tell? Sundance and Butch are good men—they just happen to rob banks.*

197

Curry is a mean, dishonest, untrustworthy . . . outlaw! It would have done no good, and I kept my peace.

Fannie and I were in her bedroom late one afternoon, sipping hot tea that Hodge had brought to ward off the chill of a late-season Texas norther. It was early March, almost time for us to head out for Steamboat Springs, and I'd found myself spending more and more time with Fannie lately. I felt a fondness for her—and a gratitude I would never put into words—and I didn't know when, if ever, I'd see her again.

"Fannie," I asked, "what are you going to do when you leave here?"

"Leave here?" she squawked indignantly, "I'm not leaving. You are."

"I know, but someday . . . when you're, well, too old . . ."

"For the life?" She laughed heartily. "Honey, I'm already too old. But I ain't got the sense to quit." Then she sobered, stirring her tea and staring down into the cup as though the leaves would give her a message. "I . . . I guess I'll go back to Stephenville, have me a little house with a garden and some chickens. . . ."

"And all the neighborhood children will call you Aunt Fannie and beg you to make them cookies," I said, laughing at the image.

She was ever so slightly offended. "That just might be, Etta, it just might. What are you going to do?" She turned the tables on me, knowing full well that the reason for my question had less to do with her future than it did with my own. "You gonna follow Sundance forever?"

I stood up, nearly knocking my cup over, and began to finger the tatted cloth on her dressing table. "Sundance says he won't do this forever . . . can't. Maybe we'll settle down . . . in Stephenville," I said with a forced laugh, "and raise our children next door to you, so they'll know their aunt Fannie."

"That's not gonna happen and you know it," she said, putting into words what I already knew. "The world's not gonna let Butch and Sundance retire peaceably."

"I . . . I heard them talk about South America," I said lamely. "Maybe there. . . ."

"Maybe," she said, though her tone was full of doubt. Then she put her teacup carefully aside, pushed herself up from the chaise, and came to stand before me. She had to tilt her head up a little to look me square in the eye, but she did, demanding, "Have you ever figured out who you are, Etta Place?"

"I . . . I'm an outlaw's woman," I stammered.

"Balderdash!" she said.

My eyes avoided hers, and I fought the temptation to leave the room. "I'm . . . I'm a girl who killed her father and who's still wanted by the Texas law," I said.

"You sure don't know yourself, Etta Place. How well do you know Butch and Sundance?"

"Pretty well," I countered angrily. I didn't want to have to tell her that I knew that Sundance would always look out for Sundance, but Butch would look out for me if he had to. Biting my lip hard, I told myself I could look out for myself. Butch would never have to take care of me.

"You don't want to hear this," Fannie said softly, "but more than you'll ever admit, you're your mother's daughter, who wants to raise babies and cook for them and have that tiny house you talk about in Stephenville."

I left the room in a hurry, angry that Fannie would see in me that soft side that I tried to hide even from myself. Behind me, Fannie stood shaking her head.

When I opened the door to the boudoir, we could hear raucous noise coming from the parlor. Fannie rushed by me, and I followed her as she stormed into the room, demanding of no one in particular, "Now what the devil is going on?"

Sundance and Butch were singing a maudlin rendition of "The Girl I Left Behind," while Annie clapped and cheered, and Joe pounded the piano keys. Sundance had appropriated a large hat with a peacock feather from somewhere and wore it perched on the top of his head, though it twice fell forward over his face. In wild pantomime, he acted the part of the girl left behind—complete with wringing hands and desperate facial expressions—while Butch overplayed the part of the heartless and inconstant lover, though he must have left six times while we watched.

I wondered that Annie could laugh, for it was clear they were playing with the idea of Curry leaving her behind. But she laughed harder than anyone, and I liked her the better for it. I looked at Sundance and thought, *By God, someday when you leave me, I'll laugh too.*

"Sundance?" I said, my tone a perfect imitation of Fannie's what-the-hell-is-going-on-here? tone.

"It's a party, Etta," he said, his voice ever so slightly slurred. "Come on . . . join the fun."

"Why are you celebrating?" I demanded.

"We're leavin' tomorrow, Etta. I know I told you that. You packed yet?"

"No," I said. Anger rolled over me. I knew we were leaving soon for Steamboat Springs—wherever in God's name that was—but Sundance had not only not told me we were leaving, he'd acted as though it were a bad idea. And now here he was celebrating because we were going.

"Etta, it's gonna be all right." Butch came and put an arm around me. He smelled of beer, but his touch was gentle when he leaned over and kissed me on the forehead. "Just trust ol' Butch," he said.

I held on to him a moment too long, partly for the comfort and partly because some current seemed to be flowing between us. Butch gave me a startled look, and he was the one who pulled away.

Sundance watched us silently, all the life gone out of his celebration for a moment. Then, ignoring me, he grabbed Annie and said, "Let's dance! Let's party!"

Sundance, I thought, *you're hiding hard from the devils that torment you.*

Steamboat Springs made every Wyoming town I'd been in look like a metropolis. The town store, housed in a shack that looked as though it wouldn't last another winter, offered so few supplies that I threatened to send Butch and Sundance back to Denver for staples. There was a saloon, though it looked so dank and unappealing I never did go in it. Sundance went once and came back shaking his head and saying, "Give me Denver." The bank, Butch announced, wasn't worth robbing.

"Why are we here?" I asked.

"Can you think of a better place?" Butch replied. "Who else but outlaws on the run would come to this place?"

I had discovered already that there were medicinal springs everywhere around this mountain town, but I was sure there wasn't a steamboat closer than the Missouri River. When I asked, sarcastically, "Whoever came up with the name Steamboat?" Sundance suddenly took me by the hand and began leading me off into the woods. When I balked, he said impatiently, "Come on."

"Where are we going?"

"To the springs," he replied, as though that was totally obvious to anyone.

We were following a deer trail, and Sundance was walking so fast I nearly tripped a time or two, keeping up with him. I had no choice, however, because he still held my hand fast.

When I asked, "How far?" he turned with a grin and said, "Women! Always complaining. It's not far. You wanted to know why the name . . . and I'm going to show you."

By now I was laughing. "Did you name it? Is that why you're so sensitive?"

He had the grace to grin. "No, I didn't name it. But I want to show you this."

We came to a clearing where a spring gurgled. It was maybe a bigger spring than some of the others, and from the steam rising from it, I judged it might be hotter—the others ranged from tepid to pretty hot.

"So?" I asked loudly.

"Shhh!" He whirled toward me, his finger to his lips.

I hushed and listened . . . and heard a sort of *chug-a-chug, chug-a-chug* coming from the spring. "So?" I finally repeated.

"It sounds like a steamboat," he said impatiently. "Can't you tell?"

I couldn't help laughing. "Sundance, I never saw—or heard—a steamboat in my life. How would I know?"

He threw his hands into the air. "Just take my word for it, just take my word!"

The country around almost made up for the town. We camped in a valley about three miles from what passed for the center of town, and all around us were mountains. In mid-March they still had great patches of snow near the tops. The trees hadn't started to bud, but the evergreens made up for that, so that we had a feeling of trees and green and forest. Sundance

201

Judy Alter

pitched our tent by an icy stream, with water so clear and cold that I sometimes thought I'd never drink my fill.

The stream was full of trout, and the meadows nearby were full of grouse and sage hens. Butch and Sundance were triumphant hunters, but I told them it was less because they were good shots than because game was so plentiful. Nonetheless, we ate well around our campfire at night, and I watched the other men wander over, drawn by the aroma of my cooking. Sometimes Butch or Sundance invited one or the other, but mostly they didn't. I left it up to them.

"I don't have to share everything," Sundance said indignantly once.

Best of all, though, was the air—clean and crisp and fresh, in a way that made San Antonio seem stale and stifling. I hadn't noticed it, or thought about it, in San Antonio . . . but once I was back in the mountains, the difference rushed at me. I woke up in the mornings full of energy—much to Sundance's dismay when I pushed and pulled until he got up to hike with me.

"Just be glad," I told him, "there's no snow on the ground. I've improved my aim."

"Probably not," he said dryly.

I took him on long hikes, so that I could stare at one majestic view after another, and we spent our days hunting, riding, and fishing. At night, we fell into bed in exhaustion.

"Your cheeks are sooo red," he told me one night, "you look like those pictures you see of Alpine milkmaids who live in the mountains."

"I am so grateful to you for pointing that out," I said sarcastically. "My face is chapped from the wind and burnt from the sun."

"You look wonderful," he said, and I knew he meant it.

All told, nearly fifty men came to the meeting Butch had called. But you'd never have known it if you were riding by— they must have camped over a circle of more than five miles. Most simply curled into sleeping rolls at night, huddled around small fires. A few, like Sundance and me, had tents—mostly they were the men who had women with them.

Elzy Lay was there—without his Maude—and I was glad to see him again. Others were names I'd heard but never put a face to before—Ben Kilpatrick, the Tall Texan, as they called him, who had a woman named Della with him. She was small and dark, with high cheekbones and a kind of dusky complexion that spoke of Indian blood. She looked, I thought, stern and "mean as an Apache." When I ventured that opinion to Sundance, he told me to hush because she really was Indian but not, he added, Apache. I never felt comfortable around her, as though I couldn't turn my back on her.

Then there was Will Carver, who had brought Lillie Davis with him, Lillie who had been at Fannie's, Lillie who'd been gone when we were there and about whom I'd never asked. Fannie hadn't volunteered, but now I knew that Lillie, who said she wouldn't be at Fannie's long, had left with Will.

Will greeted me pleasantly with. "So you're the one who's changed Sundance!" He was nice-looking enough, sort of a pale imitation of Sundance—same height, same sandy coloring, but not nearly as good-looking. But Lillie had changed—she who had been bright and charming and perpetually innocent when I arrived at Fannie's was now old. Her eyes were sad and tired, and her mouth slashed across her face in a straight line, the corners never lifting into that smile that I remembered from years earlier.

"I know why she's changed," I told Sundance angrily one day as we sat chunking pebbles into the stream and enjoying warm sunshine on our backs. "He hits her. I saw him. He didn't think anyone was around, and he just whacked the flat of his hand against her face. I've no idea what she'd done that made him so angry."

"Probably never know," Sundance said, looking uncomfortable.

I thought about Mama and all the abuse she'd taken from Pa. "I can't understand a woman putting up with that," I said in exasperation. "You ever hit me, Sundance, it'll be the last thing you ever do."

He raised his hands in mock surrender. "I already know that, Etta. Believe me, I know."

If he'd made a joke about butcher knives right then, I'd have left him—or killed him. But Sundance was smarter than that. "It's not me you're mad at. It's either Will or Lillie . . . or both."

I let out a long breath. "I guess it's more Lillie than anything. She makes me think of my mother, and not in a good way."

"Not all ladies can be you, Etta," he said with a wry grin.

We were camped several days before all the men arrived, drifting in one by one. But finally, late one night, they all wandered into a central area where Butch had built a large fire. Some lounged on the ground; others stood watchfully as though ready to bolt at a minute's fright; a few, mounted on horseback, stayed on the perimeter of the group.

Sundance had told me firmly that the meeting was men's business and I was to stay in our tent. That was, of course, all it took to encourage me to sneak out and hide behind a small cedar bush. In spite of cedar in my nose—which almost made me sneeze—and prickly branches that stuck through my clothes and set me to itching something fierce, I stayed and listened.

"We could be heroes," Butch was saying. "We'll join Torrey's Rough Riders, go down there to San Juan and beat some sense into those damn Spaniards—we'll be heroes!"

It was the same argument he'd used—unsuccessfully—on Sundance and Curry in San Antonio, and now he was trying—earnestly trying—to convince fifty outlaws to turn national heroes. It was a quixotic gesture, a naive stance taken by a man so gentle and honest that his fellow outlaws would never understand him. I knew as well as all these men how impractical, even impossible it was, but I wanted to rush out, put my arms around Butch, and protect him from ridicule.

The others knew, however, that Butch was the boss—that is, if there was a boss. And ridicule him, they wouldn't. Hoot, however, they did.

"Butch, why would we want to go fight for a country that's tryin' to hang us?"

"Hey, Butch, they'd arrest us before we could sign up."

"Butch," said one man, his voice somehow quieting all the others, "you know the governors are meeting right now."

From the startled look on his face, Butch obviously did not know. "Governors?" he echoed.

"Governors," said the man. "Wyoming, Utah, Colorado, couple other states. Tired of rustling in their states. Now, you know anybody even vaguely associated with the Wild Bunch is on their hit list. And you think they're gonna let us ride off to San Juan?"

The meeting erupted into a thousand conversations, and finally Butch simply shrugged his shoulders and waved them all away. They stood in tight little knots, talking about who knows what. Outlawry and the damned amateurs who were taking over their business, if Sundance's conversation was any sample. At last, though, they drifted away into the night to their separate camps, and the three of us—Sundance, Butch, and me—were left alone.

Sundance spoke slowly, even hesitantly. "Butch, if I'd known, I'd never have let you go out—uh—unprepared like that."

"That's why we had the meeting," Butch said, "so we could share what we knew. Ollie just knew more than the rest of us."

I realized suddenly that if the roles were reversed—if Sundance was the one who'd left himself exposed as Butch had—the result would have been tight-lipped anger and, eventually, some kind of disaster. But Butch was not bothered by embarrassment. He truly wanted to find the right path to get himself and the others out of a mess that, granted, they had gotten themselves into. Outlawry, which had started out as a lark based on youthful rebellion, had become a quagmire that threatened to pull them all down. And nobody knew that better than Butch.

"What now, fearless leader?" Sundance asked.

Butch smiled ruefully. "Well, we ain't goin' to San Juan, that's for sure."

"I'm for goin' back to Hole-in-the-Wall," Sundance said, to my everlasting amazement.

Butch narrowed his eyes and looked at him skeptically. "You got a death wish I don't know about?"

Sundance shook his head. "Naw. I think they raided it twice now—they'll know we've moved on. They'll give up."

Butch laughed and said, "You may be right. They may be just that easy to figure out."

"What we got to do," Sundance said, "is make us some plans to get a little money. Like robbing a train."

"Don't be in a hurry," Butch told him.

Chapter Nineteen

Within two days, most of the men had drifted away. Sundance and Butch seemed in no hurry, and I was still enjoying morning walks through the pines, afternoons spent fishing in the stream, fresh game cooked over a fire at night. If asked, I would readily have admitted to my ability to put on blinders when necessary—I simply banished governors' conferences and vigilantes from my mind.

Ben Kilpatrick approached our camp the second night, calling out "Hallo the camp!"

"Hey, Ben," Butch called out gladly, "come on in."

The Tall Texan ambled in, and I was glad to see that Della was not with him. Sundance gave him a cup of coffee, and the three of them hunkered around the remains of the fire where I'd cooked our supper.

"Seen a stranger lurking around last day or so," Kilpatrick said slowly. "Couple of us been watching him. Think he's a bounty hunter."

"Bounty hunter!" Sundance spat in disgust. "How low can they get?"

Butch threw him a look that would have silenced anyone else, but Sundance went on, "Lawmen can't do their own chasing ain't worth their pay." And then he rambled about amateurs and honor and all kinds of things. I longed to tell him to shut up.

When Butch finally spoke, it was slowly. "I'm obliged, Ben. Bothers me that Sundance and I didn't see him. Guess we been too comfortable up here. Actin' like we was at home by the fire."

Ben grinned. "You've every right. Pretty woman cooking good meals for the two of you . . . say, if I was you, I'd . . ."

"You'd what?" Sundance asked insistently.

Ben shrugged. "I don't know, but I don't guess I'd be watchin' for bounty hunters."

"We will now, that's for sure," Butch said.

"Are we leaving? Because of that bounty hunter?" I directed my questions to Sundance, but I really wanted to know what Butch would say.

Sundance held me at arm's length and looked me straight in the eye, his expression serious. "Etta Place, that's men's business."

I pulled away from him. "Men's business be damned. It affects me, too. If there's a bounty hunter after us, I want to know." I was angry at him, indignant.

It didn't matter to Sundance. Grinning, he said, "I don't think he's after you, Etta. You rob any banks lately?"

"Sundance," I said, my tone threatening, "you be serious with me." Then I turned. "Butch?" But he had melted into the trees.

Sundance and I'd been standing face-to-face, inches apart, and now he swallowed me in his arms, kissing me passionately in spite of a definite lack of response on my part. "I am serious," he said huskily, "always."

I pulled away, but it didn't seem to bother him.

In April, Walt Puteney and George O'Day were acquitted of all charges. By then, we were back at Hole-in-the-Wall, though I'd never have predicted that. I was delighted, though Sundance repeatedly warned me not to get too attached to any one spot. Still, I puttered in the kitchen, cooking the two of them grand meals—when they had any success hunting—and felt more at home than I had anyplace else. Secretly I knew that no matter where else we went, Hole-in-the-Wall would be home to me, in a way that neither Ben Wheeler nor San Antonio ever had been.

"Acquitted?" I asked. "Isn't that good news?" After all, Butch and Sundance and the others had raised funds for their defense, no matter by what means. That, I reasoned, meant some degree of concern.

Sundance cocked his head to one side, a skeptical gesture I was by now familiar with. "Not right now. Just means all those 'law-abiding citizens' will be madder than ever to think outlaws got off without being punished. They'd have rather seen them hanged."

The bounty hunter was still with us, having followed us during a many-day, difficult ride over the mountains between Steamboat Springs and Wyoming. He'd stayed a half day behind us all the way, and now he stayed outside the Hole, on the plains. I wondered how he could possibly attend to his bodily needs—food, sleep, elimination—because whenever I looked from the notch, there he was, sitting ahorseback, out there without any shelter. It was early April and still cold at night, but we never saw any sign of a campfire. One night it came a thunderstorm—too early for the spring storms, but nonetheless fierce. As I lay in my blankets, wrapped in the warmth and safety of Sundance's arms, I wondered if that man was still out there sitting on his horse, soaking wet, staring at the notch in the wall.

Finally, one day, after we'd been back at the Hole maybe a week, the bounty hunter rode ever so slowly toward the notch. Butch had been keeping watch, but he sounded the alarm, and Sundance and I soon joined him. So did Ben Kilpatrick, who was at the Hole with us, though Della stayed behind at the cabin and didn't come to the notch. The men all had rifles.

We watched, spellbound, as the man approached, waving a white flag.

"You go see what he wants," Butch said to Sundance. "We'll cover you."

"Me?" Sundance yelped. "I got responsibilities—Etta and all— and besides, it's you he probably wants, Butch."

Butch nodded. "I know. That's why I'm not goin'."

"I'll go," I said evenly. "He's not going to hurt me."

208

All three men stared at me. While Butch said, "You'd do that?" Sundance said, with equal emotion, "You'll not do that!" and Ben said, "I never knew a woman would do anything like that."

"Etta, you don't understand, bounty hunters . . . they're the lowest of the low. He's liable to use you as a shield . . . no telling what else." Sundance spoke earnestly.

"Sundance is right," Butch said. "Lowest of the low. Mean skunks. Can't trust that white flag he's wavin'."

"Would you all be quiet?" I asked. "Just kind of watch out for me."

"We'll have our sights trained on him all the time," the Tall Texan said.

That gave me pause. I'd assured Fannie that they never killed—and Sundance would only kill in self-protection. Well, this would kind of be self-protection, wouldn't it? That is, if they had to shoot. With that irrational thought in mind, I mounted my horse.

I waited until the man was close enough that I wouldn't have to ride far—or be exposed for too long—and then I started down the incline toward the plains. I had no white handkerchief to wave—can you believe not one of the three of them had a linen handkerchief?—but I figured my white shirtwaist and the way I wore my hat would tell him I was a lady. Anyway, I hoped so.

Once I reached level ground, I sat still on my horse and let the man approach me. Behind me, I thought I could feel three sets of eyes riveting into my back and three rifles trained on the man approaching me.

He came slowly, deliberately, showing no sign of nervousness or fear, and for that I admired him. Although I'd expected to feel nervous myself, I felt as calm as I had at the bank in Belle Fourche. It struck me, though, that Sundance had not suspected he was bringing along a female who would take these risks, and in that way I was a disappointment to him. The thought almost made me smile—which would have been the wrong thing to do.

The bounty hunter stopped some thirty feet from me and raised his hat ever so slightly. "Ma'am? I . . . I didn't expect a lady."

"Well," I said lamely, "here I am. What can we do for you?"

"Name's John Ward, ma'am. Sheriff John Ward out of Wyoming. I come for Butch Cassidy."

It sounded threatening, and I almost turned to the boys with our prearranged signal—a hand to my hat. But I managed to calm myself and ask, "What for?"

"Governor Richards wants to talk to him."

"The governor of Wyoming?" I hooted. "I'm sure he does, but Butch doesn't want to talk from inside a jail cell."

"No jail cell, ma'am. He'll meet Cassidy at the time and place of his choosing. I'm to make the arrangements. Governor Richards, he wants to strike a deal."

"A deal?" I repeated, confused. Surely this was not the result of that governors' conference we'd heard about it. They would never have all agreed to a deal. Richards must be acting alone, and that, I thought, was a sign in our favor.

"Yes, ma'am. There's got to be some way to stop Cassidy and the others from robbing everything in sight."

I stared at him. He was older than Butch and Sundance by a lot, and his face was beginning to sag at the jowls and in pouches underneath his eyes. His mouth drooped, as though he was tired—which I guess he was after chasing us so long and sitting alone out on the prairie. But his eyes looked straight at me . . . and they looked believable.

"There are three rifles trained on you," I said.

He nodded. "I figured as much."

"Throw your guns down," I said, mostly because it sounded like what I thought I should say.

"Throw my guns down? In the dirt? And ruin them?" He looked at me as though I were crazy.

I thought desperately for a minute. Then I said, "Don't move. I'm going to ride around behind you."

"You gonna shoot me in the back?" He winked as he said it, for he knew I wasn't.

"No. I'm going to watch you take your guns out of the holsters and put them in your saddlebags—carefully."

We accomplished that tricky maneuver, though it did occur to me that the men at the notch must be having fits, wondering what I was doing—and judging me a fool.

Still behind him, I said, "All right. Ride forward slowly, toward the notch in the wall."

He did, and when we were close enough, Butch and Sundance stepped out, rifles held to the side but in easy reach. Kilpatrick had disappeared—in fact, he disappeared so thoroughly that we didn't see him again. Sundance told me later that the idea of the law frightened him, and when I rode out on the plain, he said he was going to get Della and leave by the north end of the valley.

Butch and Sundance howdyed with Sheriff Ward. It seems Butch knew him, and within minutes the two of them were sitting on the rocks, talking about old times and outlaws they'd known. Sundance and I stood awkwardly around, though Sundance kept his rifle handy.

Finally Butch said, "Why you here, John?"

"Richards wants to talk to you. *Alone*."

"Who guarantees my safety?"

"I do." It was said straightforward, as though the speaker knew that Butch needed no further guarantee.

"Your word's been good," Butch said. "I set the place and time."

Ward nodded, and they worked it out. It was arranged that Butch would meet the governor—who was to come unescorted—so many miles beyond a certain whistle-stop in southwestern Wyoming. Butch described the spot exactly, down to the trail that led there and the rocks and lone tree at the place. He set the time for 3:00 A.M. five nights from then.

The two of them shook hands again. Ward tipped his hat to me and said, "Lady, you got one lot of nerve for a woman. I'm pleased to have met you." He'd never asked my name and I hadn't told him. I figured he knew who Sundance was, but no words had been exchanged between the two of them.

That night I said, "Butch, are you really going?"

He sat at the table, holding an untouched shot of straight whiskey. After a long minute, he said slowly, "Yeah. I'm going."

"Why?" I demanded angrily.

Sundance looked warily at me, as though to ask why I was so upset.

Late that night, when we lay a distance apart in our tent, he did ask. "Why're you so upset about Butch goin' to meet the governor?"

211

"I . . . he . . ." I stumbled for words. "What if he doesn't come back?"

Sundance propped himself up on one elbow to look at me. "Well," he said slowly, "that's always a possibility. It's also a possibility every time I ride away from you. But I'm not sure you'd look that way."

"I would," I hedged. "I worry about both of you."

He looked long at me. "You ought," he said with emphasis, "worry more about me. Makes me wonder."

"Wonder what?" I said faintly.

"What your feelings are for Butch," he said flatly.

How could I explain what I myself didn't understand? And how could I make Sundance believe that he was the one who roused my passion, no matter what I felt for Butch. "He's . . . he's like my brother," I said lamely. "You don't understand," I added. *And neither do I*, I thought.

And he replied, "No, I don't." Then he turned his back on me, and we both pretended to sleep.

The strain between us was evident the next day. Even Butch asked, "Hey, what's the matter here?" But neither of us told him. How could we?

Butch left three days later. He would stop to see Mary Boyd in Lander on his way, even though it took him slightly in the wrong direction. I packed some food for him—cold biscuits, a little side meat, boiled potatoes, a slice of sweet potato pie. Into his provisions I tucked a sack of coffee, a couple tins of sardines, and a can of tomatoes.

"He's not going to the North Pole," Sundance said, as he sat at the table sipping coffee and watching me. "He'll probably be fed . . . along the way." He meant, of course, in Lander.

"You never know," I said softly, "if he'll have to wait for the governor."

Sundance spit the end of a toothpick into the spittoon—a gesture he knew particularly annoyed me. "Doubt he'll wait long. Richards isn't there when he's supposed to be, Butch'll leave."

When he left, Butch kept saying, "You two be all right? Somethin's . . . ah, I don't know . . . somethin's troublin' you."

"Not a thing," Sundance said heartily. "We're just dead sure you're doing the dumbest thing you've ever yet done. But don't worry, Butch, I'll visit you in the state penitentiary."

Butch grinned and held out a hand. "Thanks. Good to know I have friends." Then he turned to me. "Try to put up with him for my sake, Etta." He gave me a soft club on the shoulder, the way men often do with each other. It was a gesture from one friend to another—Butch knew exactly what was wrong, and he was doing what he could to dispel it.

Sundance didn't miss a thing. "Etta and me are going to have a honeymoon," he said, "once we finally get the place to ourselves."

I was quiet.

Once Butch was gone, there was no more talk of a honeymoon. We went silently through the day. Sundance chopped wood, a chore he usually avoided but one that kept him out of the cabin, and I spent the day baking more light bread than we'd ever eat. I began to pray for a cold spell so it would keep for a while. We ate a quiet meal of probably the same things Butch ate on the trail—sidemeat and boiled potatoes—and then we took our coffee outside, where we sat and stared at a clear, star-studded sky.

"There's the Big Dipper," I said, pointing.

Sundance grunted.

"I always liked to make up my own figures and stories, rather than the ones astrologers talk about. See over there? Those stars are the shape of Texas."

He grunted again, and I pulled my shawl closer around me. It wasn't only the evening chill that was making me cold.

Pretty soon, Sundance said elaborately, "Well, I'm turning in" and left me alone under all those stars. There was no way I could puzzle out the whole answer to the tangle of Sundance, Butch, and me, but as I sat there, I thought I had it pretty well figured out in my mind. I did love both men, but with love that was so different that it was apples and oranges. The wild side of me, the outlaw side, the part Mama would never understand, belonged to Sundance. The part of me that was Mama treasured Butch. No, that was too simple. Maybe Butch was the protective father I'd never had, while Sundance was . . . ah, he was my lover. What I had to do was convince Sundance.

He was asleep when I crawled into our tent, and I forgot my nightly ritual of lighting the lantern and reading before I went to sleep. Slowly I pulled off my clothes and hung them on the tent's lone chair, piece by piece. Then I pulled the covers back and slid in next to him. He never moved.

I curled myself around his body, though his back was to me, and began to stroke—his shoulders, then down his back, across his stomach, and down until I toyed with his private parts. Then he moaned, not with the sound of someone coming awake but that of a man roused to passion.

"Harry Longabaugh!" I exclaimed angrily. "You were awake all the time! Why didn't you tell me?"

"You wouldn't have done that if I had," he replied, turning to reach for me. Then it was Sundance who did the stroking, and I who moaned with wanting. He teased and played with my desire, as though he were testing me, until at last I could stand it no more and cried out. Then we rolled together in a frenzy that had nothing to do with Butch or Mama or the world outside—it was just Sundance and me.

Panting, I said, "Don't you ever think I want anyone but you," and he, equally winded, managed to reply, "If this is what that thought gets me, I may think it every day."

Had I the energy, I would have hit him.

Later I thought about the differences between wanting and loving.

We began that familiar watch at the notch when Butch had been gone six days—three to get there, and three to get back, allowing of course for Lander. Before, Sundance was the one who watched; now it was me, while Sundance begged off to go hunting or take a nap and often tried to distract me.

When he asked, "Don't you want to ride up into the mountains," I merely shook my head, and he went alone. But peace had been restored between us, and it was all right for him to ride off and for me to watch for Butch. Sundance didn't really understand, but he was no longer threatened, and he knew, somehow, that I had to watch.

Butch didn't come on the sixth day, nor on the seventh, not on the eighth. I began to pick at my food and to wake during the night, imagining him in some Wyoming jail.

"Etta?" Sundance raised up in bed. "You've got to sleep . . . and to get hold of yourself. Whatever happened to him, we can't help it. And he knows that."

Unspoken, it was that lecture about the dangers and realities of outlaw life—and behind it lay the fact that it could as easily have been Sundance who disappeared into the great void of Wyoming without a trace. Sundance accepted that for himself. I couldn't accept it for either one of them.

Butch came home on the tenth day, and Sundance said to him, "I sure as hell am glad you're here. Another two days and I'd have had to bury Etta for lack of sleep and food. Worst of it was, she kept me awake all night too." He stubbed his toe into the dirt and followed it with his eyes, refusing to look at Butch.

"Nice to know I'm missed," Butch said lightly. Then he looked directly at me and said, with a great seriousness in his voice, "Thanks for worrying about me, Etta. It's nice to have good women worry about a man."

I heard the plural and knew that Mary Boyd, too, had worried. I wished I knew her. But then I would have wanted to shake her for marrying someone else, for consigning Butch to the single life he led, for not recognizing that when two people are drawn to each other the way they were it was almost a sin not to act on it. But then, if she'd acted on it, where would I stand with Butch. In my tangled thoughts, I liked him better single, even while I thought that life wrong for him.

"Well," Sundance yawned, "you gonna tell us what took you so damn long?"

Butch grinned. "Maybe, maybe not."

The governor, it seemed, had stood him up. "I sat out there by those rocks all night, and he never showed. So come morning, I moved on. Figured he'd had his chance. But it made me kind of sad, made me lose faith in politicians."

Did I see a grin as he said that?

"Come to find out days later there was track out, and he couldn't get through. Heard he wanted to arrange another meeting, but you know some things can't be done twice. What was it Shakespeare wrote, 'There is a tide in the affairs of men . . .'?"

I stared openmouthed at him. Who would ever have expected Butch Cassidy to quote *Julius Caesar*? When I collected my senses, I asked, "What would you have said to him if he had been there?"

Again that familiar grin appeared. "I'd have told him that no train or bank in Wyoming would ever be robbed by the Wild Bunch if he'd promise to call off the vigilantes and law-enforcement folks who are looking for us."

"Trouble with that," Sundance said, "is that we can't guarantee what a bunch of amateurs do. Someone we don't know would rob a bank, and then there'd be all hell break loose because you broke your promise. Besides, when you called that meeting fifty men showed up and they all thought they were the Wild Bunch. We can't control that many."

"You can't even control Curry," I said, my tone tinged with bitterness.

Butch looked at me a moment, startled. Then he said, "I s'pose you're right."

I didn't know if he was answering Sundance or me—or both of us.

After a minute, Butch brightened. "But it don't matter. I didn't have to make that promise, so now every train and bank in Wyoming is fair game."

"Did you," Sundance asked, "once promise the governor of that same state that if he'd let you out of jail, you'd never enter Wyoming again?"

Butch nodded. "But that was a different governor. I'm not bound by that anymore."

"All right!" Sundance danced a jig around me, and then Butch joined him, and the two of them high-stepped all around that little cabin, sometimes whirling me into their dance. When at last they stopped, we all three collapsed in laughter.

Later, Butch said, "Governor Adams of Colorado is in on it now. Hired a bounty hunter to find me. And I thought Colorado was safe territory!"

"A real bounty hunter this time?" I asked, remembering we had thought that of Sheriff Ward.

"Yeah, a real one. Well, sort of. A real one, but not a real smart one."

"Wonderful," Sundance said. "What we need is a dumb bounty hunter who will shoot anybody he sees."

"This one's dumber than that," Butch said. "He'll tell anyone he sees all he knows. He told me all about searching for Butch Cassidy."

We were dissolved in laughter again. Finally Sundance managed to ask, "He told you? Where?"

"Bar in Rock Springs. Never recognized me. Never even came close. Thought my name was Jim Lowe."

"Why'd he think that?" I asked.

"Because that's what I told him," Butch answered simply.

Much to Sundance's disgust, Butch had not killed, beaten, or otherwise harmed the nameless bounty hunter—"They're the scum of the earth!" Sundance protested—but had sent a wire to the governor of Colorado, explaining just how useless his bounty hunter was.

Sundance crowed with laughter. "That's making the governor eat humble pie."

Butch sobered. "Yeah, but it's not a good sign, Sundance. We're gonna have to move on, take some serious steps, go into hiding."

It appeared that going into hiding—and taking new identities—was no problem for them. What they didn't know was what to do with me. The debate raged furiously over my head, as though I had no say in my own life.

"She can go to Fannie's," Sundance said. "Fannie'd be glad to have her."

"I *won't* go to Fannie's," I said with determination.

"Etta, be reasonable, you can't stay here." Sundance threw a look toward Butch that said, *Help me with this irrational woman. Make her see some sense.*

I remembered the last time he'd told me I couldn't stay at Hole-in-the-Wall. He'd been right then, and I knew he was right now, but that didn't mean I needed to go to Fannie's. "Where are you going?" I asked.

Butch stammered. "I got a job at a ranch in New Mexico— French's WS. Told them I'd bring a crew with me."

"A crew?" I asked, my voice dripping with sarcasm.

Sundance, standing in the doorway with his back to me, threw his hands up in the air in exasperation, and Butch raised himself from the table where he'd been seated, eating the apple cobbler I'd fixed for supper.

"You know," Butch said, half apologetically, "Sundance and Elzy."

217

"And," I asked archly, "did you say to whoever is hiring you that you were bringing the Wild Bunch?"

"Aw, Etta," Butch said, his voice pleading, "I hired on as Jim Lowe. Told 'em I was bringing Harry Parker, that's Sundance, and William Lawson . . . that's Elzy."

"And Logan?" I asked.

Sundance avoided me completely, and Butch looked sheepish. "Yeah," he said, "and Curry. Gonna call him Jim Logan. Clever, huh?"

I stood with my back against the worktable where I'd prepared so many meals for them, my arms folded defiantly across my chest. I knew my eyes were burning a hole in Sundance, for he wouldn't look at me.

"All right, I'm . . . Elizabeth Parker, Harry's sister."

Sundance snorted. "You're being really difficult, you know. She is, isn't she, Butch?"

Butch didn't want to get into that argument, but he said, "We . . . well, we can't just show up with a woman at a ranch. They don't have no quarters. . . . I mean, Etta, it just isn't done."

"What's the nearest town?" I asked.

"Some place called Alma, but I doubt it's a store and two houses."

"Well," my patience was wearing thin, "the town of some size."

"There aren't any in New Mexico, except Santa Fe and Albuquerque," Sundance said, but I ignored him.

"Maybe Santa Rosa, or Tucumcari . . . maybe even Las Vegas," Butch said reluctantly. "Etta, what're you thinkin'?"

"Find out which town the WS does its shopping in, and then find out if there's a *respectable* boardinghouse there. Mr. Parker has a sister who can't be left alone—their parents being recently deceased and all."

Sundance stared at me as though he'd never seen me before. Finally, after a long silence, he asked, "And what would you do in that town other than wait for me?" His voice was a little smug as he said it.

"I wouldn't wait for you, Sundance. A man can't hardly come spend the night with his sister. . . . Oh, he can visit for tea and such. But spend the night? Such scandal! Now, Mr. Lowe . . ."

I said that to tease him and instantly realized I'd gone too far.

It was Butch who protested. "Etta! I'm only comin' for tea, with Sundance."

I tried to pass it off with a laugh. "I know that, Butch. I'm just angry at Sundance." I whirled to face him. "I can always take in sewing," I said. "I do have a few marketable skills. And I can teach."

Neither of them said much after that, but I knew it was settled. I would follow them, settle in Las Vegas or Tucumcari or Santa Rosa and wait for this next experience to pass by. It wouldn't, I predicted to myself, be long.

"Etta," Sundance asked when we were alone, "can you really go all that time without . . . well, you know . . . without being with me?"

"You mean sleeping with you, Sundance? Of course I can." Deliberately I didn't even ask how long it would be—weeks, months, more?

Reaching for me, he muttered, "I'll show you that you couldn't do it."

I pulled away from his insistent hands. "Sundance, you're the one who couldn't do it. And if anybody gives away your identity, it won't be me. I can do whatever I have to."

He turned angrily away and said, "So can I, so can I."

Chapter Twenty

New Mexico was nothing like I'd imagined, and for me it was a long, dry summer and fall. I'd thought small towns in New Mexico would be like miniature versions of San Antonio, with the gracious Spanish influence everywhere. Instead I found dust and desert and dryness. The town of Las Vegas, where Sundance and Butch ensconced me in a boardinghouse, was best described as dingy . . . or left undescribed.

"My sister, ma'am," Sundance said to Mrs. Blackburn, the frazzled-looking lady who ran the boardinghouse. "My friend and I"—he nodded his head toward Butch—"will be working at the WS, and we want a *safe, comfortable* place for my sister to stay. Ethel is"—here he lowered his voice, looked sideways at me once quickly, and then almost whispered to Mrs. Blackburn—"well, she's delicate."

Mrs. Blackburn's gray head nodded, and she gave me a long, studying look. Then she whispered back to Sundance, "Don't you worry, Mr. Parker, I'll see that she's took good care of."

I tried to smile sweetly, when every instinct in me was to bash Sundance in the head—hard!

"Ethel hopes to take in sewing," Sundance went on piously. "Is there—ma'am, do you know?—is there a need in Las Vegas for a good seamstress?"

"Oh, my goodness, yes. She can begin by mending linens for me. I'll take it off your bill." Mrs. Blackburn's hands fluttered with joy that she'd found a way to please these gentlemen in front of her. I don't think she cared one whit about pleasing me, though later she would be most kind to me.

"We'll come visit of a Sunday," Sundance said, "and if Ethel needs us before then, Mr. French will be able to find us, though"——he rolled his eyes as though envisioning the hard, physical labor they'd have to do—"we'll be out on the range a lot."

Even Butch was beginning to squirm at the show Sundance was putting on.

"Now, Mr. Parker, just don't you worry about a thing. Ethel and me, we're going to be the best of friends." With that, she came and put an arm around me to demonstrate. She smelled strongly of violet water, and it struck me that she hadn't spoken one word directly to me. Sundance had effectively managed to leave the impression that I was addled or impaired or whatever but not able to tend to my own affairs—and I'd been so intrigued by his performance that I'd stood by like a dummy and let him do it.

"I'm sure I'll be fine, Mrs. Blackburn," I said briskly. "My needs are really very few. I'll put a small ad in the newspaper for sewing, and meantime I'd be most pleased to mend your linens. If you need help in the kitchen, I can do that too."

She looked startled, as though amazed that I could talk.

They stayed, at Mrs. Blackburn's urging, for supper, though by then I was so furious at Sundance, I didn't care if he starved. Butch had hardly said a word, and for that I was almost equally mad at him. He could, I thought, have kicked Sundance in the shin or something.

Supper was a hearty lamb stew, with fresh new potatoes and carrots and—I could have sworn—a touch of red wine.

"Lamb?" Sundance asked.

"My, yes," she replied. "We got a lot of sheepmen around abouts, and its reasonable. I cook it a lot."

I knew he was thinking that he was about to work cattle and wondering if he would be caught in the inevitable wars between sheepmen and cattlemen.

221

Judy Alter

They left, Sundance and Butch both giving me brotherly pecks on the forehead, and Sundance saying gaily, "Sis, you be good till I get back next Sunday." I managed to smile through gritted teeth.

"My," Mrs. Blackburn said in a soft voice, "a girl surely is lucky to have a brother like that, one who takes care of her."

"Yes," I said distractedly.

Life settled into a routine in the few months I was in Las Vegas. During the week, I was a model boarder, mending linens for Mrs. Blackburn, setting the table for evening supper, attending church meeting on Wednesday—though I never could attend on Sunday morning when my "brother" and his friend came to visit me. As people began to know me—I went often to the general store, stopped in the milliner's, and generally tried to make friends—I got sewing jobs outside of the boardinghouse, and, as I told Sundance one Sunday, I soon had a fine business going.

"Good." He grinned. "I'll give up my business, and you can support us."

"We aren't staying here that long," I whispered fiercely. "I'm bored to death." I half suspected my landlady was just outside the pocket door that she discreetly pulled almost shut each Sunday. More loudly, for her sake, I said, "I'm afraid, brother dear, you wouldn't be able to live in the manner you prefer."

"Seems to me," Butch said quietly, "for all the risks we take, we ain't livin' very high on the hog. Most our days we're on the run or living in some run-down cabin, with Etta doin' all the cookin'."

Sundance and I both laughed, but the sound had a hollow ring to it.

On their Sunday visit, the "boys," as Mrs. Blackburn called them, sat in the parlor, which was badly decorated and uncomfortable, the chairs of stiff horsehair. Grim portraits—of Mrs. Blackburn's long-dead husband and forebears, I guessed—stared down from the walls as though they were eavesdropping, just as she was. Sometimes, as a little touch of refinement, she turned the key on a small music box just before she left the room, so that the mechanical sounds of "The Star-Spangled Banner" filled the room.

222

"See?" Butch said. "I told you we should have fought for our country."

One Sunday they reported to me that Kid Curry and Ben Kilpatrick had joined them. I didn't ask where Della was, but I knew she wasn't with them and hoped she was back in Montana. Of course, Elzy was already at the ranch.

"What a crew!" I said. "If Mr. French knew what kind of help he had . . ."

"What I know," Sundance said, "is that Butch can keep those yahoos under control like nobody else."

"And," Butch continued, "what Mr. French knows is that cattle rustling on his spread has absolutely stopped. He thinks we're the best thing that ever happened to a ranchman."

"I'll bet he does," I said, laughing to think of the joke of it and glad that they were so scrupulously honest when their honor was at stake. It was one thing I loved about the outlaw life: It had a certain honor to it, at least for Butch and Sundance. Now, Curry was another matter. . . .

Sometimes Butch would rise out of his chair and stroll to the window, standing, staring out at the nothingness of the little town. It was his way of giving us a moment's privacy—but Sundance and I found that short moment made the wanting worse instead of easier.

"Why didn't we say that Butch was your brother?" he whispered in my ear one day. "Then I could have courted you without raising suspicions."

"Only from a respectable distance," I said haughtily, pushing him away. "If Mrs. Blackburn saw you . . ."

"She'd have gossip all over this town in three minutes, and we'd be in worse trouble than we ever would for cattle rustling." Sundance laughed. "Just think, a man courting his own sister . . ."

It all came to an end when Sundance and Kid Curry decided to have some harmless fun way west. They wanted to ride to Nevada.

"Why?" I demanded.

"Because we've never been there. Hear it's a great place."

"Butch?" I said.

He shrugged. "I told them not to go, but I can't do much more. Don't worry, Etta. I'll watch after you." He said it so sweetly, so kindly, that I hadn't the heart to tell him my welfare wasn't what concerned me. I could always take care of myself—but could Sundance when he threw in with the likes of Kid Curry?

Within a day I went from worry to flat-out anger—and ruined Mrs. Blackburn's image of me forever.

"You don't have to go! It's the dumbest idea I ever heard of. It's dangerous . . . and foolhardy! Even Butch says so." I literally screamed at Sundance, paying absolutely no attention to Butch, who stood looking steadfastly out the window, and Mrs. Blackburn, who no doubt was positioned just beyond the pocket door.

"You're raising your voice," Sundance said mildly. "Butch doesn't tell me what to do, and I don't tell him." His eyes narrowed in cold anger. "And you don't tell me either."

"You've tried to run my life," I answered hotly. "You'd have sent me back to Fannie's if I hadn't made a fuss."

"This fuss isn't going to work, Etta. I'm going to Elko. I . . ." He hesitated just a little. "I'm restless, not used to working hard all summer like we have. I . . . well, I just got to cover some miles, see some new sights."

"With Kid Curry," I said scornfully. "You'll end up seeing the inside of the Nevada jails."

He shrugged. That gesture that sometimes I found endearing now exasperated me beyond words. "If I do, I do."

Silence fell on the room, so profound that I could hear each of us breathing—or thought I could. Within my own head, I heard the ragged breathing and the pounding pulse of deep anger. Distantly I thought I heard Butch sigh, but he neither turned away from the window nor spoke. Sundance stood watching me.

It was Sundance who broke the silence. "I'll see you at Hole-in-the-Wall in . . . oh, maybe three weeks."

"I don't know if I'll be there," I muttered, turning my back on him.

"That's always been your choice," he said levelly. "I . . . well, I'll say that I hope you will be." With that he came toward me, used one hand to spin me around until I faced him and the other to tilt my chin upward. Then he planted a quick kiss on the tip of my nose and turned to Butch. "You ready?"

Butch turned. "Yeah, I'm ready. Etta, I'll be by to get you first thing in the morning, just after light." His look was sorrowful, as though if he could he'd have replayed the scene just past to an entirely different script.

Mrs. Blackburn stood in the hall, hands akimbo on her hips. She watched them leave in silence, but the minute they were gone, she said harshly to me, "You'll be leaving *now!*"

"I'll be leaving in the morning, Mrs. Blackburn," I said. It occurred to me that she was afraid of Butch and Sundance now that eavesdropping had told her they were outlaws and that was why she waited to issue her proclamation.

"I won't be harboring your kind in my house," she sputtered.

I'd had enough for one day. In my most level tone of voice, I asked, "And what kind is that, Mrs. Blackburn?"

"You know . . . outlaws and their women—why, I bet you're no more his sister than I am."

"You're absolutely right, Mrs. Blackburn. I'm his lover. And I grew up in a whorehouse." With that pronouncement, I swept up the stairs to my room. And once there, finally alone, I fell to crying, even pounding the pillow in anger, though I tried hard not to make any noise for fear of further alarming Mrs. Blackburn. But, with Butch and Sundance gone, I was overcome with the unfairness of it all . . . maybe the unfairness that Sundance wouldn't—couldn't—ever become what I needed him to. I had to face the fact that he'd never change, that about him there would always be a charming, childish selfishness, a lack of responsibility that led him to do what struck him at the moment, and the devil take the hindmost.

The devil take the hindmost! It had been my phrase—hadn't I once said that to Sundance, when he'd questioned my following him? Maybe I meant it then, or maybe I'd turned responsible, though I couldn't figure why, but it seemed to me that we have obligations to those who love us. Sundance would never understand that.

Mrs. Blackburn never made good on her threat that I must leave immediately—would I have slept in the street?—but just to be safe, I stayed hidden in my room. That meant that by the time Butch came for me at sunrise, I was ravenous. Mrs. Blackburn stayed out of sight while Butch tramped up the stairs and brought down my blanket roll.

"You tell the landlady goodbye?" Butch asked innocently.

"No need," I answered. "She told me . . . last night. Says she doesn't let outlaws and their women stay in her house!"

"That right?" Butch said. "You have any breakfast?"

I shook my head.

He put the blanket roll down. "Stay here." With that he strode down the hall and into the kitchen. I could hear his voice drifting out through the swinging door. "Mrs. Blackburn, Etta . . . well, we're going to leave right now. But she surely does need some food. If you'll just give me about half a dozen of them biscuits you've baked . . . and maybe a slice or two of that ham. No, no, don't bother with the gravy—we couldn't eat it ahorseback."

Grinning like a bad child, he emerged from the kitchen with a package wrapped in one of Mrs. Blackburn's tea towels. The good lady never appeared, and Butch said later she'd supplied all he asked for without once speaking a word and without looking him in the face.

"Goodbye, Mrs. Blackburn," I called out gaily as I left. In seconds, Butch had restored my good spirits.

Riding across country a long distance gives people a certain intimacy . . . well, at least familiarity. Butch and I, who knew each other so well, reached a new level of understanding on the ride back to Wyoming, but it wasn't something we talked about or even, at the time, knew was happening. We did talk about Sundance.

"You gonna leave him?" Butch asked abruptly one night, reaching to stir the coals of the fire that still heated our coffee. We'd dined sparsely that night—canned sardines and soggy crackers bought midday in some small town—and the smell of the coffee tantalized my uneasy stomach.

I shrugged and then realized that doing so made me just like Sundance. "I might," I said cautiously. "I don't see him ever changing, ever . . . well, you know, growing up."

"So he don't have to go to Elko and raise hell?" Butch asked, and in the firelight I could see his grin.

"I don't mind the hell-raising," I said, "if I'm part of it. But I won't be treated like a convenience."

"Ah, Etta, you're never that to him. He loves you like he's never loved anyone, not even Anna Maria Thayne. But he's scared . . . and he's doing the only thing he knows to keep the devil off his back. He's running hard."

"What's he scared of?" I asked scornfully, I knew, of course, that he was scared of jail and a lot of other things, but Butch put it more clearly for me.

"That we'll find we can't do what we do here anymore. Those governors are going to beat us one way or another, Etta. We can't go on living on the dodge, making an occasional score— we'll either be killed or go to jail."

"I don't want to wait to see either one," I said, and then added, "for either of you."

He tipped his hat in my direction. "I appreciate your concern. Sundance and me, why, we might go to South America some day—take our winnings, if we've got any, and disappear." He stared at me over the fire. "We'd take you, Etta," and then he added hastily, "long as you wanted to go."

I'd heard that talk before, but that's not what I said to Butch. "You don't know that Sundance would," I said angrily. "He wouldn't even take me to Elko."

"Ah, Etta, he was going with Curry. You wouldn't have wanted to go. And it's just what I told you—a fling to take his mind off worrying. He didn't mean nothin' by not takin' you. But he'd take you to South America—that'd be more than a fling. It would mean changing our whole lives permanently."

"You won't either one live that long," I predicted grimly. Then, suddenly, I sat up straight. "Butch, why can't you and I disappear . . . right now, just leave, go someplace and take up new lives and forget the Wild Bunch and robbing trains and—"

He held up a hand. "Because not either one of us would do that to Sundance."

"He went off and left me," I fumed, "and I don't owe him anything."

Butch's voice was calm. "Think about it, Etta. If you left now . . ."

We didn't either one speak for a long time, probably the better part of an hour. But then, as Butch rose and stretched— an obvious sign he was preparing to turn in for the night—I said, "And we can't run away, because no matter what's between you and me, it's not the same. There's always Sundance, and there's always Mary Boyd . . . and nothing's going to change that."

"Not even," he said, grinning, "bad marriages or bad behavior. We're stuck with them—and that's our own doing."

"Butch Cassidy," I said, rising and moving toward him, "I really do love you." I reached up to plant a kiss on his cheek, and he in turn gave me a rough hug.

"It's mutual," he said, "and I'll always be around for you. But . . ." His last word hung in the air.

The cabin at Hole-in-the-Wall was a mess. Rodents had gotten in, split open the sacks of flour and cornmeal, and left their litter in every corner. I scrubbed floors on my hands and knees, stood on tiptoe to clean shelves, shook bedding and beat rugs until I was exhausted. It was not the behavior of a woman who planned to run away. I was there to stay, and I knew it—even if I didn't want to admit it aloud.

"Want me to help?" Butch asked twenty times.

"It's woman's work," I replied each time. Truth was, scrubbing floors did for me what running off to Elko supposedly did for Sundance. It kept my mind off scary subjects—like the future.

When I did stop to think, I couldn't decide if I was more angry or worried. But Sundance was there, on my mind, every waking moment. What would I say when he came back—or what would he say when he found me right where he expected me? My threat of leaving seemed hollow and empty, and a part of me longed to test him by making it true. But where would I go? Butch wouldn't take me to Lander, let alone San Antonio. Each night, wearied more by my thoughts than by hard work, I fell into a troubled sleep.

One day Butch rode into Kaycee for mail and supplies and was home in a hurry. "Come on, Etta," he called as he ground-tied his horse and rushed into the cabin. "Wanna go campin' for a day or two?"

"Camping?" I shook my floury hands and wiped them on my apron. "Sure, I'm ready." My energy exhausted with cleaning, being around the cabin was now beginning to bore me.

We were ahorseback and on the trail in ten minutes. Butch even complimented me on my speed.

"Where are we going?" I asked, still breathless from hurrying but glad to find myself going somewhere, anywhere, rather than sitting at home waiting for Sundance.

"Got to help a friend in Rock Springs," Butch said. "I heard about it when I was in Kaycee."

We rode long and hard, though Butch let us stop part of the two nights we were on the road. "We're in a hurry," he said, "but not that much." Still we rode after dark, under a sky so cloudy that no moon guided us. Butch rode carefully yet surely. He held back branches for me, led my horse carefully across streams, and asked constantly if I was all right.

"Butch," I finally said, "why did you bring me? You'd make better time without me."

"If Sundance had been there," he said slowly, "I'd have come alone. But you can help me. You'll see." And there was no further explanation, until we rode near Rock Springs. With Butch in the lead, we stopped at a small frame house, badly in need of paint, some four miles east of the town. The ground around the house was barren, but so was most everything else in that area. Still, this had a deserted look, as though no one cared—no vegetable garden, no chickens, none of the signs of a household.

Butch read my thoughts. "She cares," he said, "but she's old and poor and can't take care of it. Sometime I'm gonna come back here and paint it."

"She" turned out to be Mrs. Lavinia Black, former school-teacher and postmistress, and longtime Wyoming resident. A tiny woman, she peered at us through thick spectacles, having opened the chained door only a crack.

"Who you be?" she asked, her voice rising in suspicion.

"It's Butch Cassidy, Mrs. Black."

The chain rattled and the door swung open. "Butch Cassidy, I ain't seen you since . . . since you were a butcher!"

He laughed aloud. "It's been a right long spell," he agreed.

We were led into a threadbare parlor—the carpet was worn, the furniture sagged, and the room smelled musty. Involuntarily, I put a hand over my nose, but then I saw Butch frown at me. He made the introductions, and we were offered tea—Butch, who had never drunk tea as far as I knew, signaled me to accept, and we drank our tea out of fine English china cups, albeit slightly chipped.

"Mrs. Black, I hear you're having some trouble with that banker. . . ." Butch let his voice drift away.

That querulous old voice suddenly gained the strength of anger. "Trouble!" she hooted. "Gonna take my house, over a hundred dollar mortgage payment. I keep tellin' him my son'll send the money, soon as he's able. But that Cockrell down to the bank . . . the man has no soul."

Butch laughed aloud. "No, ma'am, he surely doesn't. Well, I'm gonna help you with this, but I'll leave Etta with you till I get back."

Mrs. Black smiled and reached for my hand. "We'll have a fine visit, won't we, miss? Now, where did Butch find you? Not in Lander, I know . . ." And she was off rambling.

It was almost twenty-four hours before Butch returned. In that spell, I'd managed to give the house a good airing—I don't think the woman ever opened her doors and windows, but I convinced her it was safe—and I'd washed the linens, cleaned the kitchen as thoroughly as I knew how, and tried to beat the dust out of curtains and rugs. Mrs. Black kept following me around the house, protesting, "Now, dearie, you don't need to do that." But when I cooked her a good potato soup—her supplies were limited—she seemed really grateful.

When Butch arrived, he sent me to fetch the banker. "Can't quite go myself," he said. So I went to the Wyoming State Bank of Rock Springs and asked for Mr. Cockrell. He turned out to be fiftyish, balding with a huge walrus moustache, large ears, and a self-righteous air. His hands were pudgy, with too many gold rings.

"Mrs. Black?" he said pompously. "I doubt there's any arrangement to be made. We'll simply have to foreclose on the house."

"She asked that you come see her," I said, swallowing my dislike of the man.

"I'll be there directly," he said. "I have a lot of things to take care of here."

"The son of a . . ." Butch muttered when I reported this. Between us, we took turns watching out the front window.

At length, almost at sundown, Mr. Cockrell came driving a single-horse carriage down the dirt road to the house. Even from a distance, I could see that he flicked the whip impatiently over the horse's shoulders. When he alighted from the carriage in front of the gate, he dusted his hands on his jacket and took care to straighten his string tie.

"I'm gone," Butch said. "You be sure he accepts the money and gives her a receipt."

The transaction was brief and none too cordial. I thought Mrs. Black would spit at the banker, and he remained every bit as supercilious as he had in the bank, though it was plain that he was surprised by her ability to pay. Sputtering, he made out a receipt and handed it to her, only to be rewarded with a "Thank ye, and now get out of my house!"

I hid my smile behind a hand, but when I walked him to the door I didn't offer to shake his hand nor did I bid him goodbye. He left silently.

Mrs. Black and I had settled down for the night when Butch returned, knocking ever so gently at the door and, once admitted, saying, "Let's go, Etta. We got to get away from here."

We shared hugs with Mrs. Black and then, almost before I knew it, we were on the road again.

"Butch Cassidy," I demanded, "you tell me what's going on, why we're leaving in the middle of the night like thieves."

"We are thieves," he said with a loud laugh. "At least I am. I had to go steal that hundred dollars for Mrs. Black—don't you ask where—but then, after she paid the banker, I waited for him on the road and robbed him. I got five hundred dollars back! See, Etta, we done a good deed and made a profit to boot. Can't tell me the Lord doesn't smile on outlaws!"

I was still laughing a mile later, the picture of that pompous banker rising before my eyes.

Chapter Twenty-one

Sundance was only gone the three weeks he'd predicted. Unlike the times we'd waited for Butch, when he was gone overlong and I was convinced he was dead or jailed, Sundance gave no cause for worry. If he was surprised—or pleased—to find me at the cabin, he gave no sign.

Both Butch and I watched silently as he came in, and not a one of the three of us said hello or anything by way of greeting.

Sundance stared at me a minute, then transferred his look to Butch. "Here!" He flung a roll of bills on the table.

"What's that?" Butch asked.

"My share of the loot."

"Loot?" I echoed. "You robbed a bank?" The idea that he would take that risk without planning, without consulting Butch, appalled me.

Apparently the thought never occurred to Sundance. But he was scornful when he said, "Not a bank. There's not but a thousand dollars there. We robbed a saloon . . . a damn saloon."

"Ain't that kind of like biting the hand that feeds you?" Butch asked.

I turned back to the stew I was stirring.

"That's not the half of it," Sundance said wryly. "We spent that much setting ourselves up as ranchers, men looking to invest. You know, sat in the saloon—Club Saloon, they called it—and bought folks drinks, had to have new clothes so we looked good. Bought a new suit and all."

I couldn't keep quiet. "I thought you just went for fun."

He stared at me so long without speaking that I had to force myself to keep from flinching. Finally, slowly, he said, "If I'd gone for fun, I'd have stayed with you."

"But you said . . . you said you'd never seen Elko."

"We'll talk about it later," he said firmly, his eyes ever so briefly darting toward Butch, who sat with his head down, absently whittling on a piece of stick he held.

"Should have robbed the bank," Sundance said.

"Probably so," Butch replied. "Why didn't you?"

"Curry. He got the lamebrained idea that the saloon had more money. Probably a hundred thousand sitting in that bank. Just our luck."

"Curry's luck," I muttered, wondering once again when the two of them would learn to stay away from Curry.

By the time we sat to supper, Sundance had us all laughing, but there was a hollowness to it.

A nervous Butch took himself off to his tent as quickly after supper as he could, but I piddled in the kitchen, drawing out my work, postponing the moment we would be in our tent. But then I could put it off no longer. Without a word, I headed out the door, and Sundance followed me.

He stood just inside the tent flap, hands shoved into his pockets. "I thought you'd be gone," he said.

"I thought about it." I stood before the tiny mirror he'd tacked up for me and brushed my hair hard. Then, turning to face him, I said, "But I'm not." No need to tell him part of the reason I was still there was that I didn't know where else to go; another part was Butch. Better to let Sundance think I'd stayed for him—and in a big way, I had. Whatever was between Sundance and me was far from finished, and I knew that.

"Butch?" he asked.

I shook my head. "Never. Not for either one of us." Then, wickedly, I added, "We like each other too much."

Sundance saw the joke of it, and maybe that was what spurred him to admit, "I thought about it a lot, about you and Butch. Sometimes it ate me alive, and I was ready to fight him. Other times I'd tell myself he's the best friend I'll ever have."

"He is," I said.

We met in the middle of the tent, a slow, restrained reunion that soon found us in bed together. Afterward we lay in each other's arms without speaking for a long time.

"I may have to marry you," he said at length.

I sat bolt upright. "Marry me? Who asked you?"

He chuckled. "Not you, I admit it, not you. But . . . well, maybe we should. . . ."

"Next thing," I said, "you'll be wanting an ivy-covered cottage and little blond boys who look just like you."

"And dark-headed girls who look like you," he added.

"You'll have to find another line of work," I threatened, but then my tone turned serious. "We're not that kind of people, Sundance. We've made other choices for ourselves. We can't suddenly decide to be common everyday good folks who go to church and raise their children right." I remembered my last conversation with Fannie.

He stared off into space for several minutes before he said, "I suppose you're right. But sometimes I can't see our future."

"I can see it," I said. "You'll be killed or put in jail for the rest of your life . . . but most probably, you'll be killed."

"Thanks." He reached to hug me. "It's so good to have your confidence."

"Butch talked again about going to South America."

"He told you that? Butch swore we'd never take anyone else with us."

"I'm not anyone," I said, "and yes, he told me. I don't think it'll happen. I don't think you'll live long enough."

"Maybe," he said, sitting up to kiss me soundly, "I'll just have to prove you wrong."

We slept, but sometime during the night, Sundance woke me by saying, "I told you I was going just to see Elko, because I didn't want you to know I was going to rob a bank. I figured you'd get upset."

"You went without me," I said, only slight accusation creeping into my sleepy voice. "Don't do it again."

"We'll see, we'll see."

I never did tell Sundance—or anyone else—but when he made love to me that night, I knew that he had been with another woman. I couldn't have told you how I knew, and at the moment I didn't know what I wanted to do about it. But I filed that knowledge away in my mind, storing it with other bits and pieces.

The next time they rode as outlaws I went with them, though it caused some trouble among everyone but Butch and Sundance.

Kid Curry muttered and cursed under his breath when Sundance told him, as casually as he could, "Etta's going to help us again." Curry had not been along at Montpelier or Belle Fourche, but he knew that I'd ridden with them when he hadn't. Now he glared balefully at me, and I knew he was thinking of our first encounter when I'd slapped him in the face. I didn't intend to let him forget, and I returned looks as hard as those I got.

"Guess I'll go back and fetch Annie," he muttered.

"Annie?" I asked curiously.

"Yeah," he said, his tone belligerent, "Annie from San Antonio. She's been following me around 'bout a year now. Can't get shed of her."

I looked at him as coldly as I could. "Have you told her you want to?"

He turned his back on me, and Butch muttered, "He probably likes the convenience."

They sat around the table at Hole-in-the-Wall, their eternal maps spread out before them. With the three of them were Maxwell, whom I'd never met, and Kilpatrick, the Tall Texan whom I liked a lot as long as he didn't have Della with him. I never did learn Maxwell's first name, and he never spoke directly to me, even avoided looking at me when he could.

"Etta?" Butch looked directly at me. "This is different. It's a train, not a bank." His voice held that question: Was I sure I wanted to take the risk again?

I nodded my head to tell him yes, I wanted to go, and he grinned slightly. "All right, now," he said, turning businesslike, "this is what we'll do. There's a steep grade between the Rock

235

Creek Station and Wilcox. We'll set flares here"—a stubby finger pointed out a spot on the map—"to indicate trouble on the track. Train'll make an unscheduled stop about here, just across this trestle bridge—there's a good-sized gully there." The finger moved ever so slightly. "We three"—his nod took in Maxwell and the Tall Texan—"will step out of the woods and get the crew off."

"Just where am I going to be?" Sundance asked forcefully.

Butch's answer was careful. "About three hundred yards into the woods . . . with Etta."

"But . . ." His protest died in his throat when Butch gave him a dark look. Butch had that kind of control over Sundance, just as he did over Curry and the others, but he exercised it rarely on Sundance, and it always surprised me to see it.

"There'll be a second section comin' along just behind this one," Butch went on, "and we'll have to blow the bridge over the gully quick."

"Blow?" I asked. Nothing had ever been blown up in the banks, and the idea made me nervous.

"Blow," Butch repeated. "We'll have dynamite with us. Then we'll have leisure"—he grinned at his use of the word—"to rob the front section."

"What if they won't open the mail car?" Kilpatrick asked.

"We'll tell them we'll blow the train up with dynamite," Butch answered calmly, as if there was no other possible answer.

"Would you?" I asked softly.

"Yes," Butch said.

I couldn't see that any of them looked particularly disturbed by all this dynamite, but in the same way I could not believe that Butch Cassidy would blow up a train full of innocent people. And I guess a part of me pictured each of them, blown to bits, by a charge that went off at the wrong time.

Butch went on, as though my question hadn't been asked. "But we don't want the mail car. Small potatoes, not worth the trouble. We want the express car. I specifically heard that there'll be a major shipment on June 2—fifty thousand dollars or more. That's what we want."

Sundance let out a low whistle. "I guess we do!"

Butch ignored him. "We'll have five horses in the woods. Etta and Sundance will keep them quiet, and we'll leave the train on foot, walk into the woods. It'll take them some time to get word to Wilcox and organize a posse. We should be long gone."

The meeting went on for another two hours, with endless—so it seemed to me—discussions of escape routes, hideouts, and the like. I tired of it and went to bed, long before the gentlemen retired to their tents. Maybe that was a sign that I wasn't a dedicated outlaw. Sundance would later suggest that.

Sundance woke me when he came in, not in his gentle way with love, but with a harsh comment. "Butch thinks I'm going to baby-sit you," he said angrily.

It took me a minute to come from sleep, but when the sense of what he was saying dawned on me, I murmured, "You've never had to take care of me before. Why should you start now?"

"I've always taken care of you!" he said indignantly, his voice rising.

Rising, I reached out for him. "Not at Belle Fourche," I said, "or at Montpelier, where you left me alone in the woods all day." And then, defiantly, I added, "And there's no reason for you to start now."

He looked a little shamefaced about his outburst. "I . . . Butch . . . he thinks I have to stay in the woods with you."

"It will take two people to hold the horses," I said. "Maybe it's your turn."

"But why not . . . why not Kilpatrick or Maxwell? I wouldn't want you to stay in the woods with Curry, but . . ."

I didn't point out to him that what he'd just said represented some kind of double standard—he didn't want to be responsible for me, but he wanted to decide who I would be with and who I wouldn't. Instead, I said, "That's up to Butch. You better ask him. I truly don't want to stay in the woods either, but I'll do what Butch says." And then I crawled back into bed and turned my back on him.

Sundance slept far away from me that night.

We spent one more night at Hole-in-the-Wall, Sundance and me in our tent, and the others scattered around in smaller tents. Still angry at me, Sundance spoke little and stayed away at night. I lay on my back, wide awake, my thoughts jumping from train robberies to longing for San Antonio and safety and back again to Sundance and Butch.

"Sundance?" I turned toward him and let my hand trail down his back—which was the side he presented to me.

He reached a hand behind him and swatted impatiently at my hand, as though telling me to stop, delivering a loud and clear message that he would not be seduced.

"Sundance," I said slowly, "we're going to be riding with those others for a long time. Not much privacy." My hand ventured back, this time tracing the ridge formed by his side and moving on down to his outer thigh.

"That's all right," he said gruffly, but he stirred a little, and I moved my hand back up his leg and side and over onto his stomach, reaching down from there. He moaned softly and stirred again but refused to turn toward me. By then my own need for him was growing, and I moved so that I pressed against him, so that he could feel the stirring of my body. My hands moved over him.

With a groan, he turned toward me. "You've trapped me," he whispered. "I . . . I can't deny you, even when I want to."

I nearly laughed aloud. Truth was, I guess, that we were bound to each other, whether by love, or passion, or some indefinable combination of the two. But it would have been the wrong time to laugh. His mouth was on mine, working, and as his hands moved none too gently over my body, I met his every move with needs of my own.

We were slow leaving our tent the next morning, which earned us sly, knowing glances from Maxwell and Kilpatrick, disgust from Curry, and a look of real concern from Butch. I gave him a sort of half-smile, by which I meant to say that everything was all right.

He understood. "We shoulda been gone an hour ago," he said gruffly. "You ready?" He looked furiously at Sundance, who just nodded at him.

"I'm ready too," I said, though no one had asked me.

We rode out through the notch and turned almost directly south, riding at a leisurely pace. The sun was warm on my back, and pretty soon I felt dirty, like I wanted to bathe and eat fresh fruit and dabble my feet in the creek. Instead, we kept up a steady pace for almost four hours and then stopped only to drink water from our canteens and eat the biscuits and jerky I'd packed the night before.

Sundance studiously ignored me, not wanting, I suppose, to be accused of favoring me. Curry ignored me too, but it was different, and Maxwell watched me as though waiting for me to fall from my horse in a dead faint. Their looks only made me stiffen my spine and plaster a smile on my face.

Butch was the only one of the five with a natural response to having me ride with them. Every once in a while—not too often—he'd ask, "You all right, Etta?" And when I'd nod, he'd go back to the lead, where he rode as casually and unconcerned as though he were headed to a picnic. Well, maybe he was—his kind of picnic.

Nightfall found us near the Wilcox stop, and Butch seemed to know the lay of the land. Farther north, we had crossed a good-sized gully, and I remembered that there was a trestle bridge just before the spot they planned to stop the train. We must, I figured, be on the west side of the gully, and it must've gotten much deeper as it headed south.

Butch led us at a slow walk into a grove of trees, where to my astonishment two men waited with six fresh horses. The men all howdyed, though I was distinctly left out of that ceremony, and then without much talk the two I didn't know put the horses we'd ridden on lead strings and disappeared into the woods.

Butch studied all of us for a minute, then said, "Cold camp. More corn dodgers and jerky and water. Sundance, you come with me."

Sundance threw me a look that clearly said, "See? I don't have to watch over you every minute."

Left alone with one man I barely knew, one I despised, and one I liked but didn't know well, I unpacked the food, such as it was, and unrolled my sleeping bag.

"You planning on sleeping?" Maxwell asked in disbelief.

"For a little while," I said calmly. When Butch and Sundance came back, I was asleep and only dimly aware of their talk and of Sundance's nudging me with his foot.

"Let 'er sleep," Butch said.

"Well, hell," growled Maxwell, "she's gonna have to get used to going without sleep damn quick. Tomorrow will be a hard ride."

"She's tough," Sundance said. "She'll do just fine."

I held his words close as I drifted back to sleep. Sundance would never say that to my face. I didn't even care that I heard Curry mutter, "She's a whore," and Butch warn, "Sundance, let it be."

That foot nudged me again; this time more seriously. "Come on, Etta. Time to get up."

When you sleep in your clothes, can't make coffee, don't have any way to wash your face, there's not much to making your "toilette." After a trip to the bushes, I brushed at my hair sort of hopelessly, jammed my hat on my head, and rolled up my blanket. "I'm ready," I muttered, surprised at myself that I'd slept so well.

"Here we go," Butch said, flicking open his watch. "You all keep those horses quiet, and be ready."

So Sundance and I stood, holding the reins of three horses each, hands ready to clap over their noses if there was a sound. We waited . . . and waited.

"What's happening?" I asked softly, but Sundance just put a finger to his lips and shook his head. As if men on a train would hear my whisper all that distance away! I wanted to kick him, but that indeed might have alarmed the horses.

At long last I heard a train in the distance. I almost held my breath as it came closer, the sound growing ever louder, and then we saw over the tops of the trees the red flare that meant distress on the tracks. The noise of the train changed dramatically—there was the squeal of brakes, the banging of cars into each other, the hissing of the steam as it was released.

For a long time after that we heard nothing. I looked at Sundance, but he seemed unconcerned. Then loud voices drifted toward us, angry shouting, and distantly I could hear pounding, men were pounding on the railroad cars, demanding entrance. Two shots rang out in fairly rapid succession, and I held my breath.

"Sundance?"

He only shook his head, though I could tell by the way he listened that he was paying much more attention now.

240

Then there were two explosions, one fairly soon after the other. Later I would learn that they had in rapid succession blown open the mail car and then, seeing the second section of the train approach, had blown up the trestle bridge. Then there were train sounds again—the train was moving! To be sure, it was slow and laborious, but where was it going if Butch and the others were not back with us?

"Follow me," Sundance said, and, listening carefully to the sound, he led me and the horses a little to the west. When he was satisfied we were opposite the train again, we stopped. "Mount up," he said.

"What?" My voice grew almost shrill with tension.

He gave me a disgusted look as he swung up on one of the horses. "Mount up," he repeated.

I did as he said. More loud voices could be heard, and then suddenly it grew quiet. Far in the distance I could hear shouting—the train people on the second section, I supposed, now stranded on the other side of the gully.

Then Butch, Maxwell, and Kilpatrick came walking into the clearing, Butch carrying a canvas bag, which he threw across the saddle of one horse. With no words and no time lost, they mounted and we rode out to the north. I would have thought we'd have ridden at breakneck speed, but we didn't. We kept a good, steady pace, but we never put the horses into a run, and we were miles from the train before anyone spoke.

"Probably close to fifty thousand," Butch said softly.

Sundance whistled. "No trouble?"

"Wouldn't have been if Curry hadn't taken a notion to beat the engineer," Maxwell said in disgust.

"He wouldn't move fast enough," Curry said, with almost a whine in his voice.

It was finally breaking daylight, and when I looked at Curry I saw that he was splattered with red. So were Maxwell and Kilpatrick. "You're hurt," I said. "We've got to stop." I started to rein my horse, but Butch, riding next to me, reached over to stop my hand.

"Raspberries," he said. "They blew up a damn load of raspberries in that freight car."

Sundance hooted, and even I giggled. The three stained men rode looking straight ahead, trying to ignore us.

After we'd ridden several hours, we came to a tree-sheltered creek. As if by magic, six horses waited there. With quiet efficiency, the men took saddles from the horses they now rode, saddled the fresh horses, and mounted again. Sundance helped me, so that I wouldn't slow them down, and I didn't. But just as we remounted, Butch held up a hand, and we all stopped. Each man sat still in the saddle, not moving, and though I heard nothing, almost in unison they said, "Posse!" They apparently could hear thundering hooves that I could not, not having trained myself to listen.

"Damn," Sundance muttered, while Butch said, "They shouldn't have been able to get a posse across that gully that fast. Let me think a minute."

"Let's ride," Curry said, while Sundance, almost viciously, told him to shut up.

"We'll take a stand here," Butch said, motioning his head to the other side of the creek. "In those trees. Shoot the horses, *not* the men. I don't want no killing. Etta you ride on in the direction we been going and don't stop until one of us catches up with you."

"But—" I began to protest.

"Do as I say," he said evenly, and I did, throwing a look at Sundance as I rode away. He did the unbelievable: He winked at me. I kept that wink with me for comfort.

It seemed only minutes before I heard shots, and I had to force myself to keep riding, though I stole backward glances now and then. I had ridden out of the trees that sheltered that creek and was on typical Wyoming land, brown and bare with no shelter. If a posse came after me, I decided, I'd simply stop, even if it meant being sent back to Texas. With such irrational thoughts flying through my mind, I rode on. The shots continued forever, though growing dimmer in sound—how many times could they reload?—and then there was silence. I looked again, saw nothing, and kept riding, with no idea now how far away from them I was.

To this day, I swear it was hours before they caught up with me. Sundance always said it was less than thirty minutes. But when they came, it was only Butch and Sundance. My first thought, of course, was the worst—even if I despised Curry, I didn't want to hear that he'd been killed. And the Tall

Texan—I really liked him. Still, what mattered was that Butch and Sundance were riding toward me. The only other important fact I noted was that Butch still had the canvas sack. I knew they hadn't stopped to divide their take.

They rode abreast without a word, and Sundance slapped my horse to kick him up to the speed they were maintaining. Now we rode too hard to talk, and I was left with a thousand questions going through my brain. All I knew was that they looked grim.

We must have been nearly to Casper—or so it seemed to me—when we came to a rancher's shack. Butch slowed his horse.

"Etta needs food, and so do we. We gotta stop."

"What're you going to do?" Sundance asked. "Explain nicely that we're tired, 'cause we're running from a posse, and could we please have something to eat?"

Butch ignored him. "It's a bachelor pad, no women there."

"Oh, swell," Sundance said, "now you're reading signs. How do you *know* there's no women there?"

"It plain ain't kept up good enough. If there's a woman, she's not much of one. Etta, you wait here. Come on, Sundance."

I was so tired of being told wait here, ride there, that I wanted to scream, but I waited and watched, though it was dusk now and difficult for me to make out what was happening. I heard Sundance shout, "Hallo the house!" but then I couldn't make out what was happening, except a horse and rider left in a great hurry. Butch waved me in.

"Gentlemen decided he didn't like our company," Sundance said. "Means he's headed for the law, and we can't stay long. Let's see what's to eat."

The bachelor, whoever he was, wasn't much of a cook, but there was a day-old pot of beans, cans of sardines and tomatoes and peaches, and bread so hard you had to sop it into the bean juice to be able to chew it. We ate as though we were in Brown's Palace in Denver.

While we ate, I slowly learned that they'd split up to make it harder for a posse, that Kid Curry had shot a sheriff named Hazen at the creek, in spite of all that Butch said about shooting only horses, not men. And that smokeless powder had saved their lives.

"Smokeless powder?" I echoed stupidly.

"Yeah," Sundance said, "posse can't tell where you're shooting from. Always before, they'd see that puff of smoke—they'd wait for it, the bastards—and then they'd shoot you. This new stuff, they can't tell exactly where we are."

"Doesn't the posse have smokeless powder?" I asked innocently.

"Naw," he said, "only the bad guys." But then he added, "So far."

"Man probably deserved it more than the horse," I murmured.

"Thanks a lot, Etta," Sundance said. "I nearly get killed, and you're on the side of the horses." But he was grinning as he said it, and he planted a swift kiss on my nose.

"For Pete's sake," Butch complained, "we got a lot to worry about, more than whether she's on your side or the horse's." But his anger was at Sundance, not me.

"Can't we . . . couldn't we just sleep for an hour?" I asked.

Butch shook his head. "Nope. He'll be back, bringing the law with him."

Sundance grabbed my arm almost roughly. "Come on, Etta, you wanted to ride with outlaws. Now you got no choice."

I kicked him, hard, just between his knee and the top of his boot. When he let out a yowl, I said, "Just be glad I didn't aim higher."

We rode fast again, though I could tell the horses were tiring. When it began to rain, a hard rain, Sundance let out a loud "Damn!"

"Now what?" I asked over the noise of the storm.

"Mud," he shouted back. "Makes it easier to track."

"Maybe," I said, "the rain will wash away the trail."

"Not with our luck so far," Butch countered.

I think then I realized that I was really, truly about to become a fugitive, in a way that I never had been in Texas.

Chapter Twenty-two

"We didn't want to hurt anyone," Butch said, shaking his head in puzzlement, "but that damn fool clerk . . . he wouldn't open the door."

"You coulda made a little more noise," Sundance said. "We could barely hear all that shouting and pounding."

"Wonder they didn't hear it clear to Casper," Butch said.

We were camped—a cold camp, naturally, with no fire—under a grove of trees, somewhere in western Wyoming. Butch had said we could sleep the night, and I could barely keep my eyes open to hear the story he told. And yet I wanted to know. I curled into my bedroll and listened to the two of them without saying a word.

Butch went on. "Fireman and engineer, they were all right men. We laughed and joked with them, told 'em we didn't mean no harm to anyone, even asked 'em for tobacco."

"And they gave it out of the goodness of their hearts," Sundance said. "Your guns had nothing to do with it."

"I wouldn't shoot a man for a plug of tobacco!" Butch said indignantly.

"I'm sure they felt reassured by that" was the reply.

"Curry, though," Butch said, "he didn't think the engineer moved fast enough, started beatin' him on the head with his rifle butt."

"Nice," Sundance murmured. "What'd you do?"

"Told him to stop," Butch said simply. "Don't see no reason for beating up folks."

"We heard shots," Sundance prompted.

"Yeah." Butch's voice had a chuckle in it. "I shot out the water tower. Figured that'd get their attention. But then we did have to blow the door off the freight car. The messenger just wouldn't open the door, no matter how many guns we told him we had pointed at him. So we blew it up . . . kind of overdid it, 'cause it just crumpled the whole car. Guess we used too much dynamite. That's when we got into the raspberries."

"The messenger?" I asked.

"Had to help him from the car, but he was all right. Fightin' mad, though."

"Well," Sundance drawled, "you'll surely be remembered in these parts for blowing up the trestle bridge. It'll take them a month of Sundays to build that thing again, and meantime, no trains can go through."

Butch grinned like a mischievous child, delighted in his handiwork. After all, no one had been seriously hurt.

"The money?" I asked.

"Well, look who's awake after all," Sundance said. "Don't worry, Etta, I'll get my share."

I considered kicking him again—higher. "I didn't mean that," I protested. I wanted to claim my own share, not just Sundance's, but I decided I'd best let that be for the time being. "I just wanted to know if it was worth all the trouble—all those extra horses hidden around and people to bring them to you and. . . ." My voice trailed off.

"It was worth it," Butch assured me, "it surely was. Now, Etta, you go on and get some sleep."

They sat in silence, and within seconds I was asleep. I awoke, however, minutes—or hours?—later to hear them talking softly.

"First train was pretty good, Butch, but we can't keep doing this. Our luck's going to run out."

"Yeah," Butch said, "and I'm feeling old. This ride this time, it's wore me out." He paused a minute. "And Etta, she can't do this too often."

I wanted to sit up and tell them that I could do whatever they could, but I was in one of those deep sleeps where you can hear around you and yet you can't will yourself to wake up.

"I think we ought to go to South America," Sundance said.

"You may be right," Butch answered. "We ought to think on it."

"You're damn right, we ought to," Sundance said with a vehemence I didn't expect. "I just am not ready to die."

And I was not ready for any of us to die.

Running, none of us knew that the railroad was offering $2,000 per outlaw, dead or alive, and the U.S. government matched that with an offer of $1,000 apiece. And then the Pinkertons got into it. They didn't know about me, and there was no price on my head, but there might as well have been.

I suppose if we'd known about the reward money, we might have been really frightened. As it was, we were only tired, dirty, and hungry but never frightened. Oh, maybe we were sobered. Of course, we didn't go to South America. We went all over the state of Wyoming, until I began to be grateful it wasn't as big as Texas. We even went back to Hole-in-the-Wall one night, creeping in under a cloud-covered sky. It probably was watched, but it was home to us, and we took our chances. Besides, on a practical level, it was the one place they'd all meet to divide the money Butch still carried in a canvas belt around his waist. It obviously bothered him, for as we rode I'd see him hitch and pull at it. When we finally stopped, I had to doctor the raw places that belt had rubbed in his flesh.

"Why are we creeping into our own place?" I asked, tired and angry.

" 'Cause nothin' would keep the law out of here if they thought we'd come back. We're just bankin' on their figurin' we wouldn't be that dumb."

"We may," Sundance said, "be dumber than any of us thought."

The cabin was undisturbed, but we hadn't been there ten minutes before Curry approached on foot. "Been waitin' for you," he said. "Got here yesterday. Begun to think I'd got the day wrong—or you'd forgotten." Irony laced his voice.

"We wouldn't do that, Curry, and you know it." Butch's voice was calm. "Annie with you?" he asked.

"Out in the woods," he said, nodding his head toward the outside.

Maxwell and Kilpatrick drifted in a little later. Seems they'd all three been hiding in the woods around, waiting for us to show up—well, waiting for Butch to show up with the money. By then, he had it in a sack in his saddlebags. He brought that sack in and plunked it on the table, and I left. Wasn't my business to make a fuss about my share in front of Curry.

I went to find Curry's tent and have a reunion with Annie. She looked no different to me than she had in San Antonio— pretty in a sort of hard way, and very much in control.

"I thought I might see you here," she said, and then her tone took on a bit of archness. "Harry tells me you and Sundance and Butch are inseparable." I detected—what? I didn't know— maybe envy, maybe curiosity.

"We're close," I said, "but not inseparable. Are you . . . are you getting along all right?"

Now her tone was outright defiance, no question about it. "Yeah, I'm fine. Harry's good to me, and he's gonna bring in a lot of money one of these days."

She had been half facing me, and now, as she turned, hands on hips, I thought there was a bluish mark on one cheek. I looked away quickly, so as not to stare. It struck me that she never referred to Curry by that name—the full name being Kid Curry, his outlaw moniker—but always called him by his Christian name. Was she, I wondered, trying to pretend he wasn't an outlaw?

We didn't really have much to say to each other beyond that. There were the expected questions: "You heard from Fannie?" "No, have you?" "Where are you going now?" "I don't know. You?" But it was not much of a conversation, and neither the shared experience of Fannie's or life on the outlaw trail gave us much basis for friendship.

One thing Annie said left me with the impression that she was jealous, less of me than of the relationship between Butch and Sundance. She considered Sundance kind of a second-in-command, and she clearly thought Curry should have that position. All she said was, "Harry's good at planning jobs. Butch ought to bring him more into the planning."

I didn't tell her that I thought "Harry" was trouble and would be the downfall of all of them. I went back to our tent.

Sundance woke me when he came in much later. "Almost ten thousand dollars," he whispered in my ear.

"Good," I said. "That's five thousand for me."

"For you?" His voice rose into a yelp, like that of an angry puppy.

I was awake now. "I rode, I did my part, and I should get my share," I said firmly.

"It's our share, Etta. Ours." He stretched out the last word.

"Is it twice what everyone else got?" I demanded.

He stared at me in disbelief. Finally he shook his head. "No, it's not. You . . . you better take that up with Butch."

I would, I thought, but not when Sundance expected it. Meantime, I asked, "Can we go to the Brown's Hotel?"

"Not for a while," Sundance said. "We got to ride early in the morning."

"I know," I said with resignation. "I wanted to sleep all day."

"You do that, and we might spend the next thirty years of our lives in jail," he said patiently. "There's still posses out there. We got to get out of this country."

"All right," I said, "tomorrow."

"Got some good news for you." He poked me awake again with his elbow. "Curry's gone."

"He'll be back," I predicted softly, adding under my breath, "and Annie too."

"Naw, not for a long time. Butch told him we wouldn't be riding together. Said there was no cause to beat that engineer and shoot Sheriff Hazen in the belly, and he didn't want any part of that violence."

That woke me up again, and a vision of Annie telling me how smart "Harry" was flashed through my mind. "What did Curry do?"

"Got real mad. I thought, seeing as how Butch is opposed to violence, I was going to have to take his place and defend him. Curry took a stand, like he was going for his gun—only, he wasn't wearing it. But he was . . . I think *belligerent* is the word you'd use."

"Is he gone?"

"Yeah, he rode out."

"Good for Butch," I said, and turned over to go back to sleep.

"How about 'good for you, Sundance'? After all, I saved Butch." His voice had a slight whine in it.

"I'm sure you did," I said, patting his arm slightly. We both knew Butch would have saved himself, but I didn't want to have to say that. As I drifted off to sleep, I could feel Sundance pouting next to me. I patted his arm again, and next thing I knew he was nudging me awake.

"It's time to go," he said.

No coffee, just water and hard biscuits for breakfast. As we rode away, I thought with longing of all the meals I'd cooked in that cabin, all the good food we'd eaten, and I wondered when we'd ever sit down to a meal again, the three of us together and not running from the law.

Maxwell and Kilpatrick were gone, having left, I guess, earlier than Sundance made me wake up. Once again it was Butch, Sundance, and me. "Where're we going?" I asked.

"Fellow we know has a ranch on a little creek," Sundance said, "with some great caves in the cliffs above the creek."

"Caves?"

"Etta, we can't hardly stay at the Brown's Palace right now. We got to hide out for a while."

"Where is it?" I asked wearily, hoping it was close by.

"West," Butch said.

I stared at the sun, just now rising in the sky—the sun we were indirectly heading toward. "Then why're we heading east?"

Sundance threw his hands up in exasperation. "We're never going to make a passable outlaw of you. Part of being an outlaw is that you have to do it the hard way. Can't go directly anywhere. Got to go the roundabout way."

"We're headed east," I repeated stubbornly. "Will we get there tonight?"

"Nope," Butch said. "Not tomorrow night, either."

It took us four days, and the only good things I could think of were that it had stopped raining and the weather was pleasant—not so warm in the day to make riding uncomfortable and not so cool in the evening to make me resent the slim bedroll I had with me.

We finally came to some man's ranch in the foothills of the Big Horns. I never did see anyone there, but fresh horses waited for us. We moved our pitiful bedrolls from tired horses to new ones and rode on. No rest, no food, though we did take with us some meat pie, fresh biscuits, and canned goods that had been left for us.

"Why was there no one at that ranch to see to the change in horses?" I asked.

"Man doesn't want to compromise himself. This way, he can always tell the law we rode in and stole the horses while he was gone."

"Did we steal them?" I asked.

"Naw," Butch said, "I wouldn't steal from an honest rancher. We paid him good money."

We stopped for an hour or so twice in the night, but I was so tired that when the horses walked the next day, I dozed in the saddle. Once Sundance reached out a hand to steady me.

"Thought you were going to tumble right off," he said, sort of apologetically, as though I shouldn't think he doubted my horsemanship. Then, impishly, he asked, "Having a pleasant dream?"

"Yes," I said, "of Fannie's house and soft beds and clean sheets and Julie's cooking."

Sundance sobered. "That is a good dream," he agreed.

We moved from the Big Horn Basin to the Owl Creek Mountains, climbed a steep trail up a side canyon, and dropped down into the Wind River basin, all without stopping for more than an hour at a time but also, thankfully, all without seeing or hearing a posse. It was like we had that glorious land all to ourselves—only, I was too tired and hungry to relish the sensation.

Finally we came to the Burnbaugh ranch. "Where are we?" I asked.

"On the Casper-to-Lander stage road," Butch answered.

I wanted to cry. We had ridden days without food or sleep to go what should have been an easy half-day ride from Hole-in-the-Wall!

"Etta," Sundance said gently, "there's no one on our trail. If we'd come straight here, they'd have found us sure."

It was like the first ranch—I never saw the Burnbaughs, never met them, though we ate their food and, in some sense, enjoyed their hospitality.

251

Caves aren't half bad for sleeping . . . and that was all I did, all any of us did. We ate wonderful homemade food that was delivered twice a day by two young boys—one of them told it all to the law later—and we slept and sometimes sat on a ledge looking over Muddy Creek, though it didn't look that muddy to me. We talked softly about the future.

"Can we ever go back to Hole-in-the-Wall?" I asked.

Butch shrugged. "Maybe. But we ain't ever gonna live there in peace and quiet. I'm really thinkin' we'll go to South America." But a lot would happen before we ever went to South America.

After nearly a week at Burnbaugh's ranch, Butch declared it was time to move on—and to split up. "Our welcome's wearing out," he said. "Can't expect them to feed us forever. Went down there last night, and Burnbaugh tells me Pinkerton's fellow—what's his name? Siringo or somethin'—he was here, nosin' around. He left, but he'll be back."

I'd noticed that Butch left for a while in the dark of the night and even wondered if he'd dared go into Lander to see his Mary. For all I knew, he might have done that as well as visiting with Burnbaugh.

"I don't ever want to move—I like living in a cave," I said lazily, for I was rested and well fed and content.

Then, suddenly, Butch said, "I'm going to Los Angeles . . . by way of Seattle."

We both stared at him.

"Seattle," Sundance said. "You ever thought about going by way of New York?"

Butch paused to consider the possibility. Then he shook his head. "Naw, not this time. I'm gonna ride over to Montana, take a train to Seattle, and hire on a steamer down to Los Angeles."

"Why?" I asked incredulously.

"Never been there," he said with a shrug, "and I doubt Pinkerton's will be looking for me in those places—they'll expect me to be on a horse, not a ship. I'll meet you in San Antonio in . . . oh, let's say January."

"January? This is only July," I said in disbelief. Butch gone for six months? "Sundance?"

He looked at me solemnly. "No, we're not going . . . for a lot of reasons."

Later, when we were alone, he explained the reasons to me, the prime one being that this odyssey was something Butch needed to do alone. "Breathing time," he said, "and maybe we need that too."

I wondered at the two of them wanting to be shed of each other—or was it that they needed not to be together with me? Did they need to break up our threesome? That line of thinking got so tangled, I simply put it behind me and refused to look at it again.

"Besides," Sundance went on, "I'm not spending our money to traipse around the country. Butch'll be alone, he can work his way. And I've got a different philosophy than he does—I think if we lie low, someplace out of the way, we'll be fine. In six months, we can go on with . . ."

"With robbing banks and trains?" I asked.

"We don't have that many robberies in us," he said, and for the first time I noticed the weariness in his voice. He wasn't just tired from running this time—he was bone-deep weary, the kind that builds over a long time. And this time, it built from being on the outside of the law.

"No money?" I asked. "We just robbed a train, and by your own admission *our* share was close to ten thousand dollars."

"Oh, yeah, but we can't spend it, least not for a while, not around here."

"Can't spend it?" We had gone through hell to get and keep $10,000 we couldn't spend! I was beside myself.

"It's in banknotes, traceable."

"Do you think," I asked sarcastically, "that you can spend them sometime in the next thirty years?"

He grinned. "Maybe. In South America."

There it was again—South America, looming ever larger in my future. I knew in my bones that they would go . . . and I would go with them.

Butch left us two days later. Somehow I remembered that outlaws weren't sentimental, and if that was true, I reasoned, their women shouldn't be either. But I was hard put not to cry when Butch put an arm around me, squeezed tight, and whispered, "We'll all three be together again soon, Etta, you watch and see."

To Sundance, he said, "Don't rob no trains without me . . . and, Sundance, you take care o' her." He nodded his head in my direction.

"I thought she was supposed to take care of me," Sundance said, with a perfect tone of bewilderment. "Damn! I got it wrong again."

"You sure did," Butch said, and rode off without looking back.

I was silent for three hours, until finally Sundance said, "Aren't you going to talk the whole time he's gone?"

"I will," I said, "when I've got something to say."

He chewed silently on that for a long time as we rode south to Robbers Roost, our hideout for the summer. We rode more slowly now, without the sense that we were always outrunning a posse.

"You sure Pinkerton's man isn't behind us?" I asked, not really concerned.

"I've been watching our back trail," he said, "and there's no one there. I suspect that Siringo fellow is still combing Wyoming. And he's looking for Butch mostly—and for sure not a man and a woman on a leisure ride."

"You mean that's all there was to it? We should have left Wyoming right away, instead of riding all over the damn state." I was astounded. All that riding . . . and if we'd just headed south into Colorado, or . . .

"Next time," he said with a grin, "we'll let you plan the getaway." Then he shrugged. "We did what we thought was smart, what's always worked before. Just didn't work this time."

"Next time," I said, "I'm going to pay more attention to your plans."

"Good. We can use the help." His voice dripped with sarcasm.

We rode for days, sometimes making little progress in a day, crossing rocky, barren country, sleeping at night in our bedrolls by the ashes of our campfire. But we felt safe enough to cook over early-evening fires, to stop and wash clothes and bathe in creeks—where we sometimes ended in splashing fights—and even twice to ride into small towns for supplies.

"Saw Butch's face on a poster in the general store," Sundance said after one such stop. "Didn't favor him at all. He'd be really angry if he saw how they'd drawn him."

The Roost was the one stop on the outlaw trail where I hadn't been, but I wasn't the least bit curious. It couldn't be as grand as Hole-in-the-Wall, and I wouldn't have my cabin with my spring garden, all my cooking things, my clothes. It wouldn't be home, but it would, Sundance told me, be safe.

High in the desert country of eastern Utah, the Roost was like Hole-in-the-Wall only in that it had rocky canyons and ridges, but it spread out over a much larger territory. If there were more ways in and out—and there were, it seemed to me, a thousand slick rocks and steep slopes of sandstone and hidden trails—the danger of that was offset by the wild remoteness of the place and the maze of canyons, buttes, mesas, and sandrock slopes. Left alone, I would have been hopelessly lost within an hour. I firmly believed Sundance when he said no lawman could find us once we were deep within and few wanted to try.

Like Hole-in-the-Wall, it was rugged country and beautiful in its own way, with deep red sandstone colors dominating and sky overhead so clear and bright you could see forever from the top of a cliff. But it was inescapable desert.

"We'll drop down the rockslide into Millard," Sundance told me, "then follow the Green to Sunset Pass and Poison Springs Canyon. . . . That's where we'll camp."

"Camp? In a place called Poison Springs Canyon?"

"It's the freshest, purest water you'll ever drink," he said, "and yes, we're camping in a tent. I don't know anybody's got an empty cabin there, but there'll be a good-sized tent waiting for us in some trees. You'll like it." He added the last thought almost belligerently, as though daring me *not* to like it.

"I'll like it," I said softly. Then, more boldly, "But I'd like to bathe every once in a while."

"In the spring," he said. "You can bathe every day."

Curiously I asked, "How do you know there'll be a tent?"

"I set it up with someone long time ago—outlaw communication, you might say."

We came, late one afternoon, out of the canyons onto a narrow point of land that seemed shoved out over that maze of buttes and mesas. The canyon walls all around us were shades of red and gold, from deep, sunburned tan to tawny orange and, near the tops of the mesas, bands of creamy white. But beyond us, across the canyons, was purple desert that rose to meet a set of blue mountains, so clear in that high-country air that I thought I could reach them in minutes.

"It's a long ride," Sundance said, reading my mind.

"How do you know this place?"

"It was Butch's home country once upon a time," he answered, and I thought it strange that we were here and Butch was on his way to sea.

I looked south this time and saw canyons and ridges cut back into grassy flats.

"That's where we're going," Sundance said.

We actually camped on somebody's land, in those grassy flats that turned out to be mostly bunch grass and hard grazing for the horses. All around us those brilliant colored cliffs rose steep and sharp, and I truly believed that no one could ever find us, let alone get to us.

I never met the rancher who owned the land we were on. Sundance called him Rimrock, and I sensed that they were acquaintances. He raised horses, and a good-sized herd watered at a nearby hole that Sundance referred to as Crow Seep. Sundance and I would watch them sometimes when they approached the water. Filled, they would look for soft spots to roll in and try to find bunches of grass to graze. They were wild, though, and the least sound spooked them. We had to keep our horses tied, for they much wanted to run off and join the herd.

"Instinct," he said. "Every animal wants to be in the midst of a large number of its own kind."

We spent our days wandering, mostly on foot, and doing lots of target shooting. "If you plan to ride with us more," Sundance said, "you've got to practice shooting. You were pretty good at Hole-in-the-Wall, but by now you'll be rusty."

He was right about my being rusty. He was also a relentless teacher, and I shot a rifle until my shoulder ached, my eyes blurred, and I swore at him. But I kept practicing, and within a couple of weeks my aim was acceptable to Sundance.

"It'll get better," he said, "and you'd be fine if whoever you're shooting at will stand still and wait until you get it aimed just right."

So we worked on fast shooting—with the rifle, with the shotgun, and with a small handgun he'd bought for me.

Nights we spent loving and exploring each other, physically and mentally. In almost three years together, we had never had such a long period alone, especially when we were not tensely waiting for Butch to return or some other event to move our lives forward. And we had never been without Butch this long. In that lazy summer, I almost convinced myself that I loved Sundance, not Butch.

But there was a part of me that was not at ease. I wasn't sure—it wasn't fear of the law, for I felt quite sure that no one would find us in the Roost. No, it was something else.

"You miss Butch?" he asked one afternoon as we dangled our feet in Poison Creek and watched a hawk circling above something that was evidently darting across the flats.

I thought about my answer for a minute and realized that was the part of me that was missing. Slowly, I said, "Of course I miss him. He's a part of us. But you were right about breathing space. It's good for us to be apart from the others—for us to be just . . . well, alone."

"Yeah," he said, "that's what Butch told me."

His words went through me like a knife, though I knew he didn't mean that. But his comment told me, clearly, that Butch, not Sundance, had known that we needed time alone. I had thought we would never be closer than we were right that minute—and suddenly there was a gulf between us, another chasm that would have to be crossed. Sundance never realized it.

I crossed that chasm, as I had several others, without ever letting Sundance know what was going through my mind. He loved me, I reasoned, to the best of his ability, but he was a man used to the company of other men. And I was a woman in love with two men.

Sundance began to wonder about Butch, about Pinkerton, about news of the world—and of other outlaws. He rode to the Biddlecombes—that was the mysterious Rimrocker's last name—twice a week now, and finally one day reported that he was going to ride to the small town of Hanksville for supplies and news.

"You want to come with me?" He fully expected me to leap at the chance.

I shook my head, unwilling to let the outside into my small, private world.

"I'll be gone overnight," he warned, sure now that I would change my mind.

I shook my head again. "I'll be fine."

"I'll tell Biddlecombe you're here alone," he said as he left.

I stood and watched him ride away, saw him turn once to wave, and wondered when I would last watch him ride away, knowing I'd never see him again. "Not this time," I told myself sharply, straightening a little as though that way I could get a grip on myself. I had brought one book with me—Mark Twain's *Huckleberry Finn*—and I spent the next twenty-four hours reading, washing clothes, and cleaning our campsite. *Huckleberry Finn* made me thoughtful: Where did one draw the line between Huck Finn and the Sundance Kid? How did one go from being a wild and rebellious youngster to being an outlaw? I was no closer to an answer when Sundance rode in late the next day, hollering "Hallo the camp!"

"You don't need to do that," I said, and laughed. "Nobody but you would come riding in here."

"Don't know about that," he said seriously. "That Siringo's been pretty busy." He dismounted and began pulling things out of his saddlebags—canned peaches and tomatoes, a bit of tobacco, a bottle of whiskey, some coffee.

"Oh?" I asked.

"Tell you later," he said, but I could see from his face that the news he'd heard in Hanksville had not been good. Later turned out to be the middle of the night when we lay comfortably in each other's arms, though neither of us was ready to sleep.

"They caught Elzy," he said suddenly, out of nowhere. We'd been talking of South America and the ranch we'd own there, and had, for a moment, put the present away from us. With his statement, it came crashing back.

I drew my breath in sharply. "Elzy?" I repeated, remembering his devotion to that proper Mormon wife I never met and the big gentle smile that always came over Elzy's face when he talked about his wife and daughter.

"Yeah, he and Ketcham robbed a train in New Mexico—at Folsom—and they both got shot. Got away at the time, but

Ketcham died of blood poisoning, and Elzy got caught . . . last month, August."

I was silent. There didn't seem to be anything to say.

"This Siringo fellow chased Curry's all over Arkansas, but I heard he's back in Wyoming now and Curry's still on the run someplace, maybe even Nashville."

Nashville surprised me. I couldn't imagine any of the Wild Bunch leaving the West. But I guess they did. After all, Butch went to California, didn't he? "Was Annie with him?" I asked.

Sundance's lifted shoulders indicated he didn't know and didn't care. "She knew what she was getting into," he said callously, and I wondered if he realized that others—Curry, even Butch—could with some justification be equally callous about me.

He was off in a different direction. "Some damn fool—got to be Maxwell or Kilpatrick—is spreading banknotes from Wilcox all over in Wyoming. That's why the Pinkerton guy is back up there." He sat up, moving so suddenly that I was almost tossed aside. "And no-good amateurs, people Butch wouldn't have a thing to do with, are robbing banks in his name. There's been two bank robberies since Butch went to Seattle, and they're both blamed on him." His anger was almost tangible.

"They're not leavin' us a damn choice," Sundance said angrily. "We'll have to go either to South America or to prison for the rest of our lives. And I, for one, would rather get shot in a shoot-out."

I bit my lip and turned away. It was obvious he really meant what he said, and for a fleeting moment—as though I were prescient—I saw a blazing gun battle in my mind.

Things did not look better in the morning, and we went silently about the business of cooking breakfast and making our camp as ready for the day as we ever did. Then Sundance suggested we ride, so we rode for several hours, without speaking a word.

Finally, with a wry look at me, he said, "Guess I'm sorry I went into town."

"So am I," I answered. "Who . . . how did you learn all that in Hanksville?"

"Outlaw communication again," he said. "General store kind of acts like a post office for information."

259

"Did they know who you are?"

He nodded. "Chance you always take. I guess I won't go again."

And he didn't, never again, the long months we stayed in the Roost.

We went to San Antonio for Christmas. Oh, Butch had said January, and Sundance repeated that to me. He actually said, "Butch said January."

"But," I protested, "he didn't say we couldn't go there sooner. That's just when he said he'd be there. Christmas would be a lot more . . . well, fun . . . at Fannie's than here in this lonely camp." The minute I said it I could've bitten my tongue.

"You're lonely?" he asked, and I could see the hurt on his face.

I fought for the right words. "No, I'm never lonely with you—but we'd have no Christmas tree, no big dinner, none of the things that make a holiday."

"Did you have them when you were little?" he asked.

I shook my head, and he put his arms around me. "We'll go in the middle of December," he said.

We sent Fannie a wire from Durango and took the train.

"Where'd we get the money for the train?" I asked pointedly. "I thought we didn't have any we could spend."

"I saved some back," he said, and then with a grin admitted, "Butch gave me some that wasn't from Wilcox. Still don't want to be spending that. Look how they followed poor Curry to Arkansas."

It made me glance nervously at other men in the car, but none looked like a Pinkerton agent. Then I laughed at myself: What did a Pinkerton agent look like? And, I wondered soberly, what was to stop Siringo from following us to San Antonio and Fannie's?

Fannie was as happy to see us as I ever saw her, closing the house on a weekend night for a celebration. "Not every day Etta comes home," she said by way of explanation to a houseful of girls I'd never met. I'd been gone two years exactly—it had been Christmas 1897 when we were last there—and the turnover was complete. Maud Walker was gone, I never knew where, and Annie was following Curry around. I would tell

Fannie about that later. Meanwhile, it struck me that it was pleasant to be back at Fannie's *without* Curry.

Hodge looked just a trifle older to me—maybe the hair was more gray, or the walk a bit slower. But he was nonetheless courtly as always. "Miss Etta, it's surely good to see you. Julie, she be cookin' up your favorite dishes."

"Chicken salad?" Sundance asked with a grin.

"Might be, Mr. Sundance, it just might be."

Dinner actually was leg of lamb with potatoes, peas and carrots, Julie's wonderful fresh bread, and a rich chocolate pudding for dessert. I ate like I'd never eaten before.

"You been feedin' this girl, Sundance?" Fannie asked, raising her eyebrows in amusement.

Fannie, Sundance, and I sat at a table covered with white linen. The glasses were fine crystal, the china imported Wedgwood, the flatware ornate sterling. The "girls" had eaten earlier and been sent, somewhat resentfully, to their rooms or to the parlor, the point being clearly made that this was a private party.

Sundance took it good-naturedly. "I tried, but I think she was getting tired of cooking over a campfire. She kept mentioning the Brown's Palace in Denver, and finally she threatened me that if we didn't come here for Christmas..." His voice trailed off.

"Just what was the threat?" Fannie persisted.

Sundance looked awkwardly at me, and I favored him with an expectant look. After all, he was the one who'd invented the threat, and now I was curious to hear what it was. The expected, of course, was that I wouldn't sleep with him unless and until he brought me to Fannie's, but Sundance well knew that I'd never make that threat—and he also knew that he was about to be in deep trouble if he even hinted at that.

"Well," he chuckled to lighten the tension, "she threatened to keep on doing all the cooking. What could I do?"

Fannie laughed heartily, saying, "I never claimed to have taught her to cook," and the moment passed.

Fannie and I didn't have a long, private visit until two days later, in the evening, when the parlor was full of noise and music and people, with Sundance in the midst of them, singing away, his arms about this girl and that. Fannie entered the room quietly and, with a tug on my sleeve, pulled me out of the room. Sundance never noticed.

"That bother you?" she asked as we settled in her private room. She hiked herself up onto the big bed, where she could sit propped against a thousand cushions, and I lay on the chaise, languorous from wine and a good dinner.

"No," I said truthfully. "He'll not look seriously at anyone else in this house."

"In this house?" she echoed, her voice a question.

I just looked at her. I wasn't about to tell her about Elko and his cheating, for Fannie would be quick to say, "I told you so."

She studied me for a long while without speaking, and I almost began to squirm under her scrutiny. Then, at last, she spoke. "The outlaw life still agrees with you. I'd have thought you'd have tired of it by now. Matter of fact, ever since I heard about Wilcox, I've been expecting you back."

"That was probably the worst of it," I said, "riding to get away from all those posses. But it's behind us . . . and Butch and Sundance, they're talking about quitting."

"Quitting! Man in that business can't ever quit. He either dies or goes to prison."

"Or to South America," I said.

Her eyes opened wide. "Would you go?"

I nodded yes.

She sat up straight, abandoning all those pillows so that she could look more directly at me. "Why? I really want to know. I . . . I know what drew Annie into that life—desperation and no other future. But you . . . you're educated, you could do a thousand things, and coming to work in this house is not one of them. But why do you follow him?"

It wasn't an easy question to answer, but Fannie waited patiently while I collected my thoughts. "Because I simply can't imagine life without Sundance . . . and Butch."

"Butch?" she asked archly.

"He's the best friend I've got, in a way that Sundance can't be, just because of the electricity between us. I won't say he's like a brother, because that's not quite true. I love him, but it's far, far different . . . and it's a mutual thing."

She seemed to think about that awhile. Then, "They could both be gone any day," she said tartly.

"I know that, and I . . . well, a tiny part of me is steeled to accept that if it happens. But I would never willingly give up what we have. And there's more than that . . . there's the excitement, of course. Maybe I thrive on the tension, even on the hard times. But there's that feeling of being outside the law— even if I were to go somewhere that no one knew me and become a respectable schoolteacher, I would always know that I was different, that I wasn't innocent like the children I was teaching. And I'd never be able to . . . well, to put my full weight down. With Sundance—and with Butch—I don't have to worry about acceptance or pretend to be something I'm not."

The talk went on to lighter things—the new girls she had, and how they just weren't like those of the old days. They wanted days off and this special privilege and that, and most saw Fannie's house as a step on the ladder, not a refuge from a worse life, as I had. Then there were Hodge and Julie—yes, Hodge was getting older, but Julie's cooking was as good as ever.

"I imagine," she chuckled, "Hodge'll still be answering that door when he's ninety-five years old, deaf, blind, and addle-pated. How could I ever let him go?"

Christmas came and went with Fannie's usual extravagant celebration, though this year I never felt it got off the ground. Somehow we were all solemn, in spite of José banging out "Silent Night, Holy Night" on the piano and Julie providing the best roast turkey I'd ever eaten in my life. Maybe it was because I'd been eating all that cold camp food in the Roost, but I relished every bite of that meal and told Julie so for three days afterward, until she finally said, "Hush, Miss Etta. You go on too much." I hushed.

Sundance was the one person who seemed to enjoy Christmas extraordinarily. There was a young whore—what else should I call her?—named Elise, or so she said, who hung on his every movement, stood next to him when he sang carols, laughed extravagantly when he had too much to drink and nearly set the tree on fire trying to light the candles. Sundance was by no means oblivious to her admiration . . . and I doubted he was immune to her lust. He cocked his head in her direction, watched to see if she was looking at him, smiled at her from beneath slightly lowered eyes—all the signs of a man flirting with a new woman.

I said nothing for days, waiting until Christmas was over. But I knew that Fannie was watching me. It wasn't a case where Fannie would rush in to discipline one of her girls, because the problem wasn't really with the girl. Sundance could have cut her off cold, and it would have been over. The problem was with Sundance—and I was the one who had to fix it.

The third night after New Year's Eve the parlor was unusually full of loud men and louder women, and I left early to go to bed. Sundance was in the midst of a gaggle of people, but Elise was never far from his elbow. With one look of disgust, which he never noticed, I went to our bedroom, where I propped myself up in bed and wondered what in heaven's name I would do if he went upstairs with Elise. Then I'd scold myself for being silly: Sundance would never do that. Not in Fannie's house. Just as quickly, the other side of my mind would take over, and I'd demand to know why I thought he'd never do that.

While I was in that turmoil, Fannie knocked and stuck her head in the door. "You still awake?"

"Couldn't sleep," I answered.

"I don't wonder," she said. "I couldn't either if I were you. What're you going to do about it?"

There was no use pretending I didn't know what she was talking about. "I don't know," I said. "I haven't the slightest idea. If that's what he wants—"

"It's not what he wants," she said fiercely, "but he doesn't need you to tell him that. He doesn't need you to treat him like a misbehaving child."

"That's what he is," I said petulantly.

She sat down heavily on the bed next to me. "I guess I didn't really raise you right, after all. Yes, he's a spoiled child, but you're not going to get anywhere by pointing that out to him."

"What am I supposed to do? Ignore the fact that he's falling all over a whore half his age?"

She bristled in indignation. "I don't like that word, Etta, and you know it." She was silent a long while, and I thought maybe it was her way of reprimanding me. But finally she said, "Let him know how much you love him. He'll know that what the two of you have is worth a lot more than a quick roll in the hay with that piece of baggage."

"Isn't that as bad as saying whore?" I asked.

She threw a pillow at me and left.

Sundance came in much later—but not late enough that he would have had time to go upstairs with Elise. I feigned sleep, and nearly giggled when I heard that he was singing "Auld Lang Syne" under his breath while he struggled to undo his shoes. I waited, keeping as quiet as I could, until he had finally removed his clothes and crawled into bed with me. Then I began the slow dance with my hands—up his spine and around onto his chest, down his belly, and onto his thighs, circling around until I finally touched his privates.

He moaned and squirmed, and then he muttered, "Don't, I've had too much too drink. I can't."

It was all I could do to keep from crowing, but I kept on loving, telling him that didn't matter, I just wanted him to know how much I loved him.

"You're jealous of Elise," he muttered thickly.

My every instinct was to pull back, but I didn't. I kept rubbing and stroking, and Sundance, in his poor, drunken state, muttered, "You know, Etta, I'd never look at another woman—not seriously anyway. She . . . she's young and pretty . . . but she's not you." He planted a wet kiss on my face and fell suddenly asleep.

In the middle of the night, Sundance awoke, and the effects of the alcohol had left him. As we panted together, I managed to murmur, "Elise?" and he said, none too gently, "Shut up."

Butch arrived three days later, and I was never so glad to see anyone in my life.

Chapter Twenty-three

Butch announced in July that we were going back to Wyoming for one last big robbery.

"Why Wyoming?" I asked. "There are trains and banks in Texas. Why go all the way back up there?"

With a shrug and a grin, he said, "Wyoming's home. Besides, there's all them imitators up there. We have to . . . uh, defend our reputation. Can't let 'em think we're responsible for all those botched jobs."

We'd heard of several senselessly brutal robberies—men killed after they'd turned over the money—and it bothered Butch a great deal to have his name attached to that kind of violence.

"Besides," Butch said, "the Union Pacific up there's been making a lot of noise about how they're now at the ready for trouble. No bandits are ever gonna catch them sleepin' again. I guess it's my pride, but I got to show them."

I laughed aloud, so hard that Sundance finally frowned at me. "You can stay here, Etta. We're . . . well, we probably can't go back to Hole-in-the-Wall."

Butch hooted. "No probably about it. They've got that place staked out night and day, even now. I am *not* going back there.

Now, if you two want to be foolishly sentimental . . ."

I threw a sofa pillow at him. If anyone was ever foolishly sentimental, it was Butch Cassidy.

Yet there was a surprising wrench in me when I thought about never seeing that cabin again. I didn't care about the clothes and things of mine that were still there. I'd put them behind, and I'd brought Mama's picture with me. But Hole-in-the-Wall was the place where I'd gone with great expectations of adventure and—why not?—wealth. My dreams were tarnishing more rapidly each day, and maybe I thought if we could go back to Hole-in-the-Wall, we could start all over again and things would go in a different direction. In my sane moments, I knew that wasn't true.

I studied on staying in San Antonio for several days, though I never did talk to Fannie about it and could only suppose that I would be welcome if I decided to stay. A big reason not to go with them: We would once again, most likely, ride all over Wyoming, grabbing an hour's sleep here and there, chewing on stale biscuits and always feeling the lump of hunger in our bellies.

But staying in San Antonio sounded . . . well, unsatisfactory. It wasn't that I thought I'd fall into the life and it wasn't that I cared if others thought that, but something was incomplete—the same feeling I'd lived with in the Roost. Oh, if I stayed in San Antonio, they'd come back for me . . . but things would never be the same. I wouldn't be part of both of them anymore.

"I don't want to stay here," I finally announced. "I want to go with the two of you."

"Of course you do. I never doubted it." With those words, Sundance pulled me to my feet and began to dance me around the room in grand, sweeping waltz steps that carried us the length of the parlor in three moves. Then his steps slowed and shrank, and soon we were clinging to each other, barely moving to unheard music.

"I'm going outside to ride my bicycle," Butch said in disgust, throwing a dirty look over his shoulder as he left. He'd found a used bicycle at a market one day and brought it home as proudly as though he were bringing $50,000 from a bank. After he'd painted and oiled it—with Hodge's help—he spent hours riding it through the streets of San Antonio. Then he looked at me just a moment. "I'm glad you're going, Etta," he said, and he was gone.

I wanted to call after him, to tell him it was as much him I didn't want to leave as Sundance. But Sundance was insistent on other things—and I wasn't ready to fight that battle.

We took the train to Denver and then rode north by horseback. It was an old, familiar routine by now and one that I was glad we wouldn't be repeating.

At night, around a small campfire—Butch said we weren't so desperate we needed to cold camp—they'd talk about how the West was changing. I'd fry beef we'd bought or trout they'd caught and put biscuits in a Dutch oven over the coals and listen silently to them.

"You can't disappear into the land anymore," Butch said, with real sadness in his voice.

"No," Sundance agreed, "the telephone and telegraph track you down, no matter where you go."

"It ain't like it used to be," Butch said again. "I been on the wrong side of the law some ten years now. Used to be it was fun—good to show them bankers and railroad men they weren't as invincible as they thought."

Every once in a while, Butch threw a big word—like *invincible*—into his otherwise everyday speech, and it always startled me.

"But now the fun's gone. They're houndin' a man to death. I . . . I'm gonna do this one last thing, and no more."

"You been in touch with Curry?"

Butch nodded. "He'll meet us two days out."

"I thought you wouldn't ride with Curry." I looked directly at Butch.

He never flinched. "We need him this last time, but I promise you, Etta, he won't hurt anyone."

Butch didn't know how wrong he was—or whom Curry would hurt.

"You got a plan?" Sundance asked, and Butch nodded.

When, I thought, *does Butch ever go into anything without a plan?*

He pulled a wrinkled map out of his pocket and spread it before him, and I elbowed right in between the two of them.

"Tipton," Butch said, pointing a stubby finger at Rawlins in southern Wyoming. "It's a coal station, out of the way, nobody around. And the train makes a long grade getting to it, so it has to be goin' slow."

"The getaway?" Sundance asked.

Butch's finger moved in a larger gesture. "South into Elk Basin and across to the Green River country in Utah. It'll be hard ridin', but we can do it if we stash fresh horses a couple of places." He looked up at me. "You ride that hard with us, Etta?"

I nodded and resisted the urge to remind him of the hard rides I'd already made. Proud as I was of being "one of the boys," a part of me liked the way Butch protected me.

"Sure she will," Sundance said heartily. "You know Etta can do it, Butch." Sundance didn't understand the subtleties at all, and I saw Butch look at him a minute and then look sideways at me.

We rode slowly those days, as though none of us were in a hurry to get to the last big holdup. Was it fear that this time, the last time, something would go wrong? I looked at their faces as they rode and was sure that was not it. Instead, there was almost a sense of nostalgia, a wanting to draw out as long as possible this last bit of what had been their way of life.

Somewhere in southeastern Wyoming—but beyond that I could not tell you—we stopped for horses. At night. Quietly.

"You're going to steal horses?" Sundance, who had once been wrongly jailed for stealing a horse, was incredulous. There was something honorable about robbing trains and banks, but any common fool could steal a horse—and would.

"They belong to the railroad," Butch muttered, as though that explained things perfectly. Maybe it did. "Won't nobody bother us," he said. "I arranged it."

Somehow Butch had a friend, someone who owed him for something and who was keeping the railroad horses. We left him tied just tight enough to look like he'd been blindsided but not enough to hurt him, and we rode off with twenty horses, a fine string.

"Three apiece and a little to spare," Butch said with a smile.

We crossed the desert and rode south, leaving the first bunch of horses in a meadow. Then southwest another twenty miles or so, where we camped on a small stream and left another string of horses. We rode back to the first string of horses the next day and found them well rested and watered.

"We'll camp here," Butch said. "Two days. Curry should be drifting in between now and then."

"You knew about this particular spot?" I asked, but they both just grinned at me.

Trouble began, as I'd known it would, when Curry rode in.

"What the hell is *she* doin' here?" he demanded before he'd even dismounted.

Butch opened his mouth to reply, but I jumped in, figuring I best fight my own battles. "I'm riding with you," I said distinctly.

"Not with me, you ain't," he growled, swinging off his horse to stand menacingly in front of me. "I ain't ridin' with no woman. I don't care whose whore she is."

I pulled back my hand to slap him, as I'd done before, but this time he was too quick for me. He grabbed my arm roughly and said, "You done that once and got away with it. I wouldn't try it again, if I was you." He tightened his hold, squeezing until the pain made me stifle a cry. Then he let go, so suddenly that I almost fell—and then I pretended to. As he stood there, smug in his power, I swung a boot hard into his groin.

He cried out once in real agony, and then all the breath was gone from him as he doubled on the ground, writhing and twisting, his eyes closed. The others stood and watched. No one said a word.

When at last Curry lay quiet on the ground, his face still a mask of pain, his eyes closed, Sundance came forward and stood over him. "Something you should know, Curry. She once killed a man for raping her. You might be the one best watch out."

"Give me your knife," I said to Sundance.

Curry's eyes flew open, and even Sundance looked alarmed. "What for?" he asked. I guess he figured with Curry still helpless I might be planning some gruesome but appropriate revenge.

"Just give me your knife," I repeated, holding out my hand.

He removed the sheathed knife he wore on his belt and handed it to me. Without a word, I took it and turned away. Then they all understood.

"She's armed now, Curry," Butch said. "Ain't none of us gonna come to your rescue, you get in trouble with Etta." And he too walked away.

Curry recovered enough by supper to eat the stew I had fixed from an antelope that Butch got, but as I moved about the campfire I was aware of his eyes watching me. His walk, as he approached the fire, had been slow and painful, and I knew he'd remember me for a while.

Later, Sundance said to me, "Hope you didn't mind my telling him about your pa, even if I didn't say that was who it was. I just thought he ought to know that about you."

"It's okay," I said. "I don't think I'm through with him yet, though."

"I was afraid," Sundance said with a grin, "that you'd crippled him too bad to ride with us."

"Would that be a loss?" I asked.

Sundance looked at me. "Guess not. You could take his place."

"I will anyway," I said.

And that's what I did.

The next night, just before sunset, we headed north and a little east, toward Rawlins. We rode slowly again, this time for fear of tiring the horses. They would need all their strength after the robbery, for this was the string we would ride for that first, fast getaway. If they didn't carry us successfully, it wouldn't matter how fast or rested the other horses were.

I rode next to Sundance but always a little behind, where I could keep an eye on Curry. He avoided me, almost too much so, but whenever I caught him glancing my way, I returned the coldest look I could muster. I caught myself trying to imitate the steel of Sundance's eyes when real anger blazed in them.

We reached Tipton about one-thirty in the morning, the night dark enough to hide us until we were almost to the fueling station. The company eating house was dark, and so were the few shacks scattered there for workers' families. Still, sleeping men could wake, and we were quiet.

"Curry," Butch said softly, "you take the horses and ride about a mile west. Light a fire next to the track. Use some greasewood so it'll burn good."

"I ain't ridin' nowhere," Curry said too loudly. "Make her do that." He jerked his head in my direction. "I'm gonna be part of the action."

Butch kept his voice low and even. "Last time you did that, a sheriff got killed. You'll do as I say, and you'll get your share. Otherwise . . ." He let the threat hang in the air, and I remembered Butch's promise to me about Curry. I wondered how far Curry would have to push Butch. Now, Sundance . . . that was another story.

"Etta, you come with me," Butch said, adding, "but keep your mouth shut."

I was dressed like they were, in rumpled pants, shirt and vest, a hat pulled low over my eyes, my hair tucked up under it. I fancied that I looked like a man, albeit a slight and young one. When I asked Sundance about that, he agreed with me, but his eyes danced with laughter so that I knew he was teasing me.

Just before two-thirty, when the train was due, we saw the light of Curry's fire down the track. Then I heard the whistle of the train as it began the climb up the grade. As soon as the train stopped, Butch climbed in one side of the engine and Sundance the other. I stood with my rifle trained on the door to the engine.

The conductor came down the track to see what was going on, the fire having alerted him. Instantly, Butch was out of the engine, his rifle trained on the man, ordering him to unhitch the mail, express, and baggage cars.

"I do that," the man said, "and them passenger cars will roll back downhill out of control. Might hurt some people pretty bad. Let me set the brake."

Butch nodded agreement, and he and I both covered the conductor while he set the brake. Then Butch leaped back onto the engine and motioned for me to follow. The engineer, a rifle pointed at him, moved the three cars up the track past the fire. Butch told him when to stop. We left the conductor to explain things to the passengers.

"Now," Butch said, jumping off the engine and heading for the baggage car, "get the dynamite ready."

They gave the clerk inside the car a chance to come out, but he refused adamantly. Butch nearly pleaded with him, telling the voice within the barricaded car that he was afraid he'd be hurt if he set off the dynamite, and he didn't want to hurt anyone. The man remained firm until the conductor arrived, having run up the track the mile or so we'd moved the train.

Whirling, I turned my rifle toward the man, even as I heard Butch behind me saying, "Easy now."

Holding his hands in the air, the conductor said, "Let me talk to him."

Butch nodded, and the conductor came right up to the door. "Woodcock," he barked, "don't be a damn fool a second time. They're fixing to blow this thing up, with you in or out. Get out here now."

In spite of himself, Sundance echoed, "Second time?"

"You all blew a car up around that same fellow last year at Wilcox. You'd think the fool would learn something."

Neither the conductor nor the threat of dynamite had any effect on Mr. Woodcock. He refused to budge, making me both nervous and angry. From Butch and Sundance, I knew about honor—among thieves and, I guessed, among clerks. I admired this Woodcock for his foolish but brave stubbornness—but I wished to hell he'd come out of there before he caused us real trouble.

Sundance said, "Well, hell, Butch, let's do it."

Butch nodded, and they threw two live sticks of dynamite against the door of the car. They dented the door badly but did not blow it apart. Still Woodcock did not appear. Sundance shouted—cursed, really—at the agent again, and when there was no response he threw a third charge at one end of the car. It crumpled the frame but still did not produce Woodcock. If I weren't so worried about the time we were wasting, I'd have applauded the man for bravery. I was now very curious about Mr. Woodcock.

Finally Sundance threw a charge at the other end of the car, and this time the agent came out, holding his hands high. He was a small, slim man with a green shade over his eyes, glasses perched on his nose, and a defiant stance in his body. He wasn't, I thought, the type to be a hero, and that made his stubbornness all the more to be admired.

Sundance searched him, took a pistol, and told him to stand by the engineer and the conductor. "You're a mighty brave fool," he said to Woodcock.

Two more blasts of dynamite and they had the safe open, the contents in saddlebags, and we were ready to leave. Rifles still trained on the men, we backed into the brush where Curry waited with the horses. Behind us, we left a totally demolished railroad car, it's hulk almost in shreds.

"Wait a minute," Curry protested. "We ain't checked the passengers back there." He jerked his head toward the east, where the passenger cars were still about a mile from us. "They probably got gold watches and travelin' money and all sorts of things we ought to have."

Butch spoke in that same level tone. "We aren't botherin' passengers. Never have, and there's no reason to start now. Mount up, Curry, 'fore I throw you in that saddle."

Curry started to challenge him, saw Sundance raise his rifle, and suddenly decided to mount his horse.

It would not have been practical, of course, to backtrack a mile and rifle the passengers' purses. That would have delayed us long enough for the slowest posse in Wyoming to catch us still at the robbery site. But that wasn't why Butch and Sundance didn't rob the passengers, and I knew it. Curry would never understand.

We rode nearly a hundred miles in twenty-four hours, stopping only briefly to change horses and tend to nature's needs at the two locations where we'd left the fresh strings. For sustenance, we had jerky and dried biscuits—I'd cooked an extra batch our last night in camp. For rest, we had nothing but the pounding of the horses' hooves.

"Etta?" Sundance rode next to me.

"I'm fine," I said through clenched teeth. The rush of the robbery was long gone, and fatigue made me remember why I'd thought of staying in San Antonio, why I'd sworn I'd never go on another robbery.

"You were great," Sundance said. "Steady. I watched your aim. It was perfect all the time."

I didn't tell him I'd felt my hands waver when it looked like we might never get Woodcock out of that baggage car.

We rode . . . and rode . . . and rode, through a moon-bright night and then a dusty, dry hot day. Around midnight the next night, Butch called a halt, and we camped way back in a canyon where there was a fresh spring. No food, no game, but fresh water, and that was a blessing.

"Next town we come to," Sundance muttered, "I'm going to rob the general store. Get some canned tomatoes, sardines, something to keep a man's soul together."

Butch looked up from the saddlebags where he was counting the loot. "Why don't you just pay cash?" he asked. "We took over fifty thousand dollars."

Sundance whistled, and even Curry's eyes widened in surprise.

The next day, Sundance rode casually into a small town, made his purchases—paying legitimate cash—and rode back with the news that the Union Pacific was spreading the word that only $54 had been taken in the latest robbery by the Wild Bunch.

"Damn them," Butch said vehemently. "Can't they ever play fair? Makin' us out like bumbling idiots to have gone to all that trouble for pocket change. Don't want the world to know we made a haul." As frustrated as I'd ever seen him, he picked up a good-sized rock and hurled it as far and as high as he could. It clattered and banged down the rocky side of the canyon, while the rest of us sat in stunned silence at the display of anger from Butch.

"There's good news," Sundance said softly. "Word is that there were four men involved"—he threw me a smile at that—"and that the posse totally lost track of them."

Butch shrugged his shoulders, as though that were unimportant compared to the lie about the amount of cash taken.

We slept around the embers of a campfire that night, even though it was a summer night. Canyons in that country could come up with a chill like winter, and I slept close to Sundance, my body pressed against his for warmth. Sometime in the night, though, I got up to relieve myself, going as quietly as I could toward some small bushes that afforded a little privacy.

My business concluded, I rose to return to the fire. Before I could move, a hand was clamped over my mouth and a voice muttered, "You best not make one move, say one thing."

The terror of Pa's attack came back, all those years later. The horror of helplessness, the hand that made me swallow a scream that rose in my throat and the bile that followed it, the rough hands pushing at my clothes.

"You and me have a score to settle," Curry muttered, dragging me away from the fire, even as he pulled at the pants I still wore.

Calm, I told myself, *be calm*. Breathing around that foul-smelling hand, I inhaled deeply. Then, slowly, so as not to alarm him, I reached for my waistband. The knife was hidden, nestled inside my shirt, lying on top of my belt. I went limp, making myself harder to drag, while I eased the knife out of the sheath.

"I'm gonna show Sundance he ain't nothin' special," he said, "and teach you not to be messin' in men's business. Think you're high and mighty, just 'cause they protect you . . ." He was beginning to ramble, as though anger and maybe revenge had supplanted reason.

All, I thought, *to my advantage*.

With one powerful gesture, he threw me on the ground, and I landed so hard that for a split second I feared the wind had been knocked out of me and that I wouldn't be able to move quickly enough to defend myself. But by the time he fell on top of me, I had my senses back.

When he reared back to gloat in my face, taunting, "And how do you like this now, Miss Etta Place?" I raised my hand slowly and brought the knife to bear on his shoulder. Lord help me, I never wanted to kill another man, and this time I knew enough to aim for a spot that would hurt but not kill. I sliced the skin away from his shoulder and down his back, taking with it shreds of the dirty shirt he wore.

He yowled like a hurt bear but, to my surprise and terror, neither budged from me nor loosened his grip. Instead, he struggled to reach the knife. My hand was still free, and I pitched the knife far enough that he would have had to let go of me to get it.

"I ought to kill you, you bitch," he roared, curving one hand around my throat. The other hand was disabled by my knife. Desperately I fought to loosen his fingers, but he was stronger than me, and for a second I had the real sinking sensation that I was about to die. I remember telling myself that Butch and Sundance wouldn't let me die, not when we were about to go to South America, not when we had $50,000, not when . . . not ever.

Curry's grip loosened suddenly and he fell away from me. Only later did I realize that Butch had clubbed him in the head with his rifle butt and Sundance stood behind, his rifle aimed clearly at Curry's head.

"Etta?" Sundance asked in a brittle, hard voice.

"I'm all right," I said, pushing myself to a sitting position. "You better check him. He's got a nasty knife wound. Might bleed to death."

"Let him," said Sundance. "We all warned him."

Curry was sitting up now, shaking his head as though to clear it. Angrily he looked at the two men standing over him, then at me.

"She's won," Butch said quietly, "and you won't ever bother her again. I told you before I'd kill you if you tried, but somehow I can't bring myself to do that. You're gonna ride out of here now, and you're not doubling back or any of that. If there's anything you know, Kid Curry, it's that I'm a good tracker and that I mean what I say. You come back anywhere near us, and I will kill you. I never killed a man before, but I will sure enough kill you."

Briefly I hated Butch for not killing him. *Why*, I thought, *can't he bring himself to do it?* And then I remembered that I couldn't bring myself to that terrible act again.

Curry rose on weak legs. "My share?" he asked, his voice hoarse.

"I'll count it out while Sundance covers you," Butch replied.

Sundance kept the rifle pointed at Curry, but he said, "He doesn't deserve it, Butch. If we kept his share . . ."

"I ain't doin' that to anyone," Butch said. "No matter what filth he is, I won't have it said Butch Cassidy cheated a man he'd ridden with."

Butch even wrapped Curry's wounded shoulder, and then a sullen, angry, and injured outlaw rode away from the camp, never looking back.

"I never thought," Butch said, his voice full of amazement, "that a man I trusted would do that." He shook his head, as though trying desperately to understand. Then he stood up. "I'll stand watch. You two get some sleep."

"I'll stand watch," Sundance said.

"Naw," Butch said, "I'm too angry to sleep. You go on."

And so I lay in Sundance's arms, safe but shaken. He stroked my hair and whispered, "You're one tough lady, Etta Place. You can rob a train and fight off a crazy outlaw. How did I ever meet you?"

"You stole me when I was an innocent schoolgirl." I fell asleep.

Winnemucca was my idea. That is, robbing the bank there was my idea.

From the barrenness of southwestern Wyoming, we rode into northern Utah, a surprisingly fertile land of cattle and farms—sugar beets and peas. "Beaver hunters first came here," Butch said, as though he were lecturing in history at a university. "Stashed their goods in *caches*, great caverns they dug in the earth and lined with leaves and stuff."

"Fascinating," Sundance said grimly.

As we went west, skirting the north end of the Great Salt Lake, the land grew more grim. Salt flats indicated where the lake had once risen, then fallen back, leaving land that would grow nothing.

"Want to float in it?" Butch asked me. "You won't sink. Salt holds you up."

"No, thanks," I said, looking at the gray-green water. Overhead, gulls whirled in the air and dive-bombed anything that looked like food. Fortunately they stayed a distance from us.

"At least taste it," Butch insisted. "Put your fingers in and see how salty it is."

I did as I was told and was surprised at the strong salt taste. "It really is salty. You ever taste it, Sundance?"

He shook his head but refused to dismount. "I'm exhausted, and you two are going on about some horrible-looking lake like it was one of the great wonders of the world." Exasperation colored his tone as he spoke.

"It is a great wonder," Butch said. "First white men that found it thought it was the Pacific. They talked about evil spirits and a great water spout in the middle that could draw a man clear down into the bowels of the earth."

"The bowels of the earth?" Sundance repeated incredulously.

"It ain't my phrase," Butch said defensively. "I read that somewhere. Besides, this damn lake looks to me like it's got a direct connection to the bowels of the earth, whatever that means."

Once past the lake, we were in the Great Salt Lake Desert, the salt flats, several feet deep, left by an ancient lake when it dried up. It was grim land, and we rode silently, bandannas across our faces to keep out the dust and hats pulled low to shade us from the sun. By day, we burned in the sun and wished for the coolness of Wyoming; by night, we wrapped ourselves in layers of blankets and cursed the desert night for its coldness. Thirst and a suffocating heat were our daytime companions, and Butch warned us constantly to drink from our canteens, lest we begin to see mirages.

"I think I see trees . . ." Sundance spoke in a mystical, faraway voice.

"Oh shut up," I said, and he did.

Finally we came to the foothills of a mountain range, and we knew we were through the desert. As we moved westward into Nevada, the land grew more fertile once again. We crossed one chain of mountains and then moved into Ruby Valley, just east of the Ruby Mountain Range. The eastern slopes of the valley were covered with piñon and, higher up, yellow pine. Cottonwoods grew plentifully along the streams, and the western slopes were covered with rich grasses.

"We could run some cattle here," Sundance said, his tone almost wistful.

"Yeah," Butch said, "we could." And then, apropos of nothing, "The Overland Mail went through this valley."

"They carry money?" Sundance asked. "Worth our while?"

Butch gave him a dirty look.

Occasionally we saw ranch houses, square substantial buildings set in the center of sturdy picket fences, trees planted all around to shelter the home from the wind. They were a bit of civilization obviously dropped in the midst of the valley, with mountains rising behind them.

We rode west to the Shoshone Range, and there Butch had a friend, a rancher near the town of Battle Mountain.

"Another friend?" I teased.

He nodded solemnly, all laughter beat out of him by the hard ride. "He'll feed us."

Judy Alter

Mr. Hammett was surprised to see us, no doubt about that. "Cassidy?" he asked, amazement in his voice. "I been readin' 'bout you, but way over in Wyoming. How'd you get here?"

"Hard ridin'," Butch answered grimly.

"I guess so," his friend said. "Light yourselves."

Sundance looked warily at Butch, but he followed his lead and dismounted, then came to help me off my horse. My legs were so stiff and rubbery that I nearly fell into him instead of standing next to him.

"You need some food," Mr. Hammett said practically. Within minutes we were seated around a rough pine table in a bachelor's kitchen, while a cowboy fried sizzling steaks and potatoes and Mr. Hammett poured steaming coffee into tin mugs for us.

"What you been hearin', Hammett?" Butch asked.

"You stole fifty-four dollars and killed a guard to do it," Hammett said tersely.

"We never," Butch protested, "we never killed nobody. Robbin' trains and banks ain't worth murderin' over."

Hammett looked at him appraisingly. "I knew as much. And the fifty-four dollars?"

Butch looked evasive. "That ain't right either."

With that, Hammett roared with laughter. "I didn't hardly think so," he finally said when he could speak again.

Butch could barely eat his meal for fuming. "Killed somebody! We didn't even threaten 'em, not even that stubborn Woodcock. Makes me want to bash some heads together!"

"And kill them?" Sundance asked with a grin, but Butch threw him a black look and he subsided.

Well fed, we stumbled to a bunkhouse. Hammett said that it being summer most of his cowboys were sleeping out and we could have the bunkhouse. I was flat on a bed and asleep while Butch and Sundance were still talking about who would sleep where.

Within a couple of days we were recovered—we'd slept, washed, and eaten plentifully. And yet neither Butch nor Sundance seemed in good spirits.

"Seems to me for men who just got themselves a wad of money you're mighty grim," I said, somewhat put out at them.

"You wouldn't understand," Sundance said, without even looking at me.

280

Anger surged through me, but Butch put out a hand as though to silence whatever I was about to say. "It's all right, Etta. We're just . . . well, you know, the lives we've known are over. We can't go back, and yet . . ."

"No more trains?" I asked, impertinence in my voice.

"Just leave it be, Etta," Sundance said in irritation. "It's something between Butch and me."

"I hardly think so," I said. "I've been with you long enough that I think I'm part of it too."

Butch nodded as though to agree, and Sundance simply shrugged his shoulders.

"What you two need," I said, speaking slowly and carefully, "is something to rob."

Heads whirled toward me in amazement. "We . . . we quit that with Tipton," Butch said. "Not gonna take the chance anymore. Besides, the Union Pacific probably has sawdust in their safes by now. Damn them and their fifty-four dollars story!"

"Can't do it," Sundance said. "We got no backup. Just the two of us, we can't rob a train."

"I don't mean a train," I said. "And there are three of us. Don't forget that, Sundance. I think there's something kind of perfect about it just being the three of us. I think we should rob another bank."

Sundance looked up at me, the first small sign of interest showing in his face. "What bank?"

I shrugged. "You'll have to tell me that. I don't even know where we are."

Next thing I knew, they were poring over one of Butch's wrinkled and stained maps. "Elko's too far," Butch said, "and Dunphy . . . it don't look big enough."

"Winnemucca?" Sundance asked, pointing at a spot on the map.

"Yeah," Butch said, "Winnemucca. Good-sized town, big enough to have some money in the bank but not big enough to have more than one sheriff." He was silent for a minute, looking off in the distance, and I could only guess what he saw.

Then, "Let's make some plans. We'll ride in about noon, like we always do. . . ."

"Wait a minute," I said. "The Wild Bunch always robs banks at noon. It's like the banks expect them. Let's do it different this time."

Butch looked at me suspiciously, in part, I'm sure, because I was questioning his leadership—something Sundance never did—but also because he was curious.

"Nobody expects us this far from Wyoming," I said. "Let's just ride into town and hang around for a couple of days. See what the pattern is at the bank, what's going on."

"Etta," Sundance said, smiling only slightly, "this is the sort of thing men usually decide."

Before I could voice the sarcastic remark that rose to my tongue, Butch said, "Etta might be right. Let's try it her way."

And that's how we came to camp out in an abandoned ranch shack a few miles from Winnemucca. Within an hour of our setting up camp, we had a visitor—a young boy who looked to be maybe fourteen.

"Howdy," he said. "You all come off the roundup?"

"Sure did, fellow," Butch said, grinning at the kid. Butch was a sucker for youngsters.

"That your horse?" The boy jerked his head toward the fine white stallion that Butch was riding these days.

"Yeah, it is."

"Want to race?"

"First I got to know your name," Butch said. "I never race against a fellow whose name I don't know."

Remembering his manners, the lad stuck out a hand. "Vic," he said, "Vic Button. My pa's foreman at the CS Ranch." He hesitated just a minute. "You're on CS land now . . . but it's all right. Pa won't mind, seein' as how you've just come off the roundup."

"Well, Vic Button, that's a fine horse you have there yourself. I'll race you . . . say, two out of three?"

The boy agreed and was ready to mount his horse that minute. But Butch put him off, saying he had to prepare and think about it. They'd race the next day.

Butch raced him and won, three days in a row.

"That's a fine horse," Vic would say each time he lost. "Runs better than anything I ever saw."

"Yessir, it's a fine horse," Butch agreed, slapping the horse's shoulder affectionately.

When he lost on the third day, Button reluctantly held out the reins of his horse, handing them to Butch.

Startled, Butch said, "I don't want your horse, boy. I'm gonna give this horse to you sometime."

You could hear the youngster draw his breath in sharp, then release it as though disappointed. "Go on," he said, "you ain't gonna."

"Yes," Butch told him, "I am."

In between races, young Button told us everything we could ever have wanted to know about Winnemucca, the bank, even escape routes.

"There's a shortcut," he said, "over Soldiers' Pass to Clover Valley. Not many folks know about it, but it's good travelin'. Pa says you can really make time goin' that way."

"That so?" Sundance said casually.

Button nodded affirmatively.

We ended up robbing the bank at noon, in spite of all my protestations about breaking patterns. "There just aren't as many people in a bank at noon, Etta," Sundance had said, and the bits of information we pried from Vic Button proved him right. So noon it was.

Dressed like a man, my hair tucked under a hat and the brim pulled low over my face, I sat outside the bank just before the clock struck twelve. Coming toward me across a vacant lot were two hoboes with ragged blanket rolls. They were, of course, Butch and Sundance, and inside those blanket rolls were their rifles. The plan was that they would look sort of aimless—certainly harmless. But Sundance carried it one step too far. As he later explained, it was such a beautiful day that when that cat ran in front of him, he couldn't resist chasing it. The cat proved to be a skunk, which turned on him, dousing him with spray from head to foot.

By the time they entered the bank, even Butch was about to gag. There was no need for a dramatic show of force: All those in the bank fled, holding their noses and gasping for air. One clerk remained, only because he was so violently ill from the smell that he could not move.

Judy Alter

Fortunately my job was to get the horses we tied behind the bank, so I was not exposed to the skunk smell until we were mounted and fleeing. Meantime, Butch and Sundance had scooped all the money they could from the tellers' cages, picked up sacks of gold coins out of the safe, and run out the front door to where I waited with the horses. In minutes we were pounding down the road, following the railroad tracks away from Winnemucca.

Word spread quickly, given that it was noontime. Behind us as we rode, occasional bursts of gunfire sounded, but the bullets hit harmlessly at some distance from us. Once when I looked back I saw someone on a bicycle pedaling furiously after us, but he soon fell too far behind. Besides, the man couldn't shoot and stay on the bike at the same time.

"I hear a train," Sundance called suddenly.

"Could you . . . ah . . . ride downwind of us?" Butch called back.

"No time for joking, Butch. I hear a train," he repeated.

I turned to look and saw an amazing sight: A train was indeed steaming toward us, men hanging off the sides with pistols and rifles aimed directly at us. But even as I watched, two of those hangers-on fell off the sides of the cars to which they clung. The train stopped, backed up to get them, and slowly built up speed again. After it had done this twice, we were out of sight.

Still it was not an easy getaway. Sundance dropped—actually dropped!—a sack of gold coins. Throwing his reins to Butch, he leaped off his horse, scooped up the sack, and was mounted and on his way again in seconds.

"Why'd you stop?" I asked, raising my voice to be heard over the wind and the horses' hooves.

"That's probably six thousand dollars," he shouted back. "You'd have stopped too."

"I can't believe you did that," Butch yelled, shaking his head. But he was grinning. They were both grinning and happy, and it struck me with force that it took a robbery to make them happy. If we "retired" to South America, what would they do for fun?

At Soldiers' Pass we switched to the fresh horses we'd left there, and Butch took precious time to write a note, which said, "Give

284

this white horse to Vic Button." He signed it "Butch Cassidy."

That night, as we camped well away from Winnemucca and the railroad posse, Butch said, "You know, it's a crime how easy it is to take money from people. If bankers were honest men, I'd feel guilty about it."

"Yeah," Sundance yawned, "me too . . . but not very guilty."

"Sundance," I said, "you sleep on the other side of the fire . . . and throw those clothes away."

Posses were formed all over northern Nevada to catch us, but we never saw any of them. When we stopped at Hammett's for our belongings, that genial rancher scoffed, "They'll be fightin' amongst themselves about who's responsible, who's got to pay. You all might just as well ride slow and easy."

And from the reports we heard, that was just what happened. The Winnemucca folks charged those from Tuscarora with letting us go, and the Elko County sheriff said the posse from Battle Mountain could have caught us if they'd been alert. All of them were looking for three men: As we rode north toward Idaho, I let my long hair blow in the breeze and felt very feminine.

Somewhere in Idaho, we counted our take: $31,000 plus change.

"Not bad," I said, "for a final fling."

Chapter Twenty-four

We split up. Butch wanted to go back to Wyoming, wouldn't be talked out of it.

"Every lawman in that state is looking for us and knows us by sight," Sundance argued. "You couldn't pay me to go near the place."

"I'm going," Butch said stubbornly.

"It's Mary Boyd, isn't it?" Sundance said, although he knew full well he was treading on forbidden waters.

"None of your business," Butch muttered. He wouldn't get angry at Sundance as he would have at Curry, but he wouldn't be pushed.

"All right," Sundance said, throwing a stick of wood at the campfire so hard that sparks rose and I had to beat out two that landed on my blankets. "You go on and go to Wyoming, and *if* you don't get caught, we'll meet you in—say, Fort Worth—in three months."

"Fort Worth?" I said. "Why not at Fannie's?"

"Oh, maybe we'll go to Fannie's," Sundance said. "I just feel like a change."

"Where you going?" Butch asked.

Sundance shrugged. "Maybe California, see my brother. Maybe San Antonio so Etta can see Fannie."

As it turned out, we did both.

"We'll just tell him we're married," Sundance said nervously.

We were on a train—the Union Pacific—but now we were respectable passengers, with the mail and baggage cars far from our minds. I distinctly did not want to go to California to see Sundance's brother, but I didn't have many choices. Clearly Butch did not want me going with him—and I couldn't have done that to Sundance. Fannie's was . . . well, still not an appealing idea. Caught by my pride and by the foolishness—I now saw it as that—that had led me to follow Sundance to Wyoming in the first place, I found myself headed for California.

My mood lightened when I thought of the train officials and how hard they were searching for us when we were right there, riding their train. I grinned a little. Even the rather pompous conductor inspired a smile in me. I doubted he'd be as brave as the conductor at Tipton.

"Stop laughing," Sundance said irritably. "My brother, well, he just wouldn't understand."

"Does he understand about your robbing banks and trains?" I asked pointedly.

"No." Sundance looked at the floor. "They don't know. I haven't seen any of them in, oh, twenty years. I just thought . . . I mean, if we're going to South America, I may never see them again." He looked out the window of the train, staring into the dark night that rushed by us.

I felt almost sorry for him. That touch of softness that came out occasionally in both Butch and Sundance completely disarmed me. "It's all right. I'll tell him we're married. But what about Anna Maria?" I hadn't thought of Sundance's actual wife in a long time.

"I'll tell them she died," he said, without one trace of remorse.

I burst out laughing, loud enough to turn heads. "Such a sentimental soul, you are," I said. "Not only a bigamist, but now a wife murderer."

"I didn't murder her," he said, his teeth clenched, "and could you please lower your voice? I don't even wish her harm. I just wish her out of my life."

"She is," I pointed out, "and she probably feels the same about you."

We rode in icy silence for a long time, until sleepiness overcame me and I put my head on his shoulder. At first he was stiff, but then his arm crept around me and his body relaxed. We were soon both at ease with each other and asleep.

Elwood Longabaugh was a banker! I couldn't believe it! As soon as Sundance—I had to remember to call him Harry—and I were alone, I exploded into laughter. "Aren't you tempted to rob his bank?" I asked between chortles.

"It's not funny," Sundance said stiffly. "Besides, he's only a teller. It's not like he's a banker who robs from the poor and pays the rich."

"You sound just like Butch," I said, and felt a pang of missing Butch.

"And where are you from, Etta?" Elwood asked me politely as we sat at dinner in a small café where the food was not much better than what we'd have gotten in a railroad station in Wyoming. Elwood was a bachelor—a frugal bachelor—in addition to being a banker. I'd heard of San Francisco's legendary dining—seafood, Chinese restaurants—but we were to get none of it apparently.

"Texas," I said, and offered no more.

"Is that where you met?" he asked, and I knew he was inquiring less from curiosity than politeness.

"Etta was teaching in San Antonio when I was there . . . on business," Sundance said crisply.

"Ah, yes," Elwood said, "railroads. You certainly have a fine line of work, little brother."

Sundance toyed with his roast beef. "Yeah."

We stayed five days in San Francisco, and that was plenty. Oh, when Elwood was clerking at the bank, we explored the city, wandered on Fisherman's Wharf and ate things I'd never tasted—lobster and crab—and breathed the salty air and watched the ocean. But I had been landlocked too long: Water had little appeal for me, and I found the texture of most seafood suspicious. "Give me good, chewy beef," I told Sundance.

We rode cable cars up and down the steeply pitched streets

and marveled at the houses so close together. "Texans couldn't survive here," I said. "No space around you."

"Folks from Wyoming, too," Sundance said, and we both knew that we were fish out of water, which struck me as a trite and inappropriate analogy considering where we were.

"Well, Elwood . . ." Sundance didn't seem to know what to say in parting. "I guess . . . well, I don't know when I'll see you again."

"It's been twenty years," Elwood said precisely.

"Yeah. It might be another twenty. I think . . . well, there's a business deal in South America. That's probably where we'll go next."

"You'll take Etta there?" he asked, aghast.

"Oh," I replied, "it's very civilized. I'm looking forward to it."

Elwood pursed his lips and frowned in disapproval but said nothing more.

With relief, we boarded the train for Texas.

"You know," I said, because it had just occurred to me, "we may never see Wyoming again."

He shrugged, that gesture so characteristic of him. "That's not all bad. We remember it as a great place, but I have a feeling if we went back, something bad would happen—and then it would be forever tainted. I can carry Wyoming with me anywhere I go."

I wondered if I would be able to do that too.

We went to San Antonio. But that was no more satisfactory than San Francisco. Oh, I was glad to see Fannie, and Julie and Hodge, though I thought Hodge now looked almost too old to get around. His walk had become stiff, and it took him too long to move from kitchen to parlor or kitchen to Fannie's "boudoir."

"How long can Hodge keep working?" I asked Fannie one night.

"Until he drops in his tracks," she replied without sentimentality. "What other choice does he have?"

"Would you . . . I mean, what if he simply can't do what he does?"

"You asking if I'll throw him out on the street? Of course I won't. I'll keep manufacturing things he can do as long as possible. I'm not heartless, you know." She peered at me over a pair of spectacles pulled down on her nose. Then she pulled the glasses off and waved them in the air. "Trouble is less what he can and can't do than his pride. He's got to think he can still do everything he's always done. Julie and I worry about that a lot."

"You talk to Julie about it?"

She smiled patiently. "Of course. Between us, we scheme to take care of ol' Hodge. Don't you worry about him."

Sundance threw himself into the life of the house with his usual abandon. He stood around the piano with the girls, singing heartily. He danced with this one and that, and he reported to me with great enthusiasm that "Marcy wants to be a schoolteacher" or "Sheila really wants to go to Wyoming. She says I make it sound like heaven."

Sheila and Sundance disappeared one afternoon for hours, and I paced the floor in front of an amused Fannie.

"Might as well sit," she said philosophically. "They aren't upstairs, if that's any consolation to you. But wherever they are, you've got no control over what they're doing."

"He wouldn't!" I snapped, pacing the length of her boudoir. In truth, I didn't know why I was so upset. I'd have never told Fannie, but if the right man had come along, I'd probably have cheated on Sundance in a flash. Only, the right man's heart was still in Wyoming—where I presumed he also was.

"I don't know where you ever got the idea that Harry Longabaugh is more of a saint than other men. Me, I always thought he was a little wilder than some. Mostly I've been surprised at how tame he's been with you." Fannie was still amused, while I, distinctly, was not.

I glared at her, not wanting to hear what she said. It was that same old thing again that I'd gone through with Elise just months earlier, and I still couldn't figure out my angry reaction.

Sheila came back, alone, about four in the afternoon. "Did some shopping," she said over her shoulder as she hurried up the stairs.

Sundance came limping in about an hour later. "Tried to ride Butch's damn bike," he said, rubbing one leg below the knee. "Think I wrecked the thing, and it serves him right. Maybe Hodge can fix it." He avoided looking at me.

"Where have you been all afternoon?" I asked.

"Oh, you know, just around. I figured you and Fannie were talking and I'd just go out." He stood up, that charming smile gracing his face. "You miss me?"

"Yes," I snapped, "I did. And I was downright curious about where you were."

He turned his back on me. "And you thought I was with one of the girls." It was a statement.

"Sheila," I said tersely.

He turned to look at me. "And what did you think we were doing?" Then, with a mischievous smile, he added, "And where?"

"The Menger Hotel, for all I know," I spat out.

"Nice place," he said. "It would show good taste." And he turned and walked out of the room.

Late that night, long after I had crawled into bed to lie sleepless and awake, Sundance came quietly into the room, hung his pants on the bedpost, and lay down beside me. I lay stiff and still, hardly breathing, so that he would think I was asleep.

He lay on his back, arms crossed behind his head. After a long while, he said, "Etta?"

"Yes?" I barely murmured, and started to turn away from him. One arm reached out and grabbed my shoulder. "Don't," he said. "I've got to tell you something." He took a deep breath, and I fully expected a long confession about his dalliance with Sheila. Instead, he said, "I want you to know that I have no interest in Sheila, that I have never touched her, don't intend to."

I stared at him, unnerved that he knew I didn't totally trust him.

"You don't have to apologize," he said. "I just want you to know. If I have an interest in another woman, you'll be the first to know. Now tell me what else is bothering you." He said it with an air of authority that left no room for doubt. He lay now on his back, his eyes fixed on the ceiling. "Is it Butch?"

"Butch?" I echoed.

"Butch," he repeated firmly. "Lately I feel as though if Butch isn't around, if we aren't a threesome, you aren't really happy. I want you to love Butch, but I don't want you to love him like you do me."

"Oh, I don't," I cried, my voice rising too fast in denial.

He reached over and put a finger to my lips with a quiet "Shhh."

I invented a reason for my preoccupation. "I . . . I guess I feel that we're on the brink of a great adventure—going to South America—and it makes me edgy to while away time in San Francisco and San Antonio." It wasn't altogether a lie.

"I thought you wanted to see Fannie."

"I did, but we can do all our visiting in two days—and then there's, well, there's nothing to do here. I don't know how she stands it."

At that, he laughed aloud. "It's her business and her life, that's how she stands it. But I feel the same way." Then he sat up and said decisively, "We're going to Fort Worth tomorrow."

"It's more than a month until Butch will be there," I said. "What will we do?"

"Maybe rob banks, maybe live like rich men. We've got the money."

Fannie was dismayed that we left so quickly, and as I hugged her she raised an eyebrow at me in question. I shook my head quickly to tell her I didn't know the answer to her question. It struck me that I never would know where Sundance had been that afternoon, or if he'd been with Sheila. He'd turned the whole problem back on me and effectively eased himself out of it. Grudgingly I admired his effrontery. And, probably, he hadn't been with Sheila. After all, the bike really was wrecked.

Saying goodbye to Julie and Hodge, particularly Hodge, was harder, for I knew I'd never see them again.

"You come back more often now, Miss Etta," Hodge said, and I assured him I would. Surely the Lord wouldn't mind that white lie.

We spent a month in Fort Worth. Sundance presented himself as Harry A. Place, cattleman who had recently sold a big herd, and I was, of course, his wife. We stayed at Maddox Flats again, though Sundance apologetically said several times we could stay at a better place—and maybe should to preserve the cattleman image. But we were known there and comfortable.

Because Sundance had money to spread around, we were courted by the city. We met and dined with B. B. Paddock, the colorful newspaper editor who'd brought reform to Fort Worth, at least in some areas, and K. M. Van Zandt, the Civil War veteran who was now a banker and civic leader, and Jeff McLean, a crusading reformer who was county attorney. It tickled me to see McLean trying to enlist Sundance's help—Mr. Place, he called him respectfully—in his efforts to clean up Hell's Half Acre, the city's red-light and saloon district. Sundance listened and nodded when McLean talked endlessly, and, with a straight face, Sundance expressed appropriate outrage over the flourishing houses of ill repute. I was nearly overcome with a coughing fit and had to leave the table momentarily.

When I returned, Sundance said seriously, "Such talk upsets her, Mr. McLean. She was raised delicately, you know," and Mr. McLean fell all over himself apologizing for his ill manners.

Mostly, though, I just enjoyed city life. We generally ate at Peers House, where the food was reliably good, and sometimes—well, frequently—Sundance sat in on a poker game at the White Elephant Saloon. On a warm afternoon, we might take the trolley out to Lake Como and stroll around the shore or across the bridges and stay into the evening to hear the band play. It was a far cry from Hole-in-the-Wall, but if I missed that life, I managed to keep my longing hidden from Sundance.

What I really missed was Butch, mostly because I was worried about him. Some niggling ghost in the back of my mind told me he was in trouble, but there was nothing I could do about it, and I kept that fear, too, a secret from Sundance.

Butch arrived in November, walking into Maddox Flats as though he'd just been down the street for a beer. "Hey," he said when I answered the knock on the door, "you miss me?"

"Miss you?" I cried, flinging myself into his arms. "I was frantic for fear you'd been captured."

He set me carefully back down on the floor and held me at arm's length. "You got that second sight or something?" He was dead serious.

"What're you talking about?" Sundance demanded, pulling himself off the bed where he'd been lounging.

"She thinks I got caught," Butch said, "and she's right. I did."

I gasped, my hand instantly over my mouth. "What happened?" There it was again, that sense of disbelief—all that time, they'd known that capture was a possibility. I'd never believed it . . . until now.

"Stayed with a pal just before I headed into the Powder River Range," Butch said, "and he asked me to deliver a message to somebody up on Rye Grass Creek. I did, and then I got to thinking how good that creek would feel if I was to get into it. So I hung my gun belt on a tree limb and waded in, throwin' that cool water on my face, when I heard a thunk."

"A thunk?" Sundance asked in disbelief.

Butch looked at him solemnly. "A thunk. I knowed I was in trouble right then. Turned out a deputy sheriff named Morgan had a gun on me, and my own bein' so far away, wasn't a thing I could do 'cept wait my turn. He surely took care that I wouldn't escape. Took my pistol and the shells and put them in different pockets on his saddlebag, handcuffed me, and then tied my feet under the saddle. I mean, I was helpless as a baby."

"Where was he taking you?" I asked, thinking of the Wyoming state penitentiary or some equally awful place.

"We didn't talk about that. Don't even know how much he knew about who I was. We just didn't talk beyond 'Don't try anything smart' and that kind of stuff. Spent the night at a ranch, where I had to sleep handcuffed to him." Butch grinned. "I've spent the night with better partners, I'll tell you that."

"Butch!" I said. "Get on with the story. I mean, how are you here?"

" 'Cause I'm smarter than he is," he said complacently. "Second day, we were really dry and came to a creek. His horse wouldn't drink with the bit in its mouth, and he got off to see to that. By then he'd untied my feet and taken off the handcuffs—those were his mistakes, but I didn't tell him that at the time. Anyway, I just moved my horse close up on his, got the pistol out of one saddlebag and some bullets out of the other, and while he was busy worrying with that sorry-mouthed animal, I got the drop on him."

"You shoot him?" Sundance asked coldly.

" 'Course not," Butch said. "I left him out there, told him the way to Sheridan. It wasn't more than four, five miles to the next ranch, so I knew he wasn't in much trouble. 'Cept his pride was hurt."

"And then you came right down here," I said, filling in the rest of the story for him.

"Naw," he said. "I still had to go to Lander. But I got here as quick as I could. What'd I miss? Any of the others here?"

"The others"—and that was really how I thought of them—began to drift in, each bringing a woman with him this time. First came the Tall Texan, Ben Kilpatrick, bringing with him the Indian woman, Della. She wore pants and boots and would have looked like one of the men if she weren't of such slight stature. I could swear I saw her give a scornful look to the challis dress I wore, but Sundance said later that was just my imagination.

"Are they staying here?" I asked him that night, cuddled comfortably against his back.

"Hmmm," he murmured.

"Does that mean yes?"

He turned toward me. "It means yes, they're all going to stay here."

"All?" I echoed, hating the thought of sharing Sundance and Butch with "the others."

"Curry's coming, gone to San Antonio to get Annie, and Will Carver's bringing Lillie. They're going to get married."

"Curry?" My voice turned to ice. "You said I'd never have to be near him again."

"You still got that knife?" Sundance tried to make a joke of it. Then he sobered, and said, "It's the last reunion for the whole gang . . . and, well, he's part of it. But I swear to you, Etta, he lays a hand on you, he's dead."

I'd heard that before, and I knew I'd have to protect myself.

"Will and Lillie are getting married?" I asked. "Why would they do that?"

He grinned at me. "Why do people usually get married? Because they love each other, I guess."

"Will Carver doesn't love her," I said scornfully. "He's never been around her that much, and besides, he beats her. You think he'll settle down in a nice house with a picket fence around it and raise children? Of course he won't!" I sat up in bed, propelled by my indignation, and pulled the blanket up to cover me.

Sundance let out a yelp. "Could you share the blanket? And what do you care if he won't settle down? Maybe that's not what she expects." He paused a minute. "Is that what you expect out of marriage?"

I considered whacking him with the flat of my hand and then remembered I criticized Will Carver for that very kind of treatment of Lillie. Instead I clenched my hands around my knees and thought for a long minute. "It's not what I expect from you," I said, "but it's what I generally think of marriage."

It was Sundance's turn to be silent, now that he was propped up against the headboard of the bed, half sitting beside me. "My parents have been married a long time," he said, "and I used to wonder how they stood each other after so much time."

"My parents were married a long time, and I knew the answer to that question," I said dryly.

"How do we know that wouldn't happen to us?" he asked.

"We aren't going to find out," I said firmly.

. He put an arm around me, as though to erase that memory, and shook his head. "No. I mean, married or not, how do we know that we wouldn't—well, grow bored with each other? Get up in the morning and think, 'Oh, Lord, another day.' I don't want to live that way."

I wondered if he knew there were days I already felt that way, days when I wondered what life without Sundance would be like. It was just that when I had those thoughts, I didn't know what else to do.

He nodded, grinning in recognition of the truth. "But if we go to South America, and we turn into respectable ranchers, and we get married—"

"We're not getting married."

"Well," he said, "I thought we might think about it."

"All right," I replied, "I'll think about it." And I turned away from him, plumped the skimpy pillow, and pulled the covers comfortably about me.

From behind me came a plaintive voice: "If that's what it's going to be like, forget the marriage."

We celebrated Christmas quietly in Fort Worth, sharing a dinner of prime rib at Peers House with Butch and exchanging small gifts—a fine leather bag for me and a new derby for Sundance, though he had to exchange it later for one in a smaller size. "I thought your head was bigger," I murmured.

Carver and Lillie came the day after Christmas, and I couldn't see that the prospect of marriage had made her any happier. Her eyes were still dark and sunken in her cheeks, and her smile still seemed slashed across her face. But she put on a good front, chattering with all of us about how glad she was to be married in the midst of us. Will, whom I had always thought of as decent—at least compared to Curry—stood silently by, listening and watching with a look of slight embarrassment on his face.

Butch asked him once, "You sure you want to do this?" but he said it with a grin on his face and clapped a hearty hand on Will's shoulder. Another time, Butch gave Lillie a big hug and a hearty "I hope you'll be very happy."

The mood turned less jubilant when Curry arrived. "Married?" he said in astonishment. "You need to let me talk to you, Carver. I can talk you out of this."

If looks could kill, as the old saying goes, it would have been a toss-up as to who got him first, Annie or Lillie. Curry, however, was oblivious.

"Man doesn't want to get married when he can get it for free," he went on loudly. And then he said the unpardonable. "Look at Sundance, here. He's got the right idea."

I froze, a statue half turned toward him, and the parlor where we'd all gathered turned deadly quiet. Butch cleared his throat nervously, and Will Carver stared at the ceiling, reaching out blindly to clutch Lillie's hand. Della stared impassively at the scene, but the Tall Texan looked nervously from Curry to Sundance.

It seemed an hour that we stood that way, each stopped in midmotion by what Curry had said. But it truly wasn't more than half a minute before Sundance said softly, "Etta and I are thinking about getting married, Curry." Those blue eyes had turned to steel.

Curry gave me a look that was of pure hatred.

I returned it. Anger boiled up in me that the man who'd attacked me was here among us, and no one except me seemed to think anything of it.

Judy Alter

Annie pulled Curry out of the room none too gently, and I could see outrage blazing in her eyes. Beyond Butch and Sundance and maybe me, she was the one other person in the world who wasn't afraid of Curry and his reputation, and I suspected she had an idea of what had happened back in Nevada. Curry was so dumb he might have bragged about it, even though he came out on the losing end.

Late that night, my anger exploded at Sundance. "Why in the hell do I have to be around that man?" I demanded.

"He's one of us," he said reluctantly, avoiding looking at me. "Some come and go, but the six of us—counting Elzy—we're the real thing. I'd have told Curry to beat it, but the others . . ." He shrugged, as though to show me his innocence.

Suddenly a thought crept unbidden to my mind. "He's . . . he's not going to South America with us, is he?"

Sundance's laugh was a little too quick, a little too nervous. "With us? No, of course not." But then he added, " 'Course, I can't guarantee what he'll do later on. Man's free to go where he wants."

I knew right then that Curry would end up in South America.

The wedding took place in the parlor of Maddox Flats, late on a wintry afternoon. Sundance stood for the groom, and Annie for the bride. A justice of the peace—I can't even remember his name—was hurried into the parlor, with Butch on one side and Kilpatrick on the other. It wasn't much of a fancy wedding. Lillie wore a plain blue challis dress, fitted at the waist, and someone—Annie? surely not Will!—had gotten her a small bouquet of silk flowers, which she held awkwardly, as though not sure what to do with it. Annie and I had on white waists with dark skirts, mine of wool but Annie's much more showy, of taffeta that crinkled as she walked. I wondered if she wanted to be the next bride. Della still dressed like a man.

It was the men who looked spiffy, however. Each had a new suit, with a double-breasted vest, wide ties neatly in place, watch chains obvious beneath their open jackets. And each wore a brand-new black felt derby—the others, including Butch, had all imitated Sundance and bought hats just like his

298

Christmas gift. They doffed them in respect during the brief ceremony.

And it was brief. A few murmured words, the traditional "Do you take this woman...?" and "Do you take this man...?" answered by mumbled words. There was nothing about man not putting asunder what God had joined together, just a straightforward. "You are now man and wife."

Carver kissed Lillie hesitantly, and Ben Kilpatrick immediately said, "You can do better than that, Will. Here, let me show you." With that he swept a protesting Lillie into his arms and gave her a sound kiss of congratulations.

The others of course followed suit, Curry grabbing Lillie so roughly she cried out in protest and pushed him away. He pretended not to notice and kissed her so hard, I ached for her—and longed to kick him again.

Afterward there was much champagne and a feast of quail on toast points, roasted potatoes, a fruit compote, and a high white coconut cake. We women were, I thought, a trifle solemn: Lillie looked overwhelmed, Annie looked angry, mostly at Curry, and Della looked sullen and resentful.

The men's hilarity could be measured by the bottles of champagne. "Who knows when we'll all be together again?" Butch asked plaintively.

"You all just come down to South America," Sundance said expansively.

"We should pose for a picture," Carver said suddenly. "You know, make a record of the occasion. The wedding . . . and, well, a reunion and maybe a farewell."

The others all thought it a wonderful idea, except Curry, who said, "I'm not sittin' for no picture. That's how you get caught. Somebody sees that picture and they trace it and . . ."

They scoffed at him for being fussy and scared and finally talked him into it.

"They gonna be in the picture?" he asked, jerking his head in the direction of the chairs where I sat with Annie and Della.

A pause. They hadn't thought about that. Sundance spoke up: "Will and Lillie will have their picture made, a wedding picture, but we're talking about a Wild Bunch picture."

Relieved, I sank back in my chair and watched them troop out the door. They went down the street to the studio of John

Swartz, who obliged them by taking a group photograph. Each man had a print of his own a week later, and the others hung around Fort Worth just to wait for that picture. I couldn't believe the vanity.

It is a fine picture. Sundance, Kilpatrick, and Butch are seated, Butch in an ornate wooden chair with claw feet and carved and curved armrests, and Sundance in a wicker chair with splayed legs that give a slight air of instability, as though the chair might collapse under him at any moment. Between them, Kilpatrick sits straight, at least a head taller. The bridegroom stands behind Sundance, one hand on his shoulder, and Curry is behind Butch, a hand on his shoulder. All wear their derbies, and all stare straight into the camera. Carver looks a little overwhelmed—the effect of getting married, no doubt—but Butch has ever so slight a grin, as though he knows a secret. They could be partners in a profitable—and legitimate—law firm.

"Photographer liked it so well he put one up in his window. Advertises the quality photographs he takes," Butch said proudly, as though it were the attractiveness of the subjects and not the skill of the photographer that was being touted.

"Bad sign," Curry said. "You best go rip it down, tell him we don't want no publicity."

They scoffed at him again.

Within twenty-four hours they had all left Fort Worth—Curry to Wyoming with Kilpatrick and Della for company, talking about Wagner, Montana, and the train stop there. Annie went back to Fannie's, and Will and Lillie were off to meet the bride's parents in East Texas.

They had been with us nearly a week, and we were relieved to see them go.

"Whew," Sundance said, "it was great to be with them, but I'm glad they're gone."

"That's how you usually feel about family," Butch replied.

Within a week, we heard that a Wells Fargo detective named Fred Dodge had asked John Swartz for a copy of the picture.

"Maybe," Butch said as we hastily packed, "we should have chosen a photography studio that wasn't down the block from the Wells Fargo office."

"Yeah," Sundance muttered.

We took the first train out of Fort Worth, headed east, traveling like rich folk with several trunks.

We almost got married in New York, though I would have been a reluctant bride. It was Sundance's idea. He got down on one knee in front of me, sweeping that derby hat off his head and holding it dramatically in front of his chest. He really did all that, and I was glad Butch wasn't there to see it. We were in our room at Mrs. Riley's, a comfortably furnished house in Brooklyn. Ours was a front room, with a window looking down on a skinny street where children played in a fresh but already dirty snow.

Slowly, as though his knees hurt him, he stood back up and walked to the window, staring down at the city street scene, so far from his beloved Wyoming. "I don't know," he said, "it just seems like the thing to do before we go off so far."

I decided then and there that Harry Longabaugh—Sundance, the Kid, fearless bank and train robber—was apprehensive about leaving his family, his native country, the whole life he'd known. Marrying me wasn't going to make any difference, but he didn't know that. I didn't say anything.

He turned away from the window and looked at me with a puzzled expression on his face. "It will make everything permanent. I mean, if we're going to be respectable, law-abiding citizens, then we ought to be married like everybody else."

But were we going to be respectable, law-abiding citizens? I remembered my instinctive feeling that Curry would end up in South America with us. If that happened, the law was out the window. And were Butch and Sundance going to settle down to a quiet life?

"We can pretend," I said. "We can tell everyone we're married . . . we can even have a wedding photo taken." I warmed to my idea. "Of course, I'd need a new gown.. . . ."

His expression changed. "You won't marry me! That's really what you're saying, isn't it?"

"No, I won't marry you." I knew deep in my soul that South America was an end. It would be Curry, or restlessness and boredom, or something else, even another woman, but Sundance was not going to settle down and live happily ever after. And when whatever tragedy loomed came to pass, I had to be able to bail myself out. I would survive, and I would not live out my life with Sundance.

He pouted, and I know he told Butch, because Butch asked me to walk with him one day while Sundance had gone to sit in a saloon and have a beer. "In solitude," he said haughtily.

"You know what you're doin', Etta? You hurt him a real lot."

"He'll get over it," I said. "Once he stops being angry with me, he'll find that nothing's changed. Meantime, he's ruining our holiday in New York."

Butch smiled and agreed, kicking some horse droppings out of my path as we crossed the street. New York amazed me. It was nothing like San Antonio, which by contrast seemed open and spacious. New York made me nervous, because it kept me in close quarters with strangers and its sounds assaulted my ears—peddlers and vendors hawking their wares, policemen shouting orders at pedestrians, drivers yelling at their horses, children calling to each other and nervous mothers calling to their children. Even at night, when I waked and stared out the window wondering about the future, the city was never quiet.

We walked in silence for a few minutes. Then, suddenly, out of nowhere, Butch asked, "Would you marry him if he stayed in Wyoming and kept robbing trains?"

I shook my head. "For sure not then, because I don't want to see him die. And you'd both have died if you kept that up. I guess a part of me wants always to be free to look out for me, to retreat if I have to." It was as close as I could come to honesty.

"You don't trust Sundance? You think he'll do something without regard for you?"

I shrugged. "Don't tell him that I didn't deny that."

He gave me a hug, and we walked back to Mrs. Riley's, where Sundance was peering out the front window. "Where've you been?" he demanded. "I want to go out for dinner."

In New York, we called ourselves Mr. and Mrs. Harry Place. Butch said he was James Ryan. One day Butch insisted that we go to Tiffany's, the famous jewelers.

"We going to rob them?" Sundance asked, and for just a moment I saw a flicker in his eye. If Butch had said yes, Sundance would have been game.

"No, we're goin' to walk in and buy something. I know exactly what I want."

I thought about Mary Boyd and wondered that Butch would be bold enough to send her jewelry.

The store was overwhelming, with diamonds glittering behind glass cases and snooty gentlemen in suits, with glasses perched on their noses, who asked haughtily what they could do for us. If we'd been wearing Wyoming clothes, I'd have understood, but we were in our best city clothes and looked, I thought, respectable. Butch and Sundance had on their derbies as usual.

"I want to see a lapel watch," Butch said.

The gentlemen seated us in plush chairs before a counter and disappeared for a minute, only to return with a tray in his hand. There were ten lapel watches, some studded with diamonds, one accented with rubies, some plain.

Butch studied them. "I don't know. Which one do you think, Etta?"

I was remembering Fannie's lapel pin and how much I'd always wanted one. A slight bit of jealousy lurked in my bones, but I overcame it. "I think she should have diamonds," I said. "Not too many, not too fancy, but diamonds."

He finally settled on a gold watch with a diamond-studded filigree-like decoration at the top. "Excellent choice, sir," the salesperson said, almost bowing. "Shall we wrap it?"

"No," Butch said, "just hand it here."

Startled, the man took it from the tray and handed it almost reverently to Butch, who turned to me and said, "Here, Etta, here's the lapel watch you always wanted."

"Oh, Butch!" I honestly could say no more. In minutes, with tears in my eyes, I pinned the watch on.

"I believe," Sundance said, his voice thick with tension, "that I'd like to see a diamond stickpin."

He bought it, and they both paid cash.

We went from Tiffany's straight to the DeYoung Photography Studio on Broadway, where we had an appointment for a wedding photo.

We both look solemn in the photo. Sundance is holding a top hat—replacing the derby—and wearing a black suit and tie, with just a bit of white collar showing. My dress is black, with a white jabot in front, and the lapel watch is prominent. We stand just a bit apart from each other, and I am slightly in front of Sundance. But we are looking not at each other but straight into the camera, as though staring into the future.

Really, we were looking at Butch.

Chapter Twenty-five

"You didn't tell me Butch wasn't going with us." The accusation in my tone was clear.

Sundance did what always irritated me. He shrugged. "Why should it make a difference? You and I are going to Buenos Aires."

"I thought. . . ." My voice trailed off, and finally I finished lamely, "I thought we were all three going."

"Butch will get there when he gets there. He wants to see the world."

How, I wanted to scream, can he see the world without us?

"He's going to Montreal and then to England," Sundance went on calmly. "Sounds like a roundabout way to get to South America to me, but it's not mine to say." Then he fixed me with a long look. "Not yours either, Etta."

We were silent, avoiding looking at each other. Sundance got up and walked to the window of our room in Mrs. Riley's boardinghouse. Parting the curtain to look out, he asked, "Does it make a difference, Etta? Don't you want to go if it's only me?" His voice was tight.

I answered slowly and quietly. "It makes a difference in that I'm used to the three of us being inseparable. I . . . it will take me a while to get used to this."

"Used to being with me alone?" Now he turned, and I could see the bemused look on his face. "In the old days, when we got left alone at the Hole, you welcomed it."

"And I do now, Sundance . . ." Well, it was only a small lie. "It's just that . . . South America, it's not like the Hole. It's . . . it's a foreign country!"

"Was last time I checked," he said, and then he laughed and came to put his arms around me. "Etta Place, if I didn't know you better, I'd say you were afraid."

And I had thought he was afraid! Maybe to Butch I would have confessed that I was afraid to leave our country, to go somewhere where they spoke a language I barely understood, where life was bound to be different. It wasn't exactly fear, but a great doubt that lingered in my mind that following them to South America might not be the best way for me to look out for Etta Place. But my only other choice, so far as I knew, was to go back to Fannie's, and I wasn't going to do that. So South America it was—apparently without Butch.

"Afraid?" I scoffed. "I'll show you who's afraid. You can't even speak the language, Harry Longabaugh. You'll be depending on me to tell you what to order for dinner, what time it is, even where the men's room is."

"And you," he said, smiling broadly now, "will be depending on me to take care of you." Then he paused and said, "If you're going to give me directions, are you going to pick out banks for us?"

I pulled away. "No more banks," I said. "You promised."

He looked uncertain for a minute. "I was just testing you," he said. "Wanted to know if you were really ready to give it all up."

And in that moment, I knew that Sundance would never give up robbing banks.

There was a knock on the door, and Sundance went to open it. There stood Butch, a valise in his hand.

"I got to be leavin'," he said, "but I just wanted you to know. I got word that Pinkertons know you're in New York, Kid. They think I'm in Minnesota or some godforsaken place, but they know you're here."

"We sail tomorrow," Sundance said, "and we'll stay hidden until then. I'll send Etta out for groceries."

"Good plan," Butch said as he winked at me.

Butch's leave-taking was unsentimental, as though he were going around the block and would see us in a few minutes. He told Sundance to check things out—I didn't know if that meant ranching, which he professed to want to do, or banks, which interested Sundance more.

Then he turned to me.

"Etta, you watch out for him. Without you, he's a loose cannon."

"I already told him I'd locate the men's room for him. But he says he's going to take care of me." I bit my lip.

"He darn well better," Butch said, and gave me a quick, brotherly hug.

Then he was gone, and Sundance and I were left in uncomfortable silence.

Mr. and Mrs. Harry Place sailed the next day, February 2, 1901, having eluded Pinkerton's men and survived on bread, cheese, and ham that I brought from the local market. Sundance swore he could have given his $1,000 for a good drink of whiskey, but I told him the market didn't carry it, and I wasn't about to venture farther.

Once we were out to sea by a day, Sundance couldn't have cared less about that whiskey. He was wretchedly, violently seasick, too weak to lift his head from the pillow, too nauseated to swallow even the tepid water I tried to give him. I tried scraping burnt toast into a cup of tea—it was an old remedy for nausea that Fannie had taught me. She said the charcoal and tea quieted the stomach.

Not so with Sundance. He took a small sip, spat it out, and managed to whisper, "You're trying to kill me."

Sundance stayed in his bunk the whole long trip, though by the time we neared Buenos Aires, he could take a little chicken soup or oatmeal. But after he ate, he had to lie flat on his back for a long time.

Whenever I could leave Sundance—I almost said escape from—I roamed the decks of the ship. I loved the strong ocean winds that tore at my hair and sent my skirts billowing out behind me, and I marveled at that endless expanse of water, especially when a brilliant orange sun set at the western horizon in the evenings. The captain kindly invited me to his table, with muttered condolences about Mr. Place's ill health, and I dined on all manner of delicacies, though I was always surprised at what foods they were able to keep on board the ship. When I reported on this dinner or that to Sundance, he simply groaned. Once he muttered, "He wants to sleep with you."

"What?" I said, my voice louder than I meant.

"The captain," he said. "He wants to sleep with you."

"Sundance, you better stay sick this whole voyage," I threatened, "because I will not have you insulting the man who has befriended me in your absence."

Fortunately the two never met until we were disembarking at Buenos Aires. The captain shook hands with Sundance and offered his sympathy for the difficult journey.

"It's nothing," Sundance said, waving a hand and trying hard to regain his usual casual self-possession. "My wife will have me well in no time."

"I'm sure," the captain said wryly.

As we stepped off the gangplank onto solid ground, I turned to look at the captain and saw him still staring after us. Sundance was right about the man's intentions, and I knew it. The thought gave me a little glow of pleasure and then a serious doubt—would I have been better off to have stayed on that luxurious ship?

I had tried to drag Sundance out onto the deck when the ship passed Montevideo and sailed up the Río de la Plata, with Uruguay on one side and Argentina on the other. There was, I thought, something majestic about that wide river—many times wider than the Mississippi—and that one lone hill that seemed to stand guard over it on the Uruguay side. The light-house perched on top of the hill looked like a child's toy, and I was sorry it was not night so that I could see its blinking light.

We were in Buenos Aires for three months—at least I was. Sundance kept leaving on trips of three, four, or seven days.

"Looking for land to buy," he explained, but I watched carefully when he came back to see that he wasn't suddenly spending money like a drunken sailor.

"You think I've been robbing banks, don't you?" he asked one night as we sat in the bar at the Hotel Europa where we were staying.

"Not necessarily," I replied warily. Then, laughing, "But it did cross my mind."

Sundance turned serious. "Etta, Etta. I don't know what's happened between us, but do you really have such a low opinion of me that you think I'd rob a bank without Butch—behind his back, as it were? For that matter, do you think I'd not tell you?"

I felt foolish and said nothing.

Then he laughed. "Besides, how dumb do you think I am? Dumb enough to rob a bank alone?"

"I guess I'm just nervous or . . . oh, I don't know. Sundance, I'm sorry I didn't trust you."

He looked at me out of the corner of his eye. "That's the whole point," he said. "You didn't trust me. Apology accepted . . . but the insult will linger."

That night we each slept far on the side of the bed, careful not to touch each other.

Buenos Aires was a fascinating city. I needn't have worried about Sundance's poor Spanish, for the city was full of Brits, all speaking the Queen's English. Because we were staying at the city's finest hotel and because my husband—Harry A. Place—had opened a rather large account in one of the city's banks, we were soon courted by high society. That meant wealthy English ranchers who had vast ranches—they called them *estancias*—in a region known as Tierra del Fuego or the lake district. They named these areas Río Negro and Chubut, and I never let on that I was thoroughly puzzled.

As I danced with this Englishman and that or sipped tea with their wives—who led incredibly dull lives and were limited in their interests, to my mind—my thoughts often wandered to Butch. I wondered where he was, what he was doing, and—heaven help me—who he was doing it with. Sundance was probably in more peril, riding the pampas or plains, but I rarely gave his safety a thought.

When he was in the city, we had passionate nights, and we enjoyed each other's company. Sundance liked being "Mr. Place," the rich American who was looking for an *estancia*, and he played the role to the hilt. I liked being the American wife, presumably from high society, and having everyone vie for my attention. We were a good pair, good foils for each other, and sometimes late at night we'd fall across the bed in laughter imagining the Brit's astonished indignation if they ever found out they were talking to outlaws.

One proper though overweight gentleman, a Mr. Trevalyen, asked me once about outlaws. "We have heard," he said, "that they are a great problem in your western provinces."

"States," I corrected him, and then seemed to dismiss the subject. "They prey on banks and trains, not ordinary citizens," I said. "Do you not have the same problem here?"

He shook his head emphatically. "No, we have *bandidos* who will stop travelers, but no one dares to rob a bank."

Don't tell that to Sundance, I thought.

All in all, I enjoyed my time in Buenos Aires. It was rather like spending three months in the Brown's Hotel in Denver. After two days, Butch would have hated it. After three months I began to worry about Butch, but I had made myself a steely promise that I would not mention him to Sundance, would not let him know when I worried. So it was Sundance who first began to worry aloud.

"Damn fool, off traipsin' around the world. He think we're just going to sit on our behinds and wait for him until it pleases him to appear?"

"Maybe Pinkerton caught him," I suggested, hating the words.

"Naw, Butch is too smart. And besides, it would have made the headlines even down here. Likely he's having the time of his life."

"Aren't you?" I asked.

"Me? Oh, sure. I'm with the woman I love, who doesn't trust me, and I'm riding all over Argentina looking for land, and I'm hot and I want a drink of whiskey."

"Me, too," I said.

Sundance turned sweet—something he did less these days—and covered my hand with his. "I found some land last week," he said.

"Last week? And you're just now telling me?"

He shrugged. "I'm not sure how you'll like it. It's remote, and you . . . you're liking life in the city."

This time I was the one who shrugged. "I'd give it up," I said, and then added, "to be with you." But inside I wasn't sure I would. In Buenos Aires, alone, I could make a life for myself.

Several wealthy ranchers had almost openly asked me to be their mistress, and I could always become the Buenos Aires equivalent of Fannie. Neither of those ideas appealed to me, and I searched my mind for other opportunities. A fine dress store? Sundance had always picked my expensive clothes. A fine restaurant? My cooking was strictly country style—corn bread and beans, not haute cuisine. In some senses I was trapped by myself.

But Sundance knew none of that. He thought only that I wanted to go anywhere with him. "Good girl," he said, heartily pleased. "This is in Chubut Province, a place called Cholila. It's just this side of the Andes, halfway down to the tip of Argentina."

"Halfway to the end of the world," I said. "How far from here?"

He avoided my eyes. "Sixteen hundred miles, give or take a little." Then, persuasively, he added, "Pinkertons will never find it." He was silent for a long time, and then he said, his voice tentative, "Etta? We could . . . ah . . . leave instructions for Butch and go on."

"If that Frank Dimaio from Pinkertons can't find it, neither can Butch. We're not leaving without him." I said it decisively, and Sundance turned angry.

"Butch," he said. "Which one of us are you with?"

"Sundance," I replied wearily, "let's not have that argument again. I'm with you, and you know it. I'm Mrs. Harry Place. But I won't leave Butch. And you wouldn't either."

"I know," he said, and called for another drink.

Butch arrived about two weeks after that conversation, banging on the door of our suite in the middle of the night and, once entered, grinning as though he'd been gone only a day.

"Damn," Sundance said without rising from the bed, "you stay away forever, and then you come back just when I don't want to see you."

Butch looked instantly hurt. "I thought you'd be asleep," he said.

"That's what I meant," Sundance told him.

"Turn your back," I told Butch, and he did while I slipped into a robe.

"All right," I said, "now tell us all about everything."

"Yeah," Sundance said, "where the hell you been?"

"England," Butch said, crooking his little finger and pretending to hold a dainty teacup. "It was soooo vehhhry . . . well, it wasn't Wyoming," he finished lamely.

I laughed. "You needn't have gone all the way to England. They're lots of Brits in Buenos Aires. I've been drinking tea and talking racehorses and all that right here."

"How do you stand it?" Butch asked. "I got tired of it pretty quick."

"Oh," I said lightly, "I'm adaptable."

Sundance had tired of our light bantering. "I found a place for us near Cholila, in Chubut Province," he said. "We'll leave in two days. I got all the supplies, everything we need."

Butch slept the entire single day he was in Buenos Aires. When I thought about it later, I realized there wasn't a lot I would have shown him, not much that he would have liked. And I didn't want to make farewells to all those ranchers I'd been partying with. Who knew if I might need to call on them sometime? Butch—much as I loved him—might have tarnished my image, for he truly did still look like an outlaw from Wyoming.

We went by ship from Buenos Aires to Madryn on the Gulf of Nuevo. Sundance was pale and quiet, but never as desperately sick as he had been on the long voyage. Still, he stayed below, while Butch stood with me at the rail, staring at the endless water.

"You and Sundance been all right?" he asked, his voice too casual.

"I guess," I said. "He was gone a lot, and I . . . I was the belle of the ball in Buenos Aires." I gave a little whirl, as though promenading for him.

Butch grinned. "I can't think of a better belle," he said, "but I don't know how you stood it." Then, seriously, he asked, "Are you ready to go back to living far away from civilization? I mean, after New York and Buenos Aires?"

"I am because I'm not ready to leave you and Sundance," I said.

He interpreted my words his own way. "But someday you may be?"

I nodded. "Someday. Maybe. If you go back to robbing banks."

"You loved it! You wanted to be part of it, asked me," he protested.

"I did love it, loved the excitement. But now, from a distance—and it's not been all that long—I see the folly of it. I don't want to see the two of you hang or spend your days in jail . . . and I sure don't want that for myself. So I'll do what I think I have to whenever."

"To take care of Etta?"

"Who else is going to do it? Not Sundance. Not really, when the chips are down."

Butch put his big hand over mine. "I'll always take care of you, Etta, the best I can. But I can't promise that'll be enough. And I can't offer you what you really want and need."

The ghost of Mary Boyd of Lander rose between us again.

From Madryn we went by horseback to Trelew in Chubut, and suddenly I was back in Wyoming—or felt that I was. The three of us rode horseback, leading packhorses. Sundance had had furniture and supplies shipped to Cholila, but we had supplies for the trip—which took over a week—and our personal possessions. We crossed Patagonia from the coast, heading directly west. Endless plains of lush grass stretched all around us, and the sky was clear and cloudless, like a giant canopy cover hanging over us. The wind blew constantly, as it can in Wyoming, and we saw occasional dust devils.

It was by then early May, the beginning of winter in Argentina, and the nights were cold, the days sometimes damp. I was thankful for the Wyoming woolens I'd packed, and at night I was glad to share my covers with Sundance. Butch always tactfully slept on the far side of the fire, and we never did have to make a cold camp because we were being followed. I'd thought it pure luxury compared to camps I'd known, but in my dreams I often returned to the Hotel Europa. Strangely, Sundance was never there with me.

Occasionally we saw gauchos, with their funny narrow-brimmed hats that they held on with straps under their chin. They wore colorful ponchos with silk handkerchiefs around their necks.

"They're like us," Sundance said, "outlaws."

313

"I thought they were just cowboys in funny clothes," Butch said.

Sundance spoke with lofty knowledge gained from his weeks of exploring the pampa. "The cowboys are vacqueros, and they don't look as . . . well, as dirty. The gauchos, they trade in illegal hides."

"I'd rather rob banks," Butch said with a grin.

"We got something in common," Sundance said. "They're disappearing. They can't survive in the modern cattle world, just like we couldn't survive in Wyoming anymore."

Butch gave his hat an imaginary tip, as though acknowledging a certain brotherhood.

"There, but for Etta, go you and me," Butch said.

Sundance looked at him a long minute, then at me, and finally said, "I don't think so." Then, jokingly, "You sure there's no Pinkerton man following us?"

"Better yet, you sure you know where you're goin'?" Butch asked.

"I've been here before," Sundance said, and he used that same unerring sense of direction that had taken him safely all across the western states.

Finally the land began to rise and break into foothills, and I remembered my first approach to the Rocky Mountains when Sundance tried hard to explain to me about distance and foothills and the nature of mountains. Eventually, the Andes, mountains so much higher that they make the Rockies look small, rose before us in all their majesty, and we rode through a region of beautiful clear lakes set amid hills that gradually grew into the mountains.

"This is what they all talked about! Tierra del Fuego!" I was overwhelmed with the landscape. "It's better than Wyoming!"

"Heresy!" Sundance said.

"What'd you say?" Butch asked, and I repeated the Spanish slowly for him. He mouthed it after me, but his pronunciation was awful, and he was embarrassed when I laughed.

Throughout the long journey, Butch had kept his distance from me. Once in a while I'd see him glance in my direction, and when I caught him he'd smile or wink. But he did not, as he once would have, come to sit next to me at the night's fire, and he spun no tales of England for me, though I longed to hear them. When, twice, I asked, he just shook his head and said, "It was different, Etta, really different. But there's not much to tell." This from the man who'd spun magical tales about being accused of stealing a pair of overalls or jumping off a moving train. I couldn't believe his British trip was as dull as he said. That shared moment of intimacy on the deck of the boat to Madryn was gone as though it never existed.

In the night, when he thought Butch was sleeping, Sundance was passionately insistent, and I responded—but always with an ear cocked to hear if Butch was still snoring.

"Quit worrying about him!" Sundance said one night, as he turned away in anger.

We reached Trelew, a small city, none too soon. Mr. and Mrs. Place soon had private rooms at the Globe Hotel, and Mr. Cassidy was left to entertain himself while we stayed locked in our room for an entire day. I matched Sundance's passion minute by minute, but I did it in a detached way that was analyzing myself even as I responded to his touch, his kisses, his insistent thrusting. A part of me would always love Sundance, there was no doubt about that, and I would not hurt him for anything. Another part of me, the impersonal part, reveled in the pure physical pleasure of our coming together. But the most complicated part of me was that which knew that for the time being I was irrevocably with Sundance—unless I wanted to cross those pampas by myself and head back to Buenos Aires alone—and it was only practical to make him feel I loved him. That I succeeded was testified to by his dazed look of happiness when we sat in the bar with Butch late that night.

"You have a good day?" he asked Butch.

With a blush and an embarrassed nod toward me, Butch said, "Probably not as good as yours."

I kicked him in the shins under the table, and he yowled. "Sorry, Etta, I just couldn't resist."

We stayed only long enough at Trelew to be certain that supplies were being shipped, and then we left on horseback for our *estancia*.

Sundance played the guide with a kind of superiority that amused me. "It's not like the—what do you call them, Etta?"

"*Estancias*," I supplied.

"Right, *estancias*"—he mispronounced it—"but it's a substantial ranch. We can raise sheep and cattle, and there's a good solid house. Better than at the Hole."

With this he shot me a long look, and I knew that no place would be better than the Hole, and the actual building had nothing to do with it. While he and Butch talked about the advantages of our new property and whether or not Sundance had driven a good deal, I let my mind go blank and concentrated on the mountains ahead of me. They almost made me homesick.

Our ranch was near the town of Esquel, and it was indeed 1,600 miles from Buenos Aires and 400 miles from the nearest railroad. We eventually had 300 head of cattle, 1,500 sheep, eight or so horses—the number varied from time to time—and two gauchos to help with the work. Once settled there, we felt so safe that we used our own names. The people of Esquel were a combination of Spanish-speaking natives and Welshmen who had come farther than we had to seek freedom. All of them welcomed us, and we became somewhat celebrities.

"Etta," Sundance said one day in a tone that was only half jest, "do you have to wear breech pants and show everyone how you can shoot a rifle? It's not the way ladies behave here."

"Makes people notice me," I said. "I like that."

"We spent a lifetime trying not to be noticed," Sundance said, now speaking in exasperation to Butch and ignoring me, "and now she's become a . . . a . . . what's the word I want?"

"A showoff?" Butch asked helpfully.

"An exhibitionist," I said calmly.

"You are not!" Sundance said. "Least, as far as I know you always have clothes on!"

I giggled at him. "I'm just having fun," I said, "and the townspeople like it. I'm even teaching some of the ladies to shoot. Can you imagine that their men have never taught them?"

"With good reason," Sundance said, and even Butch chimed in with "Great! Now we'll be surrounded by armed housewives. I think I'd prefer Pinkertons."

"Bite your tongue," I warned him.

Actually, for two years, there was no need for Butch to bite his tongue. We lived in peace with other ranchers, we went to carnival with our neighbors before the Holy Season—I could never get either Butch or Sundance to church, not that I missed it much myself. But I thought it was the thing to do in that community and for that way of life. I was strangely anxious to blend in, to be one of the people. I did learn local recipes from the other women (Butch particularly liked a bean-and-pork stew that was traditional). I danced at the weddings, smiled brightly at christenings and wept at funerals. It was almost like we lived in that rose-covered cottage that I would never have, not with Sundance, not with Butch.

We lived in harmony among ourselves too. Butch and I, privately and apart, came to some sort of acceptance. We joked with each other, and sometimes we exchanged wry grins, but we kept our distance. I let Sundance fill my life, and he, sensing a change in me, became less testy, more the old fun-loving Sundance, the man who'd captured my heart in San Antonio. Oh, I still longed for Butch, but I guess I learned that life is a series of compromises. And I was ever watchful for change, for something that would force me to move. For the time being, in peace, I was content, if not wildly happy. After all, I had the two men I loved all to myself.

"Sure is a good life," Butch said one night, seated on the veranda of our small house, his chair tilted back against the wall even though I'd warned him three times that evening alone that he'd break the chair by tilting it that way.

It was dusk of a warm February night—winter in Wyoming, but summer in Argentina—and we sat sipping coffee laced with just a bit of whiskey, a luxury we still treasured from the Hole days.

"Yeah," Sundance said from the stairs where he sat smoking his cigarillo so the smoke would go in the other direction. He'd acquired a taste for cigarillos in Argentina and often tried to convince me that the smoke kept bugs away. I had tried smoking one and found it unpleasant, to say the least. Butch had laughed when I spit and choked.

"It's peaceful. And you know what amazes me? I'm not bored." Sundance sounded purely surprised at himself.

"Thanks," I said.

"You know what I meant, Etta. I don't miss the old days, don't miss being on the run, don't even miss the high of robbing banks and trains. Guess I'm getting old."

"We all are," Butch said. "Sometimes I get homesick"—we knew that meant he longed for Mary Boyd and, probably, for the family he loved but rarely had seen in those last years—"but not enough to go back and take those chances. My running days are over."

And I began to believe that. I truly thought there would be no bank robberies, no trains to hold up. If they had changed—mellowed?—so had I. I was through with adventure and excitement. I'd had wild and crazy, I told myself, and now I wanted peace and quiet. Sometimes I thought our new life was too good to be true, as if the Lord or someone would reach down from heaven and smite us, not for sins of the past but just because people were not meant to be that happy. And then I'd scold myself. *This is the way we'll live the rest of our lives*, I told myself firmly.

I should instead have listened to that warning voice.

Butch came riding hell-bent for leather one day from town. "Sundance!" He was hollering before he ever reined that poor horse to an abrupt stop. "Sundance? Where are you?"

Sundance came lazily out the door, with me close behind him. "You see a ghost?" he asked.

"Damn right I did," Butch said, taking the steps two at a time. "A ghost named Apfield."

Sundance was unperturbed. "Pardon me? Apfield? I don't think I know that particular ghost."

Butch threw himself in a chair, his hands nervously twisting the gloves he carried. "Trouble is, he's not a ghost. He's a flesh-and-blood cattle buyer."

"Oh. That makes sense," Sundance said, grinning.

"Was a sheriff in Wyoming," Butch said. "Mean and greedy son of a bitch. You know there were a lot of sheriffs I liked real well. He wasn't one of them."

Sundance was more serious now. "And you saw him? Where?"

"In Esquel," Butch said, his voice now weary. "He really is a cattle buyer."

"He see you?"

Butch nodded his head. "I'm almost positive. I tried to sidle away, but I felt his eyes staring at me even through my back."

318

With certainty I knew that I had been right. People were not allowed to be as content as we had been for long.

Finally, Sundance spoke. "No sense acting in panic. Let's give it a couple of days, see what happens. Etta, tomorrow you ride into town, casual, and shop or do whatever. See if you can find out if anyone's been asking about Butch."

I nodded.

Next morning, wearing my breech pants and a gaucho-style hat, I raced into town, coming to a dramatic stop in front of the mercantile store, as was my usual habit. People stared, but then they always did because I was more than a bit of a showoff. Were they staring differently today?

In the store I asked for cigarillos for Sundance, thread, and chilies. The storekeeper knew we bought such things as sugar, flour, and coffee in bulk, so it was no good asking for those. He was cheerful getting them for me—a trifle too cheerful, I thought. And the ladies who greeted me, weren't they too friendly? Everything struck me as unnatural and posed, and yet I knew my senses were heightened enough to give in to imagination.

Still, when I arrived back at the ranch I said, "He was asking. Everybody was polite and . . . it was like they were trying to be natural and couldn't. Something's changed." I was then, and am now, a firm believer that the slightest change sets off a reaction until there is a huge eruption—and that, I knew, was what was about to happen in our lives.

Butch and Sundance paced the floor, argued and talked and discussed and banged their fists on the table in anger for two days, and never did decide what to do. The provincial authorities decided for them.

"Visitors," Sundance said, rising to stand to the side of the window, as I'd first seen him do all those years ago in Hell's Half Acre. "Police, provincial police."

"You got your gun?" Butch asked, and Sundance nodded. "Loaded?" he insisted, and Sundance nodded again. Then, to me, Butch said, "Bring that whiskey and some glasses."

By the time the police—a commissar and three men—rode up to the house, Butch was standing on the porch, welcoming them in his still-broken Spanish. My Spanish was only too good—I understood clearly when the commissar, a man named

Tasso, announced that he was here to arrest "Butch Cassidy and Harry Longabaugh." He pronounced the names peculiarly, but I was in no mood for giggling.

"Would you like a sip of whiskey?" Butch asked.

The commissar and the three men behind him all shook their heads to reject the offer.

I stood in the doorway, looking from one to the other, fingering the small hand revolver in my pocket. When I took my eyes off the scene in front of me, I raised them to those majestic high mountains and wondered if they offered as many hiding spots as the Rockies.

"Why do you want to arrest us?" Butch asked.

"You steal, in the United States, you rob banks and trains. There is a reward."

"And who gets the reward?" Butch asked.

"The man who told us who you were," the police officer said, always most polite.

"Apfield," Butch spit out. "Dirtiest sheriff ever wore a badge in Wyoming."

"That may be, senor, but I am not here to judge his competency as a sheriff. I am here to arrest you."

"Why arrest us?" Butch asked. "True, we did steal, but only from the greedy and powerful, like the people who owned the railroads. We never took a penny from poor people. Sometimes we gave our money to them."

"That is noble—"

Tasso, never got to finish the sentence, because Sundance interrupted. "We're not going with you." He said it calmly and quietly, but he left no doubt he meant it.

Casually, Sundance drew his Colt revolver and shot a couple of bullets in the air. Just as casually Butch, who was now on the ground, off the veranda, picked up a rock and tossed it in the air. Instantly the rock was shattered by a bullet from Sundance's gun.

As though they'd rehearsed this a thousand times, Butch threw Sundance a rock, which he then pitched in the air. Butch's shot shattered it before it reached the arc of its flight. They repeated this only twice, and I knew they were saving the bullets. After all, they were the ones with guns in hand. The officers would have awkwardly had to pull out revolvers or rifles from their cases. Clearly, Butch and Sundance had the advantage.

"Pardon us for shooting rocks," Butch said. "We do this every day because we are bored."

"Sí, señor," the commissar said. "We are sorry to have bothered you."

And they turned and rode away.

We left the *estancia* that night, under cover of darkness, leaving behind most of our possessions and a note giving the livestock to the two men who worked for us. We were on the run again.

"Dimaio will be here in no time. Probably already in Buenos Aires, if I know Apfield," Butch said.

We were camped in the mountains. A small fire glowed at our feet, and we clutched cups of coffee laced with whiskey. Whatever else we left behind, Sundance had remembered the whiskey.

"Can't we go to Bolivia or Chile? Someplace else, anyplace?" I asked.

Sundance shook his head. "They're onto us. I think we could go to Egypt, and they'd find us."

"Or join a monastery," Butch said glumly.

"I suppose," I said, trying to add a light note, "I'd have to get myself to a nunnery."

Then Sundance laughed aloud, a hearty natural laugh. "I think they'd see you coming a mile away, Etta," he said. "No, we'll have to think of another plan."

"Well," Butch said, "we can't hide in these damn cold mountains forever. Winter's coming. And we got no money. We left everything at the place. I guess we'll have to rob a bank."

Sundance's eyes suddenly glowed with the light of interest. "Now, there's an idea! I wonder why I hadn't thought of it myself?"

"You said no more banks," I reminded them, drawing my skirts close around my legs and, in effect, drawing into myself.

"That was then, and this is now," Sundance said glibly. "Now we have no choice."

I knew there must be a choice, but I didn't know what it was.

Chapter Twenty-six

That was why I went to Rio Gallegos with them—no choices. I couldn't stay in Esquel at the *estancia*. Dimaio would rather have caught Butch or Sundance, but he'd have taken me if he could. And in the back of my mind always hovered the fear that if I were captured for being with the Hole-in-the-Wall Gang, someone would find out about Pa's murder in Texas.

I couldn't get to Buenos Aires—even I was not foolhardy enough to set out across the pampa on horseback by myself. Nor could I go over the mountains to Chile—no one in Tierra del Fuego could, for there was not yet a pass. The only pass was far to the north at Mendoza, a place that I did not know then but would know too well one day soon. So I went to Rio Gallegos, in the southern tip of Argentina's coastal Patagonia region, a land less intriguing to me than Tierra de Fuego. The Andean range there breaks up into rocky bays and islets, and deep canyons break the windswept plateaus. It is sheep farming country, and Sundance told us that wool was shipped north from Rio Gallegos to Buenos Aires.

"When they've just shipped a load of wool, there'll be money in the bank," he said triumphantly. "We'll watch for the right time."

All I cared about was that the wind blew constantly and I wanted it to stop.

As we neared the small city, though, I began to care about something else—my safety. "We've got to have a plan," I announced one night as we huddled around a campfire. I thought I spoke with some authority. What I really meant was that I didn't intend to get captured or shot doing this, and I wanted a plan to avoid that.

"Excuse me?" Sundance said. "Who put you in charge?"

A furious reply died on my lips when Butch said softly, "Of course we do, Etta. I know that . . . and I got a plan. I'm sorry I haven't told you about it yet. Didn't know you were worrying."

"I was," I admitted.

"Well," he said, "here it is." And he proceeded to lay out a plan so simple yet so perfect that I laughed aloud. "It's your chance to wear those breeches and ride like hell," Butch said, and then, "Pardon my language, Etta."

We camped three miles from the town for almost three weeks, and twice a week we rode into town for provisions. We did not ride leisurely. We rode as though the devil himself was after us, racing, calling to each other, urging our horses to greater speeds. More than once I beat both of them, and I would pull my winded horse to a stop and stare triumphantly at them. Butch laughed, but it made Sundance angry.

The townspeople of Rio Gallegos, needless to say, were taken aback. They watched us openly. They stared. Some women averted their eyes from mine, as though they couldn't believe a woman would behave so. These were not the rich women of Tierra del Fuego *estancias*; these were women whose men were shepherds or worked on the docks where the ships came to get the wool. The women themselves worked hard cleaning and washing and cooking for their families. I doubt any of them had ever been allowed to ride a horse, and it made me want to shout at them, "I can teach you to shoot a rifle!" After all, I'd taught the women of Esquel.

Butch talked me out of that idea rather quickly, and Sundance said, "You're doing a swell job of making a spectacle of yourself, Etta."

"That's what Butch wants," I said serenely.

323

But those rides into town told us what we wanted to know: We soon learned when the next big shipment of wool would go out—prepaid, as it were. The bank was a small one, a stucco building with a fading tile roof and a wooden hitching rail in front. It had a verandah covered by a wood roof that sat on wooden poles. Several old men gathered daily on the benches on this verandah to talk of wool and ships and weather.

"Will they be a problem?" I asked softly one day, nodding in their direction.

Sundance was scornful. "You think I can't outshoot those old men?"

But Butch was reasonable. "They have no guns," he said. "They'll be upset, but they won't bother us." And when the time came, they didn't.

When we weren't riding hell-bent for town, we were bored. In our haste to leave Esquel, I had brought no books or magazines. There were no streams for fishing, no small game to hunt, nothing to do. Butch had a deck of cards, and they played endless rounds of anything they could think of, from gin rummy to poker. I spent a lot of time thinking about the future, but it got me nowhere.

Finally the day of shipment came. The next day when we thundered into town we had all our belongings rolled behind our saddles. We hit the bank at noon—some of Butch's habits never changed!—and were out within minutes, carrying 20,000 pesos and a tin box with gold ingots in it. I had done my part, training a rifle on the cashier and guard, and I bet it was a long time before the people of that small town stopped talking about the *norteamericano* lady bank robber. I just hoped Dimaio never ventured that far. Then I realized that was a foolish hope—once the robbery was made public, he'd be down there.

The perfect thing about Butch's plan was that when we galloped out of town, no one paid us any mind. After three weeks they'd gotten so used to our loud craziness that they just went about their business. Even the old men didn't realize anything had happened as we ran out of the bank, vaulted onto our horses, and took off at a dead gallop without a backward look. Just like every other time, we shouted. Only this time, in English, we shouted out loudly about our success. We were probably twenty miles away before anyone thought to organize a posse.

We made cold camps at night—we just hadn't bought all those provisions in Rio Gallegos for nothing—and sometimes we rode at night. Just over a week later, we were back in Esquel—or near it. Under cover of dark, Butch rode in to see friends. When he returned, the news was not heartening.

"Dimaio's been here, and the federal authorities have warrants for us. We can't stay."

"Can we go to Madryn and take a boat to Buenos Aires?" I asked.

Sundance hooted. "Show up in Buenos Aires? Now that they know who we are, we'd be in jail before we had our first sip of whiskey in the Hotel Europa."

Reluctantly I realized that he was right. We were on the run again. *We might as well have stayed in Wyoming,* I thought bitterly.

We rode north, edging along the mountains, until we finally cut east to Neuquen, a town in the middle of the pampa on Rio Negro. Butch and Sundance robbed the bank without ever once having ridden into the town.

"That's stupid," I raved the night before when they told me of the plan. "The dumbest thing I ever heard of."

Even Butch was grinning. "Thank you, Etta. I appreciate your confidence."

"Butch—"

Sundance interrupted. "You got to admit it beats other plans just for sheer excitement."

"I'm not looking for excitement," I said angrily.

"Why, Etta," he said smoothly, "I always thought you were."

"You aren't coming with us this time," Butch said. "It'll make it look different if there are only two of us, and I . . . well, I don't want you to take the chance."

That was something new! Was he worried about me or was he sensing that my own newly developed worry might make me cautious and therefore a liability at robbery? Or did he sense that one day, probably soon, they would be caught or killed? I shivered. I didn't want an answer to those questions right away.

I waited on horseback for them to come roaring into camp. They passed me without stopping, and I spurred my horse to catch up with them. We disappeared into the tall grass of the pampa, but I was not pleased with my companions.

We were exhausted by the time we made camp that night, and Sundance and I quarreled over the placement of the sleeping rolls, what there was—or wasn't—to eat, almost anything we could find to pick at each other about.

"You two need some time alone," Butch announced. "I'm going over yonder." It had been almost a month since Sundance and I had slept together, and Butch apparently thought that was why we were getting testier with each other by the minute.

Sundance grinned at his longtime friend. "I don't think that's going to solve the problem," he said. "But thanks."

I remained silent.

Sundance was right. It didn't solve the problem. But neither did I regret a minute of that long night, nor did I mind riding across the pampa in a sleepless haze the next day. Every once in a while Sundance—who was bright and chipper, blast him!— would look at me and laugh. Butch kept his eyes either straight ahead to where we were going or behind to see if we were being followed. We weren't.

We were next headed for the bank at Mercedes, on the railroad line between Buenos Aires and Valparaiso, Chile.

"What happened to hiding out between times and letting things quiet down?" I asked.

Sundance favored me with a withering look. "Things aren't going to 'quiet down,' as you so delicately put it. Our philosophy this time is to hit 'em hard and run."

"Run where?" I asked sarcastically.

"Bolivia," Butch said calmly. "I figure we'll just rob our way north until we can get passage to California. And if we make a big splash in Bolivia, then the Argentina authorities will know any robberies that happen here weren't committed by us."

Only later did it occur to me that they could have ridden right over the mountains at the pass at Mendoza. They would have been in Chile, headed for Valparaiso and easy passages to California. No, they wanted to give it up and go home—but not quite yet, thank you. At the time I thought they were protecting their reputations.

"Nobody else down here robs banks," I pointed out.

"Never can tell," Sundance said airily. "There might be other visitors."

Why, I wondered, did I feel as if someone had walked on my grave? And when did they have time to plan this all out without my knowing it? Were they whispering while I was asleep? Clearly, whatever and however, the two of them had made plans without taking me into their confidence.

"You going with us to Mercedes?" Sundance asked innocently.

"We could use a third person, Etta," Butch said. "This is a bigger bank than Neuquen. But not, Etta, if you don't want to. . . ."

"I'm with you, aren't I?" I almost spat the words out, and then I felt instant remorse over having been harsh with Butch.

Butch chose to ignore my sharpness. "Good," he said, "this is what we'll do." And we hunkered around a fire and watched him trace pictures in the dirt. How he knew to plan a robbery in a town he'd never checked out is beyond me, but I think Butch operated by finely honed instinct a lot of the time.

We rode into Mercedes just before siesta. I have to admit that Butch's noontime habit was a good one in South America, where everything closed down after lunch for a siesta. We ate a good lunch—beef and beans—in a small café, and Butch and Sundance each had one local beer. No more. In that heat, I thought even one was taking a chance on dulling their sharpness, but Butch pointed out that everyone would think it strange if they did not have a drink with their meal. I drank water.

We robbed the bank, but not without incident. As had become usual, I trained my rifle on the cashiers, lined up against a wall, while Butch and Sundance rifled the cash drawers and explored the safe. Since it was siesta, we didn't have to worry about either customers or an officious bank president. Whoever he was, he was home having a siesta.

But one cashier was determined to be a hero. He was a slight and young man, though already balding, and he wore great round spectacles—an unlikely-looking hero. But if I turned my head the least to the right, watching the others, he began to edge toward his cage. I whipped around, pointing my rifle at him and waving him back. We did this three times, until even

327

I was losing patience with this foolish man. But I knew what he did not: I would never shoot him.

Then he began to yell as loud as he could, "Robbery! Help, robbery!"

That brought Sundance and Butch both on the run, and Butch flattened the man with one hard punch to the chin. All the starch went out of him, and he sank to the floor.

"Let's go," Butch said, his tone edging closer to frantic than I'd ever heard from him.

We were mounted and out of town in seconds, and we rode for a long time without speaking. Finally, when the horses could hold the pace no longer, Butch signaled for a walk, though he kept looking nervously over his shoulder.

"You should have shot that blasted fool," Sundance said, turning to me angrily.

"That would have brought attention faster than his yelling," I replied. "Besides, I'm not going to shoot anyone."

"If you're not going to use it, you shouldn't carry a rifle," he answered in an irritatingly smug tone.

"I never in my life shot a man," Butch said quietly.

Sundance stared at him. "I don't want to ride with either one of you unless you decide you can use those damn rifles. I'm not risking my life for your principles."

When we made camp that night, Sundance made a big show of pulling his bedroll off to one side of the small clearing we'd chosen for a cold camp. Deliberately I laid my roll out where I'd be between the two men—and some distance from Sundance. Nights were cool on the pampa, even though we were moving north toward the warmer climate of northern Argentina. I settled down into the warmth of my bedroll with a small sigh of satisfaction, the only comfort I'd known all day long.

"Etta?" Butch whispered my name as he crept toward me on all fours.

Instantly I sat up. "What is it?" I demanded aloud, sure that we were surrounded by *federales*.

"Shhh!" he whispered. "Don't want to wake Sundance."

From across the clearing came a clear voice. "It's all right. I'm awake. You two just go on and do whatever you want to do." Sundance's tone had a bitterness to it that was familiar to me by now.

"Ah, Kid," Butch said. "I just want to talk to her."

"Be my guest," came the reply.

Butch reached out and brushed the hair off my forehead, his touch ever so gentle. For a long minute he just stared at me with a look as tender as those Sundance gave me in the early days of our togetherness. At last he spoke. "You aren't going on any more jobs with us, Etta. I . . . I don't want you to face that kind of danger."

"You think I've lost my nerve, don't you?" I whispered back.

He shook his head. "You've always had more nerve than any twenty women I know, Etta. It's not that. It's just that it's time for it to be over for all of us. Sundance and I, we don't have a choice even here in South America. We thought we did, but Pinkertons has hounded us down here. But you do. From now on, you'll wait for us at safe places."

"We could leave," I ventured.

He stared off into space. "We can't, but you could. And if you want to, I'll see that happens. But I guess I hope you'll go north with us, and finally we can all go back to the States together."

I reached for his hand and was surprised by the electricity that flowed when we touched. "I'll stay," I told him, "because I love you."

"Ah, Etta!" He was once again the bashful, brotherly Butch.

From behind me came a plaintive. "What about me?"

"Go to sleep, Sundance," I said, but I was laughing as I said it to make it a joke, and he took no offense. Or if he did, he was silent about it for once.

What bothers me to this day is that, Pinkertons or no, they could have left. They just couldn't bring themselves to give up the only way of life they'd ever known, no matter how much they talked about new lives.

We rode west to San Martin, keeping parallel to the railroad tracks, but always out of sight. Then, at San Martin, we hitched the horses in front of a store and left them, knowing someone would care for them. We boarded the train for Mendoza, which really wasn't much farther.

"Why didn't we just ride there?" I asked.

"Because they'll be looking for us to be horseback. They won't expect us to arrive by train."

"It would be better if I had good clothes, wouldn't it?" I said.

"Yeah, but you don't."

In Mendoza we checked into a small, old hotel. The lobby had a stone floor with dirt between the stones, and the stucco of the walls showed great gaps and cracks. The clerk at the worn wooden counter was as bored as he could be and barely gave us a look as Butch signed us in. If asked later, he'd never know he'd seen the famous *norteamericano* outlaws. While we stood waiting for him to figure the room rates, a pig ran squealing through the open area, chased by a young boy of about ten who was yelling at the top of his lungs. Butch and Sundance were not impressed, but I was—and not favorably.

Sundance and I shared a tiny room, the space almost entirely taken up by an iron bedstead. The linens looked slightly gray, and the quilt was worn. I stared at it in distaste. The only other furniture in the room was a straight chair and a small, scarred chest of drawers that held a pitcher and a basin.

"I guess," Sundance said, "we won't be upright much in here." Then he began to pace around the bed. Just to get out of his way, I jumped onto it and heard the loud squeak of springs. He looked at me and almost grinned like the old Sundance, but then he said, "It's all falling apart, isn't it?"

"What? The bed?"

"That too," he said, "but I meant you and me." He looked hurt, surprised, uncertain, and in that moment I probably loved him as much as I ever had.

Loosening my hair, which had been bound up under a hat, I said, "I don't know, Sundance. It surely doesn't feel like it did in Wyoming."

His laugh was wry. "Maybe we were Wyoming lovers."

"We did all right in Utah," I reminded him, "but New Mexico was not good."

"What's happened, Etta? I still . . . I mean, you can still set me on fire."

"And you can me, Sundance. I imagine if we're both around at eighty, it'll still be true. But I don't think that will happen to us."

He shook his head. "I know it won't. But we're here now, Etta. What's happened?"

"I think it's what I told you in New York. I know you can't give up this life."

He was honestly perplexed. "But you . . . you were the one who loved it, loved the excitement, begged to go with us."

"I guess I've changed." I wanted to suggest I'd grown up, but I knew that was the wrong thing to say.

He tried anger. "It's Butch, isn't it? You're in love with Butch."

It made me weary to think we would fight that battle again, and I rose from the bed and walked to the window. "Whatever I feel for Butch has nothing to do with this. Butch is . . . well, for me, he's a might-have-been, something that never could happen. You're what happened, and if you don't know the difference, I'm sorry for you."

Instantly he was beside me, and I was in his arms. "I know, Etta, I know. . . . I just don't want to lose you."

There was no way I could bring myself to tell him that he was going to lose me, no matter what. But I had no need to talk. Within seconds we were peeling off our clothes and jumping into the bed, like old times. In spite of squeaking springs, which I was sure everyone in the hotel could hear, we spent a wild and wonderful afternoon, and when we went to supper—late, because South Americans don't dine until nine or ten—I asked nervously if my lips were red and swollen.

"It looks becoming on you," he said smugly.

Butch was already seated at a table, and without looking at us he shoved the menu across the table. "Doesn't look promising," he said. "Better stick with the beef."

Before I could even look at the menu, I heard a familiar—and unwelcome—voice.

" 'Bout time you all got here." Kid Curry stood before us, as ugly as he'd ever been. Before I could speak, he nodded his head in my direction and said, "The whore even followed you to South America, I see."

"I thought," I said in measured tones, "that you were killed in a Tennessee shoot-out."

"Newspapers got the wrong man," he said smugly.

I turned to Sundance, but he was staring at the floor, his hands knotted in his lap, his expression one of discomfort. "You knew!" I exploded. "You arranged for him to come here!"

Judy Alter

Sundance remained silent, and I turned to face Butch.

Butch was honest, but his very honesty forced him to admit that he had lied to me, or at least deliberately not told me everything he knew. "I knew he was coming, Etta. I . . . I advised Sundance against it."

My thoughts were exploding in my brain. "He's been here a while, hasn't he? That's why you knew there might be robberies other than those you committed."

Now both men stared at the floor, afraid to look at me.

"Why the hell are you lettin' her treat you like this?" Curry demanded.

Sundance suddenly rose to his feet, his fists clenched. "Shut up, Curry!" he said, his voice so loud he was almost shouting. "Get out of here. I . . . I'll talk to you later."

By then I was shaking with anger. I shoved the menu away from me, pushed back my chair, and rose to leave.

"Etta?" Sundance's voice was plaintive.

"When's the next train for Valparaiso?" I asked.

He looked crestfallen. "You wouldn't."

"I would . . . and I will." There was no need to tell him that joining up again with the man who had nearly raped me was the ultimate betrayal.

Butch rose. "Sundance, you go see Curry. I'll see to Etta."

I was almost as angry with him. "I don't need 'seeing to,'" I said. "I can take care of myself."

"I'd like to buy your train ticket," Butch said, his voice ever gentle. He led me out of the dining room, while Sundance went in another direction to look for Curry. Sundance had started toward me, and then he apparently thought better of it. I didn't know if he was cowed by my anger or by Curry's scorn, but I wanted to believe it was the former.

Butch went with me to pack the few belongings I still had with me.

"You got a skirt in there?" he asked, nodding his head toward my skimpy roll.

"Why?"

"They might be looking for a lady in breeches," he said. "I think you best wear the skirt."

And so I put on a wrinkled skirt of corded cotton, but I still had my boots, a dirty white shirt, and my gaucho hat.

"You're sure about this, Etta?"

"Damn sure," I said, still angry.

Butch took my hand and held it but said nothing for a long time. "I don't think he can help himself," he finally said. "I think the lure of it is too much for him. . . . Curry isn't the only one of us who is that tempted by it, so tempted that common sense goes out the window."

"I thought you were going along with them."

"I will, for a while. But I'm like you. I don't want to die. They won't quit until they do. And you're smart to leave us. I only hope I can leave at the right time, before it's too late."

I literally threw myself into his arms, right there in that tiny hotel room. "Come with me now," I begged. "We can go back to the States, start over as new people—we'll be together." For just a moment, I lived that wonderful fantasy.

"You know I can't do that to Sundance, Etta." He disentangled himself from my arms and put a brotherly arm around my shoulders. "I'll get there sometime."

It turned out that the passionate afternoon I had spent with Sundance was our farewell. I didn't see him again before I boarded the train. "Tell him," I said to Butch, "that I love him, and that I'm . . . Oh, never mind, don't say any more than that. Anything else sounds stupid."

"Were you going to tell him you're sorry it turned out this way?" He was leaning against a bench at the train station, and I sat just a bit apart from him.

"I guess so, and it would be true."

"Then I'll tell him."

And so it was Butch who kissed me goodbye—only the second on-the-mouth kiss I'd ever had from Butch, and this a lingering one that made me want to pull my bags off the train and stay.

"I'm sorry, Etta," he said. "As sorry for you and me as I am for Sundance."

And then he was gone, and I was looking frantically for him as the train pulled out of the station. In the dark shadow beyond the lit area I saw him slouched against the wall, his hand raised in farewell.

Epilogue

In 1911 the newspapers carried the headline, "US Bandits Killed in Bolivia," and I knew before I read further that Sundance was dead. The article said that Butch Cassidy and the Sundance Kid, leaders of the Hole-in-the-Wall Gang that had "terrorized" Wyoming for many years, had been killed in a shoot-out in San Vicente, a small rural community in Bolivia.

"Robbing the bank," I thought, "and it probably didn't have a thousand pesos all told!" I wept for Sundance, wept that he had died in a hail of bullets, and then gave thanks that he had not died on the gallows or spent long years in prison, which would have killed his spirit. He died, I knew, the way he wanted to.

But Butch? Just as surely as anything, I knew that it was not Butch who died with Sundance. It was Kid Curry, who deserved, to my mind, a much worse fate than a quick death by gunfire. I also knew that Butch was alive and well someplace and that someday he would come to find me. I just didn't understand how long it would take him.

Butch came to see me yesterday. Oh, the girl who announced him called him Mr. Phillips—William T. Phillips—but I knew it was Butch the minute I set foot in the parlor. Sixty-something—the year is 1937—he still had the round, innocent, baby face he'd had in his twenties when he first started robbing banks and trains. Now, though, his hair is streaked with silver, not the sunlit brown I remember, and yesterday he wore a proper business suit, not the denim and flannel of our days in Wyoming. The only other times I'd ever seen him in a suit were when Sundance made him wear one to pose for that picture in Fort Worth.

I stood in the doorway for a minute, fighting for self-control. "You didn't die," I said.

He grinned lopsidedly in a way that I remembered so well. "No, I didn't. Didn't you know that?"

I nodded. "Sundance died," I said.

"Yeah. You'd have heard from him if he hadn't."

And then I was in his arms, my face pressed against his shoulder, my tears dampening that good suit.

"Etta, Etta." He spoke gently, stroking my hair, calming me as he always had done.

"It's Eunice now, Eunice Parker," I said, regaining my senses and backing away from him a few inches.

"You'll always be Etta to me."

And he would always be Butch. "Why did you wait so long?" I asked, and my anger flared.

"I thought if I found you, they'd find both of us."

There was no need to identify "they." It was the law. Probably even to this day there were warrants out for both of us—and for Sundance—across the West. I just hadn't thought about that for a long time.

"How did you find me?" I asked.

"Long story. I knew that business about you dying of appendicitis in Denver wasn't true. You were as healthy as ever when you left us in Bolivia. Lately, I been thinkin' about how you always wanted to live in Fort Worth, and I knew you'd be running a house. Been here a few days poking around."

"This isn't a whorehouse," I said, my voice suddenly cold.

He grinned again and shrugged. "You've changed, Etta, but you haven't. That quick anger—it's still there."

"If you'd been Sundance and said that to me, I'd have picked up the nearest vase and thrown it at you."

He laughed aloud. "You may still throw it at me," he said.

We sat on the sofa, companionably close and yet not touching. Slowly Butch told me that he'd married and had a son. They lived in Seattle, where he was a respected—and honest—businessman.

"Then why," I asked, "come looking for me now, when it's all some twenty-five years over?"

"It was time." Then he grinned again. "I . . . well, I had to find you once. I promised Sundance, you know."

"Sundance doesn't stand between us anymore." My voice was almost harsh. "Neither does Mary Boyd."

He winced when I said that. "No, but a lot of other things do. Not just my family, but . . . oh, hell, I don't know, Etta. I didn't come for any big reunion, and I'm no more after your skirt than I was when you was with Sundance." He was at a loss as to how to go on.

"I guess," I said softly, "there's some things you can't ever get back, Butch. And what could have been between us but never was is one of those things."

"I guess you're right," he said, "and it's one of the biggest regrets of my life. I don't worry over the trains and the banks, but I do worry over how I hurt my family . . . and what I missed with you."

There wasn't much either of us could say. I kissed him quickly and rose from the couch. We talked a little after that, mostly about nothing, but pretty soon he said he guessed he'd better be going. Now that he'd found me, he was going back to Seattle the next day.

"You got a picture of that son of yours?" I asked.

Almost shy, he produced a picture of a boy who looked to be about sixteen, with his father's baby face and stocky build.

"Tell him never to go to Nevada or Utah or Wyoming," I said. "Old-timers will take one look at him and hang him."

Butch laughed and kissed me quick on the forehead. Then he was gone out the front door. I stood on the porch and watched him walk away, and I thought to myself, *Damn! There really are things you can't capture ever again. What's that line from Shakespeare? "There is a tide in the affairs of men"?*

Butch and I had missed the tide . . . and the boat.

MATTIE

The Spur-Award-winning novel!

JUDY ALTER

Young Mattie, poor and illegitimate, is introduced to an entirely new world when she is hired to care for the daughter of an influential doctor. By sheer grit and determination, she eventually becomes a doctor herself and sets up her practice amid the soddies and farmhouses of the Nebraska she knows and loves. During the years of her practice, Mattie's life is filled with battles won and lost, challenges met and opportunities passed.

___4156-1 $3.99 US/$4.99 CAN

A BALLAD
FOR SALLIE

JUDY ALTER

Longhair Jim Courtright has been both a marshal and a desperado—and in Hell's Half Acre, the roughest part of Fort Worth, he is a living legend. His skill with a gun has made him a hero in some people's eyes . . . and a killer in others'. As soon as young widow Sallie McNutt steps off the stage from Tennessee, her refined manners and proper attire set her apart from the other women of the Half Acre. And it isn't long before something else sets her apart—someone wants her dead.

___4365-3 $4.50 US/$5.50 CAN

Legend

LOREN D. ESTLEMAN, ELMER KELTON, JUDY ALTER, JAMES REASONER, JANE CANDIA COLEMAN, ED GORMAN, ROBERT J. RANDISI

For the first time, these amazing talents—combined winners of 14 Spur Awards!—have joined forces, and the result is truly the stuff of legend. Together they recount the life of Lyle Speaks, from his hardscrabble boyhood in Texas to his later years as an aging cattle rancher in Montana, years in which his colorful past may yet come back to haunt him. From one end of the West to the other, Lyle's exploits made him famous—admired by some, feared by others. But now Lyle wants to set the record straight. No matter what the cost.

___4496-X $5.99 US/$6.99 CAN

Jane Candia Coleman

I, PEARL HART

It is while she is awaiting trial for an armed stagecoach robbery that newspaper reporters dub Pearl Hart "the Bandit Queen." That is before her desperate escape from jail and her dramatic recapture. Before she is done, she will earn the dubious honor of being the first woman sent to the infamous Yuma Penitentiary in the Arizona Territory. Award-winning author Jane Candia Coleman has written this gripping, uncompromising narrative in Pearl Hart's own unique voice. Based on the memoirs of the woman who lived it, this drama goes behind the headlines to follow the Bandit Queen's journey from her home in Toledo, Ohio, to the boom camps of the Arizona Territory, to the hard scrabble life of an outlaw.

___4794-2 $4.50 US/$5.50 CAN

Dorchester Publishing Co., Inc.
P.O. Box 6640
Wayne, PA 19087-8640

Please add $2.50 for shipping and handling for the first book and $.75 for each additional book. NY and PA residents, add appropriate sales tax. No cash, stamps, or C.O.D.s. All Canadian orders require $5.00 for shipping and handling and must be paid in U. S. dollars. Prices and availability subject to change. Payment must accompany all orders.

Name_____

Address_____

City_____ State _____ Zip_____

E-mail _____

I have enclosed $ _____ in payment for the checked book(s).

☐Please send a free catalog.

CHECK OUT OUR WEBSITE! www.dorchesterpub.com

MOVING ON
JANE CANDIA COLEMAN

Jane Candia Coleman is a magical storyteller who spins brilliant tales of human survival, hope, and courage on the American frontier, and nowhere is her marvelous talent more in evidence than in this acclaimed collection of her finest work. From a haunting story of the night Billy the Kid died, to a dramatic account of a breathtaking horse race, including two stories that won the prestigious Spur Award, here is a collection that reveals the passion and fortitude of its characters, and also the power of a wonderful writer.

___4545-1 $4.99 US/$5.99 CAN

Dorchester Publishing Co., Inc.
P.O. Box 6640
Wayne, PA 19087-8640

Please add $1.75 for shipping and handling for the first book and $.50 for each book thereafter. NY, NYC, and PA residents, please add appropriate sales tax. No cash, stamps, or C.O.D.s. All orders shipped within 6 weeks via postal service book rate. Canadian orders require $2.00 extra postage and must be paid in U.S. dollars through a U.S. banking facility.

Name_____
Address_____
City_____State_____Zip_____
I have enclosed $_____ in payment for the checked book(s).
Payment <u>must</u> accompany all orders. ❑ Please send a free catalog.
    CHECK OUT OUR WEBSITE! www.dorchesterpub.com

MAN WITHOUT MEDICINE
CYNTHIA HASELOFF

Daha-hen's name in Kiowa means Man Without Medicine. Before his people were forced to follow the peace road and live on a reservation, Daha-hen was one of the great Kiowa warriors of the plains, fabled for his talent as a horse thief. But now Daha-hen is fifty-three and lives quietly on the edge of the reservation raising horses. When unscrupulous white men run off his herd, the former horse thief finds himself in pursuit of his own horses and ready to make war against the men who took them. Accompanying him on his quest is Thomas Young Man, a young outcast of the Kiowa people. During the course of their journey, Daha-hen adopts Thomas and teaches him the ways of the Kiowa warrior. But can Daha-hen teach his young student enough to enable them both to survive their trek—and the fatal confrontation that waits at the end of it?

___4581-8 $4.50 US/$5.50 CAN

CYNTHIA HASELOFF

THE KIOWA VERDICT

In 1871 Satanta, a Kiowa war chief, boasts at the Kiowa-Comanche Agency that he has led a war party against a wagon train of freighters. When he repeats his boast to General W. T. Sherman, who is on a tour of frontier forts, the order is given for his arrest along with two other chiefs who are implicated. The killing, torture, and mutilation of the freighters is said to have been a ghastly crime. But never before have members of an Indian war party been put on trial to defend their brutal actions. The chiefs will be tried in a Texas courtroom, with a former Indian fighter to defend them. Will a fair trial even be possible in such a setting? And will the outcome be justice . . . or vengeance?

___4767-5 $4.50 US/$5.50 CAN